W

This book is a work of fiction. Names, characters, places and events are a product of the author's imagination. Any resemblance to actual names, characters and places are entirely coincidental. The reproduction of this work in full or part is forbidden without written consent from the author.

Electronic Edition
Copyright 2020 Merrill David

Dedication

This book is dedicated to those unfortunate beings who found themselves at the Great White concert in the Station nightclub in West Warwick, Rhode Island, on February 20, 2003. About three years prior, I lived in a rental house around the corner from where this tragedy occurred. I knew at least one of the victims, as well as one of the survivors. As a fan of that band, I probably would have been at the show myself, had I not moved out of state a few months earlier to chase a job opportunity. God rest their souls and may their families and loved ones find peace…

Part 1 - Trials and Tribulations

Modern humans are characterized by their erect posture, bipedal motion, and manual dexterity. They are equipped with larger, more complex brains than their predecessors - brains that feature a particularly well-developed neocortex, prefrontal cortex and temporal lobes - all of which enable high levels of abstract reasoning, language, problem solving, sociality, and culture through social learning. These characteristics contributed greatly to the evolutionary success of the homo sapiens.

But what does it really mean to exist in this world as a human? Most would unequivocally agree that every human life span contains some percentage of felicity and anguish, with many choices to be made along the way. These ultimatums may lead to more celebratory events and/or pitfalls, depending upon which path was chosen.

Granted, one is unable to choose their starting point or rooting grounds, by whom or in what location they will ultimately be nurtured and grown. Depending on where your spin on the wheel-of-fate lands and places you, and the conditions and tribulations attached to your existence, you undoubtedly will resultantly endure some amount of physical and emotional pain and suffering in your life span.

The human existence is like a vast stretching spectrum. Some may be monumentally blessed with riches, fame, and glory while others are quite satisfied with the simplicities of life. These qualities are quite commonplace and often under-appreciated; the ability to breathe freely and unassisted, to not just see beauty in nature with the eyes but also to recognize and appreciate such actively, to sense changes in the environment such as a breeze on a balmy summer afternoon; to be able to think and strategize, capable of feeling emotions and expressing the same.

Many humans are content to exist in the simplest terms possible, satisfied to be able to enjoy these simple comforts of life. They thrive on being good persons, exuding of character and caring for their fellow man.

But to others the desire to be the greatest, to dominate, the possession of power - consumes them. They launch their quest for that which they seek, risking all they possess and at whatever cost possible. Some, upon realizing their goal is unattainable, destroy those who possess the prize so that person may no longer have what the desperate man cannot.

Each human at one time or another will peer between the cracks in their virtual fence to catch a glimpse of what exists on the other side. Some are searching for fame, riches, or glory while others lust excellence and relevance. The strength, power, and immortality they seem to lack appears in yonder yard much like grass that appears greener; the fruit from that orchard across the way manifests itself to be riper, juicier, and tastier.

Most possess the wisdom in knowing they can always fertilize their grass to brighten its sheen. They may plant and nurture new fruit bearing trees that may yield a harvest equal to or even rivaling that of their neighbors. This comforts them and they move on with their current existence.

But there will always be those that continue to overindulge

and attempt to reach through that crevice in the divider, hoping to grasp that for which they long. Some reach their trophy with a few minor scratches but without suffering excess harm.

Others get their wrists snatched and find themselves being pulled through the partition only to be violently attacked by seemingly mindless dead folks who ultimately chew out their throats and then snack upon their well-developed neocortex, prefrontal cortex and temporal lobes.

And then, there is a minute percentage of society who are quite amenable to the concept of exchanging everything up to, and including, their lives for the opportunity to be celestial, God-like, supernatural.

And so, the decadence and decomposition of man begins....

Chapter 1 - Listen to the Blowflies

Earle Cabell Federal Building and U.S. District Court, Downtown Dallas
(Present Day)

It was January 18th in what the locals call "the Big D," the city of Dallas, Texas. Along with its neighbor to the west, Fort Worth, the two combine to make up the giant urban center known as the "DFW Metroplex." Dallas is also the home of the Earle Cabell Federal Building and United States District Court, located in the downtown area at the corner of Commerce and Griffin.

It was 1:35 p.m., and outside the temperature was 50 degrees Fahrenheit - a typical early afternoon temperature for the month of January in this region.

Anomalous, however, were the large black masses slowly passing in the midday horizon. These were not nimbostratus clouds or flocks of crows. They were not balloons, nor banners being towed behind small, single-engine planes, advertising Crazy Ray's prices at the Furniture Warehouse. These were insects of some sort - large masses of them.

They had been spotted throughout north Texas and had made their way into Dallas County over the last few weeks. However, the masses went unnoticed by most and got no attention from the local news media whatsoever. These were blowflies, and they had a story to tell, but no one was listening.

Inside the Cabell Courthouse, in the courtroom of the Honorable Presiding Judge Curtis J. Parker, a murder trial had been ongoing for the past nine weeks and was about to conclude. The man sitting in the defendant's seat was one Jacob "Jake" Hathaway. He was a large Caucasian male, at 6'3" in height and weighing in at 230 pounds, with brown hair cut in a military or crew-cut style, and crystal blue eyes.

He wore a black and white horizontal striped Dallas County Jail prisoner jumpsuit with a ballistic vest over the top of that to protect his upper torso, should he be shot at. Even in this attire, it was apparent from all the onlookers that Hathaway's physique comprised solid muscle, with very little body fat.

Hathaway had always taken pride in his body and had trained hard, accruing his sculpted muscular mass through years of hard work and weight training. Not nearly as strong as his core was Jake's mind. Throughout the years, he had acquired a case of Post-Traumatic Stress Disorder, a condition which made it difficult for his mind not to wander during times such as this. This was a moment when he would have been best served fully concentrating on the circumstances unfolding.

Jake began to take a mental voyage, visiting the time his story began:

Born on July 15 thirty-five years earlier, Jacob "Jake" Hathaway was the first offspring of Charles and Clara Hathaway. Five years later, Jake's brother Richard (Rich) was born.

Jake's parents, Charles and Clara, were devout Catholics, and they raised their sons Jacob and Richard in the same manner, sending them to Catholic schools throughout their early impressionable years. The boys were taught everything the public-school kids learned, while also studying and memorizing prayers, religious concepts, making bi-weekly confessions, receiving their first holy communion, and eventually earning their confirmation in their late teen years.

This happy middle-class family of four lived in the small town of West Greenwich, Rhode Island. This was a quaint New England town of about 6,000 residents and was one of the least densely populated towns in what was the smallest state in the United States.

West Greenwich was in Kent County, along the western half of the state. It was about a twenty-minute drive south of Providence and about thirty minutes east of Connecticut. Residents on either side of that Connecticut / Rhode Island border found that where you were situated in relation to that line played quite a powerful role in the way your life eventually played out for you. Much of your life was predetermined for you and depended greatly upon which side you grew up on. It was somewhat of a Mason/Dixon line for this neck of the woods.

If you were on the Rhode Island side, you lived in a state where one could drive from one corner to the farthest end in less than an hour. In the "Biggest Little State in the Union," you were very likely to root for Boston Red Sox baseball in the spring and lounge on the sands of your favorite ocean side beach in the summertime while enjoying an ice cold Del's lemonade.

You would be fond of the fall foliage yet grow tired of the annual parade of leaf peepers, and then bundle up for the harsh winters while consuming bowls of steaming clam chowder and rooting for the New England Patriots football team. You were also considered to be a "New Englander", and you washed down your Maine Lobster and blueberry pie with Sam Adams' Boston Ale, and you wouldn't have it any other way.

Being a New Englander, particularly a Rhode Islander, was like belonging to an elite private club, a fraternity whose members had their own beliefs, language, phrases, culture, and accent.

There, submarine sandwiches were called "grinders," water fountains in the elementary school were referred to as "bubblers," athletic shoes were "sneakers," and if someone claimed something was "wicked" they weren't calling it evil, they were using the word as an equivalent to "very," only stronger.

If you were living on the west side of the line, in Connecticut, you behaved like and held yourself to be more like a New Yorker. You most likely spoke with a thick accent, that bad attitude and quick temper New Yorkers are rumored to possess. You had to ride those dirty subway trains and be loyal to one of those big city sports teams (but you still had to decide if you would be for the Yankees and Giants or the Mets and the Jets). Your pizza was thinner - and you loved living in the New York groove, listening to Billy Joel's 52nd Street album repetitively, with a good dose of Sinatra mixed in as well.

When Jake was in his early pre-teen years, his grandfather on his mother's side, Grandpa Bill, moved in with the family after suffering a major stroke which limited his mobility and self-reliance. Grandpa Bill, "Pops", had a completely bald head caused by Father Time; no shaving was involved as would become a fashion trend later with men actually taking razor to scalp for the very same look. Pops wore dark framed glasses and utilized a four-legged walking cane to traverse about the house. He was a Camel brand cigarette chain smoker and a boxing guru.

As a young adult Bill boxed as an amateur and after that he trained some of the up and coming youth at a local gym that his good friend owned. Bill was a great fan of local Rhode Island boxer Vinny Paz, previously known as Vincent Pazienza, an Italian-American former world champion in the lightweight and light middleweight classes. However, Paz was probably best known as the "Pazmanian Devil."

Now that Grandpa Bill's training days at the gym were over, young Jake became his new personal boxing prodigy. Punching a speed bag, skipping rope, and jogging around the neighborhood under the watchful eye of his Pops, Jake's after-school activities consisted of training and working on these exercises, with an occasional smidgen of homework mixed in.

Jake would always treasure the time spent training with his Grandpa Bill - inspiring him to eventually work his way up the ranks until he was boxing competitively in his early teens. Jake would enter boxing tournaments down at the closest YMCA in North Kingstown where, at the age of 15, he met his best friend, a red haired and freckle faced white kid named Jimmy Griggs.

Jimmy Griggs hailed from the nearby town of Exeter. He was not blessed with the size and athletic ability that Jake possessed. However, where Jimmy may have lacked talent and girth, he made up for it in aggression and effort.

Jimmy's father was a Rhode Island State Police Trooper, he was tough and disciplined and he always raised his son to instinctively act with a similar mindset.

Jake and Jimmy had much in common. They shared a passion for pretty girls (and covering their bedroom walls with posters of the likes of Heather Locklear and Heather Thomas). They were both huge Sox and Pats fans (however Jimmy's favorite professional sports franchise beyond compare was the NHL team, the Hartford Whalers). They dreamed of someday riding in or better yet, owning the cool fast cars that they read about in the magazines, and they were all about the rock music of the times; rock bands such as the Scorpions, Van Halen, Whitesnake, Dokken, Ratt, Great White, Guns N Roses, and so on.

But their favorite band of all derived from England and was known not as much for their hair like the previously mentioned bands as they were for their psychedelic lyrics and sound. The music group was Pink Floyd. The two teens particularly admired "The Wall," an album the band released in 1979, which was followed up by a movie based on the same.

The main character in "The Wall," a rock band lead singer named Pink, found his walls and world closing in on him as a result of his combined drug use and mental health issues. Pink lost his father (killed in World War II) at an early age, and as an adult rock star he experienced suffocation due to the swarm of stalking fans constantly smothering him and seeking a glimpse of the star.

When the boys were 16 years old, they enjoyed hanging out together on the weekends and enjoying the outdoors by swimming, playing baseball and basketball, riding bicycles, and so on in the summertime. Playing ice hockey, sledding, and skiing occupied much of their time in the winter months.

On one Friday night in July, the teens decided to go camping on an abandoned piece of property not far from the Griggs' house, and on the edge of Beach Pond.

They pitched a large tent and built a healthy campfire from available kindling the elder pine trees had discarded during the December solstice a year earlier. Being young, adventurous, daring, and dumb, they decided it would be cool to down some beers that they had 'appropriated' from the mini fridge in Mr. Griggs' grungy garage/man cave.

Around 1:00 a.m., and after they had consumed about four Narragansett beers apiece, the duo decided to commandeer a canoe leaning against a nearby stack of four-foot fireplace ready logs and set out rowing into the dark, to the deepest midpoint of the murky pond.

Then, as if they had not already made enough poor choices that evening, Jake excitedly requested, "hey dude, you wanna hear something really loud?"

Slowly, with his right hand, he pulled a surprise out from the front pocket of his blue jean jacket. Jimmy's eyes got large as he noticed that in Jake's hand was a quarter stick of dynamite, otherwise known as an M80.

"Oh, hell yeah, man - let me light it!" was the reply from the smaller, even more intoxicated Jimmy.

Jake handed Jimmy the explosive and a small red Bic lighter. Jimmy sparked the rusting lighter and held the flame to the wick of the waiting M80. The wick hissed as it caught the flame and the ember gradually worked its way toward the mini powder keg.

Jimmy yelled "WOO HOOO!!"

He moved his left arm back and prepared to launch the explosive forward with a baseball pitcher's type of motion. But just before he could release the explosive, he clumsily struck the bill of his ball cap with his left hand, causing the boom stick to fall down into the collar of his green and white Hartford Whalers hooded sweatshirt.

Jimmy was slow to decipher the magnitude of what had just happened, and by the time he realized his mistake and struggled to remove the M80 from his shirt, it was too late.

The gunpowder sparked and BOOOMMMMMM!!!!! The small red stick exploded just centimeters from Jimmy's skin, causing a large chunk of his neck to be ripped from his body as massive amounts of blood gushed underneath his Whalers shirt.

The now unconscious lad was thrown into the water, having suffered extreme trauma to the left side of his neck and his lower chin area. Jimmy sank like a rock into the cold lake, and Jake did not hesitate to jump in after him.

Being dark outside and the water being quite diluted, Jake found it hard to see and navigate in the cloudy depths of water below him.

He called out loudly, yelling "JIMMY!!! WHERE ARE YOU?? JIMMY!!!!"

Young Jake tried to rely more on his sense of touch, feeling around with both hands in an effort to locate his buddy, but to no avail. The search was fruitless.

Jake abandoned the capsized canoe and as quickly as he could, paddled back to shore and ran all the way to the Griggs' house about a quarter mile away.

Jake pounded on the front door and was quickly greeted in the doorway by Trooper Griggs. "Jake, what's wrong? Where's Jimmy?"

Sobbing and in a panicked frenzy, Jake disclosed the details of the incident in the lake. Trooper Griggs threw on some sweatpants and a jacket and raced back to the scene, with his foot-long metal law enforcement Streamlight brand flashlight in hand to aid in the search for his son.

A countless number of fellow police officers, firemen, and caring neighbors responded to help in the search. The inquiry would continue for hours, stretching into the daylight hours and until all involved were exhausted and unable to continue. In the end, the expedition was all done in vain. Jimmy was nowhere to be found.

Authorities returned days later and dredged the body of water to reveal Jimmy's lifeless, blood-drained body in the dungy depths of Beach Pond. The Medical Examiner's Autopsy Report would later indicate that the cause of death was not drowning - rather it was exsanguination, or death by excessive blood loss, which did Jimmy in.

Jake always felt guilty about and second guessed the events leading up to Jimmy's death. What if he had not suggested that they drink some beers and suppose he had not provided the M80.

What if Jake had just brought some Playboy magazines instead? The boys probably never would have made it to the water and would have been content in downing some cold ones and ogling Miss July in the centerfold.

Why couldn't he have been a stronger swimmer? If only he could go back in time and change any one of these circumstances, Jimmy could possibly still be alive today.

Jake spent countless months after the incident in which he remained depressed, sluggish, unmotivated to do much at all. That is, until he met Kristin Ramey.

Jake and Kristin met in high school when Jake was a senior and Kristin was a junior. They were classmates in Biology and US History and were in the same Home Room. Kristin was a cute, bright eyed, long haired brunette from North Kingstown and was quite taken with the small-town boy at the back of the class.

Jake and Kristin became friends quite naturally and by the mid-semester point they had become a couple - the traditional high school sweethearts. He was a starting linebacker on the varsity football team and Kristin was on the cheerleading squad.

Kristin was the missing link in the young man's life. She offered him the caring and concern that he lacked and needed. This sustenance was something Jake's stoic New England family could not or did not provide. His parents rarely spoke, hugged, or showed any type of emotion. Later in life this demeanor would be adopted by Jake as well. But back then, he gratefully absorbed every drop of devotion and attention that Kristin provided.

The last time Jake saw Kristin was in June, the month after he graduated high school. Jake was 18, Kristin 17, and he was about to set foot on the plane that would take him to South Carolina to begin his life as a Marine. The couple vowed that they would keep in touch, that this was not goodbye, just a temporary setback in their lives, this would be a true test of their relationship which would most likely make them long for and want to be with each other that much more.

Jake began his tough, regimented Marine training and quickly found himself back in a similar state of melancholia as he was after the Jimmy tragedy and before he happened upon Kristin. Clouds constantly hovered above him, doubt and insecurity following his every move. Being away from his home, family, Kristin; and facing a new challenge – conditioned him this way.

And as if he wasn't already down in the dumps enough, now there was a new ultimatum Jake would encounter. One requirement Jake had overlooked and not anticipated could now stand in his way of achievement; his class had just been told that they would have to demonstrate their ability to swim well, in waters deep, over long distances and for great lengths of time.

Jake wasn't much of a swimmer even before the Jimmy

incident, and for years afterward he never cared to go back out into the water at all. But now and at this point in his Marine training, he would have no choice in the matter.

At that point, Jake had to make a conscious effort to overcome his weakness, to ignore the images he still had of Jimmy's limp body submerging in the lake water. Jake challenged himself to persevere and was able to transform himself into a more than adequate swimmer, successfully completing the rigorous and grueling amphibious assault training that the Marine Corps offered.

Earle Cabell Federal Building and U.S. District Court, Downtown Dallas
(Present Day)

Now the former Marine and Dallas Police Department Sergeant sat in the defendant's chair, dressed in his black and white horizontal striped jumpsuit, ankle shackles restricting his leg movement and an electric shock wire strapped around his abdominal region.

This device was controlled remotely by sheriff's deputies guarding Hathaway, to be activated should he attempt to flee. A 50,000-volt jolt of electricity would convince anyone to revisit their initial thoughts of escape.

United States Prosecutor Michael Ferron had been assigned the task of presenting the facts of this case before the chosen jury. His goal was to secure a guilty finding by the jury and in convicting Hathaway of the multiple murders he was accused of.

Ferron had already spent the last nine weeks presenting evidence in the case and introducing witnesses and 'experts' to testify against Hathaway, and he now addressed the jury with his closing arguments.

"Ladies and gentlemen of the jury, I stand before you today representing the people of the United States of America. More specifically, the people of Dallas County, Texas. And furthermore, I speak for the two persons who cannot be here to speak for themselves; Richard Hathaway and Holly Ann Jones - Hathaway, were so callously taken from this world in the primes of their lives on that fateful February eighth.

"I want to thank you all for the time and attention you've put into this case. I think we can all agree that yours has been a very difficult and trying task. This case has been different from most cases, actually very different from any other case.

"For the last three weeks you each have had to live with these details and images you have been introduced to. These have been some of the most horrific crimes, with some of the most graphic violence, ever perpetrated against any other human beings. It's unfortunate that we must deal with crimes of this nature and that you have to view these horrific photographs, hear the witnesses' grizzly first-hand observations and descriptions of the devastation and killing.

"Although we may be able to take some solace in the fact that our lives will never be as irrevocably affected as those of the victims and their families; we are all victims here. Every resident of Dallas has been taken advantage of, short changed and cheated by this defendant who appears before you."

Ferron continued; "Jacob 'Jake' Hathaway is a man who swore before you when he took his oath of office as a Dallas Police Officer that he would do everything in his power to protect life and property and the rights, liberties and freedoms we have all been afforded as citizens of this great city and country. Well, he lied to you all. He betrayed the trust you all instilled in him.

"So now all of you have been assembled here to do one thing, to hand out some justice. Each one of you is here in part because you told this court under oath that you could base your decision in this case on the evidence brought before you-the evidence that came from the witness stand, documents, and photographs, everything that was presented to you during the trial.

"This is the information you must weigh and base your decision upon. Our duty as prosecutors and representatives of the State is to prove to you beyond a reasonable doubt that Jake Hathaway is guilty of all charges. Use your common sense, apply it to the evidence that you've seen and heard; and you will recognize that we have proven our case.

"The defendant is charged with three crimes; you just heard them described by Judge Parker. He's charged with two offenses of capital murder and with one count of kidnapping - all felonies. And, folks, we are here to assert that justice in this case calls for guilty verdicts on every one of these charges.

"Now I would like to spend some time with you talking about all of the elements of the two capital murder crimes. As Judge Parker mentioned to you, when a person murders more than one person during the same criminal transaction, it is considered to be a capital murder, punishable by a sentence of life imprisonment without the possibility of parole or by death from lethal injection. It is alleged that Jake Hathaway committed these ruthless, brutal murders."

Ferron's words were just white noise to Jake Hathaway, who sat in his designated defendant's seat, wondering and praying that this was all just a very bad dream. Or could these be hallucinations? Jake frequently experienced these as a result of the Post Traumatic Stress Disorder that he acquired during his tour of duty in Iraq during Operation Everlasting Freedom.

In March of his ninth year in the Corps, Jake was still enlisted and active in the war, but found himself wallowing in depression. He was unable to function or perform even the simplest of everyday tasks without breaking down mentally. He often heard rambling, cryptic voices inside his head. Soon afterwards Jake found himself honorably discharged from the Marine Corps.

In his current state of bewilderment and confusion, Jake was unable to comprehend what was transpiring around him, unable to communicate with his defense attorney or to inquire about the way this trial seemed to be playing out.

Nothing that occurred since the birthday party and through the current trial procedures made any sense to Jake. That whole period had been like a blur - as if Jake had been teleported to a different time or place.

He had seen similar scenarios before on some of those classic Twilight Zone episodes and Planet of the Apes movies. Where people voluntarily or involuntarily traveled through time, either into the past or the present, via time travel experiments or by some unknown factor or force of nature. Jake would not have been surprised if at any second, a six-foot gorilla soldier in military garb and battle gear appeared on horseback, breaking through the courtroom doors and chasing him about, cracking a large horsewhip in Jake's vicinity.

Jake recalled earlier in the morning seeing a large statue beside the front steps leading to the courthouse. Having not paid close attention to that landmark at that time, he now wondered if the bronze cast might have been Lady Liberty herself buried up to her navel in sand and pebbles accumulated over a time lapse of several centuries.

Something had changed in the world, something seriously wrong was going on here, and it could not all be taken back and made right again with the push of a button on a remote control.

Equally stunned, sitting at the rear of the courtroom, was a young man in his mid-twenties. His name was Kelvin "Mack" McElroy, and he was a fellow police officer and co-worker of Hathaway's. McElroy was trained by Hathaway in more than one phase of the four phases of a six-month long Field Training Program instituted by the Dallas Police Department.

McElroy began to reflect upon some of the better days he and Hathaway had together, and Mack also wondered where he would be right now had Hathaway not influenced his training and life the way he did....

Chapter 2 – 'X' Marks the Spot

Kelvin McElroy was the product of an interracial marriage, and he grew up a small southern town kid from Pass Christian, Mississippi. He spoke with a slow, down-south drawl and, as some southerners are known for, he too was known to throw around a colorful phrase now and then to express himself in a way those from other parts don't always quite understand.

His father being African American and his mother being Caucasian, he was occasionally picked on and sometimes bullied as a youngster. He recalled being in town with his mother and hearing his mom being called names from ignorant town-folk. But he wasn't one to let these things bother him much and he still had his share of good friends of both black and white races. Friends with whom he shared time within various forms of recreation such as fishing, football, playing dominoes, hanging around and sometimes getting into minor trouble as kids can do.

He became heavily involved in sports as a teen and played on his Pass Christian High School Pirates' baseball and football teams and became affectionately nicknamed 'Mack' by his teammates.

After high school, he attended a local junior college for a couple of years but really had no clue what direction he wanted his life to go in. That was until one day he heard that a Dallas Police Department recruiter was going to be in town at the local Marriot Hotel.

After he met with the recruiter, McElroy liked what he heard. Being a police officer was his opportunity to be able to help people in need, to protect them from others who would victimize those older, smaller, or weaker - basically anyone they could take advantage of in order to make a buck or benefit in some way.

This sounded like a great chance for Mack to find a career that would challenge him and one that he could be proud of. Mack flew to Dallas a month later for three days to undergo DPD's thorough hiring process, which consisted of a written exam, a physical agility test, a polygraph test, drug screen, medical checkup and psychological evaluation.

The physical agility test proved to be a particularly memorable experience for the young police officer applicant, as one of the tests was a fifty-yard dash which was conducted in the basement of an old downtown building that used to be the Dallas Police Headquarters. It was in this very underground basement back on November 24th of 1963 that Dallas nightclub owner Jack Ruby shot Lee Harvey Oswald, the alleged assassin of President John F Kennedy.

McElroy returned home to await the test results, and about three weeks later he learned he had passed every step of the process. So, at the tender age of twenty-one years old, Kelvin McElroy was hired by the Dallas Police Department, and his world was about to flip upside down. This tiny-town kid was about to be paid to police one of the largest metropolitan areas of the country.

It was a cool, rainy December day when McElroy rolled into 'the Big D' with all of his worldly possessions in the back of his grey Chevy S-10 pickup and the small white and orange six-foot-long U Haul trailer being towed behind it.

McElroy had already made quite a name for himself back in

his hometown, being the first in his family to get a college degree, let alone the first to attend college at all. So, it was also quite a monumental achievement for him to be moving to Dallas to start a new exciting career and to begin training in the Dallas Police Academy.

Dallas Police Academy Class 226 consisted of twenty-six recruits, twenty men and six women of all races and ages and hailing from all parts of the United States.

On day one of the academy, Mack instantly noticed one of the other twenty-six recruits. Her name was Megan Anderson. *Everyone* noticed her.

This twenty-year-old, captivating Caucasian female had long, flowing, naturally curly dirty blonde hair. At 5'3 and 115 pounds, she was an avid Crossfit and weight trainer and was equally as excited about her tattoos. Approximately one third of all of her skin was currently canvassed, and she had one or two more ink projects pending as soon as she had the money to pay for them.

Mack graduated from the academy with the highest grade-point average in his class, and he and Megan, along with three other rookies, were assigned to the downtown area known as the Central Business District, on foot patrol.

The Central Business District, or "CBD," consisted of an area on the west side called, quite appropriately, the "West End," another section on the east side called "Deep Ellum," and a Farmers Market to the south.

Mack was slated to be trained by Sergeant and Field Training Officer Jake Hathaway, who was advised he would be re-assigned to the K9 Unit after McElroy's training was completed.

Mack felt very fortunate in having been assigned to Jake Hathaway for the first and last phases of the four total phases in what is a six-month long Field Training Program. Senior Corporal Hathaway had the reputation of being a great, hardworking street cop who had a nose for sniffing out criminal activity.

His reputation as a no-nonsense, tough, training officer preceded him, and was one which the rookie officers in the academy gossiped about and feared. For he had failed many a rookie officer in the Field Training phase when they fell short of his stringent standards. On the other hand, he had played a prominent role in the instruction of more than one new officer being nominated by their peers as the outstanding Rookie of the Year.

On the first day of field training, Mack showed up forty-five minutes early. He had left his house very early, not wanting to risk the chance of running into some bad traffic and being late on his first day. His navy blue Blauer uniform pants and shirt were freshly pressed, his 5.11 black tactical boots polished, and spit shined, with his hair cut short and high. His Glock was still coated in the factory oil and his Taser brand electroshock weapon was new and as bright yellow as a bumble bees butt.

Some of the senior officers (often referred to as 'old heads') around the station observed Mack and his academy classmates lined up in the hallway and began to cut up, laughing and joking about how they "looked and smelled like fresh new rookie cops straight out of the academy."

The first couple of weeks in the Field Training Process allowed for trainees to primarily observe their trainers on the job, giving the rookies time to get acclimated to their new beats. It didn't take Mack long to learn the Central Business District.

Mack soon came to learn that "Deep Ellum" was best known for its live music, hole-in-the-wall bars and performance halls, as well as its many tattoo parlors. Hathaway and his rookie would eventually spend many Friday and Saturday nights patrolling this area, breaking up fights and investigating car burglaries, pick pockets, and robberies each night until, like clockwork, one of the clubs would blast the song "Closing Time" through its indoor and outdoor patio speakers at 2 a.m.

But most of McElroy's training would derive from the many hours he and his trainer would spend patrolling the West End. This was an area that consisted of restaurants, a mini indoor mall that also had a movie theatre, as well as office buildings and a Greyhound bus station. More notably, though, were the Dealey Plaza Historic District and Sixth Floor Museum, as well as a Holocaust Museum.

Many historians believe the shots that killed President John F. Kennedy had been fired from the southeast corner window of the Texas School Book Depository (now known as the Sixth Floor Museum), and that an assassin fired the shots. Texas Governor John Connally was also severely wounded in the assault, as the gunman fired upon a presidential motorcade that drove through the now-famous Dealey Plaza on the early afternoon of November 22, 1963.

Although most believe the shooter in this case was Lee Harvey Oswald, an employee of the Texas School Book Depository, others speculate Oswald was merely the sacrificial lamb offered to conceal what was in reality a United States government involved conspiracy.

Nonetheless, in its present state, the Sixth Floor Museum, which is located on the sixth and seventh floors of the building, explores President Kennedy's life, legacy, and various theories about his murder.

Mack had to chuckle to himself every time he thought about walking the beat with Jake in the downtown area, often having tourists walking up to them to ask where Kennedy was shot. This would be Jake's cue to sarcastically take his own right index finger, point to the back of his head, and exclaim "right about here!"

The tourists usually would at that point become speechless. Either they were in shock from the tasteless comment or possibly thought the officer was a dumbass and didn't understand they were looking for directions to the *physical* location where Kennedy was killed, not the part of his body which was impaled by a fast-flying, lead projectile.

Jake would then usually pause to get the most out of the tourists' reactions before saying "only kidding - it was right down there," and point to the large white "X" spray painted onto the roadway in the exact spot where Kennedy sat in his open limousine when he was sniped.

Field Training went well for McElroy, as he made every effort to absorb everything of value he possibly could from his trainers. He studied the Texas Penal Code and Code of Criminal Procedures on his time off, as well as the department's general orders and standard operating procedures. Mack continued to work out in the gym, weight training and running to keep his body as fit and strong as his mind.

Perhaps most importantly of all, through a great deal of hard work and repetition, Mack was able to learn how to initiate his own activity and to make quality proactive arrests while keeping his own and others' safety as priority number one. He made mistakes during training, but he accepted them, learned from them, and vowed to never make the same mistake twice.

On days when Mack would make it through the first half of his shift without screwing something up too badly, Jake would reward him by buying the recruit's dinner at Hathaway's favorite restaurant, the Steak Pit. This dark, dirty, roach-infested eatery on Harry Hines was not fancy, the staff wasn't overly friendly, and the food wasn't good either. But the place was *Jake's*.

It was where the patrol sergeant could go every single late night to escape from all of those people flagging him down to ask directions, the citizens who thought it was funny when they were around cops to point at their friend and say, "Hey officer, he's the one you're looking for- he's got warrants out. Haa haaa."

Mack didn't get Jake's attraction to this place. Mack hated the place. But being a good rookie who didn't want to piss off his trainer, he went along for the ride.

One incident would forever remain with Officer McElroy.

It was a Saturday morning around 2:15 a.m., when Mack and Jake were walking the beat in the Deep Ellum area of downtown. The officers got flagged down by a citizen who worriedly exclaimed, "There's a fight going on down that alley!"

The officers began to head that way. They knew that they were getting close to the disturbance when they noticed that several people had just noticed them and were now running away down the opposite end of the alley. Mack was smart enough not to instinctively chase after the first person he saw running away. Rather, he scanned the area to ascertain who the real catalyst of this disturbance was. He then noticed as one male who was apparently high on drugs or intoxicated from alcohol, dressed in all black, failed to see the law officers nearby. He then sucker-punched an elderly man who had been camped out on a corner, begging for handouts.

Mack ran toward the assailant and leapt at him, launching his body forward and airborne. This was a diving tackle that would have made many NFL players proud. The assailant was knocked to the ground, with Mack landing on the guy's back. A short struggle ensued, but Officer McElroy was able to use his physical strength and prowess to subdue the assault suspect.

Jake stood back a couple feet, watching the rookie act. But upon further observation, Jake noticed that the suspect in black appeared to be very nervous. He was much more nervous than your run-of-the-mill drunk who had just left the bar and decided to smack some homeless guy who looked at him the wrong way for not giving up some loose change.

Mack got off the suspect but failed to handcuff him right away or even maintain a strong hold on him. The opportunistic suspect sprang to his feet and began to scan the area around him, most likely preparing to react as most humans do when they respond to stress or as criminals do when they are about to be detained, apprehended, or arrested by law enforcement; responding typically with a fight- or-flight instinct kicking in.

Mack instructed the criminal to put his hands behind his back, and Jake noticed that the subject was hesitant to respond and looking down at the front of his pants. Hathaway observed that the intoxicated male had a bulge inside the front of his trousers, and he was starting to reach down in that direction with his right hand.

Jake drew his Glock .40 caliber and aimed it at the suspect, saying, "Don't fuckin' move, you piece of shit! Mack, handcuff him! Now check his waistband carefully."

Sure enough, the offender had a switchblade knife in his pants and was about to attack Mack with it. He knew he had an outstanding parole violation warrant issued by the Texas Department of Corrections and was not wanting to go back to prison.

Jake never put this incident in his training records or mentioned it again, but Mack would never forget. Jake knew that Mack had just gained more from this experience then he ever would from reading the same teachings in a book or hearing it in a lecture. This was a prime example of 'failing forward', turning mistakes into invaluable life lessons.

From that day forward when Mack contacted anyone suspicious or otherwise, he always carefully maintained eye contact with the subject. He watched closely and paid particularly close attention to others' hands to ensure they were not reaching for a weapon.

He also learned that you could learn much about what someone was thinking or planning by the way they acted - through their body language. One could learn a lot by studying persons' subconscious facial expressions, hand movements, gestures, postures, even eye pupil dilation.

However, this was not an exact science. For there was one

instance when Mack noticed that a person whom he was interviewing was acting peculiar and began to reach toward his crotch area. Mack grabbed a firm hold on the male's arm and said, "What are you reaching for down there?"

Mack noticed a large bulge in the man's pants and did a pat-down in that area to feel what seemed like a cantaloupe in the front of the guy's pants.

It turned out the dude had a huge tumor in one of his testicles, and the man and his gestures were completely harmless. But as Jake would always tell his rooks, "It's better to be safe than to be sorry."

Chapter 3 - Beckoning of the Berserkers

Dallas County Jail, Downtown Dallas (Present Day)

Soon after being charged with the murders, and not financially stable enough to afford some high-dollar attorney, Jake hired the cheapest attorney he could find. Jake did not think he had anything to worry about anyways, so he wasn't concerned that his new representative, Duy Tran, was fresh out of the Southern Methodist University Law School, with no real trial experience to speak of.

Before the trial had started, Tran met with his new client in a Lew Sterrett visitation room and warned the accused Hathaway that this case would not be an easy one to defend. For, although he believed Jake's story, there were several obstacles in the case which they would have to navigate around.

For one thing, the bodies of Rich and Holly had mysteriously vanished before any testing or further evidence collection could be achieved.

Another troubling issue Tran had discovered involved the prosecution's key eyewitness, Mrs. Gladys Torrence. She was the victims' next-door neighbor who witnessed the slayings. Surely, she would be able to set the jury straight about the incident and establish Jake's innocence.

However, even during discovery and pre-trial motions, she often seemed to be testifying as if reading from a prepared script and was testifying with statements that were contradictory and misleading. Something was very wrong with that woman's reliability, which could work in one of two ways. Either (A) the jury could totally dismiss anything she says out of their lack of confidence in her, or (B) they could be gullible and fall for the load of crap that she was shoveling onto their shoes.

"Well, you better figure it out. I'm depending on you, and so is my family," Jake told Duy as he chugged down a gulp of warm water from a styrofoam cup.

Jake wondered how a small-town kid like himself could find himself in a predicament such as this. It was going to take much more than his personal strength to survive this ordeal. Jake considered himself fortunate to still have his faith after all these tribulations. He had been raised by parents with a strong Catholic influence. For now, he would be relying upon much higher powers than himself or his attorney to intercede in this volatile situation.

Jake was baptized as a baby. As a child, his life was consistent with that of any other Catholic raised kid. He attended mass each Sunday, learning and memorizing all the assigned pertinent prayers. He learned lists of religious concepts, and at the age of fifteen he had his Confirmation. This was the ceremony in which a young adult begs for God's mercy, they say their penance (reciting the prayers that they have memorized) and profess their personal commitment to the faith.

Being Catholic also meant Jake found himself at the church giving Confessions every Wednesday and Sunday. He would also 'say the rosary' - touching each bead on a rosary necklace and saying a corresponding prayer for each one. Jake had a working knowledge of all of the saints as well.

For example, one of the many Catholic saints was Saint Michael, the archangel patron saint of police officers and soldiers. Jake felt it appropriate to have the image of Saint Michael tattooed to his left peck on his chest when he finished his service with the Marine Corps and learned he had been hired by the Dallas Police

Department.

Jake often wore a white gold chain with a silver crucifix as well, reminding him constantly of his commitment to and relationship with God.

Earle Cabell Federal Building and U.S. District Court, Downtown Dallas
(Present Day)

Prosecutor Ferron continued: "Now, let's talk evidence, starting with the direct evidence we have in this case. What is direct evidence? Direct evidence is one of two things. You have an eyewitness who saw a person commit the offense and can identify this person. We have that. Or, you have someone say, 'Yeah, I committed those murders.' It's called a confession. And we have that too.

"So, what else could we possibly need? Nothing. That's all we need. But we have more ... physical evidence; it's DNA and fingerprints, the weapons used to inflict the injuries and cause the deaths. It's any other type of physical evidence. And we've got all of that, too. And finally, there is circumstantial evidence, which is everything else. We have plenty of that as well."

"When you hear from the defense, I anticipate they will attempt to sway you by saying that the defendant was committing the act of self-defense and was in imminent fear of death or serious bodily injury and acted to stop such action against him. This is the defense's attempt to create doubt in your minds.

"They do this to try and confuse you, make you question what you know is true.

"But the TRUTH is that Jake's actions were willful and deliberate - and that in his premeditated state, he killed more than one person. He was the one and only principal party responsible - inflicting fatal injuries to poor Rich and Holly Hathaway - Jake's own brother and sister-in-law, ending their lives."

Jake, incensed at the accusations leveled at him, leaned over to speak to his eager but slightly overwhelmed, young representative.

"Duy, how can they do this to me? These are all lies!"

He began to feel light-headed, his blood pressure like a

heartbeat pulsating loudly inside his head. Jake felt as if his brain was swelling within his skull. The sensation was maddening.

He had felt this way before - and found that retreating to a safe place in his mind could sometimes pacify him. He closed his eyes and replayed in his mind's eye several cheerful memories from when he and his brother were young.

He recalled the snowball fights they had out in the front yard during some of those long, cold winter snow days when school was canceled. Then there was the tree fort they built in the woods together, and the dark, scary nights they endured when they slept overnight out there during the summer breaks. And of course, there was the unforgettable experience of sitting side by side with their dad on top of the left field wall, better known as the Green Monster, at a Red Sox game at Fenway Park.

Rich, considered by most to be the smarter of the two brothers, grew up with the hopes of someday being a lawyer. He started his freshman year of college at Brown University in Providence, Rhode Island, in the fall following his eighteenth birthday. Rich aspired of obtaining a degree in engineering.

During spring break in the following March, Rich and some of his college buddies loaded up a Chevy Astro van and headed south to Daytona Beach, Florida. They had the typical youthful intentions of drinking heavily and being in proximity of many tan, beautiful, scantily clad sorority girls.

But when Rich returned to New England, for some unexplained reason, he was very different.

Within a month he had dropped out of school, moved out of his parents' house and started living in his brown Chevy Malibu.

Subsequently, he was found wandering around naked through the neighborhood - on more than one occasion. This led to his being arrested for public lewdness and public intoxication.

Rich's criminal history soon expanded to include an arrest for shoplifting, as well as for assaulting a peace officer, which is a felony in the State of Rhode Island.

As a result of this felony charge (and conviction), Rich spent six months in the ACI - Rhode Island's Adult Corrections Institution; the state prison.

Shortly after his release, Rich was compelled to move away from the Northeast to get a fresh start. As a resolution, Rich's roll of the dice, figuratively speaking, resulted in him moving to north Dallas to be closer to his older brother.

There Rich found for himself a small one-bedroom apartment and began working full-time at a local Whataburger restaurant, where he met associate burger slinger Holly-Ann Jones, a cute little long-haired redhead with permanent fake eyelashes and a strong east Texas accent.

Holly, who was the same age as Rich, had previously been married to her high school sweetheart, Kent Jones. Holly and Kent had a son together, named Austin Waylon Jones. Several months after Austin's birth, Kent overdosed on methamphetamines and Holly was left alone to raise their son.

Rich and Holly soon became inseparable, hanging out together after work and eventually cohabitating for a while at their rental house in the "M Streets" area of upper Greenville Ave. They were soon married, just four months into their relationship.

Austin, who is now 11 years old, grew to be very fond of his new stepdad. And in that same year, Holly gave birth to her second child, presenting Rich with the gift of a handsome baby boy named Carson.

Suddenly, the prosecutor's roaring voice echoed through the chambers as he continued. "Remember the testimony from defense witness Gerald Fitzpatrick? You may recall that Fitzpatrick was in the Marines with Jake Hathaway for five years. They trained together, performed top-secret missions together."

"The defense team called Mr. Fitzpatrick to paint the defendant as a hero – like Captain America. And then the defense called some police officers that worked with the defendant to talk about his career as a police officer. Again, they would have you think Jake Hathaway is about the most daring, law-abiding, Super Cop that ever lived."

"But then I cross-examined Mr. Fitzpatrick, asking the pertinent questions that the state did not want asked - and we heard the truth. Fitzpatrick hesitantly admitted to you that, while in the Marine Corps, he and Jake were trained to *KILL*. There you have it. Finally, someone is telling the truth about our defendant, the trained killer. Now, I will reveal to you MY character assessment of the defendant."

"He was nothing more than a camouflaged hit man employed

and paid by the United States military. And he continued that legacy as a patrol sergeant for the Dallas Police Department."

Jake's jaw dropped – or at least to him it felt that way. He expected to hear a thud as his cleft chin hit the table in front of him.

The shock of Ferron's words took his breath away. Jake had always taken pride in doing what he believed to be admirable and ethical. He didn't consider himself to be any kind of hero... just a Marine doing what Marines do every day. But since when does defending your country mean that you are a "hit man" – a murderer?

At the conclusion of his senior year in high school, Jake had signed a four-year commitment to the United States Marine Corps, having no desire to go to college or join the workforce.

So in the month of June and at the age of 18, he began the first of twelve humid summer weeks of hell in boot camp at the Marine Corps Recruit Depot in Parris Island, located within Port Royal, South Carolina. There all recruits are required to endure and satisfactorily complete a 54-hour simulated combat exercise known as "the Crucible."

After completing boot camp, Jake was sent to Camp Geiger in North Carolina for more training in the School of Infantry. This course instills all basic infantry skills and some advanced infantry skills for those Marines who are going out to the fleet.

From there, Jake transferred to Camp Pendleton in San Diego, California. There he spent several more weeks learning amphibious assault techniques.

Amphibious warfare is a type of offensive military operation that uses naval ships to project ground and air military power onto a hostile or potentially hostile shore. Throughout history these operations were conducted using smaller boats from the larger ships as the primary method of delivering troops to shore.

More recently, specialized watercraft such as fast patrol boats, rigid inflatable boats called zodiacs, and mini submersibles were designed for this purpose. The Marines are credited with being the earliest in the American military to adopt a varying range of maneuver-warfare principles which emphasize flexible execution.

Considering more recent warfare that has strayed from the Corps' traditional missions, it renewed an emphasis on amphibious capabilities.

After Jake's amphibious warfare training was completed, he was assigned to the West Coast 11th Marine Expeditionary Unit (MEU) based out of Marine Corps Base Camp Pendleton in San Diego.

Each MEU consists of a Command Element, a Ground Combat Element; separated into a Battalion Landing Team that includes three rifle companies, a weapons company, and a battery of artillery and platoons of the following: combat engineers, light armored reconnaissance, tanks, Force Reconnaissance and amphibious assault vehicles), an Aviation Combat Element; built around squadrons of 25 to 30 Marines per CH-53E heavy lift helicopters, light attack helicopters and Harrier attack jets.

There was also a Logistics Combat Element, who supplied additional support for the MEU. Jake was one of the 1,200 Marines assigned to the Ground Combat Element- specializing primarily in the operation of amphibious assault vehicles.

MEUs deploy aboard an Amphibious Ready Group (ARG), composed of three naval ships specifically designed to provide the Marines with a mobile base of operations. MEUs spend at least six months training for a variety of amphibious operations before they are deployed. Then, for six months at a time, Marine Expeditionary Units embark upon United States Navy warships and prepare to launch a range of missions—from humanitarian and peacekeeping missions to full-scale combat engagements, on extremely short notice.

The 11th MEU was one of three units that maintained a presence in the Pacific Ocean, Indian Ocean, and Persian Gulf. Due to the nature of their expeditionary mission, they were able to deploy anywhere in the world.

In the early months of Jake's fourth year of enlistment, the three Marine Expeditionary Units were summoned to Afghanistan to begin training for an operation which would later be termed the "Operation Everlasting Freedom."

They eventually would play a large part in dismantling the Taliban and wiping the slate clean of al-Qaeda in the entire region.

Although Jake's unit saw much wartime battle action in that operation, Marine 1st Lieutenant Jake Hathaway had become heavily involved in another, much more classified project.

A group of Five Star Generals had assembled to form a committee to address the issue regarding a recent trend of Marine recruits who washed out of the boot camp training regimen due to being too mentally and /or physically weak.

Also, some who successfully completed training had to be discharged soon afterwards when they were deployed in third world countries and thrown into battle only to subsequently fold under the pressure.

All the branches of the armed forces were seeing the same characteristics in this new wave of recruits. These "millennials" were coming into training camp with the initial appearance of being ambitious, achievement-oriented, and seeking out new challenges.

However, this group also appreciated being kept in the loop, were not afraid to question authority, and craved attention in the forms of feedback, praise and guidance.

These traits were contrary to the timeless American military tradition of discipline, chain of command, and doing what you are told without question, and without questioning why.

So much for the old school, hardcore military drill sergeant's cadence of, "yours is not to question why; yours is but to do or die!"

This new committee was formed with the objective of developing a plan to turn the new generation of soldiers into modern day 'Berserkers'. Icelandic and Scandinavian historians alike wrote of their description of Berserkers as soldiers who were as strong as bears or wild oxen, and as mad as dogs or wolves, and feared nothing and no one.

They rushed forward suddenly into battle in a demoniacal frenzy and without armor. Neither edged weapons nor fire could deter them. They furiously bit at and devoured the edges of their shields, eager and anxious at the chance to slay and destroy.

They would rush through the perils of crackling fires; gulping down fiery coals by snatching live embers in their mouths and letting them pass down into their innards. And when they had ravaged through every sort of madness, they turned their swords with rage against the hearts of their enemies.

So now the wise men of this US Marine Corps panel decided to appoint someone to head a project with the goal of turning modern day Marines into medieval times 'Berserkers', under the guise of forming a 'Strength and Conditioning, Health and Nutritional

Wellness Plan.'

Considering his personal commitment to physical fitness and weight training, Hathaway seemed like the obvious choice for the person to head up this new Marine venture.

He was given a team of scientists and physicians to assist him in his testing and planning, as well as three volunteers who signed waivers, relinquishing them of any opportunities of filing liability claims in the future should the experiments go awry.

The volunteers, or perhaps a more accurate depiction for them would be the 'volunTOLDs,' were highly encouraged to accept these assignments or find themselves in even fewer desirable positions in the very near future.

These were quite possibly the three guys in the unit who were nothing more than the most expendable of the group. The thought being that if these soldiers ended up damaged somehow or for some reason, there really wasn't much of a loss. These were already considered to be the least dependable and/or talented soldiers they had.

But if somehow these treatments did transform these men into 'Invulnerable Warriors,' then it would be a win-win all around.

This trio of selected soldiers would include men with just about the most opposite up-bringing possible:

Barrett Blackhoof was birthed by a single mother and into the Shawnee Tribe of Native Americans in eastern Oklahoma. The Shawnees are a federally recognized tribe, once considered part of the Cherokee Nation.

After his father walked out on the family, and then his young mother died of a drug overdose about six months later, the ten-year-old Barrett had no family to turn to and nowhere to land.

He was eventually scooped up by a state-run Child Protective Services agency that placed Barrett in a Caucasian foster home outside of Shawnee territory. He was often bullied and chastised for celebrating his family heritage, making him want nothing more than to someday be able to rub it all back in their faces, make his name become a household word. A name that people would never forget.

Levi Fiedler grew up in a small town of roughly 5,700 people, in Chadron, Nebraska. He was a goofy-looking, tall, slender and freckle covered Caucasian kid with large ears who had never really had any friends growing up.

He joined ROTC while in high school and then upon graduation, he immediately met with a recruiter to sign enlist in any branch of the military that would show interest in him first.

Fiedler could have cared less about defending his country and the freedoms that it promises. He was hoping to become a part of something, anything, much larger than himself. He desperately wanted to belong to someone or something, and to be a part of a cause.

The third volunteer was an interesting character named **Daniel Camacho**, one who would become very influential in the actions and lives of the previously mentioned soldiers.

As a collaborative effort and after much thought, the team dubbed this new endeavor the "Zeus Project." This moniker was inspired by the Greeks, who considered Zeus the King of the Gods; who supervised the universe, to include the sky, lightning, thunder, law, order, and justice. The name seemed fitting as the goal was to turn some loser GI's into Immortal, "Invincible Warrior" GODS.

As a result of his hard work and dedication in this new assignment, Hathaway was promoted to Captain on July 15th in only his fourth year of service in the Corps.

It was an unprecedented leap in rank in what was the beginning of what could have been a great military career, had it not been for an unpredictable turn of events that would follow.

The arrival of November marked the start of Operation Everlasting Freedom, and Jake and Camacho, as part of the 11th MEU, were deployed to Afghanistan, where their unit played a prominent role.

The combined forces encompassing the U.S. military and its allied forces established their first ground base in Afghanistan, known as FOB Rhino, to the south west of Kandahar. These troops went on to further destroy the Taliban and suspected al-Qaeda in that region.

In early March of the following year, the 11th MEU, as part of the United States military, joined with allied Afghan military forces. They conducted a large operation in efforts to destroy al-Qaeda in an operation code-named Operation Anaconda.

It would be during this deployment that Captain Hathaway would find himself in a scenario that would eventually change his and many other lives forever....

Chapter 4 - Mutiny Within

Earle Cabell Federal Building and U.S. District Court, Downtown Dallas (Present Day)

Prosecutor Ferron took a deep breath, then stood up from his perch before taking a prolonged stroll which ended adjacent to the jury box. There he paused momentarily before resuming his closing arguments.

"You heard from our witness, Holly and Rich's next-door neighbor named Gladys Torrence. Thank God for people like Gladys Torrence.

"She was a close friend of the victims. She testified that she remembered when Rich and Holly moved into their modest three-bedroom red brick ranch house next door. Soon afterwards Holly gave birth to baby Carson. Gladys even babysat little Carson occasionally. But soon-after that, Mrs. Torrence noticed the couple appeared to be having some marital problems. Several times she heard yelling and screaming coming from the couple's house - their bedroom was at the end of their house closest to Torrence's residence.

"Shortly after Carson was born, Rich and Holly separated, and Rich moved out. Gladys doesn't know where Rich moved to, but she saw him return usually on weekends to visit. Rich appeared different, though. She alleged that maybe he was drinking alcohol or taking drugs. And I propose to you jury members that Rich was using these drugs to escape the fact that he knew his brother Jake was having an affair with his wife, Holly."

The large group of trial observers gasped as one, and Jake began to hemorrhage with a wrath unequaled. It was bad enough he was being framed for two murders, but now he was being painted as an adulterer as well. And with his sister-in-law, nonetheless!

He turned his head to stare directly into the moist eyes of his girlfriend and soul mate, and he shook his head side to side to refute the cheating allegation and to let her know it was a sham. Tears rolled down Amanda's cheeks. She placed her face down toward her lap and in the palms of her hands.

The prosecutor continued to spew his lies and falsities.

"Of course, Rich's drinking and drug use cannot be confirmed - but nevertheless, Gladys affirmed there was a change in Rich's posture. His overall manner and appearance had deteriorated, as well as his hygiene.

"Gladys also noticed on several occasions that there was a different vehicle going in and out of Holly's garage, which was attached to the house. This car was white and large - looked like a police car. It definitely was not Rich's tiny little blue Mazda Miata with the soft-top convertible.

"And remember what she saw on that afternoon of February Eighth? Gladys recalled at about 12:35 p.m., she was in her vegetable garden on the west side of her house. She was just fifty yards from Holly's yard. A large white and blue police SUV pulled in front of Holly's house. A white cop and his police dog walked into Holly's driveway, then walked up to the front door.

Ferron continued. "The cop didn't knock, didn't yell 'search warrant' or nothing. He just kicked the door in with one kick of his boot. Gladys was terrified for the safety of her neighbor, Holly. She even feared for her own safety. Gladys ran into her own house and grabbed binoculars. She investigated Holly's home through a variety of open windows. She could not believe what she saw next."

"The cop and his police dog were inside the front of the residence. Meanwhile in the back-kitchen area, Holly was trying to feed baby Carson some birthday cake. Suddenly, the vicious dog just started jumping up on Holly. The dog was biting, clawing, tearing, and shredding the flesh on Holly's arms and upper torso. Then the cop started shooting her!"

"Yes, you heard that right! A young mother simply attempting to have a nice birthday party for her baby gets gunned down in her own kitchen! My god..."

Ferron took a dramatic pause, shook his head side to side and sighed before proceeding.

"Holly toppled onto the floor – dead. She dropped the baby. The cop picked the baby up and used only his right hand to hold

Carson by his foot, dangling the baby upside down. The bad white cop then walked back outside with his killer k9. He put the baby in the front passenger seat of the police truck and walked back toward Holly's house.

"Gladys continued to watch as Rich appeared in the front yard and tried to rescue his baby boy. He soon found himself under attack. The defendant then commanded his vicious K9 police partner to attack Rich. I believe Gladys described the dog as a 'hellhound'. The dog was viciously tearing away at Rich's body with his huge fangs. Here we have a so-called lawman using his trained killer police dog as a weapon! But it gets worse.

"Gladys then watched in horror as Jake used his taser to shoot Rich in the face, filling Rich's noggin with 50,000 volts of electricity. Then he drew his Glock automatic .40-caliber pistol and shot Rich five times in the chest. But that wasn't even enough for Jake. He didn't even stop there. The defendant was so filled with anger, hatred, and jealousy that he was not satisfied with just murdering his victims. He wanted overkill!

"He removed his large Marine issue K-Bar fighting knife with the seven-inch carbon steel blade from the sheath on his left ankle. He then viciously stabbed the blade into Rich's forehead, nearly taking off the top half of Rich's head!

"Rich would not take another breath of air after this. He would never live to see his baby son Carson blow out the candles on a birthday cake ever again. This murder happened right in the front yard - in front of an eyewitness – Gladys. Thank God the crazed defendant did not see Gladys watching. Who knows what he would have done to her!!!"

A dramatic cessation followed, as Prosecutor Ferron acted all choked up. He took a swig from the tall glass of ice water on the table in front of him. He swallowed the water and then set the glass back down on the table before continuing.

"After the murders, Jake and his deputized hellhound kidnapped baby Carson and drove away. They offered no medical attention to their victims. Jake left them there to rot where they lie."

At no point in Ferron's statement about Witness Torrence did he mention that she was no longer alive. That detail and the story behind it were just a couple more facts that failed to see the light of day during this presentation by the prosecution team.

Ferron continued: "Now, you also remember the testimony given by FBI Agent Danny Camacho, don't you?"

"Danny Camacho." Just hearing that name again infuriated Jake, causing his blood to boil and pop within his veins. His heart began to pound rapidly, and his breathing became deeper. Jake found himself taking oxygen into his body through flared nostrils and between clenched teeth.

Danny and Jake shared some history together years earlier in the Marine Corps. But these two would never sit down together amiably and drink beer together – that's for sure.

Young Daniel Camacho was the oldest of three siblings born to Hector and Maria Camacho. This young couple, just five years before Daniel's birth, had been filled with the ambition to someday find full-time, well-paying jobs for each of them. Like many other couples, they had hopes of being able to afford the cost of raising a family. For this reason, they knew they had to flee the poverty and insecurity of Mexico. So, they illegally crossed into the United States in pursuit of their dreams.

The family settled in the Compton area of southern Los Angeles. It was a rough neighborhood, to say the least. One had to be physically and mentally tough in order to survive this urban jungle. Young Danny struggled to endure life in this difficult setting. And to make matters worse, at the young age of just seven, he lost the only real male role model in his life. Danny's father was killed in an automobile collision, leaving Maria and the children fending for survival on their own.

In June the year following Jake's enlistment, Danny Camacho entered the Marine Corps and reported to the Recruit Depot in San Diego. Like most new Marines, he was full of piss and vinegar and eager to get boot camp past him. Camacho could not wait for the opportunity to be deployed and see some real combat time.

Danny was what some would describe as a 'gym rat'. He had spent most of his time growing up bench pressing and lifting weights in the backyard of his mother's modest Compton residence. The yard was enclosed by a six-foot chain-link fence and was protected from within by two aggressively trained pitbulls named Schwarzenegger and Ferrigno.

As a result of his backyard benching, Danny's six-foot two-inch frame was muscle packed and ripped. Although his last name was of Hispanic origin and he had a brown complexion, Camacho spoke little Spanish. The extent of his Espanol was "Nachos Bell Grande and Burrito Supreme."

After completing boot camp, Camacho was sent to Camp Pendleton in San Diego, California. There he spent several more weeks in the School of Infantry, followed by several more strenuous weeks of learning amphibious assault techniques.

At the conclusion of this training, Corporal Camacho found himself assigned to the West Coast 11th Marine Expeditionary Unit (11th MEU), as was Jake Hathaway. They were two of the 1200 Marines in the Ground Combat Element that specializes in light armored reconnaissance.

Jake and Camacho often trained together in teams. Camacho quickly gained a reputation of being cocky. He seemed to be a self-centered prick who cared much more about his individual fame and glory than about the unit or the Corps or defending his country.

But as large as the unit was, Jake was able to avoid Camacho as much as possible when it came to 'down time' away from the base. And when it was time to resume training and get back to the grind of Corps life, Jake was able to maintain a professional working relationship with Danny. This was possible, although Jake considered Camacho to be nothing more than a pompous, obnoxious, douchebag.

Later that same year in the summertime, some of the drill sergeants from the base got together and planned a boxing tournament. The motivation behind the fights was in an attempt to create some competition, team building, and pride in all the troops.

Jake had continued to box in his spare time for fun and as a way to keep up with his cardiovascular training. He still had the endeavor to someday become a professional fighter after defending his country. For that reason, Jake naturally jumped at this opportunity to compete again, even if only for a month-long tournament.

Although he had never boxed in a ring, Danny Camacho was quick to sign up for the tournament as well. He wasted no time in starting his trash talk, making it-known to everyone within earshot that he was going to "kick everyone's ass and win the whole thing."

Danny and Jake each fought and beat two other opponents on the way to the championship fight, where they met to battle for what would soon become an annual tradition, the crowning of the title "Pendleton's Semper Fi - King of the Ring."

In their much-anticipated championship bout, Jake jumped out to an early lead. He was flying off the ropes and ripping off punches with his right hand to Camacho's torso primarily. A couple of good headshots got mixed in as well.

Jake Hathaway was obviously a very good fighter; his skills were polished and evident.

Camacho's style was quite contrary, as he was very strong and punched very hard. Danny's problem was that, due to his wildness, many of his blows did *not* land on their target. He still had knocked out his previous two opponents easily. Neither of those fighters, however, had exhibited the boxing prowess of Captain Hathaway.

Jake was taking his time, placing his shots, stepping to the side looking for an opening that he might not see in front. Through the first couple of rounds, he proved to be the early aggressor, with the punch numbers favoring him, landing 30 punches to just 17 for Camacho.

Camacho was becoming winded, making it more difficult for him to slip punches. He was strong and tough but was starting to feel Jake's multitude of quick jabs that were beginning to slow him down. He knew that his time was quickly winding down. He knew he had to connect with some power shots to knock his rival out and end this thing.

Camacho now was depending less on his ability to sidestep away from Jake's blows but rather was doing his best to block the shots with his gloves. He was attempting to pick his spots, and to pace himself until the right moment presented itself. He was waiting for the precise second in which he could unload with a power strike.

By round three, Jake was in the zone, throwing combinations, coming at Camacho from different angles. Danny was not able to anticipate these shots. Jake was showcasing a very smart fight.

This was just like Jake had always dreamed: fighting in front of a large crowd. He was showing off some of the skills he had obtained through years of sparring at the Y. And moves he had picked up through the close guidance of Grandpa Bill.

Jake's momentary lapse in focus startled him. He knew he had to rid his mind of any distractions, so he took a step back to get out of Camacho's line of fire while he regained his composure. This awkward back step caused Jake's boot to drag on the canvas and he staggered backwards.

Jake spun around to catch himself from falling, and he stood straight up with his back now facing Camacho. Jake quickly bladed his body then turned to face his opponent. Camacho's right gloved fist pummeled Jake's left side of his jaw. POWWWWW!!!

The Marine Captain heard the echo of the collision in his skull and felt the pulsating vibrations of pain racing throughout as well. The muffled sounds of the crowd yelling "get up!" were what clued Jake into the fact that he had been knocked out and was lying face down on the mat.

He had never been hit this hard, never been knocked out. Stars were swirled around his head, and they were not the stars some of the generals in the arena wore on their collars.

The referee began to give a standing eight count as Jake staggered to his knees and wobbled onto his feet like a newborn fawn standing on its own accord for the first time. The referee reached eight, then moved back two steps and instructed Jake to walk toward him and held his arms out. Jake lifted his gloves but was still unsteady on his feet, and the referee ended the bout, ruling that Camacho had won on a TKO.

For the rest of his military career, Jake would continuously be reminded by Camacho of the fight in which he 'pummeled Jake into submission' and won the title of "Semper Fidelis - King of the Ring" for that year.

Chapter 5 - The Village Idiots

Operation Anaconda, Al Anbar Province, Iraq (approx. 8 years earlier)

Since the Invasion of Iraq in the previous years, U.S. military forces had been stationed in and around the Al Anbar province of Iraq. Their primary objective was to control the Haditha Dam, a major hydroelectric installation. The area had seen several clashes between U.S. forces and insurgent groups since the beginning of the war. Hundreds of fatalities were lost on both sides. Conditions had been deteriorating under military rule. Attacks on U.S. troops as well as executions of suspected informants were common.

It was November 19th in the eighth year of Jake's service. An improvised explosive device, or IED, composed of 155 mm artillery shells and explosive-filled propane tanks was buried under loose dirt and rubble in a roadway heavily traveled by the US troops in the Al Anbar province.

When a Humvee transporting the 3/2 Kilo Company, 3rd Platoon Marines drove through that portion of the byway, the vehicle rolled over the device. This caused the IED to explode, splitting the vehicle in half and ejecting three of the squad. They were killed abruptly when their heads contacted the hard-compacted desert ground and/or by being struck with the flying Humvee debris.

Naturally the troops were all devastated by the loss of their comrades, and particularly affected were the guys from the killed soldiers' unit. This included those from the West Coast 11th MEU, such as Jake and Camacho and their team.

For the 11th MEU had been assigned to perimeter control in and around the Al Anbar Province and had been fighting valiantly to protect the lives of those who resided in the region and were thought not to be outwardly evil or militant. These citizens seemed for the most part to be victims of circumstance, just in the wrong place at the wrong time.

They were just like those of any other culture, trying to live their lives out in peace in a world better known for its violence and inhumanities.

Corporal Camacho was the first to learn of the Humvee bombing, and he, along with two of his comrade soldiers set out to the Province to get answers as to who may have initiated such an attack.

They arrived in the hot dusty region of Al Anbar in their olive camouflage Jeep. But before Camacho and Privates Fiedler and Blackhoof could even exit their vehicle, the sneers and jeers from the village people rained down upon the truth seekers.

Unexpectedly, the villagers seemed to be celebrating and rivaling in the death of the United States soldiers. An American flag-burning demonstration was occurring in front of them, and despite them, in the town square.

Never one to turn the other cheek when provoked or slighted, the hot-headed Camacho took the incidents unveiling before him as a personal attack. Not known to be one who ever acted for the love of his country or even just because it seemed like the "right thing to do," Camacho cared only about what was good for him or his personal cause, or because it would be fun.

It is unknown which of these reasons incited the ignorant one to act, but Danny jumped from his driver seat, his M16A4 service rifle in his left hand and a FGM-148 Javelin anti-tank guided missile strapped over his left shoulder.

Camacho was followed by Fiedler and Barrett Blackhoof, who were similarly armed. The trio of doom began to walk through the streets of the villa, firing their semi-automatic rifles into the crowds of once jubilant picketers.

With casualties and the incapacitated injured lying all about on the ground, those Iraqis who were capable began to flee the streets in pursuit of shelter within their simple structure homes.

Despite the bloodshed they had caused thus far, the GI's were not yet satisfied in their redemption. They continued their rampage, throwing grenades onto the roofs of houses, with the subsequent detonations causing the structures to collapse. Untold numbers of adult and child occupants were left lying beneath the resulting dust and rubble.

The Americans decided to enter the fragged shacks in pursuit of those avoiding retribution. The first three buildings they infiltrated appeared to be uninhabited, or at least unoccupied at the time. It was hard to tell the difference between the two because even houses that were lived in had very little furnishings or personal effects.

Next, they set foot in the first structure in which the three soldiers encountered people. A large family appeared to be taking shelter in a corner behind their dining table which was propped up on its side. The square table these Iraqis normally broke bread over was now being utilized much like a large wooden shield to protect them from harm.

Fiedler pointed his M16A4 muzzle in their direction and began to apply pressure to the sensitive hair-trigger when Camacho boomed "NO!! I've got something better."

Camacho pulled an empty syringe and a small medicine bottle out of his green canvas backpack and stuck the needle end into the bottle to load the syringe.

The unstable commando then walked over to the corner of the room where the clan attempted to shelter themselves. Camacho, holding the syringe in his left hand, grabbed hold of the table with his right hand and slung the wooden furniture piece across the room and into a wall, the collision causing it to smash into a magnitude of timber fragments.

"Hold them fuckers still!" Camacho instructed his cohorts.

Fiedler leapt forward and placed hands one at a time on the mother, father, and four children of ages ranging from four to fourteen, holding them still while Barrett Blackhoof steadily pointed the firing end of his assault rifle at them all and Camacho injected each of them in the neck to shoot them up with a substantial dose of the bottle's contents.

Captain Jake Hathaway had left the base as soon as he heard gunfire coming from the nearby village. He arrived on the scene just in time to see his three comrades exiting the shanty in which the injected family resided.

Camacho held the medicine bottle in his left hand and with his right hand, he threw the used needle to the dirt ground and stomped on it with his standard issue size 11 combat boots.

"What the hell did you do?" Jake interrogated.

"Well sir, you know these vitamins and supplements we have been volunteering to take for the last year and a half or so as part of your so-called Zeus Project? It seems like you were right about them making us more muscular, energized, and with a higher tolerance for pain. So, we figured what's good for us should be equally as good for our friends here!" Camacho articulated.

Hathaway was furious, his face beet red and his top about to blow. "Do you know what you have done? You guys have crossed the fucking line! We are here to protect these people! Whether you like them or their politics or not, we have a job to do, and what you guys have done is committed war crimes. Murder! This is the kind of shit that the United Nations gets involved in. You guys are fucked and rightfully so!"

Camacho doubled over as his grin quickly turned to a hideous cackle. "It doesn't matter, Captain, 'because we were all fucked when we started taking your Zeus Juice. Funny how you neglected to warn us about these side effects that all three of us are now experiencing."

Fiedler added, "Yeah, Captain, with all due respect, I must say that as your guinea pigs, you have fucked us up! I'm angry all the time, like I want to kill something, someone, anyone - even these guys I work with here. I feel inhuman - like an animal. I've been having dreams in which I was eating the flesh of somebody. I'm not sure who though."

Fiedler expressed his concerns as well.

"Yeah, boss – the same goes for me. I have been feeling powerful as hell, wide awake, robust as shit! But I have some issues too. Like, for example, I got some fingers and toes that are turning blue and the skin is getting hard and I'm starting to lose feeling there. It's kind of like parts of me are slowly dying."

Camacho joined back in. "So, we figured, you know what, if Captain Hathaway says this 'Zeus Juice' is so good for us, let's give some to our friends here in the village. They certainly could use some supplements like these. Ain't that what friends are for?"

Jake realized that the senseless murders his soldiers had committed in the town square and the injection of an innocent family could result in the allegations of war crimes. This would undoubtedly draw negative attention internationally. Jake became enraged.

"Go straight back to camp and prepare a memorandum about the role each of you played in this incident! And don't be surprised if you end up locked up or discharged after our investigation!"

The media soon caught wind of this incident and began to investigate, reporting their findings to the Pentagon, who then launched their own official United States criminal investigation. As a result, it was determined that 27 unarmed Afghanistan civilians - including children as young as two years old and women - were killed by the three members of the 11th MEU.

During an interview with Pentagon officials, Corporal Camacho and his co-defendants all insisted that upon their arrival into the village, they were fired upon by multiple insurgents in the street. The three Americans returned fire, killing several of the enemy assailants.

When several of the gunmen fled and ran into houses to hide, the GI's began searching door to door for them. After clearing each house and determining it was vacant, they would blow the structure up with a grenade to prevent the enemies from circling back around and occupying it for shelter.

At no point in the investigation was there any discussion regarding the details of what transpired six family members who were injected. Apparently, no one knew about this incident other than the GI's involved. The family in mention had completely vanished. It was as if they had fallen through a crevice in the earth's crust and were now trapped within the inner core.

As a result of their investigation, Pentagon officials and their Intelligence Squad determined that their photos and witness statements provided by the Iraqis were inconsistent with the three Marines' report of a firefight. There was no evidence to suggest that the three American soldiers had encountered any form of resistance or attack and that there was probably no threat to begin with.

Camacho, Barrett Blackhoof, and Levi Fiedler were all court marshaled on 27 counts of murder in what the prosecutors characterized as the Al Anbar Massacre, and Captain Jake Hathaway was subpoenaed and testified against the three accused.

Prior to the trial, Corporal Camacho made a deal with the military prosecution team and testified against Fiedler and Blackhoof in exchange for probation and an honorable discharge from the Marine Corps. Camacho testified, blaming the entire incident on the other two. Fiedler and Blackhoof each got twenty-year prison sentences while Camacho walked away without so much as a blemish being added to his record.

Months went by, and Jake heard no mention of Camacho. Even Jake's military connections, who kept close tabs on everyone even after they left the Corps, had no idea where Camacho had gone. It was almost as if he had vanished, disappeared from all sight and sound.

In the middle of Jake's second year with DPD, he had just started training his recruit, Mack McElroy when he heard the rumor from his Corps buddies that Camacho had resurfaced. He had been accepted into the Federal Bureau of Investigation as a rookie special agent.

Jake found this revelation to be quite disturbing. Camacho was not mentally stable enough to be trusted greeting people at the door of the local Walmart, never mind being a special agent for the FBI.

Chapter 6 - Holy Cadaver

Earle Cabell Federal Building and U.S. District Court, Downtown Dallas
(Present Day)

Ferron continued his closing arguments: "Camacho told you what happened when he and his companion agents tracked the defendant down as he returned to the Dallas Police Central Division station house ... the agents arrested Jake without incident.

"You saw photos of his appearance at that time - blood and brains sprayed across his face - a bite mark on his right shoulder where victim Holly tried to defend herself from this killer. Jake's uniform was taken as evidence - the blood and brain tissue matter all contained DNA that tested back to both Holly and Rich.

"Jake was also in possession of a Taser. The same one he used to sadistically electrically shock victim Rich's face. Then, Jake finished off his victim in a vicious stab to the head with a huge metal Marine knife. Jake still had this knife on him when he was detained by the agents.

"And as for the other deadly weapon he used - that vicious trained assassin k9 named Roscoe - you saw the pictures taken of Roscoe when the agents first saw him back at the station. Much like the defendant, Roscoe was covered with blood, skin, and tissue on his face and all over his matted fur."

Ferron produced large blown-up color images of Roscoe for the jury.

"Look at the teeth on this dog - look at his body. This is not a police officer K9, this isn't no hero dog like Lassie or Rin Tin Tin - if you are old enough to recall who they are. This is a seventy-five-pound musclebound, trained-to-kill, Belgian Malinois that the defendant Jake used as a weapon of destruction to attack and injure victims Holly and Rich.

"Roscoe was used to incapacitate both victims - chewing, gnawing on, and biting their extremities and torso so they could no longer move their shredded arms and legs to defend themselves. Roscoe's deadly dagger-like teeth tore those two-innocent people to bits.

"Mr. Swanson, the professional Police K9 trainer, explained how these dogs are controlled by their human partners through verbal commands. Roscoe wasn't motivated on his own to attack Holly and Rich. Roscoe didn't wake up that day and think to himself, ``Hmmm, I think I might go to that baby's birthday party and attack some harmless unarmed humans for no reason.

"This is all on Jake. Jake gave the orders, and Roscoe complied like a soldier. Like the trained killing weapon soldier dog that he is. And when Holly and Rich could no longer move to flee the onslaught or defend the attack, Jake finished them off – causing one final devastating blow to each of them - stabbing Holly in the face with a kitchen knife and then by thrusting that seven-inch stainless steel blade of his K-Bar knife through Rich's skull."

Jake sat – still dumbfounded by the way he was being portrayed and that the prosecution was weaving their lies into their arguments to manipulate the jurors into accepting this was not self-defense. Needing a brief respite from the corruption, he looked over his left shoulder to see his lovely lady sitting just three rows behind him.

Amanda appeared trance-like, probably in shock from the venom that was being slung about the room. Amanda looked at the heavily shackled Jake and fought back tears, mouthing the words "I love you" for Jake alone to lip read. Jake instantly found himself wandering off to a happier place and time…

Philly Fogg's restaurant, San Diego California (9 years earlier)

It was July 19th. Marine 1st Lieutenant Jake Hathaway was

being promoted to captain, a rank he had been trying to obtain for quite some time. That evening, Jake and some Corps buddies decided to enjoy a night out on the town and to celebrate the substantial promotion.

The rowdy Marines found their way to a sports bar not far from downtown called Philly Fogg's. This bar/restaurant featured a British-style food menu including fish and chips, Irish stew and shepherd's pie. Also, in stock was a large variety of worldwide beers.

The place was hopping, and the food was quite tasty. But Jake was not one who enjoyed being the center of attention. And this being Jake's party, and guys being guys, his comrades were yucking it up and doing just about every stupid thing possible, cutting up like crazy.

These were good dudes. They meant well. But Jake missed some of his buddies from back home in New England. He recalled a few fun evenings from the past with his Yankee pals (referring to friends from the Northeast, not the baseball team - *not that baseball team*). They were all regulars at another sports bar, the best and most notorious one in Boston – the Cask 'N Flagon. It was located right outside of Fenway Park.

Jake recalled stopping in there at times, sucking down a few Sam Adams beers before heading up the street to take in a Red Sox game.

Quickly his mind was brought back to the barstool where his body was propped, as an ice-cold stream of West Coast ale was poured from a beer pitcher onto the top of Jake's brown high and tight buzz cut. The beer streamed down his cheek, waking Jake up from his Fenway trip.

Jake was highly agitated by this prank. It had crossed the line of good-humored harmless horseplay. He quickly stood up and turned to look behind him to figure out which jester he was about to beat down. Behind Jake stood Danny Camacho, one of the newest members of the 11th MEU.

"What the fuck, Camacho - you fuckin asshole?!"

"Baaaaaahaaa!!"

Camacho began laughing loudly and hyena-like, not so much because he thought it was funny but more so because that was just the kind of person he was.

Camacho was like the anti-Jake, who loved nothing more than attention from wherever he could draw it.

Everyone in the sports bar turned toward the cackling sound coming from Danny's pie-hole. Many of the other women in the establishment began to watch him and were quite attracted to the show. Some even considering taking a spin on the Camacho amusement park ride. He was a good-looking dude with dark brown hair, medium complexion, and a body built by Jake (not Jake Hathaway - that other Jake guy that used to be on the fitness commercials).

One person sitting in the bar was not so impressed with the Danny fiesta that was unfolding around her. She did not even do so much as glance over at the spectacle. She was the type who would drive past a train wreck or rolled over SUV and not look at them because everyone else was doing it (and they were causing traffic to slow down by doing this, so she was getting pissed off).

Her name was Amanda McKnight. A gorgeous twenty-three-year-old long-haired brunette with sizable brown eyes, this Fort Worth, Texas, native was 5'5" and weighed about 130 pounds. She was the offspring of a Caucasian mother and a Hispanic father who decided to go out for a pack of smokes and never return when Amanda was just three years old.

When her father split, Amanda's mother had a difficult time dealing with the separation and requested her mother, Ava's grandmother, to watch over the young girl for a couple of years.

Eventually Amanda's mother remarried a Caucasian man, Amanda rejoined them, and they moved to the southwest Dallas neighborhood of Oak Cliff, an area known for its crime, poverty, gang violence, and Stevie Ray Vaughn.

Amanda had no choice but to quickly acclimate - to learn how to put on a tough appearance in order to survive and not be eaten alive in this rough part of town.

Amanda became a very popular figure at Sunset High School where she was on the yearbook staff for two years and a cheerleader for three years, before being accepted to attend San Diego State, which brought her to the West Coast.

Now this brown-skinned beauty was dressed casually in a modestly cut pink blouse and a tight pair of designer jeans. She sat among three other women at a small round table in the corner. Amanda was easily the prettiest girl in the bar but did not know it. She was comfortable with and accepting of the fact that she was attractive, but by no means did she act like she was the hottest babe in the place, which she was.

Unintentionally, she caught Camacho's eye (and everyone else's - including the newly promoted captain) although it was not in her game plan.

Amanda was much like Jake - cool and fun but in a low key, under the radar manner.

She didn't like to be the center of attention, really **didn't like** going to places like this because she was uncomfortable around large crowds. But she was dragged there that night by her friends who were celebrating her birthday.

What Amanda *did like* was '80s rock music, Mexican food with margaritas, the Dallas Cowboys ... and Jake. She had been eyeing him from afar all night long.

Jake had noticed Amanda as well, but figured she was in a league all her own - way too good for him and she *had to be seeing someone...*

Camacho strolled toward Amanda's table, and he began to remove his shirt. He started dancing and gyrating around like out of those Chippendale dancers might have done before they learned how to dance - and if they were on crack. Danny had no rhythm at all and was also quite tanked.

He made a veil attempt at singing the Def Leppard song "Pour Some Sugar on Me" ... and he was staring directly at Amanda, obviously aiming the lyrics toward her. He was making overly suggestive gestures, pointing at the dazzling brunette and then pointing toward his package and acting as if he were air-humping.

Amanda felt compelled not to pay the boisterous one any attention. He was like a bad car crash- a train wreck.

Danny was fortunate with his choice of music. Amanda did dig her some Def Leppard.
She did not, however, appreciate the way he was butchering the song, or much else from this performance for that matter.

Jake was also noticing the disgusting display. He was a few sheets to the wind and still pissed off about the beer poured over his head. Jake stood up and began to walk in the direction of Amanda's group celebration where Camacho was still shaking what he had.

"Yo, Camacho, what are you supposed to be - a circus monkey? Where's your organ grinder?"

Camacho, not happy that his mating ritual had been interrupted, chimed in.

"I got an organ for you to grind on!!!"

He used both hands to shove Jake backwards, sending Jake landing on his ass on the floor in a puddle of beer and God knows what else.

Jake stood up as quickly as his wobbly drunk body could propel itself. Jake and Danny stood face to face, eye to eye. Two large muscle-bound Marines with nothing in common but their assignment in the Corps and both being plastered.

And that twinkle in the eye of that fine lady Amanda.

It was that spark that they both sought to obtain. Without hesitation they both made ready to settle their differences right there and then, clenching fists and preparing to battle as was done back in the Gladiator days.

Three burly surf boarder looking bouncer dudes - almost as large as the two Marines - ran up and grabbed the two adversaries by their collars and escorted them to the front door, then shoved both men outside onto the sidewalk.

There the combatants prepared to continue the clash of titans. Amanda and her friends exited the bar and walked outside, then began attempting to hail a cab.

Danny quickly lost interest in the epic battle.

"Ladies - hey ladies, you don't need a cab, I can give you a ride ... or at least one of you I can!!! I'll take you home, beautiful, but your ugly friends are on their own..." Camacho squawked as he stared at Amanda.

Amanda whispered something to her girlfriends then strolled over to the concrete octagon where Jake and Danny were squaring off seconds earlier.

Confidence overwhelmed Camacho, who anticipated that he would soon be taking the sexy brunette home and then probably getting some action after that.

Camacho took his car keys out of his back jeans pocket and was about to point her towards his vehicle. Amanda, clutching a small piece of paper between her right index finger and thumb, instead obtained entrance into Jake's space with her pleasantly perfumed presence.

Amanda put her left open palm on Jake's six-pack abs and then with her other hand, she tucked the paper note into Jake's front right jeans pocket, securing the document deep in the pocket. Amanda's whole hand was in Jake's pocket now as she seemed to be either playing pocket pool or just protecting the note from being dislodged prematurely.

Her girlfriends were able to get a blue and yellow Charger Cab stopped and Amanda recognized this as her curtain call. Planting a peck on Jake's right cheek, she made sure that Danny was paying close attention as she said, "I'm Amanda - call me."

Then, with her *not trying to be sexy* walk - but failing – she strutted her stuff over to and into the cab. Camacho and Jake watched as the taxi slowly drove away.

Chapter 7 - Meat and Greet

Earle Cabell Federal Building and U.S. District Court, Downtown Dallas (Present Day)

Prosecutor Ferron stood from his chair and began to walk toward the jury as he contemplated his next strategic move.

"Now let's talk about the physical evidence we have in this case. Physical evidence doesn't lie. This is a very, very compelling physical evidence case.

"The FBI responded to this scene within a matter of minutes. Inside the house they collected bloody fingerprints from the baby's highchair, a large kitchen knife, the cardboard birthday cake box, and a living room wall. Whose fingerprints did these come back to after running comparison tests? The defendant - Jake Hathaway.

"The blood in the prints was not his, but that matched up through DNA analysis as being the blood of his first victim, Holly Hathaway, Jake's own sister-in-law.

"Agents found pieces of skin tissue in the dining area from where his victim Holly had tried with all her might to scratch her attacker in a failed attempt to defend herself from the onslaught. More of the defendant's skin was found under Holly's fingernails and even on her teeth.

"That is how desperate this woman, Holly, was in trying to save herself. She had to resort to biting her assailant when scratching was not effective. Unfortunately, the biting could not save her either. (Dramatic sigh). This skin contained DNA that was tested to be Jake's.

"And lastly, we have the Marine issue Ka-Bar fighting knife with the seven-inch carbon steel blade. This was the very instrument of death that Jake used to thrust into the forehead of his brother Rich, killing him instantly!

"And on the knife handle is the DNA from Jake's sweat, as well as his fingerprints. And on the blade is the blood, skin, and hair that contain DNA that tested to be Rich's.

"Some evidence such as witness testimony may be contradicted. You saw the defense team try to create some confusion in your minds by offering their so-called version of what really happened on that fateful day. However, physical evidence is not that way" Ferron said.

"When you have fingerprints, when you have DNA evidence, when you have skin and blood samples placing the defendant at the crime scene like we have in this case, none of those have been contradicted.

"You have not heard anybody take the stand and say, 'no, that wasn't his fingerprint.' Or, 'no, that wasn't really his knife. No, that really wasn't his DNA, blood and skin.'

"And of equal importance was the fact that no other physical evidence from anyone else - identified or not identified - was found. None. Meaning no one else was there to help with or commit these unthinkable crimes. It was Jake Hathaway. And no one else. Uncontradicted.

"I say that because in our instruction to you, we talked about our responsibility of proving the defendant's guilt *beyond a reasonable doubt.* It's not necessary that the elements of the offense be proven by direct evidence alone, it can be proven by circumstantial alone or combined with direct. But with this case -

you have it all.

"You have witnesses that testified before you that Jake is the killer. You have circumstantial evidence provided by witnesses as well.

"And finally, but not least of all, we have a confession. After the FBI agents picked Jake up at his workplace, and the previously mentioned evidence was seized from him, agents interviewed Jake in a recorded session. You heard that audio recording. You heard Jake say that he and he alone killed both Holly and Rich.

"He tried to say that he was defending himself - that he had no choice in the matter. That's absurd! Defending himself? From a young mother who was feeding her one-year-old boy some birthday cake. Please..." Ferron rolled his eyes.

"But most importantly, you have this undisputed physical evidence that just stands up on its own merit. It all points directly at that defendant and screams 'beyond a reasonable doubt – HE IS GUILTY!!!'"

Ferron stood up and enthusiastically pointed at Jake to add a dramatic flair to his last statement.

"This is a simple case of love and sex and jealousy. Jake had an affair with his sister-in –law ... I know - pathetic, isn't it? Then when she shut the relationship down, he couldn't stand it. He was so eaten up with jealousy that he decided that if he couldn't have Holly, then no one would.

"He went to her house to murder her in cold blood, and when Rich happened to show up, Rich tried to stop the killer of his wife - his own brother! And where did this get him? Dead –that's where.

"Because Jake is a cold-blooded killer, and he destroyed the life of his brother without even a second thought. He had no hesitation whatsoever. Hard to believe, but it's true.

"So now the case is about to go to you so you may do your part. The overwhelming evidence before you prove Jake to be guilty of two counts of capital murder and one felony kidnapping charge. And folks, that is what we ask you to do - return a verdict of guilty on all four of these charges.

"Thank you for your attention and thank you in advance for handing out justice on behalf of these victims, their families, and everyone in Dallas, Texas. Everyone in America, for that matter.

God bless you all."

Jake was escorted to his accommodations, otherwise known as block C, cell #52, in the Lew Sterrett Justice Center (the Dallas County Jail), where he spent what could turn out to be his final evening of captivity before learning his fate.

He fully anticipated that the following day he would find himself back in his seat at the Earl Cabell United States Courthouse and hearing the jury foreman read aloud before God and all mankind that he was not guilty of any of the murders he was charged with - that he was merely defending himself and protecting baby Carson from harm.

But Jake had to be realistic too. There was the chance that the jury could be duped and buy into this crock-of-shit theory that the prosecutors and Feds were dishing out.

Jake lay flat on his back on his cell's bed (a block of concrete with a half-inch cushion on top disguised as a mattress). Realizing he may never be able to enjoy the warmth and compassion of being in the unconfined presence of the love of his life, Amanda, ever again.

He began to reminisce about their earlier days and the months following their initial meeting during his promotion party years earlier.

San Diego, California (9 years earlier)

Leaving Philly Fogg's that night, the newly promoted captain was feeling pretty good about himself and his life in general. Not only had he just received a promotion in the career of his calling, he had just scored him the phone number of that exquisite lady that he had been admiring all night from afar.

Jake waited a couple of weeks before even coming close to calling Amanda.

Although he had not called sooner for fear of sounding too eager, he could not wait to see her again. Jake finally contacted the lovely brunette on a Monday night, and they made plans to see each other the following Friday evening.

That first date went off without a hitch. It went so well that it was followed up by several more, and before they knew it, six months had transpired.

On a chilly January southern California evening, the second

Friday night since they met, Jake picked Amanda up at her apartment. He was driving an army green unenclosed Jeep that he had borrowed from the base.

"Where are we going tonight?" she inquired.

This Friday night would soon deviate itself from the previous ones.

What are you doing?" Amanda queried, as Jake tied a dark handkerchief over her pleasingly bulbous brown eyes.

"I don't want you to see which direction we are headed. I'm going to show you something I've never shown any other woman" Jake said as he began to drive.

"Your evil Siamese twin?" Amanda asked.

"Haaa, funny. No." Jake replied.

About twenty minutes later, the Jeep came to a squealing-brakes stop. Jake removed Amanda's blindfold, revealing what appeared to be a military base with armored planes, trailered sea vessels, and brown and green camouflaged ground vehicles gathered all around.

"I decided to finally take you home with me" Jake pronounced with a smirk on his face. "Welcome to Camp Pendleton!"

The two were alone in the outdoor vehicle and equipment storage facility. A brilliant full, red blood moon shone down in all its glory upon the love-struck couple.

Jake led Amanda on a private tour of the complex, and then he asked her if there was anything else she wanted to see. One vehicle struck Amanda's fancy.

"I want to go in that one" she said, pointing to one of the several Amphibious Combat Vehicles (ACVs) that were congregated there.

Jake recommended Amanda take her sandals off as they climbed up the ladder attached to the rear of the vehicle. They then descended through the hatch that led to the vehicle's interior.

Jake explained that this was a special, unique combat vehicle that was unlike any other.

"It was designed to self-deploy from an amphibious assault ship about twelve miles from shore. It can carry up to seventeen Marines on board and is able to travel eight knots or faster through seas with waves up to three feet" Jake said.

"When approaching land, it operates much like a tank. It's

able to contend with a full range of direct fire, indirect fire, and landmine threats while also destroying other combat vehicles similar in size."

Amanda yawned and remarked somewhat sarcastically "wow, some pretty cool stuff ... but does it have a radio? I want to hear some music."

"Umm, no" Jake said.

Amanda, seated in the ACV's driver seat, turned the driver seat around facing backward, toward Jake. She began to unbutton her light blue blouse, revealing her shapely bronze bosom.

Jake removed his shirt, revealing his two black ink tattoos. One of the images was a crucifix on a chain hanging in the center of his pectoral muscles. The second, larger tat was located on his heart and bore the image of St. Michael, the archangel patron saint of soldiers and police officers.

Amanda was in the process of completely removing her blouse and then her lacy beige brassiere when she commented on Jake's artwork. "Nice ink."

Being a Catholic-raised girl herself, she was quite familiar with both images.

Jake sensed that Amanda appreciated his tattoos and he began to tell her where and when he had acquired them. He was quickly interrupted by her left hand, which Amanda abruptly placed over Jake's mouth.

"Shut up and help me," she commanded as she unbuttoned her Levi's jeans. Jake smiled, highly excited and glad to oblige. He tugged at the legs of her skintight jeans to get them off her before Amanda similarly assisted with his.

It had already been hot, moist, and sultry within the military vehicle. It was about to become nothing less than blistering.

Suddenly the Whitesnake song "Slide It In" began to play, softly but loud enough to create just the right mood for what was to follow. Because there was no AM/FM radio in the vector, the origin of this epic tune could not be identified.

The passion continued to flourish inside the sweltering armored love chamber for about an hour. Afterwards, the exhausted soldier decided that this might be the most opportune time for him to act on something he had been contemplating since he began to really know Amanda personally.

Jake prepared to propose to Amanda, to beg her to take his hand in marriage. But he was terror-stricken. He had not experienced much in his life nearly as impactful enough to place fear in his heart.

Not snakes or spiders or deep water, vicious dogs or things that go bump in the night.
Not the thought of going to war or the potential of being wounded or killed in battle. Not being alone without backup and facing Osama Bin Laden - types in deep underground sand cave dwellings.

But the whole concept of pouring his heart out to and devoting his attention and focus on one woman, leaving him open to the possibility of heartbreak and rejection- was terrifying.

The night before, Jake had been rehearsing the scene in his mind, convincing himself to follow through with his plan. He would get down on one knee and remove an engagement ring from the watch pocket in his jeans.

"Will you please marry me, Amanda McKnight?" his wobbling voice would question.

Speechless and caught off guard, Amanda would then most likely retort with something like, "Oh my God! Are you serious?"

Jake would then reassure her by nodding in the affirmative, responding with, "I couldn't be any surer of it than I am now!"

Jake's scenario preparation ended there, as he had no idea what to expect in her answer. All he could do at this point was go through the motions and hope for the best.

So, the time had come. Jake had his girl right where he wanted her. The evening had gone great, they had just made love in an Amphibious Combat Vehicle. The mood was set.

The lovestruck young man reached down to pick up his crumpled pair of Levi's jeans off the vehicle floor to remove an engagement ring from the front pocket. Alarmingly, a shrill sounding air horn began to wail. Flood lights darted about the base. Jake knew that in a matter of seconds, military policemen would be buzzing all about. The young Marine threw on his pants and said, "we got to go."

It was three o'clock in the morning. Jake took his lady home and returned the muck-encrusted Jeep back to the base before anyone realized it had been commandeered.

And that was about the closest Jake would ever come to

proposing to Amanda McKnight ever again.

Chapter 8 - Taking it All in Vein

Dallas County Jail, Downtown Dallas (Present Day)

Jake counted the ants scurrying around below his concrete bunk. He dropped crumbs from his uneaten bologna sandwich onto the cold, solid, concrete floor to provide food for his newfound insect friends. This was just one of the various menial tasks that preoccupied his time since his incarceration in the Lew Sterrett - Dallas County Jail.

Jake's mind was racing, flashing strobe-like images of Amanda blinked in his mental monitor. He thought about his love for her and about some of the difficult times they shared as well. Although they never married, they had been living together, practically married, for a couple of years now.

She was a very jealous woman. That temperament had been brought on undoubtedly by a cheating ex who tainted her before Jake came into the picture.

When the couple had gone out in public, she would watch him closely. Often, she accused him of making intentional eye contact with other women, staring at them. Jake often felt inclined when other women were in the area to look down at the ground to avoid such accusations.

Early in their relationship, Jake's high school crush Kristin called Jake once just to say hello and to see how he was doing. She was excited to hear his voice and to share the latest news in their lives.

Amanda overheard the conversation and was obviously upset by the thought of Jake speaking with another woman. So much so that Jake later wrote Kristin and said he could not have anything to do with her anymore because his girlfriend was so jealous. That was the last communication ever between Jake and Kristin.

Looking back on that decision now, the heartfelt Hathaway had much regret for having done that to Kristin. He felt as if he had betrayed their friendship and the commitment he had made to always be there for her. Jake missed Kristin badly and highly doubted that she would ever have anything to do with him again.

Jake's meditation was abruptly shortened when one of the jailers yelled "yo, Hathaway. You got a visitor. "

Jake was escorted into a large room with chairs lined up in a row and facing each, with a solid wall of shatter-proof glass in between. Jake sat down where instructed, then waited for his visitor to arrive.

Having seen her in court earlier in the day, Jake yearned for a chance to talk to Amanda. He hoped she was about to breeze into the room on the other side of the glass.

The moment was quickly ruined when Jake watched his caller embark upon the visitor's room and sit down across from him behind the glass partition. Jake tried not to act disappointed, for his visitor was not Amanda. It was his buddy, Dave. This was still a pleasant surprise, much better than counting insects.

Dave Talucci owned a successful sports bar / restaurant called "the Hail Mary." The business was in Addison, a small but thriving suburb just north of Dallas.

Talucci was 40 something years old, short and dumpy, with a receding hairline and thin moustache. He was usually dressed in the finest and latest jogging suits with matching tennis shoes, and a gold chain hanging from his neck.

A native of Chicago, Dave was divorced and had no children. He had lived in the house across the street from Jake and Amanda for a couple of years now, and the neighbors had begun a gratifying friendship. Dave and the couple often joined up to watch football, cook out, or just to talk about the latest news and gossip from the neighborhood.

Now, sitting across from Jake, Dave was shocked to think that his good friend, the tough seasoned veteran cop could have murdered his own brother and sister-in-law.

Jake seemed to be distant and distracted. Dave knew he had to carefully choose his words. He realized this might be his only chance to converse with his friend.

"Jake... I know what the media is saying about that day. I'm curious to hear it from you. What *really* happened?"

The imprisoned one spoke, explaining the circumstances that led to his being here. Or at least he described it as well as he could, considering he did not completely understand much of it, himself. Dave attempted to comprehend the tale he had just heard, then had some news of his own to disclose.

"Since your incident, a lot of strange events have been happening. And they seem to be quite like what happened to you. Just the other day I saw a local TV news story about a crossing guard out in Tyler. She was about 65 years old and wearing a reflective traffic vest, helping kids cross the street after exiting the bus.

"She was holding up traffic with this handheld stop sign when three creatures came out of the woods. They were slow, walking at less than normal walking speed. Two men and one woman. At least it sounded like they used to be.

"They got right in the roadway, making cars swerve around them. Someone yelled 'everybody run!'

"The crossing guard lady swiveled in time to see the trio of dead *things* right behind her. She yelled at the kids, screaming, 'get back on the bus! Back on the bus!'

"She bought the kids some more time by throwing herself into the path of the monsters, and they soon lost interest in the children. All of this was captured on the school bus video system - they showed it on the news!

"The blue-haired sweet grandma was soon being devoured by these dead-looking people who were tearing her face and arms to shreds with their nails and teeth. They tried to bite through her plastic vest but were unsuccessful - so they clawed it off her then proceeded to feast upon her chest - ripping and pulling on organs.

"One creature bit through her intestine then began pulling at the slimy organ with its teeth. The intestine stretched several feet, originating from within the lady's inner cavity. Another thing attacked her head, pulling her brain out through the top of her skull and feasting on it! The kids re-boarded the bus, and the driver accelerated down the road, leading them all to safety. But that crossing guard lady died a hero!"

"Oh damn." Jake reacted. "Sounds a lot like what I experienced!"

Jake paused to further comprehend Dave's message and horrific description of the zombie attack.

The jailer standing in the doorway behind Jake said "five more minutes."

Jake blurted out what had been on his mind all along. "How's Amanda?"

"Oh, Amanda. Umm - she's not good." Dave knew that sugar-coating the truth would be wrong and that Jake would see right through it.

"I understand she's working as an assistant to some wealth management banker downtown. Apparently, there's a customer who's like an incredibly wealthy oil tycoon, and he's got a thing for her. He keeps asking her out. But don't worry she's not... that's the last thing on her mind is starting over. She still can't accept the fact that you're here. She's still in shock.

"Also, she has been having problems with Carson – she said that he didn't seem normal. Maybe he can sense what happened to his parents. He is always fussy and cranky and not wanting to drink his milk or eat his jarred baby food.

"As for Austin, he keeps skipping school and getting into fights. He's constantly cursing and blaming you for killing his mom and Rich. When Amanda defends you, they get into fights and he runs away from home. She suspects that he has become close with the girl who used to babysit Carson. She apparently has run away from home and has been missing for a few days now."

Dave knew his timed visit was running out, and he changed the topic to discuss all the bullet points he had in his mental discussion agenda.

"By the way, I am so sorry to hear about Roscoe..."

Jake looked up, stared into Dave's solemn face, and said "what about Roscoe?"

"I figured Mack, or someone must have told you." said Dave. He now regretted bringing up the topic, as he wished he did not have to be the one to give the lousy news to Jake. Jake already had enough shit to contend with in his life.

"There was a demonstration outside the police station. People were picketing, handing out fliers. They were all fired up, demanding that Roscoe be put down because he was so vicious -

tearing up Holly and Rich the way he did…"

Jake was stunned and devastated.

"What!!?? Roscoe didn't even come into the house with me when I was attacked by Holly- or what *used to be* Holly. He was in the truck until the Rich-monster tried to eat me in the front yard. Roscoe was defending me like he was trained to do. Dogs aren't cognitive- they can't think about or premeditate their actions. They do what they are trained and told to do. He was protecting me - nothing more."

Jake asked Dave whether Mack was aware of all the hype surrounding Roscoe, and if Mack was planning on taking any action to save the canine.

"Well, that's the other thing I needed to tell you." Dave looked at his feet as he reported the news. "Mack is still really having a hard time understanding why you had to do what you did out there."

"But he saw them," Jake said. "I called Mack to come out there as I was leaving to get Carson to safety. I know Mack went out there."

"He did go there," Dave said. "But the Feds beat him to the scene and had already hidden the bodies somewhere. Which I don't understand, by the way. I thought you cops were all supposed to leave crime scenes intact until video and pictures could be taken and the bodies marked with chalk outlines and such. Mack said he got there quickly and there were Federal Agent types already cleaning it up."

Jake scratched his head. "Yeah, that's not protocol by any means. Dave, can you tell Mack what really transpired there. Rich and Holly were not themselves. Please ask Mack to investigate this further so he will understand. He must believe me. And for God's sake, please ask him to save Roscoe from being destroyed. If he doesn't want to do it for me, he can at least do it for Roscoe."

Dave nodded in agreement. "I'll do whatever you need, buddy. Don't worry, I'm going to pass the message along to Mack. Somehow, we will get you out of this mess. And Roscoe, too."

Dave made a fist and held it up to the thick bulletproof glass that separated the visitors from the prisoners. Jake gave Dave an imaginary fist bump by holding up a meaty balled-up right fist against his side of the smudged glass partition.

David Talucci walked away from the Dallas County Jail with thoughts and plans running through his mind. He was now a man on a mission.

Jake had known Dave to be a good friend and neighbor. Dave was smart, educated and a good conversationalist. But Jake had no idea Dave had the drive and determination in him that he had just exhibited. Jake now felt very assured that Dave was going to do whatever he could to keep his promises.

Quickly, the convict's thoughts turned toward Roscoe, Jake's K9 police partner and best friend for the past year and a half.

When Roscoe was a mere ten months old, Jake's department purchased the Belgian Malinois dog from a breeder in Illinois. The breeder specialized in training these animals to be serviced as K9 police dogs. Jake traveled to the puppy farm to spend about six weeks training with the new dog.

It was important for Jake to learn a set of commands in the German language and then to practice using them with the dog, while also serving the dual purpose of developing a rapport with the young animal.

All of the Dallas K9's up until this point had been German Shepherds. Roscoe was the first of what would be many more Belgian Malinois dogs to come, patrolling the streets of the 'Big D' with their human partners.

Right from the beginning, Jake was impressed by this new dog. As with all purebred Belgian Malinois dogs, Roscoe was medium sized and square proportioned.
Roscoe's base color was fawn, and his short coat made him and his breed less prone to heatstroke.

He had black erect ears and a black muzzle. Roscoe would eventually grow to his maximum weight of between 64 and 75 pounds.

This dog was active and friendly, and exhibited the high energy levels the breed was famous for. It did not take long for a friendship to develop between Jake and this dog, and Roscoe soon became very protective of his new master and partner. Their connection was as strong as ever. If anything, the bond may have been too strong.

These two were practically joined at the hip, they lived and worked together for the next five years. However, Jake knew that Roscoe's role was not the same as that of a human police officer partner.

Roscoe, like any officer, was trained to take on action that could place him in immediate danger. His job was to protect the lives of his partner or any other human who needed to be protected from loss of life or imminent bodily injury, even at the risk of sacrificing his own life for that of a human. Jake had been able to give Roscoe the commands that put the K9 in danger in order to save human lives. But he prayed that no harm would ever come to his K9 partner. He knew the guilt he would feel would be unbearable.

Fortunately, Roscoe had been able to overtake the enemy and avoid injury each time he was called into action.

But now Roscoe was in danger. With angry citizens rioting and demanding that the police dog not only be taken out of police service but also that he be destroyed for his part in the so-called "murder" of Rich and Holly.

And Jake was not in any position to rescue his unjustly condemned partner. A partner who just over two years earlier had miraculously saved the young human police officer's life.

Chapter 9 - Angry Brain Hungry Face

Dallas, Texas (Six years earlier)

Jake only had less than two years on the job and had only been paired up with his K9 partner for a couple of months. It was rare for such a young officer to be accepted into the K9 unit as a handler. This role was typically one filled by officers who were much more seasoned and experienced, in the primes of their careers.

In their short time together, man and man's best friend became precisely that. Best friends. Jake and Roscoe were inseparable.

They trained together with regularity, with Jake and other K9 officers using seized dope for training purposes. The handlers would hide seized baggies of cocaine, marijuana, heroin, and meth in various locations to test their dogs' sense of scent. Sometimes they hid the dope in undercover cars in a parking lot. Other times they stowed the drugs inside pieces of furniture scattered throughout their training facility.

When Roscoe and the other dogs located the drugs, they gave whatever alert they had been trained to give. Some just sat still; others scratched at or snorted around the area they sensed that the drugs were in. Roscoe had a particularly keen sense of smell, not only for narcotics but for crime in general. He was always alert for activity and gifted in his first impressions of people, seemingly able to sniff out not only those committing criminal acts but those even with bad intentions.

The handlers and K9s also practiced their tracking skills. It was essential for them to be able to pick up the scent of a missing person or suspect of a crime at one location and then follow that scent in order to pinpoint the person's current location.

Upon the K9 finding the drugs or tracking down their target, whether it be in training or in real time police work, they were rewarded with their own personal toy. Some dogs liked to chew on a plastic hose, others preferred their favorite tennis ball thrown their way. But it was always their handler giving the dog the reward and no one else. It was a pact shared and honored between these teammates.

On a cold winter November Dallas morning, Jake and Roscoe were patrolling the mean streets of a southwest Dallas neighborhood called Oak Cliff. There were hardly any calls for service coming in due to the temperatures. Some of the other officers on the shift were trying to keep busy with self-initiated activities such as performing traffic stops and / or patrolling commercial storefronts to prevent crimes.

It was about 3:00 a.m. when Jake finished assisting a stranded motorist with a flat tire and decided to stop somewhere to take a short ten-minute break. After he warmed up, he and Roscoe could park the squad somewhere dark and set out on foot in the nearby business complex to try to catch some burglars in the act.

Frequently around this time of morning and in this part of town, burglars were known to smash out the front windows of closed offices and steal the computers and monitors to sell for drug money.

Jake pulled his black and white police SUV into the parking lot of the 7-Eleven store at Jefferson and Davis. He parked the vehicle, leaving it locked but running so the heater would keep Roscoe warm in his back-seat area cage.

As Jake walked toward the convenience store, he was eagerly anticipating a nice hot cup of dark roast coffee. But he soon realized he had not marked out on the radio to advise the dispatcher of his location. He realized that if he were to get into some shit storm and need assistance, no one would know where he was.

But before Jake could key up the mike on his portable radio on his duty belt, he heard what sounded like a male's voice yelling from around the corner, "Give me all the fuckin' money, bitch!"

The numbed, weary lawman gripped the handle of his now unholstered Glock. He cautiously peered around the corner of the wooden six-foot fence that separated the 7-Eleven from a Whataburger restaurant directly behind it. Jake found himself about fifty feet away from the drive thru lane at the rear of the burger joint. There was not a single car or customer in sight.

Upon a closer look, Hathaway noticed a masked bandit who had the front half of his upper body completely inside the drive-thru window. This skinny black-garbed perp was holding a large ten-inch-bladed steel kitchen knife and was pointing at the head of the Whataburger employee - a shaken teenage girl who realized this job was not worth the minimum wage she was earning.

Jake advanced about thirty feet without being noticed and took cover behind the wide concrete base of a large metal streetlight pole in the same parking lot.

"Drop the weapon!" Jake yelled at the violent criminal, who suddenly became aware of the police presence.

The disguised man quickly backed himself out of the Whataburger drive-thru window and took off running north through a trashy, unlit alley.

Without hesitation, Jake took off on foot after the fleeing felon. He keyed up his portable radio as he ran and somewhat excitedly reported, "this is 437. I'm in foot pursuit, headed north through the back alley."

The dispatcher was quick to respond, saying, "I copy, 437. What is your location?"

Preoccupied with the situation, Jake did not respond with his location. He instead reached into his pocket for his key fob, hoping to electronically open the rear door of the police squad car to release Roscoe from the vehicle.

But before he could push the button on the fob, it flew out of Jake's cold, numb hand and dropped to the ground, out of his reach and hidden from his view.

"Motherfucker!" he thought to himself, for he knew now that his K9 partner Roscoe would be unable to help him.

Jake soon lost sight of the perpetrator in the darkness and he stopped running, slowing his pace to a walk so he could search the area methodically rather than running blindly into a hiding and waiting armed suspect.

Jake knew he had called for the cavalry to assist him, and he began to wonder what was taking everyone so long to get to him. For in the heat of the moment, Jake still did not realize he had never properly checked out with an accurate address or landmark.

Jake had left his flashlight behind, charging it in the vehicle so it would have been fully charged when he was attempting to apprehend burglars in the act, after his coffee break.

He held his weapon close to his body in a ready, 'Sul' position so that the suspect would not be able to grab onto his extended arm to take the weapon away.

Jake began to hear sirens echoing through the Cliff, and he knew that his comrades were looking for him. It was just a matter of time until they located his parked vehicle at the 7-Eleven and set up a perimeter from there to locate him and the scumbag.

Jake stealthily made his way through the alley, slowly and carefully searching behind trash cans and propped-up wooden pallets. He made a valiant effort to use the darkness to his advantage, but his location was quickly compromised when his police radio blared out: "437- what is your location?"

As if on cue, the desperate criminal now knew exactly where his pursuer was located and leapt out from within a slimy, garbage filled dumpster. He crushed the officer's skull in with a swift blow to the head from a cold steel black tire iron.

Sgt. Hathaway collapsed to the refuse covered tar alley surface, his head draining thick blood through its newly sustained gash.

Jake awoke seconds later to feel a tugging at his holster as his assailant was attempting to rip his duty weapon from its holster. The wounded officer knew that just because he was down, he was not out of the game. If he were to succumb to these circumstances, he surely would be killed.

Jake rolled over onto his weapon side to throw the criminal off him and to keep from being disarmed. The frantic hoodlum was thrown off balance and tried to get steady on his feet when Jake jumped up into a fighting stance and began pummeling the dirtbag with a variety of punches to the face and throat.

The criminal descended to his hands and knees, unable to see through his swollen blood-filled eyes and spitting out blood through freshly loosened teeth.

Jake took time to mark out properly with the dispatcher and within seconds he heard the once distant sirens suddenly growing nearer.

Jake was standing over his arrestee, about to place a set of steel handcuffs on him, when a white, older-model Oldsmobile Cutlass Supreme raced up the alley straight toward Jake.

Hathaway dove out of the center of the alley, and the car slammed on its brakes to a skidding sideways stop. Another concealed, black garbed subject then stepped from the driver's side of the vehicle and pointed a large black .45 semi-automatic handgun at Jake.

"You never should have left the donut shop, pig! Now you're gonna die!"

Jake had nowhere to go from here. He was not close enough to dive behind any form of cover nor even anything to offer concealment. Jake knew his chances of being able to reach this man before he could fire off a shot were very slim.

Suddenly, as if appearing from out of nowhere, 75 pounds of Belgian Malinois muscle leaped toward the perp. Roscoe's open mouth closed onto the right hand of the thug, causing him to release his grip and drop the pistol onto the ground.

Roscoe continued chomping on the hand until the bad guy began kicking at Roscoe's head with steel-toed boots. Roscoe dove at the criminal's face and neck, biting with an unseen ferocity and tearing away chunks of meaty flesh.

Sirens and squad cars were now raining on top of Jake and Roscoe as their partners had located their comrade. They collected the trash (metaphor for bad guy), and Jake was transported to the hospital for the large gash on the front right top side of his head, which would later result in a very large and noticeable scar.

Jake never was able to arrive at an explanation as to how Roscoe found his way out of the locked police truck.

Perhaps it was through some miracle from God or from Jake's guardian angel, but somehow the door was ajar, and Jake's life was saved by his best friend and partner, K9 Officer Roscoe.

Chapter 10 - Dead to Rights

Earle Cabell Federal Building and U.S. District Court, Downtown Dallas (Present Day)

As the conclusion to this marathon-like trial drew nearer, Jake was finding it difficult to remain focused and attentive to the court proceedings. Although his body was still sitting in (and shackled to) the same chair that it had been over a span of the last three weeks, his mind was wandering. Hallucinations became the norm, and Jake was metaphysically bouncing around from one place to another.

Were these symptoms of his PTSD, or was it just a safe place for his mind to travel to in order to avoid the lies and travesty that he was facing? Or perhaps it was a combination of these conditions.

Prosecutor Ferron addressed the judge, but Jake, in his state of insanity, was instantly mentally teleported to another earlier time and place. He found himself sitting in a reclining easy chair in his parent's Rhode Island living room, watching the cartoon trial scene from Pink Floyd's "The Wall" movie.

Suddenly Judge Parker became more alive than Memorex. He slammed his wooden gavel down onto his large oak desktop: "Defendant!!! Mr. Hathaway!!!! Are you awake over there??!

"Sir, do you realize what is happening here??? Defense attorneys- please be sure that your client isn't daydreaming over there - he needs to be cognizant of these procedures. The jury has informed me that they have arrived at a verdict."

The jury members were slowly escorted back into the courtroom.

Judge: "Members of the jury, have you reached a verdict?"
Jurors: "Yes, we have." Judge: "Does the foreman have the verdict form?"
Jury Foreman: "Yes, I do. In the United States District Court for the District of Texas, Criminal Action No. 2011-TX-78, United States of America vs. Jacob 'Jake' Hathaway. We, the jury, upon our oaths unanimously find as follows:
"Count 1, first-degree murder of Holly Ann Smith-Hathaway, **guilty**.
"Count 2, first-degree murder of Richard Alan Hathaway, **guilty**.
"Count 3, kidnapping of Carson Hathaway, **guilty**."

Judge: "Sir, was this and is this the jury's verdict?"
Jury Foreman: "Yes". Judge: "Members of the jury, you have determined by your verdict that the evidence established the guilt of Jake Hathaway on these charges beyond a reasonable doubt of crimes for which death is a possible punishment. We will reconvene tomorrow morning at 9 a.m. for the sentencing phase."

Jake's head began to spin, he felt light-headed and sweated profusely. His mind raced, filling with thoughts and feelings of a wide range of emotions to include **shock, disbelief, and sorrow.**

Shock: because he knew that he took pride in always trying to be a stand-up guy, a class act, a Christian. He was once a dedicated soldier who fought against some of the worst evils in the world with love for his country and with so much pride in being a United States Marine that he could hardly refrain from showing it.

Jake would never hurt so much as a mosquito that didn't bite him in the butt first and drain out a drop or two of blood. Now if someone had it coming - messing with him or his family, victimizing some innocent person who was unable to protect themselves - or, God forbid, they took any type of enemy action to attack his country - that was another story...

Disbelief: the way the prosecutors for the State failed to openly disclose facts about the case that revealed the truth - that Jake truly was defending himself against people who changed somehow and were not human any longer.

The hair on their heads was straggly and thin and missing in spots. Skin from their heads to feet appeared to be rotting and falling off, smelling of a combination of decay and compost.

Their eyes had no warmth or humanity behind them - the pupils dilated and black, appearing in size and color much like small circles hole-punched from a sheet of black construction paper.

The teeth were yellow, also decaying, and blood drenched, with a stench coming from the creatures' mouths that could only be described as what might emerge from below the floor drains of an unregulated slaughterhouse.

The fingernails were unkempt, long, claw-like and yellow, and the toenails were probably the same, but the bare feet were so covered with caked-on blood and other body waste that the nails were not very visible.

Both were slow, dragging and shuffling their feet and moving lethargically as if half dead. They had no emotion, no expressions, nothing whatsoever that hinted these were living people.

These were obviously not Holly and Rich - or even humans for that matter. And it did not take someone who knew them personally to realize this.

Sorrow: Not only for Holly and Rich, but also for Holly's parents and Jake's own parents. Charles and Clara Hathaway had not only lost their youngest son Rich to whatever it was that turned him into that creature, they had now lost their oldest son. Not only had he been found guilty of two murders, he was about to be sentenced to either life in prison or death.

Jake agonized over how Rich and Holly's children Austin and Baby Carson would be affected. With both parents taken away from them, and their Uncle Jake accused of killing them- their lives would never be the same.

Thank God Austin wasn't there at the birthday party to witness the horrible scene.

Luckily Carson will have been too young during the incident to remember the events of that tragic, fateful day.

Earle Cabell Federal Building and U.S. District Court, Downtown Dallas

In open court the following day - 9:00 a.m.

Prosecutor Ferron: "Since their introduction of the death penalty, Texas has always required the jury to decide whether to impose the death penalty in a specific case. Once each side has pleaded its case, the jury must answer two questions to determine whether a person will or will not be sentenced to death:

The first question is whether there exists a probability that the defendant would commit criminal acts of violence that would constitute a continuing threat to society. 'Society' in this instance includes both inside and outside of prison; thus, a defendant who would constitute a threat to people inside of prison, such as correctional officers or other inmates, is eligible for the death penalty.

The second question is whether, taking into consideration the circumstances of the offense, the defendant's character and background, and the personal moral culpability of the defendant, there exists enough mitigating circumstances to warrant a sentence of life imprisonment rather than a death sentence."

The jury was escorted out of the courtroom and into the jury room to deliberate these two questions posed of them which would ultimately decide the fate of Jake. At approximately 10:30 a.m., the jury indicated they had decided and were led back into the main courtroom.

Judge Parker: "Members of the jury, have you reached a decision on this defendant's punishment?"

Jury: "Yes, we have your honor."

Judge: "Before we proceed, I want to caution everyone here that there must be no audible or visible reaction to the punishment when it is read. When the jury returns, the punishment decision will be handed to me and I will read it. Now, any person violating this order will be removed from the courtroom. Mr. Foreman, please hand me the jury's punishment verdict form."

At this point, Jake was midway through his latest prayer, still outfitted in his striped pajamas with his torso covered by a bulletproof flak jacket and shackles that bound his ankles together. His head lowered, hands clasped together with fingers interwoven, eyes closed. Jake was pleading with God, begging that this nightmare would end abruptly, and he would awaken to find himself in his bed beside his sparkling love, Amanda.

Amanda was present watching the proceedings as she had been every day. She was seated on a bench just twenty feet behind Jake and the defense team's table. Dressed in a black Cardigan sweater and black long flowing dress with conservative flat-bottomed shoes, Amanda sat staring at the back of Jake's head.

She hoped the love of her life would turn around and take a glimpse in her direction so that she could get another look at his face. Amanda hoped to capture such an image to store in her memory files. This could possibly be one of the last opportunities she may ever have to see Jake again outside of a prison cell.

Beside Amanda sat Jake's best friend and former police partner, Mack McElroy.

Mack sat staring straight ahead at the proceedings but really wasn't very in tune to what was being imparted. For he had a couple of different emotions he was debating within his head, much like the scales of justice teetering slightly from one side to the next. He was attempting to decipher which one he should be feeling at this juncture.

Like the proverbial tiny angel sitting on one of his shoulders, Mack heard in one ear a voice that was urging him to feel *guilt* - for Mack had kept a secret from Jake for several months leading up to the birthday incident.

It seemed like not that colossal of a deal back then. But as the prosecutors' theory developed and they revealed Jake's supposed "motives," Mack came to realize that if he had disclosed his secret to Jake's counsel, they could have used that information to blow holes in the prosecution's story.

Meanwhile on Mack's other shoulder sat a micro-devil who was whispering into Jake's other ear, advising him he should be feeling nothing more than *hatred*. Jake had murdered Mack's lover, Holly.

Maybe all along Jake knew of this relationship and was pissed off that his brother's wife was messing around before her divorce was final. Or perhaps Jake wanted Holly for himself. Or maybe Jake was just a racist asshole and didn't want his Caucasian sister-in-law to be with a black man?

The debate raged on in Mack's mind until it was obvious the little devil guy had won. Mack could not find it in him to forgive Jake for slaughtering Holly - a petite, beautiful young woman who was merely throwing a birthday party for her one-year old child. It made no damn sense.

Mack and the entire crowd in the courtroom took notice as the Judge took the punishment verdict form from the Jury Foreman and began to read aloud.

"We the jury find that there does exist the probability the defendant would commit criminal acts of violence that would constitute a continuing threat to society, be it inside or outside of prison. We find no sufficient mitigating circumstances exist to warrant a sentence of life imprisonment rather than a death sentence."

The judge looked graciously at the jury and thanked them for their efforts. "Mr. Jake Hathaway, you are hereby sentenced to death by lethal injection at the Texas Department of Corrections in Huntsville. May God forgive your soul. Do you have any final comments before your transfer to death row?"

"Yes."

Jake wriggled his shackled, ballistic-vest-covered, electric-shock-collar-wearing body closer toward the defense attorneys' microphone.

Looking much like Hannibal Lector straight out of the movie scene where he was wheeled around on a dolly and outfitted similarly, Jake imagined what Jesus felt while wearing a crown of thorns and having a huge wooden cross strapped to his back.

He never claimed to be anyone's savior, but right about now he sure as hell felt like a sacrificial lamb.

"During the trial, I was advised by my attorney not to testify on my own behalf. I did not, and now I regret that. I guess he thought that my story – the truth – was too far-fetched, unbelievable, impossible. If you had told me that my brother and sister-in-law would somehow turn into - whatever they turned into, I might not have believed it either. Some sort of sinister synthesis. But it happened! I loved Rich and Holly, and I never would have hurt them. But these *things* that attacked me that day were not Rich and Holly.

"And why is everyone covering the truth up? No one showed

the jury any pictures of their entire bodies. They showed extreme closeups of the injuries I caused when I had to use force to protect myself from being killed. But there were no pictures of their faces. They didn't look like humans. Their eyes were large and swollen, pupils dilated and tiny and jet black. Their hair was starting to fall out, their skin was corroding and falling off.

"Why were there no pictures of Holly's other injuries? She had large bite marks on the side of her neck and on her upper body! These were not caused by me. I sure as hell didn't bite her! Those are not normal human bites. And they were not caused by Roscoe either. Roscoe didn't exit the Tahoe until I was struggling with Rich- what used to be Rich- on the front lawn.

"Why is that witness Gladys lying and saying that Roscoe went inside the house with me? Why didn't we hear anything about forensic tests being done on the bite? DNA could have been taken from the skin tissue there. The teeth marks should have been compared with mine and with Rich's teeth. This would have proven they were not mine and probably from Rich!

"No one showed my police cruiser in-car video camera footage that showed the creature trying to bite my heart out in Rich's front yard. Where is that video? The taser I use contains a tiny video camera mounted to the grip that was programmed to record a ten-second video clip automatically when the taser was fired. Where is that video? If I was a murdering scumbag like you all portray me to be, why didn't I go on the run? Why did I drive right back to the police station? I knew the FBI would be wanting to interview me. I figured they would believe me.

Jake continued. "The evidence all points in my favor - that this was self-defense! But none of this evidence was brought out in court. And then the prosecutor, in need of a motive, invents this crazy story about me banging my sister-in-law and then seeking revenge when I can't have her? Fuck you, Ferron, you piece of shit! How dare you insinuate that I did anything inappropriate with my sister-in-law. You're a sick asshole. Judge, please tell me what the fuck this is – because this sure isn't fuckin justice!"

Judge Parker stood and shouted "Bailiffs, remove Mr. Hathaway from this courtroom at once!"

Filled with fury due to his unjust treatment, Jake yelled "This is bullshit!" and struggled to free himself from his restraints before an electric current flowed through his body from the shock collar on his neck down to the tips of his toes.

The shock made him piss in his striped jail jumpsuit. The once proud Marine and Police Sergeant was humiliated in front of the world. He lay on the courtroom floor, his muscles twitching and giving out due to the electric current as he basted in his own urine.

Court bailiffs flooded the room and circled around the sentenced one as other Deputies escorted the trial observers out into the safe confines of the building.

Amanda attempted to make her way to her fallen boyfriend, yelling "Jake! This is all wrong! We're going to fight this! I love you, baby!"

Her words echoed as she was shoved outside of the grand solid oak double doors and into the hallway, as Jake struggled to mouth the words, "I'm sorry! I love you" before being kicked in the teeth by an occupied size 12 1/2 black tactical boot.

Part 2 - Life After Death Sentence

The "human condition" is the reflective nature of Homo sapiens that allows for deep thinking and reflections upon conditions that may to one extent or another affect man's contemplations, and therefore his decision-making process.

Concerns of human beings vary, ranging from theories regarding the meaning of life, the search for gratification, and their sense of curiosity, the inevitability of isolation and the awareness of the inescapability of death.

These are all key concerns to the self-aware man, mysteries which he may never be able to resolve or fully understand. Yet, the unique feature of the human brain and the cerebrum within is that it allows for the analysis of these existential themes. The results of this analysis quantify the owner's point of view, and thus affects one's thoughts, attitudes, and actions accordingly.

The plans that you make and steps you take could very well depend on which of your cerebral hemispheres, the left or right, you depend upon or favor more heavily.

There are those whose allegiance runs with those whose blood runs black. This is the type of person who is more apt to take a bone saw to your jugular than to lend a helping hand to their fellow man when society is crumbling, a festival of mutilation surrounds you, and humanity is dying. Their lawlessness, selfishness, bullying of the weak and laziness should all be considered mortal sins rather than mere capital vices.

Chapter 11 - As Humanity Falls

Dallas County Jail, Downtown Dallas (Present Day)

Jake was still housed in the Dallas County Jail, awaiting his transport to Huntsville. The transfer was expected to transpire sometime over the next couple days. Word quickly spread throughout the facility that there was a cop who was being held there on two murder charges.

So much for trying to keep a low-profile in there. Jake knew some of his counterpart inmates would probably remember him and would consider it worth the risk of getting additional sentences to cause him some pain or worse.

Dressed in his regular daily attire, a white jumpsuit with lateral black stripes, inmate #978658 began to do some people watching. He did not for fun or for entertainment purposes, but rather as a way of protecting himself from any type of attack.

He noticed some prisoners shooting dice. Other inmates were making up rap songs about the injustices in the American penal system. Still others were soaking paper towels in coffee, only to let them dry, then cut the paper towel into smaller strips in order to roll them up and smoke them.

Apparently freebasing caffeine produces a high comparable to that of crack cocaine, since both are central nervous system stimulants. The high achieved when freebasing caffeine is immediate, but the duration of the high is shorter than that of cocaine. Jake pondered what he had observed.

How do people come up with this shit? It takes some real ingenuity to figure out and experiment with these things – if these guys are smart enough to find ways to get wasted smoking coffee, imagine what they could do in the real world if they had set their minds on it...

But this was no time for Jake to mull over how and why prisoners get stoned smoking Folgers. He had to appraise his current situation thoroughly. He was only days away from being transported to the Texas Department of Criminal Justice's Polonsky Unit in Huntsville, where the state's male death-row inmates were housed until they were eventually put to death.

He had to replay in his mind the extremely troublesome events that led to his murder arrest and convictions if he was going to be able to possibly make any sense of it all.

Back on that fateful February eighth, Jake was on duty as Dallas Police K9 Sergeant. He had been trying to call his brother Rich for two days straight to find out what time to be at his brother's house for his one-year-old nephew, Carson's birthday party. Jake was never able to get Rich to answer his phone.

So, at about 12:30 p.m., Sgt. Hathaway went to Rich's North Dallas house in the "M Street" area of upper Greenville to make an appearance at his baby nephew Carson's party. Rich's blue Mazda Miata convertible was parked on the street in front of the house, and Holly's red Kia Rio was in the driveway.

Jake parked his Chevy Tahoe police truck on the street behind Rich's car and left his K9 partner in the vehicle. Roscoe was friendly enough with the family, but Jake knew Roscoe would be so tempted to lick the birthday cake.

Jake knocked, but there was no answer at the door, and he then found the front door unlocked. He went inside to see an undetermined red liquid splattered all over the living room floor, walls, and even the ceiling. Inside the dining room was a square chocolate frosted birthday cake carved into eight even rectangular slices. However, the cake had been flattened - much like a powdery layer of fresh snow that someone belly-flopped onto to make a snow angel.

Jake tried to take comfort and convince himself that the red liquid all over the living room was ketchup or paint. But Jake was also cautious and knew the red could very well have been blood and that something might be very wrong. He drew his service weapon and held it in a ready position as he walked through the house looking for his brother, sister-in law, and nephews.

"Hello? It's me, Jake. Where is everyone?"

Usually when Jake went to their house, Austin was the first to answer the door. Austin thought it was cool to have an uncle who was a cop, and he especially liked to see Jake play ball with Roscoe in their large back yard. But today there was no sign of Austin, or anyone else for that matter.

The sound of baby Carson's shrill cries suddenly emerged from the dining room around the corner. Jake rounded the wall to see the one-year-old squirming and kicking, strapped into a highchair that apparently had been tipped over in a disturbance. The toddler was struggling to get free, grunting and squealing like a wild pig that had just stepped into a steel jaw trap.

Jake began working quickly to unfasten the straps on Carson's seat. Then, with his peripheral vision, he saw what at first appeared to be a human shape rounding the corner from the kitchen. IT was trudging into the dining area toward him. The form moved slowly and had long straggly hair. IT appeared to be female.

This THING was covered with blood from head to toe, growling and snarling like a mother black bear coming out of her den to protect a cub. It smelled of rotting flesh, its yellow decaying teeth were glaring.

The sergeant did not recognize the figure and began to back up. He tripped over the highchair leg and fell to the tiled floor. The she-monster grabbed Jake by the arm and began lunging at and biting near Jake's head.

"OH FUCKKKKKK" Jake yelled as he ducked just in time to avoid a face bite but instead was bitten deeply on his right shoulder, causing instant pain and massive bleeding.

The right-handed cop tried to unholster his Glock .40 caliber handgun from the holster on his right hip. But because of the injury he sustained, Jake was unable to grip his right hand on the weapon strong enough to remove it from the holster. The desperate lawman lunged with his left hand toward a large kitchen knife lying on the table beside the flattened birthday cake.

He grabbed the utensil by the handle and swiped the blade toward the still-biting figure, stabbing it in an upward motion through the side of ITs face. The creature continued biting, with the blade side of the knife visible in its open breathy mouth and its left eye socket.

Jake removed the knife and stabbed again, striking IT in the forehead and sinking the blade about five inches deep. This final blow finished off the creature, with IT dropping to the living room floor.

Jake closely examined this THING. He discovered that under its putrefying, oozing, bubbling, soggy, rotten skin was what he thought he recognized as what was once his sister-in-law, Holly.

Jake was normally as cool and calm as can be in strenuous situations, but at this juncture he was quite shaken and hoping that what had just transpired was not reality. Maybe this was just a figment of his PTSD hallucinations. Jake walked back outside and aimed his trembling body toward his waiting patrol car parked on the street.

K9 Officer Roscoe was in the back-seat area of the Chevy Tahoe, barking loudly and viciously while pressing his face against the tinted glass. Roscoe sensed that his partner was in serious trouble. At this point, if Roscoe could speak like a human, he would have pointed with his paw and yelled "Jake - look out!!! Behind you!!!"

Another dark form had emerged from around the east side of the house. IT was now just several feet away from Roscoe's human partner. This creature too was snarling, biting, reaching. IT was acting as if it wanted to eat Jake.

This THING appeared to be starving, craving for the sustenance that human flesh would provide. Jake turned suddenly to see what he recognized as something that appeared somewhat like his brother Rich. But it also looked like the miscreation he had just slain with the frosting-covered butcher knife inside the house.

"Rich!!! Rich!!! It's me, Jake!!! What are you doing? What the fuck is going on?!"

The Rich/monster dove at Jake, seemingly attempting to swallow him whole in one enormous bite.

Realizing that this was not the same person he knew as his brother; Jake began thinking aloud. "I gotta get to the car, gotta get the less-lethal..." referring to a Remington 12-gauge shotgun covered in orange paint to signify that it was armed with bean bags instead of buckshot slugs.

Jake didn't make it to the car or the orange shotgun. The creature tumbled on top of him, about ten feet away from the police truck.

Armed with his Glock handgun, his yellow plastic taser, black metal asp baton and a can of Law Enforcement strength pepper spray, Jake used his left hand (now his only working hand) to wrap it around the hungry carnivore's throat. ITs yellowish flesh and blood saturated incisors were mere inches from Jake's face.

His right hand was no longer able to grip a weapon. However, Jake was able to use that hand to apply enough pressure to push his vehicle's K9 door release button on the keychain in his back pocket. K9 Roscoe's door popped open and the anxious police dog sprang into action. As always, he knew his job was to give his all, including his life, to defend his partner.

Roscoe began tearing into the Rich/monster's torso, arms, and neck area. He was ripping out mouthfuls of flesh, shaking his head side to side while biting non-stop.

The creature seemed not to be fazed. IT was still making every effort to feast on Jake's face.

Jake's strength was waning. He recalled the only thing that seemed to stop the Holly/monster was a swift stab to the forehead. Jake knew he only had one chance of surviving this encounter.

A neighbor came out of a house next door (Gladys Torrence). When she saw what was happening, she began to scream with panic "AHHHHHH!! OH, MY GODDDDDDD!!"

This was just the break Jake needed. The distracted Rich/monster turned toward the shrill sound for a split second. This was all the time Jake needed. He released the throat of the beast with his left hand and then quickly reached for his Taser X26 CEW (Conducted Electrical Weapon), holstered on his left side.

Aiming the Taser into the pizza-sauce-looking, sore-popping, stinky face, he pulled the trigger. Two dart-like probes stuck into ITs head, filling the beast with 50,000 volts of electricity.

Rich/monster's body began to fry and sizzle. This filled the cool February air with a stench that could best be described as rotten Spam sautéed in sewage and sizzling on a hot tin roof. IT jumped back a couple of feet, it's central nervous system obviously tweaked. But it still didn't go down for the count.

Exhausted and weak from the large amount of blood lost from his shoulder, Jake had to use his left hand to de-holster his Glock from the right-side holster. Still left-handed, Jake fired five 10 mm rounds into what was once his brother's chest. This too was ineffective, and the attack continued.

Jake dropped his Glock to the ground, then used his left hand again to remove his large Navy Seal SOG knife with partially serrated 7-inch blade from the sheath on the inside of his left pants leg. Jake stabbed IT in the forehead repeatedly until IT was moving no longer.

Jake picked his Glock and Taser up off the front lawn grass and returned inside the house of horrors. He released baby Carson from his highchair restraints. Jake took hold of his exhausted nephew and carried him out to the awaiting DPD Tahoe. Jake opened the driver's door and climbed up into the seat, his large muscular left forearm pressing Carson snuggly against him, his strong left-hand supporting Carson's small head and neck.

Roscoe jumped back into the vehicle via the still-open back driver side door. Roscoe laid down on his specially customized doggy seat as Jake slowly drove away. Jake turned his head to look back at the house, still in amazement of the events that had just transpired.

Jake began to drive back toward his house, where he knew Amanda would be able to care for the newly orphaned one-year-old. The rattled sergeant used his cellphone to call his best friend and peer Officer Mack McElroy to tell him about the incident.

"Mack - dude! Are you at work? I need you to get over to Rich and Holly's place now!"

Mack responded, "Sure, what's going on? Is Rich beating on Holly again?"

"You wouldn't believe it if I told you." Jake said. "Just get over there quick and secure everything until I can get back there. First, I gotta take Carson home to Mandy, where he'll be safe."

Jake clutched his nephew close to his chest as he sped the ten miles straight to the house he shared with Amanda. Jake parked in his driveway, ran into the house with Carson, and handed the baby off to his unsuspecting lady.

"What's going on babe?" Amanda asked.

"I wish I knew, Mandy, but I don't even have an explanation for what's going on. Please just take the baby and care for him. He has no one else now. I've got to go back there. I'll fill you in later. Love you!"

Jake began to return to Rich and Holly's house, and he called Mack's cellphone while he was driving. "Hey, man, are you out there yet?" Jake asked.

"Yeah, I got here fast, but the FBI beat me to it. How the hell does that happen? You didn't even call this in on the radio, so they couldn't have picked up on it over their scanner. I made it inside the house, and there were agents crawling all over the place.

"Jake, they were scurrying about like ants. They were moving items around, covering stuff up with tarps. As soon as they saw me, they told me they didn't care whose jurisdiction this was, they were taking over the investigation. They kicked me out. Jake, where is Holly? Is she with you? What the hell happened out here?"

"I need to meet you somewhere, tell you what happened. I'll be behind the closed down factory on Industrial Ave in five minutes."

Just as Jake ended that call with Mack, an incoming call on Jake's cellphone caught his attention. Jake did not recognize the number on his display, but he answered the call, nonetheless. "Hello?"

"Jake, it's Chief Snippet." The Dallas Chief of Police sat comfortably reclined in a brown leather-bound chair, his cowhide boots resting upon the desk as his beady bald head was covered by his white ten-gallon cowboy hat.

"Hey, boy. I hear you got yourself in a jam back there. Why don't you come in and tell me what happened?"

"Chief, I don't know what the hell happened to those people, my brother and sister-in-law. They weren't themselves. I had no choice."

"I know, son, no one here thinks you did anything wrong. You know I always take care of my own. Come on into the station, we will make this all right for you, okay?"

Although he had heard other officers refer to the chief as a snake in the grass, Jake never learned the reasons why. He had never encountered any negative experiences on his own, so he had no reason to not trust the old man now. Jake somewhat reluctantly agreed to meet with his chief, and he began to respond back to Central Headquarters.

Jake arrived within twenty minutes and parked his police SUV outside the main entrance. Before he could even remove his key from the ignition, the vehicle was surrounded by jet-black Tahoes with red and blue wig wag low-profile LED lighting systems activated in full. Suddenly, dark-sunglass-wearing field agents began to pour out of the SUVs like jesters from a clown car underneath the big tent.

"Sgt. Hathaway?" one of the suits demanded.

"Yeah, that's me..."

"We need to talk to you about what went down at your brother's house."

"Sure, follow me inside to the chief's office and I'll tell you the best I can, but I really don't understand much of it myself..."

Suit One responded with, "Your Chief doesn't give a shit what you have to say. He told us he would get you here and then we could cuff you and stuff you and throw away the fucking key. Unquote."

The agents escorted the police sergeant over to their waiting pursuit-rated police package Tahoes with heavily tinted glass, where they promptly grabbed Jake's arms and hands before advising him that he was under arrest for the murders of Rich and Holly Hathaway.

Jake was disarmed, handcuffed, and thrown into one of the Fed's SUVs. The driver of that vehicle promptly sped off to transport Jake in a short ride to the Dallas County Jail. Jake was subsequently booked in on capital murder charges and spent the night in an isolated holding cell.

What the fuck is going on here? How can they not possibly comprehend what happened back there? Jake thought to himself.

He was trying to make some sense of the madness that had prevailed as he found himself surrounded amidst the caged chaos existing within the Lew Sterrett jailhouse walls.

Dallas County Jail, Downtown Dallas (Present Day)

Jake had been kept in solitary confinement since his arrival in the Dallas County Jail. This was partially to assure the safety of the onetime cop to safeguard him from being attacked by anyone who was not so fond of his kind.

But the confinement was also assuredly meant to keep Jake from talking about his case and spreading the word about the odd sequel of events that had occurred at the birthday incident.

The good thing about this alone time meant the wrongly convicted Sgt. Hathaway had plenty of time to think, plan, and strategize. Sitting alone in the confines and solitude of his cold, lonely concrete square, Jake began to feel as one with the darkness.

Although he was devastated to be completely detached from the love of his life, Amanda, he was beginning to feel somehow as if his other human emotions and qualities were beginning to escape him.

Where the solitude, darkness, and cold of his surroundings would make some men break, Jake could feel himself changing slowly. Or had this begun long before the ' Birthday Incident'?

Was it his current predicament that had him changing mentally within? Or was something physically occurring within his body after having sustained that vicious bite from the Holly / creature? He had not been eating nearly as much as he had prior to his incarceration, yet he was not feeling hungry like before.

His strength suspiciously was not waning, although he was eating less and not working out as he did when that was part of his daily regimen. Jake could tell that something was just not right about him, but only time would unlock the mystery.

Chapter 12 - Dead Giveaway

I 45 South, Buffalo, Texas

The aged grey Bluebird bus, Dallas County Jail's prisoner transfer vehicle, motored its way south on Interstate 45. This was a major thoroughfare running north and south through central Texas. This would be a long, lethargic pilgrimage to Huntsville. To be more specific, the Allan B. Polunsky Unit of the Texas Department of Corrections. This was the facility where male death row inmates are housed until the day of their execution.

The bus had now traveled about two-thirds of this three-and-a-half-hour journey. It was now traveling through Buffalo, Texas, where the highway narrows to two lanes in each direction.

The driver, named Bob, was a weathered, salt-and-pepper-haired and bearded Dallas County deputy. He had two other similarly uniformed individuals seated behind him, one on the driver's side of the center aisle named Grover and one on the passenger side of the aisle named Pete.

These two were armed with .40-caliber Glock pistols and 12-gauge shotguns. They were strategically perched in seats that positioned them facing the opposite sides of the bus from where they sat. With a half turn of their heads in either direction, they could observe either the sixteen prisoners at the rear of the bus or the steaming black asphalt Texas roadway in front of them.

The prisoners were all adorned in steel silver wrist and ankle bracelets. These were attached to heavy chains that ran through a large eye bolt. The eye bolt was welded to and extruded upward from the vehicle's floorboard near each of the prisoner's feet.

A large galvanized steel cage surrounded the prisoners, and a large thrice-padlocked door separated them from the 'first-class section.' That was where the deputies sat at the front of the large bus.

The sixteen prisoners consisted of two women and fourteen men, one of whom was former Dallas Police Sergeant Jake Hathaway.

Jake was not receiving any special privileges or treatment. He was being treated the same as every other convict. However, even the transport deputies did their best to keep Jake's identity secret from other prisoners. They realized that many of these convicts would jump at the opportunity to "welcome" a former cop.

The deputies remained ever watchful of their surroundings while also multitasking and listening to the bus's AM radio. A national news syndication was reporting the multiple reported sightings of large black insect masses over the last few weeks. These were spotted particularly in the warmer climate regions of the southern ends of both coasts.

Government scientists confirmed these insects were flies but claimed to be baffled as to what species they belonged to. There were many theories being floated around as to where they came from and why they had become so prevalent recently.

Jake had his eyes closed for much of this long trip. He wasn't napping. He was still trying to sort through the details that led to his being here. Suddenly he felt a nudge as the prisoner to his left was elbowing the left side of Jake's rib cage. Jake opened his eyes and turned to his left to see the striped guy gesture with his head and eyes toward the front.

Without turning his head, Jake shifted his eyes to the right. He observed the two guards both concentrating their attention on an older model flat black Dodge Ram crew cab. It had dark tinted glass and no license plates and had just raced past the bus.

The 4X4 truck had a lift kit, large knobby off-road tires, and a matching black push bumper and grill guard. It swerved directly in front of the bus and was slowing down with its red brake lights illuminating brightly. The bus driver slammed on the brakes, slowing the bus' speed from 60 mph to 40 quickly to avoid striking the pickup.

The Ram cut back into the lane to the left of the transport vehicle and slowed greatly to find itself lined up parallel with the bus. The guards appeared tense, squeezing their shotguns and preparing for the unknown.

Deputy driver Bob became distracted by the Ram as well, failing to notice a person dressed in a black ski mask, black T-shirt and black tactical BDU pants that had just come out of the woods.

The woodsman tossed a spike strip across the roadway in front of the massive Bluebird. The tires rolled over the sharply spiked device as the rubber in the bus's front tires ruptured. The sounds of two mini explosions were followed by the audible rush of hot air from each front tire.

The bus driver jerked the steering wheel to the left, hoping to avoid the back tires running over the spike strip as well. However, the old steel vessel was not agile enough to make this maneuver and flipped over on its right side. This motion threw the un- seatbelt-fastened guard, Pete, down against the side of the bus that was in contact with the freeway.

Pete's head went out the nearest open side window and was promptly grated into the highway asphalt. Soon the roadway was littered with bus debris and brain matter as the aged metal behemoth slid about 120 feet before coming to a halt.

The bus lay still, lying across the highway and blocking both southbound lanes. The black Ram's white back-up lights appeared as the dark truck was thrown into reverse, squealing tires and burning rubber in the process. It then stopped just south of the bus, intentionally stopped sideways with the passenger side of the Ram facing the front of the fallen transport vehicle.

The salty old driver Deputy Bob, who was hanging sideways by his seatbelt, was also unconscious either from a concussion suffered in the vehicle roll or maybe from a heart attack. Grover, the guard who kept his head, began to crawl toward the open bus door when gunfire erupted from the Ram.

AK rifle-fired bullets careened through the open bus door. Grover returned fire with his Glock pistol, then reached across to Pete's headless torso to take two extra magazines full of .40-caliber bullets from Pete's duty belt. Pete wouldn't need them anymore. But Grover would.

Unbeknownst to Grover, a dark blue Chevy Express van with limo window tint had just pulled up. It was behind, and on the north side of, the prison vehicle. Three individuals dressed head to toe in SWAT gear with full facial masks and helmets carried assault rifles as they exited the van. They walked in separate directions and rounded the downed prison bus vehicle, walking towards the bus door.

The leader of the tactically dressed unit approached the Bluebird's accordion style door with an entry shield. He instantly began to take rounds from Grover's pistol. The rounds ricocheted off the shield and were effective in slowing the renegade threesome's approach. But then Grover's weapon ran dry. Grover thumbed the magazine release button to drop the empty magazine as he had done so many times during combat firearms drills during training.

Holding a full Glock mag in his left hand, Grover began to

insert the mag into the weapon. He then was struck in the head by the team leader's shield. The magazine didn't sit properly in his weapon, and as Grover attempted to fire the weapon again the top bullet didn't feed properly into the chamber. The gun jammed. The Glock did not fire, and it was rendered temporarily useless until it could be properly cleared.

Knowing he did not have the time to correct the malfunction, Deputy Grover threw the weapon down, and dove behind Pete's body.

Grover began to remove the firearm from Pete's duty belt when the team leader placed the red dot from his AR-14's laser sights between Grover's eyes. "Unless you want to die now, stand up and go unlock that fuckin' convict cage."

Grover stood up, limped over to the cage, and removed a keychain from one of the keepers on his belt. He then unlocked the three padlocks with three separate keys.

Then he was told, "now release that white cocksucker there - the one that used to be a cop."

Jake could sense the eyes of the fifteen other inmates all looking around, wondering who among them used to be 'Johnny Law' - their enemy.

Deputy Grover used yet another key to unlock the Peerless cuffs from convict Hathaway's wrists and ankles. Jake remained seated. He was unsure of what was happening and what these SWAT-looking guys had planned for him.

The renegade leader said, "Thank you for all of your help, deputy" and promptly fired the AR-14 at Grover's forehead.

The helmeted commander then pointed the rifle at Jake's head and thundered, "GET THE FUCK UP!"

Jake complied and was ordered into the back of the Chevy Express. As Jake climbed into the back of the van at gunpoint, he was struck in the back of the head with a blunt object. This knocked Jake unconscious. His body slammed face first onto the solid steel floor of the back of the van.

Blue Elbow Swamp at Old Hwy 90, just east of the Texas / Louisiana Border

Jake awoke to feel his face pressed against the cold, damp

earth just east of the Texas/Louisiana border and south of Old Highway 90. He was also on the edge of the Blue Elbow Swamp, not that there were any signs posted or landmarks around. Jake had no clue as to exactly where he had been dumped, much like a box full of unwanted newborn tabby kittens.

Jake sat up and looked down at his own body to notice he was still wearing the striped Dallas County Jail jumpsuit. Beside him was the clear zip lock property bag which contained his wallet with his flat DPD Sergeant badge inside.

His head was throbbing from the thump he had been dealt to his cranium. Jake was now sporting a huge goose egg on the back of his head.

A dried blood trail connected Jake's wound to a path of grass flattened by a heavy vehicle with large knobby tires. Jake followed this flat-grass path for quite some time, while wondering who the hell had sprung him free from the prison bus. Was it friend or foe?

Seems like a friend would understand that Jake was wrongly convicted and have set him free to buy Jake some time. With that time, he could search for the proof necessary for a retrial. Either that, or he could just stay in hiding to avoid being executed.

But an ally would not have crushed him in the back of the skull before throwing him into the Arkansas woods either. An enemy would have enjoyed causing the head trauma to Jake, but why would such an adversary set him free?

Although he had been shed from his prison cell and shackles, Jake knew he would not be able to communicate with Mack or anyone else without compromising his location. In this modern day of cell phone pinging, smartphone mapping and so on and so forth, tracking a person was just too easy. The desperado contemplated what his loved ones and friends were thinking about his situation, his guilty verdict.

Do they believe the prosecution and Feds? How could they? They know me better than anyone else does. Surely, they can see that something is seriously wrong here and that I was unjustly accused and sentenced for murders that were clearly self-defense? Will anyone be willing to sacrifice their lives and freedom to help me regain mine? And even if I could ask them to do so, I would feel so friggin' guilty if the same were to come upon one of the people who mean the most to me....

Dressed as he was, Jake decided it would be best to stay off of the highly traveled highway. He decided to travel east through the swamp region instead, until he could acquire a more suitable means of transportation to get him out of the area and back to the northeast.

The stiped journeyman grabbed his wallet and stumbled across the murky marsh for what seemed like hours. Eventually he came upon an abandoned air boat, floating atop the swampy water just a few feet from the marsh on which Jake traveled. Surely the owner of this vessel had to be close by.

Jake was correct, for what remained of the owner was just yards away. There was a pile of entrails and a pair of mutilated Lee jeans crumpled up into a ball nearby. That was all that remained of whoever this was.

Hathaway had no idea that an epic battle had transpired on this very spot just twenty-two hours earlier.

Chapter 13 - The Blue Elbow

Blue Elbow Swamp (22 hours earlier)

Junior Swanson was a native of Thibodaux, Louisiana. Born and raised there, he had never gone outside of the southern half of the state. He had no reason to. He lived in a humble houseboat that was docked upon the Blue Elbow Swamp, and spent a great portion of his days there, hunting gators from aboard his pride and joy – an American Air Ranger airboat.

This was not your everyday run-of-the-mill fan boat. It was equipped with a supercharged 502 big block engine and three composite propellers enclosed in a protective metal cage.

This cage prevents objects such as tree limbs and branches, clothing, passengers, or wildlife from coming in contact with the whirling propeller. This could cause devastating damage to the vessel and traumatic injury to the operator and passengers.

The propellers are the key driving force in these vessels. They produce a rearward column of air that propels the airboat forward upon the driver's command.

The operator and passengers of this boat are seated in elevated seats that allow visibility over swamp vegetation. The improved visibility permits the operator and passengers to observe floating objects, stumps and animals in the airboat's path.

Above the cage on this model of Air Ranger is an observation platform. This higher vantage point is ideal for sportsmen like Junior who need such an advantage when doing what they do best - hunting the American alligator.

By perching about ten feet above the swamp level, one may more readily locate the largest reptile in North America. The American alligator loves nothing more than to bask in the sun or snack on one of their favorite meals from their diet of crabs, fish, frogs, birds, nutria, beavers, snakes and turtles.

The larger specimens Junior would capture alive. He would rope them with lassos as if rounding up young steers at a rodeo, except for the fact that the gators are much more slippery, slimy, elusive and deadly. They are then duct taped around their powerful jaws and loaded into a pickup truck for transport to a live gator farm.

The hatchlings he would simply scoop up with a net and toss into a large plastic beverage cooler containing a few inches of swamp water. Eventually they would be shipped to a taxidermist in town who would transform the little fellas into keychains, hats, and other trinkets to be pawned at the local Jiffy Marts to tourists who are just passing through.

On this fine fall afternoon in August, Junior sat upon the observation platform of his Air Ranger. The boat was stationary, floating in the frothy green swamp water approximately forty feet out from the nearest tract of low wetland.

Binoculars in hand, the hunter spotted what appeared to be a series of large black bumps projecting out of the water among a patch of lily pads. It was halfway between the airboat and the marsh.

Junior knew those bumps well. They belonged to the back of an American alligator, and probably a good-sized one from what Junior could tell. But directly in Junior's line of sight with the binoculars, about twenty feet behind the gator, there appeared to be an outline of a person stumbling around in the low marsh.

The person appeared to possibly be intoxicated or stoned,

staggering around and repeatedly falling face first. As Junior watched, the person fell repeatedly in the thick inundation of grass, sedges, cattails and rushes.

Upon further observation, Junior identified the form as a man dressed in a grey suit and with a pink and blue striped power tie. And now the impeccably dressed one was staring straight at Junior and wading through the swamp vegetation, walking in a beeline for Junior and his boat.

Junior found it incredibly odd that a man in a suit would be mucking through a swamp. But he also realized that the odd one did not see the gator between himself and Junior. Junior did not want to startle the gator by yelling or making a loud noise, but somehow, he needed to alert the man that he was ambling directly toward a large gator.

Suddenly a wood sandpiper with its long legs, dark brown upperparts and white spotted breast obliviously landed upon a log. The log was floating in the same lily pad cluster as the hungry alligator.

The gator lunged forward with its broad snout and open steel-trap-like jaws, snatching the piper by its white rump and black-barred tail. The panicked native swamp foul began to flap its wings mightily, flying out of the mouth of death and barely escaping alive with only the loss of a handful of tail feathers.

Junior highly expected the possibly drunk man to retreat after seeing the gator in action. However, just the opposite transpired. The suited one began to stride faster, his eyes locked in on Junior and paid no heed to the crock. Junior began yelling.

"Hey man – no!!! Go back!!! Get out of the water!!! There's a gator right there!!!"

The suit began moving at a faster pace, still awkward and unbalanced but with a look of determination on his face. He was up to his waist in the thick goopy vegetation. He was completely ignoring the gator.

The nine-foot reptile was highly disappointed in having lost his tasty piper treat. It turned his long head sideways and clamped its 74-mini dagger-like teeth into the upper left thigh of the stranger, and a black liquid oozed and squirting from the new row of holes in the strange one's side. These holes perfectly matched the row of razor-sharp incisors in the gator's mouth. The thick black coagulation of fluid was flowing into the swamp water like crude oil.

Junior couldn't stand by and watch as this guy who was possibly mentally challenged or wasted got eaten. Junior moved the boat closer and held out a ten-foot-long wooden pole toward the injured man. "Grab a hold of this. I'll get you out of there!"

The bitten one made no effort to reach out for the lifeline, and Junior noticed his entire left leg was hanging by just a few tendons. Tendons that looked like rubbery strands of well-done pasta between the torso and the severed appendage.

But the suited one continued forward. He was hopping on his one good leg under the water and using both arms to steady and balance itself in the green swampy froth.

The gator again snapped at the man, grabbing his left arm. Its teeth clamped down harder and harder, severing muscle, tendons, and veins. The loud sound of bones popping, and snapping could be heard clearly. And with the gator's mouth still clamped upon the arm like a vice, he jerked his head suddenly, yanking the mindless one's arm off in a split second.

Junior grabbed his shotgun from a storage compartment underneath his airboat seat and blasted the gator in the face with a 12-gauge shotgun round. The gator bellowed an intense B flat chorus of intense infrasound and released the arm, which floated off with the currents and into a clump of swamp grass.

The severely wounded reptile rolled over on top of the water, baring its cream-colored underbelly before submerging into the deep dark depths of the swamp.

Junior exclaimed, "My god, man, are you okay?"

The odd man, now hobbled and with only one arm and one leg, did not answer. He was unfazed by the loss of his limbs, not exhibiting any fear or shock or pain.

Junior had not heard any news stories about these once-human creatures that were turning up in random locations throughout America. But he knew now that this suited amputee was not human. Far from it.

Junior reached for the Air Ranger's gear stick to start its powerful engine and rotate its propellers. This would produce a column of air and create forward momentum. But before Junior could complete the motion, the creature pushed off with its one existing leg, leaping up out of the froth and into the airboat.

The apparition opened its mouth and chomped on Junior's neck, removing a mouthful of skin tissue and blood. Junior was traumatized and in shock, trying to comprehend how he went from attempting to rescue a stranger from a gator, to now having that same stranger actually be a monster who was now dining on Junior's flesh.

The force of the attack caused both Junior and his attacker to careen off the air boat and into the murky water.

The monster stood in the water, its only arm holding the Cajun around his gorged neck area. IT began to chew at Junior's face, removing his eyeballs with his teeth.

Then IT reached into the now empty orbital sockets with its tongue and teeth. The THING was using ITs mouth to pull out chunks of the brain. IT began to feast upon the morsels like a young child enjoying bite-sized portions of carnival cotton candy from a large swirl of the product on a stick.

The evil dead thing finished snacking on Junior's face and head. Then IT began to tear into Junior's torso, biting into his vital organs. IT was severing the body parts and gorging at the tender meaty vessels.

Once the creature's hunger was satisfied, IT dropped the lifeless, hollowed shell of a carcass into the muck. IT began to hop back in towards the shore.

Without warning, the pissed-off gator re-emerged from behind the creature. The right half of his snout and face was completely blown away from Junior's shotgun.

With his mouth wide open in mid-flight, the gator dove at the crippled zombie. With one ginormous chomp, the gator dismembered the head from the body of the THING's cadaver. Then the monstrous gator belly-flopped back into the sludge.

The zombie head was still in the large reptile's mouth, ITs zombie eyes fluttering up and down and ITs mouth still opening and closing.

A deafening silence filled the air as nature and all her participants maintained a stillness unprecedented.

The silence was soon muffled by the sound of a 300-pound gator with only half of a face, which began to stroll from the tide and wobble up onto the marsh to enjoy his midday zombie head delight.

The gator finished his treat then dove back into the darkness of the deep. The smell of spleen spirit was still pungent and wafting about the Louisiana Bayou a day later.

Blue Elbow Swamp (Present Day)

Jake continued walking east out of the swampland and soon encountered a clearing with a large dirt parking lot. Here motorists parked their vehicles during the daytime to either share rides or jump on a bus. After a quick scan of the lot, Jake spotted a beat-up yellow Olds Cutlass Supreme with the windows rolled down parked at the rear of that lot.

Fortunately, the driver's side of the car was facing away from the more heavily traveled side of the parking area. He eased his way to the vehicle and slid in through the open passenger window. Jake wormed his way into the driver's seat and then slumped down while looking around in the glove box and console for whatever might become useful. Nothing but junk was in there.

However, Jake located a large flat-head screwdriver down on the back-seat floorboard. This was just what the doctor ordered! Who needs a key when you know how to pry open the steering column and start the ignition with a screwdriver? During his police career, Jake had recovered many stolen vehicles that had been taken in just this fashion.

Jake fired up the Cutlass and then took a longer glimpse into the back seat to behold a welcome sight. The owner of this fine vehicle had also been gracious enough to leave behind a greasy old outfit. This would help Jake blend into his new surroundings much better than his striped jumpsuit.

Hathaway slipped into the grease covered white wife-beater tank top, torn blue jeans, and "Git-er Done" ball cap. Now he felt like he really fit in splendidly here, in what he would soon learn from a road sign, to be Pine Bluff, Arkansas.

Jake drove that stolen Cutlass Supreme with a purpose. He avoided the main thoroughfares and took to the back roads when possible, only returning to the freeways when he needed gasoline.

For the most part, and when he could get decent reception on the FM radio, the prison escapee listened to classic rock radio stations. They were playing many of the songs Jake grew up loving. These tunes posed as a gentle reminder of the life he once had and would most likely never experience again.

When the rock stations faded away from bad reception, he went to the AM side and listened to the news. Jake was curious as to whether the news agencies were reporting the story of his prison bus takeover from earlier.

He did not hear any reports about himself, but another news flash struck his curiosity. There was an account of a naked Florida homeless man who apparently went into a cannibalistic feeding frenzy and ate another guy's face off. As the story recounted, this apparently 'crazy' person spent eighteen minutes ravaging his victim, devouring over 75 percent of the other man's face.

Supposedly a video camera from witnesses captured the growling and vicious attack. The suspect was filmed eating his victim's nose, mouth and eyes before being shot four times by a responding police officer.

Federal investigators determined that the suspect was not mentally ill. Rather, he was extremely 'mind altered' as a result of smoking a dangerous new street drug known as "bath salts."

This news report troubled Jake greatly. Not so much the story itself, which was damn frightening, but even more perplexing was something the reporter said at the end of the story. The reporter closed the news report by indicating that the incident was being investigated by federal agents, who were attributing the behavior to the abuse of a new drug.

Once again, this was not an occurrence that required a federal investigation. It had not occurred on federal property; the suspect did not cross state lines. There was no reason whatsoever for federal agents' involvement.

But Carson's birthday party nightmare did not rise to the level of requiring a federal investigation either. Sure, Jake was there, and he was a government employee for the City of Dallas, and as a result, it could not be investigated by his own agency. But that meant that it should have been investigated by an agency at the state level - say, the Department of Public Safety or the Texas Rangers.

Jake was seeing a pattern. Why were the United States Government taking over these investigations when they were not required to? This was very unlike federal workers, who usually are hard pressed to even do their own jobs, never mind picking up extra assignments (he reflected upon his last visit to a US Post Office to arrive at this conclusion).

Another recent news story came to mind. Jake recalled a few months earlier in San Francisco, another naked man was filmed running wild through the 16th Street BART Station. The long-haired 24-year-old former circus acrobat was seen attacking several commuters. The attacks came in between some impressive acrobatic maneuvers, such as the backflips he was executing on top of turnstiles.

And again, a federal investigation into the incident was conducted. Their "analysis" led them to report their conclusion that the individual "had been through a lot of stress. He seemed to be having a nervous breakdown."

People have mental breakdowns and do unreasonably odd things all the time...you don't see the FBI getting involved in those incidents.

Jake concluded that these three events were probably all somehow related. This could be just the tip of the iceberg.

Something is going on here. What do the Feds know and why do they not want everyone else to know about it?

Jake was very familiar with conspiracy theories and government scandal and corruption talk. Afterall, he had spent all that time working the very Dallas beat where President John F. Kennedy was murdered. That was one of the most often debated crimes in American history. Movies and tv shows based on that incident and the surrounding theories are still being produced today.

The secret government Area 51, also officially known as Groom Lake, also came to mind. This is a famous remote detachment of the Edwards Air Force Base in the southern portion of Nevada. Its primary purpose, according to the Central Intelligence Agency, is to support development and testing of experimental aircraft and weapons systems.

However, the intense secrecy surrounding the base has made it the frequent subject of conspiracy theories and a central component to unidentified flying objects folklore. This has never been declared a *secret base*, yet all research and occurrences in Area 51 are 'Top Secret, Sensitive Compartmented Information'.

Jake wondered if right across the street from Area 51 was another top-secret government operated airplane hangar with a small handwritten sign marked "Area 52" hanging from the front doorknob. Inside could be where the bodies of what used to be Holly and Rich lie, along with other possible victims of whatever it was that changed them.

A team of scientists clad in white plastic hazardous material jumpsuits picking and prodding at the corpses, scraping flesh samples onto rectangular glass slides to be analyzed beneath a microscope.

When the Area 52 guys run out of supplies, they must go next door to the Area 51 people and ring the doorbell to ask if they can borrow latex gloves and scalpels.

Jake caught himself trying to put a humorous spin on what has been a way too serious past year or so. A nice brief lapse of reason could take him away from the grim realities surrounding him. Even if it was only momentarily.

Chapter 14 - Time for A Reunion

Reunion Tower, Downtown Dallas (Present Day)

Reunion Tower was a 561-foot-tall structure. It featured a towering, rotating spheroid at the top that was covered with evenly spaced, bright fluorescent white lights. The tower and the Bank of America Plaza, a 72-story skyscraper with miles of green lateral fluorescence illuminating laterally upon its magnificence, combined to beautify the nighttime view of downtown Dallas' skyline.

Just down the street a short distance was Reunion Arena. This was a massive dome styled structure which had now sat empty and alone for several years in the southwest corner of downtown Dallas. This building lies just west of the colossal convention center and south of the "West End "entertainment district. The infamous historical landmark turned tourist trap known as "Dealey Plaza" is just around the corner, to the north.

This arena was formerly the home of the NBA's Dallas Mavericks and the NHL's Dallas Stars. It has long since been replaced by a larger, more modern facility named the American Airlines Center, about one mile north of the old arena.

Reunion Arena had been the topic of many conversations within the Dallas City Council regarding the plans for its future. Perpetual discussions and debates waged onward over whether the prodigious superstructure should be demolished, modified and attached to the convention center, or converted for other uses.

However, unbeknownst to the massive general public, the arena had a new occupant already. The NCEAID, the National Center for Emerging and Infectious Diseases, had recently moved into the unoccupied space.

This was Washington's answer to combat the looming "Infection Armageddon". It was practically what Jake had pictured when he mused about an "Area 52."

Still intact and in place were the arena's multiple rows of chewing-gum-stuck-on-the-bottom seats. Electronic scoreboards still hung from the rafters and displayed a long past contest between the Mavericks and Minnesota Timberwolves, which the Mavs won 107-93.

In sections where lower courtside floor seats once stood, these areas were now bare of the stadium seating. Makeshift cubicles had since been assembled and erected there. These cubes served as quiet areas for those scientists and pathologists requiring some privacy during their down time. Down time for them meant they were taking a break from experimenting on flesh hankering creatures or infected sickly persons.

The wooden parquet floor that once served as the home court for the Mavericks was now the new laboratory where teams of lab-coat-wearing scientists worked in shifts. They worked around the clock, attempting to determine the causes of the infection. Some were tasked with obtaining specimen samples for study, while others experimented with various drugs to develop a vaccine which could cure or reverse the effects of the infection.

Unmarked Ford Crown Victorias and Chevy Suburbans

regularly flocked into the underground loading dock area of the domed building. They were delivering countless infected beings to be quarantined, poked and prodded, and experimented on. They would remain at this location until they eventually "switched" and had to be put down.

Similar vehicles carried out the remains of those who had already been euthanized. Their infected carcasses were hauled off to a nearby "burn site" or incinerator, to be properly disposed of.

The NCEAID had been sent to the Dallas Metroplex area to create a base for their operations. This location was chosen for a couple of reasons. First of all, Dallas was a nice central location within the U.S., with close proximity to a major airport. Secondly, this was where one of the first 'zombie' type incidents were reported. There had been previous incidents in Florida and California, but those situations were easier to write off as "nervous breakdowns'' or "bath salt abuse" cases.

The public was being fed information that the Dallas story was actually a 'love triangle murder', with Jake taking the fall as the bad guy. This was the feds' attempt to conceal their involvement in the origin of this infection. Meanwhile, behind the scenes and concealed from the public, the NCEAID was fully aware of the truth. They were under the strict orders of the President to make this issue go away before it became leaked and got completely out of control.

The agency was tasked with researching the infection outbreak, arriving at a solution, and creating a vaccine to destroy this vicious virus.

The head of the NCEAID was a pathologist and epidemiologist named Dr. Adil Subramani, an American-born 50-year-old man of Indian descent. His parents immigrated to the United States just months before Adil was born.

Dr. Subramani was used to working with short timelines and under a great amount of stress. But this assignment was unprecedented. Never had the fate of a nation and perhaps of an entire continent or more rested upon the outcome of the doctor's and his teams' work.

Adil divided his agency into two groups, tasked with diverse but equally consequential studies and duties. Subramani's goal was for Team A to track the virus and contain it. Meanwhile, Team B worked simultaneously on the development of a vaccine or cure. Adil's goal was to within one year be informed on how to attack and destroy this plague, and to be prepared and able to do the same.

Team A wasted no time, aiming their focus upon analyzing various data accumulated from the regions of the country affected and infected. They would gather reports and news stories about incidents and events that could possibly be related to exposures to the infectious strain. They consulted with hospitals and paramedics, reviewed police records. They scoured the web for reports of subjects experiencing sudden onset of fever, chills, headaches, coughing, swollen or enlarged lymph nodes, and a general feeling of discomfort, illness, or uneasiness whose exact cause is difficult to identify.

They also began studies on the possible variables that could regulate a greater or lesser probability of infection in a region. These factors include altitude, temperature, hydration of the terrain, and vegetative growth.

Meanwhile, Team B steadily analyzed the infected specimens brought to them to learn as much as possible about the characteristics of this strain. They had high hopes of developing a particularly effective panacea.

This arena, a one-time entertainment mecca, is now buzzing with activity. It resembled a beehive that was alive and active at the pronouncement of a new spring, with much pollen to be retrieved and harvested.

Mack's residence, East Dallas

It was a Tuesday morning, no different from any other. Officer McElroy found himself lifting Olympic weights in the stuffy garage turned weight room of his east Dallas townhome.

Killswitch Engage was blaring away on his portable CD player boom box, so he did not hear his cellphone when it rang. However, he did see it bounce off of the shelf and fall to the rubber matted floor, vibrating and rotating beside his beer-filled mini fridge.

Mack looked at the caller's name appearing on his smart phone's screen. He recognized that the call was coming from one of his cop co-worker buddies, so he answered.

"Hey, man. What's going on? I'm in the garage pumping some iron. What's that? No, I haven't heard anything. What happened?"

The voice on the phone began to speak and was quickly interrupted by Mack's utterance of shock.

"Oh, no!! Fuck no!!! This shit isn't funny, man."

Mack paused and intently listening to his coworker on the phone, who was in the middle of describing the news flash he had just heard on the radio.

"Dude, they reported that 'convicted murderer' Jake Hathaway made an escape attempt while being transported from Dallas County Jail to the Death Row housing unit in Huntsville.

"The plan failed, and Hathaway was shot and killed by the transport guards. Those deputies are being hailed as heroes. They are calling this the second greatest shootout in history between cops and criminals next to the famous Bonnie and Clyde finale."

Mack was still devastated by the loss of Holly and had not spoken to Jake since the day of the incident. And although he was angry and hurt by what transpired that day, Mack suddenly became overwhelmed with grief and sadness that he knew would not be leaving him anytime soon.

He also knew that he should be the one to notify Amanda in person of the devastating news. He should be the one she hears it from rather than to let her hear about it on the radio or the TV.

Mack showered and dressed quickly, then drove across town to Amanda's house. He knocked on the front door seemingly for several minutes. Mack had not seen Amanda since Jake's sentencing at the courthouse, so he had no idea how she was handling her lifestyle of being alone.

Amanda opened the door, obviously having just been awakened. She was dressed in flannel red and blue pajamas, her long brown hair up in a ponytail. She looked thin and pale, as if she had not been eating enough or sleeping well. "Oh, hi, Mack. What's up?"

Mack's face was solemn, and it was obvious he was not at Amanda's for a social call.

"There's something I need to tell you, and we probably need to go inside and sit down for this."

The two sat in the living room as Mack struggled to choose the appropriate words. There would be no easy way to break this horrible news.

"The prison bus that was transporting Jake and others down to Huntsville crashed. Then apparently some of the prisoners tried to escape and there was a shootout with the deputies. Amanda, I'm so sorry. Jake is dead."

Amanda paused and reacted awkwardly, as if she had just been pranked.

"No, I know you're just joking. Did Jake put you up to this? This isn't amusing, Mack. It's bad enough that he has been locked up and sentenced to death for bogus murder charges. But now you're gonna tell me he's dead. That's not cool, Mack."

Mack's face was unwavering as he clenched his jaws tightly.

"You are messing with me, right? Mack, tell me you're just joking. Oh my god, you're *not* joking! Mack! NOOOO!!!!!"

Amanda began sobbing fiercely, tears streaming down her lovely cheeks.

"Why would he try to escape? That makes no sense. He just told me the other day that his attorney was going to appeal his conviction because he could prove that the witnesses lied. He said that the feds were trying to cover something up. He promised he was going to get the conviction overturned and all charges would be dropped."

Amanda wiped her eyes with a tissue and blew her nose.

Amanda continued; "then after he was freed and his record was expunged, we would have been together forever. We made plans. Everything from what we were gonna do the first night of his freedom to where we were going to retire. And somewhere in between those two events we were going to get married. We had it all planned out. I didn't even get a chance to say goodbye."

Sobbing, Amanda questioned the powers above. "How could God do this to us? It's unfair to Jake. He should not have been cheated out of a long life like that. And it's not fair to me, because now I am left here to live the rest of my life without him. Without my best friend, soul mate, lover. Gone."

Amanda hugged Mack tightly, her clenched fists behind him.

"Mack, I know you were Jake's best friend. But the prosecutor said that Jake was having an affair with Holly, and that was why he went over there to her place and did what he did. Please tell me the truth. Was Jake really cheating on me with Holly?"

Without hesitation, Mack replied, "Absolutely not."

"As a matter of fact, I think I need to confess something to you. I have been feeling guilty about this for quite some time now, and I need to come clean."

Mack leaned back on the sofa and cleared his throat, preparing to tell a long and difficult tale.

"It all started back in April of 2007. Jake's brother, Rich, and his wife, Holly, were in their house arguing and yelling. Rich was being verbally abusive towards Holly.

"Their next-door neighbor, Gladys Torrence, called 911 to report that a man and woman were fighting next door.

"I was dispatched to a disturbance call, having no knowledge that Jake's brother lived there. Upon arrival, I learned that the male, Rich, had already left the location. The woman was still present, and she identified herself as Holly Smith, Smith being her maiden name. She made no mention of being Jake's sister-in-law, and she told me about her marriage troubles.

"Holly explained that her husband Rich had physically abused her in the past, but she never called the police or made a report because she didn't want to get him into trouble. But she was afraid of Rich, especially when he was in his 'altered state.' She insisted that sometimes he didn't seem like himself, like he was a totally different being. He was always a little weird, but she thought it was just because he was from up north" Mack said.

"Anyways, I got enough information to make an incident report, and I told Holly to call 911 anytime Rich was acting violent. A few days later, Holly called the police station asking for me, saying she had some more information for my report. When I received the message, I responded back over to Holly's address.

"I arrived and walked up to the front door, which was wide open. I called out, 'Mrs. Smith? It's Officer McElroy, Dallas Police Department... Mrs. Smith?'

"The sounds of yelling and screaming emerged from the back bedroom. I ran back into the house and pushed open the partially ajar door to see Holly lying on the bed face down. A television on the dresser was blaring full blast with an old rerun episode of 'Married ...With Children.'

"Al Bundy and his wife Peg were getting after it in regular fashion, yelling at each other, hurling one insult after another, making a total sarcastic mockery of the show's theme song 'Love and Marriage' by Frank Sinatra.

"I found it peculiar that the TV set was on with the volume up so loud. It seemed like Holly should have been expecting me, listening for a knock at the door or a doorbell ring.

"Holly was sobbing - her head in hands, loudly bawling - so loudly that I was not sure if she even realized I was there. I found it odd that she was dressed the way she was – in black lingerie - not pajamas, no robes, no fuzzy slippers.

Mack continued; "she looked my way, and I tried not to let her see that I was looking at her body. I tried to maintain some professionalism and not let the animal magnetism I was feeling distract me from my duty. I was *supposed* to be making sure she was not injured or in danger.

"I asked her: 'you okay? Mrs. Smith? Did Rich go crazy again? Did he do something to you?'

"Holly rolled over and looked hungrily at me, smiling like a Cheshire cat. I was startled and couldn't help but to look again at the lingerie; her low-cut lace-decorated brassiere that revealed just enough of her large, supple breasts. Tiny- lacy thong panties that color coordinated perfectly with her bronze tan."

Mack noticed that Amanda looked quite awkward about all the specifics he had related.

"Oh, sorry - got a little carried away. The point of the matter is that Holly wasn't exactly intending on filing a police report."

Mack continued.

"Then Holly replied wrathfully: 'no, Rich didn't do anything to me. He never does. That needle-dick asshole never even looks my way anymore. I don't even think he's human. Maybe he's not attracted to me anymore. Do you find me attractive?'

"I was relieved that Holly was not really distraught or hurt. And I was about to leave when she grabbed my arm and said 'officer, I've been such a bad girl. I think you need to punish me.'

"I called my boss and said I was sick and needed to go home. But I stayed right there" Mack said as he continued to fantasize about the events of that sweltering evening.

He recalled Holly putting both of her hands on him, feeling his arms and biceps first before making her way to his chest and down to his lower abdomen. At that point, Mack became aroused.

He felt as if his large rechargeable Streamlight flashlight had suddenly appeared in the front pocket of his uniform pants. He knew that could not be the case, however, because he had left his flashlight inside the patrol car.

Mack recalled warning Holly about her abuse of the 911 system and he did his best to discipline her in an appropriate manner. Discipline that was dished out repeatedly and with pleasure, into the early morning hours.

Mack snapped out of his fantastically distracting memories and continued his conversation with Amanda. "So, over the following months, Holly and I continued this relationship, since she and Rich were officially separated.

"About a month into the relationship, Holly finally revealed to me that she was related to Jake through her marriage into the Hathaway family. She begged me not to tell Jake about us because she didn't want the family to know that there were problems with the marriage. So neither me nor Holly ever told Jake or anyone else about our relationship."

Amanda was relieved to hear that her Jake had not been unfaithful. But she also seemed taken aback by the details of Mack's story. Amanda acted as if she was fanning her face with her hand and joked, "damn, is it hot in here or what?"

She paused and continued.

"I'm only kidding. But seriously, why did you say that you feel guilty about this? If Holly and Rich were separated, you didn't do anything wrong."

Mack confided in Amanda.

"I just keep replaying it in my mind, like it's on a never-ending loop. I can't stop seeing the image of the judge reading aloud the verdict in Jake's trial. I must wonder what would have happened if I had come forward with my story right then.

"Maybe I could have disclosed my secret to Jake's attorney. This revelation could have then been brought before the judge and jury in open trial. The prosecution would have had to manufacture some different motive. Maybe the jury would not have been as easily swayed and Jake might have never been convicted."

"Don't beat yourself up over it too badly, Mack." Amanda sympathized. "It's all a moot point now. It seems to me that the feds had it out for Jake and would have found one way or another to frame him with murder. I just don't understand why."

"I don't get it either, but I sure as hell am gonna find out for you. I promise."

Mack got up from the couch and escorted himself to the door. He left Amanda alone to continue crying in her brown leather La-Z-Boy recliner.

Although he was still bitter about Holly being taken from him like she was, Mack owed it to his recently departed partner and friend to fully investigate the incident. It was not fair for him to wrongfully convict Jake in his heart without having all the facts first. Mack would do the same for any accused criminal whose case he was assigned, and it would be unjust not to grant his best friend the same courtesy.

Even though Jake's explanation for killing Holly and Rich had seemed impossible back then, similar news stories of the "undead" had been emerging of late and rising to the surface. Mack wondered if maybe there was some unsolved mystery lurking here. Regardless, Mack made a promise to Amanda he would investigate the case, and that was exactly what he planned on doing.

Chapter 15 - Carnivore Conspiracies

Mack's residence, East Dallas

Mack was anxious to begin his investigation into the Birthday Incident, as he had promised Amanda he would. He had already attempted to track down Jake's in-car video and body-worn camera video from that date to see if any of the events had been captured. These video files had already been opened and deleted, as had the ten-second video clips recorded each time Jake's taser was fired.

Mack had one last source to check for any possible evidence.

On the day of the Birthday Incident, after receiving the call from Jake and responding to Holly's house, Mack went inside and was quickly halted and told to leave by the FBI.

Mack turned around and quickly grabbed a small Panasonic digital video camera that was sitting on a living room bookshelf. The red recording light appeared to be on, and Mack abruptly snatched the device with his left hand, hiding it within his palm as he walked straight outside to his vehicle and drove away.

Mack had not mentioned to anyone that he possessed this object. He had not reviewed any of the recorded footage earlier out of fear that he would see something he did not wish to see. He previously thought he could not bear to watch Jake slaying Holly, Mack's innocent, lovely, girlfriend.

But now he was ready to watch and learn what really happened that day. The anxious young lawman turned on the Panasonic camcorder and set it to play mode. He backed the recording up to the beginning of the most recent recording, which was time stamped February 8th. It was the date of the Birthday Incident.

That recording started at 11:01 a.m., and the shot was pointed directly at baby Carson sitting in his highchair. The camera angle never changed, the picture never zoomed or panned out, and it was apparent that someone had just set the camera on the bookshelf, pushed record, and left it there.

The toddler was fussy and cranky. Perhaps he was not enjoying the way his pointed cardboard Spiderman birthday hat with the tight rubber band felt strapped around his chin. A small paper plate with a rectangular wedge of chocolate birthday cake lie on the tray in front of Carson. But he seemed much too distracted by something outside of the camera shot to be sampling the confection.

Suddenly at 11:10:07 a.m., disturbing sounds emerged from the near background. Mack listened closely and heard what could best be described as loud growling and moans. These sounds were followed by what he recognized as Holly's voice yelling, "Rich!! Stop it!!!"

Holly entered the picture briefly and stood beside Carson, as if trying to shield him from harm. She wore a white jogging bra beneath blue coveralls, her shoulder length dirty blonde hair worn up in a bun and held together with a baby blue scrunchie.

A greenish colored pair of arms and hands, possibly belonging to Rich, were seen reaching for Holly. She jumped backward to avoid being grasped, and her upper torso bumped into the highchair, knocking it onto its side.

Carson screamed bloody murder as he remained strapped into the seat but was now hanging by the restraints. Holly stood up, screaming for her life, and was jerked backward when the same grotesque set of hands snatched her up by her hair and pulled her out of the video shot.

Over the next few minutes, more stumbling around and groaning was audible. Holly's voice again yelled out from another room, begging "Rich – STOP!!"

Chewing, munching, and slurping sounds followed. Then there were long moments of silence. Only Carson hanging sideways in his chair, squirming and crying, was present on the recording until 12:35 p.m. At that time, the voice of Jake Hathaway was heard coming from the direction of the front entryway.

"Hello? It's me, Jake - where is everyone?"

Mack continued to watch the video as Jake appeared on screen, in uniform and without Roscoe. Carson cried harder and louder as Jake noticed the tipped over highchair and began to unstrap his nephew. Growling and snarling noises became apparent, and Sgt. Hathaway looked to his right, then stood up. An overwhelming look of fear and surprise was displayed on his face.

Jake stumbled backward and tripped over the seat legs, falling back onto the tiled floor. A possibly female creature wearing tattered blue coveralls over a bloody and black substance covered jogging bra, grabbed Jake's arm.

Mack focused his eyes intently on the small screen.

Is that - was that - Holly? OH, MY GODDD!!

The she-creature's jaws were opening and closing, intent on biting Jake. Jake was able to avoid being chomped on the face but was unable to elude the strong beast biting him deeply on his right shoulder. Blood gushed out of the severed limb.

The injured sergeant stumbled out of the picture. This was followed by the obvious sounds of a physical struggle and combat. Off camera the combined animal-like grunts and sounds of warfare continued until a loud THUKKKK!! sound was followed by a THUMPPPP!!

Jake's heavy breathing and gasping for air followed. Then once again the images of Carson squirming in his rolled over seat continued for about eight more minutes. Jake reemerged on the screen, appearing exhausted, shaken, and in a great deal of pain. Jake set Carson free and cradled him in his arms as he walked out of the frame.

Within fifteen minutes, FBI agent Camacho appeared on the recording. Mack recognized him from his testimony in Jake's criminal trial.

Other agents arrived and began moving items around and covering stuff up. Soon afterwards, Mack showed up on scene and swiped the camera from the bookshelf as he was escorted back out.

McElroy sat shocked at what his eyes and ears had just been exposed to.

Jake was not a murderer, and that was not Holly that was trying to eat him. Maybe at one time that creature was Holly, but not by the time Jake arrived. So, if Holly was no longer herself, there's a good chance that Rich wasn't himself either.

The inquisitive investigator in Mr. McElroy then decided to review chronologically all previous recordings on the camcorder. He was hoping to find some further evidence in the sequence of events leading up to the birthday.

The earliest recording on the camera was of a rock concert at the Providence Civic Center in January from two years earlier.

Rich must have snuck his camera into the event somehow and recorded portions of the performances by the bands White Lion, Dokken, and Aerosmith.

The next recording on the camcorder was dated March 11th, the year before the Birthday Incident.

Mack pushed play and watched intently as a disheveled Richard Hathaway appeared in the video.

His eyes were bloodshot, his hair was matted down flat. In places, hair from his head appeared stuck to his face either with dried vomit or some other similar substance.

Rich was alone in the recording, and he appeared to be outdoors. The specific filming location was unclear. Rich was barely dressed, wearing only a pair of underwear boxer shorts that were dirty and soiled.

He began to speak slowly, with a voice that was weak and wobbling.

"HHHollyyyy... ahem... "(clearing his throat) ...

"Holly. I want .... you to know .... how sorry I am about ... my behavior ... lately. You ... didn't sign up ... for this, and you have no idea .... what you have gotten yourself into by ... being with me. It's all my fault though ...for never telling you... how were you supposed to ... know?"

The barely audible recording continued as Jake's younger brother took a pack of Camel cigarettes he clutched in his left hand and lightly tamped the box onto the ground. He continued tapping to pack the smokes tightly. Then he removed one cigarette from the pack. Rich lit the Camel and began smoking away as he continued his recording. He then began to discuss his vacation in Daytona Beach, Florida, during a spring break from college.

"It was about four in the morning...I was still drunk from the kegga we had that night... I left the beach house to go for a walk ... and burn a couple Camels. It was beautiful outside ... probably about 70 degrees, slight ...breeze blowing through the palm trees. So, I'm walkin'... down the street, and a white van pulls up. These two.... titanic friggin' dudes all in black, with their faces covered with ski masks, jump out of the back. They jumped me, beat ...my ass, then threw me ...in the back of the van."

Rich took a couple drags before resuming his tale and recounting what he observed upon awakening.

"I musta...lost consciousness in the vehicle, 'cause I don't remember anything... until I woke up ...who knows how much later. My eyes opened... and I was lying on my back... on a gurney or hospital bed of some sort. I noticed about twenty... other people around me ... also lying on the same beds. Some men, some... women, of all different races and ethnicity.

"They all appeared to be sleeping or dead. Then I noticed .... they were all hooked up to some... kind of intravenous lines, connected to a bag filled with a dark red liquid. I also discovered I had the same ... tubes hooked up to my right arm, a similar red ...liquid being pumped into me.

"I tried to sit up straight, but my mobility was restricted. It was... then that I realized - I was shackled to the bed with leather cuff restraints around my wrists and ankles."

Mack sat still- fascinated, watching the recording of a ruffled Rich.

Rich then finished his cigarette and rubbed it out on the dirt ground beside him before continuing his tale.

"I was very groggy... from the drugs, and I had no idea where I was... but I knew that this was not a normal ...hospital or health care facility. I pulled the tube out of my vein, causing the... red fluid from the tube to spill all over me and onto the white tiled floor.

"A fifty-something year old ... Middle Eastern man in scrubs then came in at the far end of the room and I ... acted as if I were comatose or dead, whatever state the others were in.

"Luckily the guy didn't stay long ... then as soon as he left the room, I was able to shift my weight to the edge of my gurney, making it jump, inching ... closer to a nearby supply cart. Even with my wrist secured, I was ... able to reach over with my left hand and grab a disposable plastic handled green ... scalpel.

"I stuck the blade from the scalpel into the keyhole ... on my left wrist shackle, utilizing it like a key to unlock the clasp and free my left arm, then ... the right arm and ankle shackles."

The video clip continued, with Rich seeming more delirious as it progressed.

He began to talk about escaping out of the "bright, white room" and into an office cubicle type section of the building. He said he then went out into the parking lot and into the night. He described feeling weak and dizzy, barely able to walk. He was hiding in a nearby wooded area as security guards with flashlights shining and guns drawn began to flood the immediate vicinity.

Before long, military looking vehicles in their drab olive-green paint jobs began arriving and searching as well.

The hunted one could hear the blaring portable radios of those searching for him, with an unknown person on the other end who was shouting.

"Has the patient been located yet? Someone tell me if we have him yet!!"

Another voice replied, "No, sir. Not yet."

The leader's voice returned, sounding displeased with the predicament. He instructed all of the staff: "shut the place down now! Terminate all of the patients and burn the facility down!!"

Rich paused, his story interrupted by a low-flying police helicopter with searchlight, passing above.

"Shhhh!! Don't let them hear you!" Rich said into the camera as if talking to an actual person by his side.

After the copter was out of earshot, Rich resumed his video confession. He described hiding in a tree while seeing the entire facility go up in flames. Rich noticed all the security and military people were out of the proximity now. They were probably still looking for him, but thinking he was further away.

Rich said he began thinking about all the other people he saw strapped down to their beds. Some were unable to flee the smoke and flames within, so Rich ran back inside. He hid behind the bushes beside the building as scores of fleeing staff members cloaked in scrubs headed for their cars.

They obviously were eager to get the hell out of there before the place blew up or before the police arrived. Or both.

Awestruck, Mack eagerly continued to view the recording as Rich concluded his story:

"I went inside ... expecting to find all of the other bedridden ones murdered like ... the voice had instructed, but they were all still alive. I guess the staff decided ... the patients were going to burn to death anyways ... since they were all restrained to their beds, so they didn't kill them first like instructed. They just smashed chemical bottles all over and ... lit the place on fire.

"I was able ... to free some of the other people, not sure exactly how many ... some were unconscious, and I had to carry them out fireman style over my shoulder. Others who were in better shape, I ... told them to help me free others. Some of them helped, others just hauled ass.

"Anyways, Holly... It turns out I was in that hellhole for about eight days. I'm not sure what ... they did to me back there, but at least whoever... they don't know who I am, because I left my ID back in the ... beach house and I had nothing in my possession to identify me. I never told any of my ... buddies what happened to me either – when they questioned where I went that week, I told them I met some girl and ... spent the week with her.

"I tried to resume my ... normal life when I returned to Rhode Island, but I could not study or work. I kept seeing ... my buddies from the trip. It brought back those horrible memories. So, I moved down here to Texas to get a clean start..."

Rich continued to duck down in the shadows and to look all around him as he wrapped up his message for Holly.

"So, babe, I need to cut to the chase because they are getting closer. I can't go back to my job at DQ, because 'they' know ... I work there now. You are probably wondering who 'they' are... so am I. 'They' could be military people or CIA or something, but whoever... those people are, they're somehow connected to the lab in Florida.

"And somehow, they found me, and have ... been following me home from work the last few nights. There are several of them, and they have a few different cars.... I know it's just a matter of time ... until they get me and kill me.

"It's been three years since Daytona, and I know ... I had a hard time with what happened to me at first ... but I thought maybe it was all a mental thing. I really thought a change of scenery; coming to Texas ... would fix me.

"But it didn't. I have changed, Holly – I swear I wasn't always like this. I'm sorry I got violent with you at times, lost my temper so often. At times I ... feel kind of inhuman, more like an animal. Lately I have been conflicted, thoughts of ... killing and murder run through my mind. An overwhelming desire to eat human flesh ...

"You can see it's essential for me to leave. I can't risk anything happening to you or ... the kids, so it's for the best that I ... leave you alone. You must understand - I don't want to be apart from you. I love you so much!"

The recording concluded and was followed by blackness and static. Mack wondered how the camera and the recording made their way back to Holly's house if Rich really had left with them that night.

If Mack had not seen the birthday video, he would have had to question the validity of just about everything he had just seen on Rich's last video diary. But knowing what Mack knew now, anything at all was possible.

There were no further recordings on the digital camera. Having reviewed the clips and knowing now what he knew, Mack began to put the pieces of the puzzle together.

Rich and Holly had changed into something like ... zombies. As crazy as that seemed, Mack could not better define what he saw with his own eyes.

The video of the birthday incident lined up perfectly with what Mack knew of the incident from Jake's cell phone call as Jake left that day. The video also corroborated what Mack saw with his own eyes when he arrived at Holly's house. Anyone else watching this birthday clip might have assumed they were watching a scene from a low budget horror film.

This meant that Jake was innocent of murder. This should have been obvious to the feds who had access to Rich and Holly's bodies, as well as all of the evidence which supported the fact that this was not a premeditated murder.

Mack could not comprehend why the FBI was not treating this case as an obvious example of self-defense. Perhaps some military or government types had been stalking Rich in his final days leading up to the birthday incident.

It's possible they were planning on abducting and/or killing him so he could not talk about what had happened to him at that Florida lab just three years earlier.

But Rich changed to a zombie before they got to him.

That would explain why the FBI was able to respond to the birthday incident within minutes. They were possibly already in the area trying to hunt Rich down.

Then when Holly ended up dead as well, they had no choice but to frame the first person who showed up, Jake, for the incident. They made it appear as though this was a domestic type murder scene. All so that they could cover up the fact that two people had turned into zombies as a result of some crazy government laboratory experiments.

What Mack struggled with and made no sense to him was the whole laboratory and experiments scenario. Why would the government be abducting and then conducting experiments on innocent people? What could they possibly hope to accomplish by turning healthy humans into hungry, human-eating cannibals?

Previously Mack had been guilt ridden about not revealing to the court the fact that it was he who had been in a relationship with Holly, not Jake. For the prosecutor had alleged that when Holly broke it off with Jake, Jake sought revenge. He went to her house to slay Holly and killed Rich when he showed up to rescue her.

But now, considering this new information obtained through his investigation, Mack wondered what would have happened if he had spoken out about this relationship. As crazy as things have been, this information may have just encouraged the prosecutor to name Mack as an accomplice to the murders. After all, Mack was the second person on scene, not counting the feds.

Had Mack shared his story in court, he might have found himself abruptly taken into custody and seated right next to Jake. He could have found himself wearing a matching shock collar and leg irons.

If the government was so eager to throw the book at an outstanding Marine war hero with nothing but commendations in his file like Jake, they surely would not hesitate to do similar or worse to Mack.

The rookie Dallas officer now became more determined than ever to get to the bottom of this outrageous display of government corruption and conspiracy. He had to clear the name of his best friend.

Chapter 16 - Abracadaver

The Hail Mary, North Dallas (Present Day)

Officer Kelvin McElroy was off duty and had just made some astonishing discoveries relevant to his investigation into his best friend's murder trial. Needing some time to relax and collect his thoughts, he made his way to his favorite drinking hole, a sports bar named "the Hail Mary." The pub was owned by his and Jake's good friend, Dave Talucci.

This was an establishment that many off-duty Dallas Police Officers and Dallas Firefighters frequented. They were welcomed by the ownership and employees who recognized and were thankful for these heroes' service, dedication, and professionalism.

Mack and Jake went to this establishment on many occasions after work or on their nights off. It was a great place to unwind, shoot some billiards, throw darts, tell tales and drink beers – whatever method one preferred in order to relieve some work-related stress.

Mack sat alone at a corner booth drinking one Shiner beer after another. He looked up from his beer nuts to see a familiar face had emerged.

Dressed in a red plaid half shirt, Daisy Duke blue jean cut-off shorts, and a pair a black leather cowboy boots, Megan Anderson strutted forward.

"Hey, Mack! Long time no see!"

"Megan! Hey girl! How's Northwest Station treating you?" Mack stood to give his former rookie school classmate a hug.

"You know, it's okay. Same old stuff as you see down here in Central, just different faces. How have you been, Mack?"

Hesitating slightly before responding, Mack in his Shiner haze answered, "I'm doing okay, I guess, considering all that's happened. What about you? You still married?"

"Unfortunately, I am. He's such a dickhead. I should have listened to my mom when she told me I was too young to get married."

"I'm sorry to hear that. Really sucks. Hey, you know about Jake, right?" Mack invited a response from his cute former colleague.

"Yes, I do, and I still can't believe it. Wanna hear something I never told anyone before?"

"Of course,"

Megan paused, her eyes filling with tears.

"Okay, well, please don't share this with anyone. You know, there was that time during field training when my regular FTO was out sick for the whole week and Jake filled in as my trainer? You were gone doing observation days in Investigations and Crime Scene, Property Room, etcetera.

"Anyways, Jake and I hit it off right from the start. He was several years older than me, but it didn't seem like it. We talked a lot, really got to know each other. We remarkably had a lot in common, with similar interests in fitness and weight training, tattoos, and music.

"I could tell he was the kind of guy who doesn't show emotion or talk much about himself or his life. But for some reason, Jake really seemed to open up around me. He talked about his girlfriend, how they met, how good their relationship used to be. But he also talked about her jealousy, her failure to trust him and her constant accusations of him being unfaithful. I think maybe I caught Jake at a very vulnerable juncture in his life.

"And it was obvious we were each completely and utterly physically attracted to the other. We never said a word to each other in that regard, but the feeling was powerful, some might describe it as an animal-like magnetism.

"It was difficult, but we kept the training days professional. We were both in a relationship at the time, and it was as if we each knew that it might jeopardize what we had with our significant others if we got to know each other better. So, we kept the contact very minimal, and we never again spoke at great length, only saying hello occasionally in passing and brief small talk in the hallways about calls for service we were on together.

"Soon afterwards, I completed my field training phase and was transferred to the Northwest Division out near Bachman Lake.

"I often think about our one week together and pondered what might have been if we had let nature run its course. If we had gone along with our initial feelings and attraction.

"Mack, I fell in love with Jake in that short time we had together. Since then at times I thought about contacting him somehow and expressing my feelings for him. But I was too intimidated by him and afraid to tell him how I felt. I also didn't want to jeopardize his relationship because he seemed to be very much in love with Amanda, despite her inadequacies.

"So, as you can tell, I am devastated by the news of his passing. I will always love him."

"Wow," Mack said.

"What?"

"Jake told me similar things about you after y'alls' time together. He told me you were the first person he met since Amanda that he really felt drawn to. It was like there was a real connection. He truly was afraid of spending much more time with you because he feared he would only end up wanting you more. I don't think he had any clue you felt the way you do, though."

"Oh, I think he figured it out," she added while her frown flipped up into a devilish grin.

Mack did not tell Megan he was investigating Jake's supposed death, because he did not want to get her hopes up that he may be still alive.

The two caught each other up on the latest news involving other classmates they had in the same academy class, all of whom were subsequently spread throughout the seven Patrol Divisions in the city.

Megan said, "I should rejoin my friends at their table, but it was so good to see you again, Mack. Let's keep in touch!"

She gave him her cell phone number and retreated to the opposite end of the restaurant.

Dave made his way over to the booth, sat down across from Mack, and said, "Who's the hot chick?"

"She's with DPD, went to the academy with me, but now she works out of Northwest. Her name's Megan - really a sweet girl."

Dave nodded in the affirmative, then became still and silent. He acted as if he had something to say but couldn't find the words.

After a lengthy period of silence, Dave eventually looked down at the table and spurted out, "I can't believe Jake's dead. It's all over the news...you know I went down to Lew Sterrett and saw him just a few nights before it all happened?"

"No, I didn't know that..."

"Yeah, he was down, rightfully so. He really wanted me to talk to you and tell you something that bothered him to the point he could not sleep. He wanted me to stress to you that when he went to Carson's birthday party, Holly was not her normal self. There was something terribly wrong with her and Rich. I told him by the time you got to the scene the feds had covered the bodies up so you could not see for yourself how they appeared."

"I believe him now," Mack said. "I came across some evidence that I had not been privy to before."

"What kind of evidence?" Dave asked.

"Dave, I think it would be in your best interest and for your own safety that I do not say everything I know. But I have reason to believe that the feds, FBI, military branches, and who knows who else, are all involved in experiments that were turning people into...basically, zombies. As crazy as that sounds.

"And they are all working together to keep all of this covered up. I don't even know who I can and cannot trust in my own department, because some of them may be connected as well. But I still don't understand what anyone could possibly gain from such experiments. I plan on figuring that part out soon enough."

A bug-eyed Dave was caught off guard by Mack's remark. "Wait- back up. Did you just say zombies?!"

Duy Tran, Jake's young legal adviser, had just entered the bar. He saw Mack and Dave and instantly made a beeline towards them.

"Guys - tell me what I heard about Jake is not true. Hold up - did you just say something about there being zombies?"

Mack and Dave recapped their conversation for the "Dew-man," as his closest friends called him, to get him caught up to speed. Since the trial, Duy had found himself to be despondent and guilt-ridden. He accepted full blame and responsibility for the outcome.

Although he was new to the criminal defense circuit, he felt it was a case he should have won. Hearing now that the trial and evidence against Jake seemed to have been fixed and based upon lies, deception, and a government cover-up, Tran's emotions switched to anger.

One of the things Tran had always loved and admired about America was the Constitution the United States had in place. He admired the written Preamble calling for the establishment of a "more perfect union" by "ensuring domestic tranquility," "promoting the general welfare," and, above all else in Duy's mind, "establishing justice."

The United States legal system should ultimately operate as the means and system through which it guaranteed that the protection of every citizen's rights and freedoms would be sustained.

Tran could not say the same for the legal system utilized in his native country of Vietnam. However, at this point, Tran was not so sure about this American system either.

Duy Dong Tran was born in Da Nang, Vietnam just twenty-five years earlier. When he was three years old, his father and mother moved with Duy and his sister Tien from Vietnam to the United States. They were in pursuit of the American Dream; the opportunity to obtain stable, well-paying jobs, with health care benefits, and the ability to provide a better life for them all.

They first landed in Alaska. There, Duy's father spent a couple of years employed as a fisherman. He made a living catching King Crab off the Alaskan coast.

After that, his parents were eager to relocate the family to

Texas. Once there, they appreciated the warmer climate and reasonable cost of living. They decided to establish roots there, so they settled down and had a family.

Duy's mother and father both acquired their cosmetology licenses, and soon afterward they realized their American dream; by opening their own nail salon in Arlington, a city just west of Dallas.

At the age of ten, Duy and his younger sister were in the salon with their parents one Saturday afternoon. Two armed masked men made their way into the store. They never fired a shot, but they did plenty of damage. The fear they placed in the Tran family that day would never be forgotten. That incident would always act as a psychological scar on their sense of safety and freedom.

Duy then vowed he would dedicate his life to justice. His original intention was to become a police officer. But when he learned his poor eyesight would prevent him from achieving this goal, he altered his plan. Instead, he earned himself a law degree at Southern Methodist University in Dallas.

Now, armed with that certificate, Duy was striving to become one of the best attorneys in the Metroplex. He was hopeful he could make a difference in the lives of those who had no one else to turn to.

So, the more Duy heard Mack speak of the lies and falsities by the prosecutor and witnesses against Jake, the Dew-man became that much more furious. For example, Mack revealed that the prosecution and witness Gladys had lied about Roscoe going inside Rich and Holly's house and they claimed that Roscoe had attacked Holly.

Mack's investigation revealed that on the day of The Birthday Incident, Roscoe was equipped with a GPS tag on his collar, and every move he made could be tracked in a live computer feed and recorded to review later. Mack reviewed this footage for the day and time of The Birthday Incident and discovered that Roscoe never made it inside that residence.

And speaking of witness Gladys Torrence, Officer McElroy learned some very interesting information about her when he attempted to track her down following the trial.

Chapter 17 - Thin Mints and Maggots

M Streets, Dallas TX (Two weeks earlier)

Witness Gladys Torrence was a widower who lived alone with her eight small indoor dogs of varying species. After her testimony, Torrence was driven home by an unknown government official in a plain white Chevy Impala with U.S. Government plates.

A month later, little Stacey Hall, a twelve-year-old Girl Scout from troop #695, made a gruesome discovery.

One Tuesday evening after school, Stacey was dressed in her freshly ironed mint green vest, white shirt, and matching green skirt. She left her house with the good intentions of selling some cookies to benefit her troop. Stacey towed behind her a red metal Radio Flyer wagon loaded down with cases of the various popular flavors she had to offer.

Stacey approached Torrence's house with the high hopes of selling some of her thin mints. But she quickly noticed all of the windows were wide open.

Some had screens still intact while others had been removed or possibly just dropped out.

Jet black flies poured in and out through the open windows. From the front sidewalk, the scout was overwhelmed with a horrible scent.

Stacey was a senior scout; curious, kind-hearted, and always eager to do whatever it took to acquire another merit patch. She sensed something was not right here, yet the young scout knocked on Gladys' door anyways. But she did so with slight trepidation.

Stacy waited patiently for someone to respond. She began to make observations of the scene, as a good Scout should.

She noticed what appeared to be ants and other insects crawling out of the mail slot on the front door. Stacy used her green and white pencil to lift the mail slot cover upwards so she could get a better peek inside.

She soon wished her curiosity and desire to do good had not gotten the best of her.

For lying within a foot of the front door was the half-eaten remains of a carcass of what was once possibly a poodle. The head was intact as well as its tail and vertebrae, but the meatier parts of the body appeared dissected and its little torso was gutted.

An infestation of maggots wriggled in and out or their minute masticated holes throughout the gutted poodle pup.

Scout Stacy promptly disgorged her chicken taco lunch all over the front door. She quickly wiped her mouth clean with a Fiesta Mart sales flier that was lying on Torrence's welcome mat before using her cell phone to call 911.

Police officers and firemen responded to the location and, after donning full haz-mat suits, went inside. The overwhelming scent of ammonia, animal feces, urine, and death filled the air.

The emergency responders, although they were all wearing breathing apparatus, could still detect the odors floating around them like clouds. Animal feces from the small dogs and from unseen critters such as rats or raccoons was piled up and smeared all over the brown shag carpet found throughout the residence.

Gladys' surviving canines were standoffish, hiding under masses of filth or huddled together in corners. They barked and howled steadily with their shrill, scared little dog voices, indicating to the humans that they were traumatized, frightened, and hungry.

Upon closer look at the mutts, it was apparent their matted facial and body fur was soaked in blood and covered with what appeared to be human flesh.

The response team made their way into the back bedroom of the ranch house and discovered a wall of stacked white plastic Walmart shopping bags that were filled with human excrement.

Gladys had to resort to relieving herself this way when her water and electricity were shut off months ago. It was at that time that she opted to discontinue paying the bills in favor of spending the money on thrift store treasures and dog food.

Behind the wall of plastic bag poop was what appeared to be Gladys' mutilated body curled up into a fetal position on the floor. Her tongue was missing from the body, and it became apparent that her eyes had been plucked from their sockets. The item possibly used to remove her eyes, a blue and white ball point pen inscribed with the words "Bingo Palace, Tyler Texas," was lying on the floor near the body.

The first emergency medical technician to see Gladys realized through his extensive training alone that there was no sense in trying to revive the elderly woman. She appeared to have been at one time bound and gagged with duct tape and was clearly way past reviving.

Closer examination revealed the tape that had restrained her wrists and ankles had been chewed off. The gag from her mouth had been clawed away from her face.

With all these dogs around in the house, it seemed as if one or two of them had removed Gladys' restraints, trying to rescue their master.

Just as someone was about to throw a sheet over the elder's remains, the cadaver snarled loudly.

"GRRRRRRR!!"

ITs snout pointed skyward up into the air as if sniffing something tasty.

In ITs cadaverous condition, and having no eyes, IT began to wave its arms around, feeling around for something. IT was apparently trying to reach the nearby morsel that it was smelling. The startled EMT yelled "FUCK!!!" and ran out of the house without looking back.

One of the first responding police officers inside the house saw this unthinkable incident occur. He unloaded at least four rounds of 9 mm bullets into what was once Gladys' head, causing the abhorred to finally come to rest.

After the corpse was removed from the residence, animal control officers responded to the scene to take custody of the abandoned animals. They were now feasting on Stacey's chicken taco regurgitation.

An autopsy report would later conclude that after she was bound and gagged, approximately 20 percent of Torrence's body was eaten by her small dogs. A smaller percent was devoured by a small collection of unidentified rodents.

Most likely the eating/chewing of the cadaver occurred postmortem. But it was possible that some occurred prior to her death. As for the eyes and tongue being removed from the victim, it could not be positively determined whether this had also been done by the dogs. This would have been extremely rare, nearly unheard of.

Another possibility was that this was done by another person. Possibly it was done by the same person who murdered Gladys. And she was most likely killed to shut her up, so she could never speak the truth about what she saw and heard next door.

One thing was *not* found in the report. There was no type of explanation or theory provided as to how Gladys was reborn or transformed into the creature that the EMTs and police encountered.

In the days that followed, town health inspectors found the Torrance house to be uninhabitable and a safety hazard for all within a nearby proximity. The odors and contamination emanating from within made it dangerous for anyone around. The structure was condemned and slated for destruction.

The Hail Mary, North Dallas   (Present Day)

Dave and Duy were floored with the news Mack had just revealed. Dave quizzed, "What was that Gladys lady's last name again?"

"Torrence."

"Oh, wow, I thought so. There were some off-duty firemen here drinking beers the other night. I overheard one of them talking about the fire at the Torrance house.

"He said the house had already been bulldozed, demolished per a court order. The fire department ordered to go over there to perform a 'controlled burn' of the existing structural remains.

"He said trenches had already been dug around the property line borders to prevent the flames from jumping over to the grass or other portions of neighboring lots. The concrete foundation was not visible, nor were the tremendous amount of collected items, garbage and trash the hoarder-woman who had lived there accumulated over the years. All that was visible were the downed walls and roof, broken and battered, lying over the top of the previously described assortment that lie beneath.

"So, they start burning this pile of shit and they abruptly become inundated with smoke and the stench of what the fire guy described as a backyard carcass barbecue. He said there must have been a bunch of animal remains or something like that inside. It smelled like death and feces combined, being cooked over a tremendous open flame for the entire neighborhood to inhale.

"But apparently there were some that did not mind the odor as much, and were attracted to it, like a moth to a flame. Suddenly these creatures started stumbling out of the woods at the rear of the property, staggering about and acting as if they were trying to find the buffet they were smelling. They began to walk right into the fire at first, but I guess they saw the fire dudes and began to go after them.

"A couple of the older, more seasoned, firemen retreated to the cab of their firetruck and radioed the police. But this one young rookie fireman named Donny, fresh out of the fire academy and full of piss and vinegar, grabbed one of those axes. I think he called it a 'Denver Tool'. He took it off the side of the truck and went after the mis-creations.

"This Donny guy starts thrashing those dead fuckers upside their heads with his axe, splitting some of their skulls in half and completely decapitating others. Luckily, he had his helmet and face shield on, because they said it was like a black bloodbath, zombie blood muck and head and skull fragments rained down upon him and even splattered the windows of the adjacent fire truck.

"Sounds like this Donny kid was a bad-ass. He was young, big and strong. He wiped out about fifteen of those walking corpses before he started to tire. He must have realized his energy was waning as he began to backtrack toward the truck. But then one of those fuckers circled around behind him and was lurking in the shadows between Donny and the rig. The beast grabbed the rook and bit at Donny's shoulder. Luckily the monster couldn't bite through the fire coat. But then IT started clawing at Donny's face shield and helmet, knocking them off Donny's head."

"The zombie was just about to bite the fire rook's face. Then one of the elder crewmates, Earl, climbed out of the enormous red Pierce fire truck. Earl speared IT between the eyes with the forked end of a 30-inch tri-bar forcible entry tool. The creature dropped to the ground like a sack of potatoes."

Dave concluded the story.

"Then that old Earl guy looked at the rookie and said, 'someday you'll learn, kid. Nothing you do out here means shit unless you make it back to the station alive at the end of the shift. Now get in the damn truck.'

Dave got up from the booth and walked behind the bar to fetch another round of cold ones for himself, Mack, and Duy. He returned with the ice-cold bottles, returned to his seat across from Mack, and dealt the drinks.

Mack had already depleted a six-pack and began to nurse number seven as he prepared his companions for the somewhat irrational statement he was about to give.

"I don't think Jake is really dead."

Duy and Dave looked at each other in amazement and in unison they glanced back at Mack and said, "Whattt?"

"I'm serious, y'all. After I got word that he was dead, I attempted to track down the location of Jake's body to confirm the report. I kept getting the runaround with everyone I contacted. I began to question the media report in which the Feds announced Jake was slain in his 'escape attempt.' I got to thinking - what if Jake's still alive and this is just another attempt on the government's part to cover something up?

"Maybe I'm just losing it. After all, I haven't gotten a full night of sleep since this whole thing started. I guess it couldn't hurt to tell you guys all that I know. I was hesitant before because I thought maybe someone might think you know too much and shut y'all up. But you need to know the truth.

"You know, I wasn't there for the Birthday Incident, when it transpired, but Jake called me right after it happened. He told me about the nightmare that had just unfolded. He had to leave to take little Carson to a safe place and he asked me to go to Rich and Holly's place to secure the scene.

"I got there pretty quickly and went inside, but the G Men were already on site. They had the two bodies covered up with tarps, and they were cleaning up blood and other bodily fluids, skin and flesh, off the walls and floors. A video camera had been set up on a bookshelf to record the area where Carson's highchair had been placed. I grabbed the digital video recorder and found it to still be recording. I tucked the camera under the front of my shirt and walked out the front door with it just as some big asshole Hispanic agent told me they were taking the investigation over and the PD was not needed.

"Later that night I watched the recording" Mack said. "I sat in my seat, stunned by the disturbing scenes that were unfolding before my eyes on the birthday video. I saw *what used to be Holly* attack Jake, causing him to fall backwards into Carson's baby dining chair. Jake looked scared to death, but he was obviously not going to leave his nephew alone there with whatever Holly had turned into. I kept replaying the split second repeatedly in which she was on screen. I tried to freeze it, but the image was blurry.

"But from what I could see, it appeared that Holly had somehow morphed into a monster. Her body was covered with rotting or burnt flesh which was hanging off her body. But most disturbing to me was her face. She no longer seemed human. She wore a hungry, emotionless expression and was more like an animal than a person. This image burned into my brain, and I cannot get it out of my mind for the life of me. It still gives me nightmares.

"But now, the thing that bothers me most is that I have no idea if Jake is really dead like they are reporting. It doesn't make sense to me that the Feds would have plotted an escape from a prison bus in order to kill Jake when he was already scheduled to die by lethal injection on death row. So maybe he is alive somewhere and someone is holding him captive. Or maybe he's out there on his own, on the run, being hunted like some big game wild animal whose head would be mounted and displayed like a grand trophy above the fireplace mantle of his executioner.

"I keep thinking about poor Amanda, now left all alone with Jake being gone. And little Carson, with his parents out of the picture now, he really needs the love, guidance, and support of his aunt and uncle, cause there ain't nobody else."

Mack paused before revealing a sensitive side that he tried to avoid using whenever possible. But by now this transparency was unavoidable. "I don't have a wife, no family nearby. I have decided to take a leave of absence from the PD in order to get to the bottom of this craziness. One way or another I am going to track Jake down. If he's dead, then I will find his body. If he's alive, I'm gonna let him know I have the evidence that can get his conviction overturned.

"But the first thing on my agenda is to go set Roscoe free. It's bullshit that they are talking about having him destroyed. Hopefully when we get there to release him, he will not treat me like he did the criminals out there on the streets of Dallas. This dog is one mean son of a bitch. But if he remembers me and will go along willingly, he could prove invaluable in my travels and search for

Jake. So, if anyone wants in on my mission, y'all are welcome to join."

"Count me in for all of that!" proclaimed Duy. "I'll go with you to save Roscoe and for whatever else comes after that. It's the least I can do for Jake. I still feel like I could have done a better job defending him in court during his murder trial.

"And my law practice can wait. Besides, if things don't change anytime soon, I may be completely out of a job. It seems as if the more the infection spreads, the less need there will be for legal proceedings."

"You know, Duy, you really shouldn't beat yourself up about how that trial went down" Mack sympathized. "I think you guys would have lost no matter what you said or did. They had the deck stacked against you, the whole thing was crooked and fixed. The government needed to make Jake their scapegoat in order to cover up their role in the whole infection thing. They had to get rid of him to shut him up because they know he has the inside scoop on the scandal."

Mack was grateful to have Duy's support and asked, "okay, what skills do you possess besides your legal prowess? Are you into martial arts or have any experience with weapons or anything?"

Duy paused briefly before responding.

"Well, I'm afraid of guns and can't fight, but I'm kind of into knives. You know, butterflies, switchblades, machetes, hatchets - basically, anything with a blade. When I was a kid, I had a set of throwing knives that I would chuck at a target in our backyard. I'm not too bad at it. Had a blowgun too that I made from bamboo, but I need a little more practice with that."

Dave said, "I'd be happy to assist you guys on the Roscoe mission. I can't leave my business for an extended length of time to go searching for Jake, though, as much as I'd love to help with that as well.

"And Mack, I have a talent that might benefit us nicely. I used to be a landlord over some crappy apartment complexes, and over the years I became quite gifted at picking door locks. But why are you asking the kid about weapons training and martial arts and shit like that? Are there guards surrounding the puppy pound or something?"

"Naw, man," Mack assured. "The pound is out in the middle

of nowhere. There's no one out there at night. I don't anticipate any problems at all."

"Well fuck, then" Dave said. "Let's go do this thing right now!"

City of Dallas Animal Services Department, South East Dallas TX

The animal shelter was located several miles from downtown, in the southern part of the city. The Animal Services Department Building was in a desolate industrial district, neighboring the Southside Water Treatment Plant just to the south and the McCommas Landfill directly to the north.

The building was surrounded by old native elm trees and backed up to the Trinity River, the longest river that flows entirely within the State of Texas. This body of water was given its name in 1690 by Alonso De León, who called the stream the "La Santísima Trinidad," or "the Most Holy Trinity."

There were no single-family dwellings or multifamily apartment units in this tract. The only structures nearby were the manufacturing plants and commercial industrial businesses that were closed at night. No one should be in the area or be alerted if the building's audible burglary alarm was activated or all the dogs began barking loudly during the rescue.

Dave parked a block away from the facility. The trio were all in dark attire, with Mack and Duy clothed in black T-shirts and BDU tactical style pants while Dave chose a more athletic fashion with his Adidas sweatpants and matching jacket which covered his flabby frame. All three wore matching ski masks over their faces, and they exited Dave's crew cab F150 pickup truck to begin their short jog toward their target.

Dave carried a small metal box, Duy had a large pair of bolt cutters in hand, and Mack had his Glock .40 holstered at the ready. He also carried a wooden handled sledgehammer just for good measure.

The team arrived unnoticed. Duy, realizing that many burglar alarms depend upon the telephone landlines, promptly utilized his cutting tool to snap the phone cables running up the exterior wall of the building.

Dave approached the glass front door with his locksmith kit in hand. He wasted no time in working the lock and within three minutes he had the door open. A welcome surprise followed as no audible alarm sounded and they made their entrance.

The desperados proceeded through the lobby and encountered two sets of parallel hallways. Each corridor led to a separate ward of seemingly endless aisles of indoor dog kennels.

"Which way should we go?" asked Duy. "Should we split up to find Roscoe or stay together?"

"We don't even know what he looks like," Dave remarked.

"He's one bad ass Belgian Malinois who looks like a friggin attack dog" Mack said. "He should still be wearing his brown leather collar with the little K9 police badge attached."

Mack suggested, "Let's stay together, you guys, just so we don't have to track everyone down when we do find Roscoe. Let's just move quickly."

Upon selecting a point from which to commence, the soldiers of fortune found countless cages containing the wrong canine. Soon, half of the kenneled mutts broke into a loud barking frenzy as the caged animals howled their disapproval of being woken in the middle of the night.

But the men eventually located their prize.

Roscoe was lying on the cold concrete floor at the rear of his cage, at the opposite end of the cell away from the door and empty food and water bowls. The muscular animal lay on his stomach, motionless and with his eyes closed shut.

"That's him?" Duy asked. "He looks like death warmed over. Is he even breathing?"

With a solemn look on his face, and in a voice that hardened as he spoke, Mack murmured, "we may be too late."

Mack grabbed the large pair of bolt cutters from Duy's grasp and began to work on the padlock, to no avail. Dave offered to try his hand at picking the lock with his locksmith kit, but Mack said, "Hold yer horses. Hand me my sledge back."

Mack clutched the timber-handled maul and with one powerful, mighty swing he aimed the steel anvil into the inferior locking device, which promptly exploded with shards of aluminum and metal hovering through the air.

This blast echoed through the facility. Now every fleabag in the joint was bellowing. Every dog except for Roscoe, that is. Roscoe opened his eyes and looked up at Mack, who had one foot in the doorway of the pen.

"Dude be careful," urged Dave. "I'm not sure he recognizes you, and he seems out of it. He may bite the shit out of you!"

Mack ignored the pleas and continued to enter the canine coop. "Roscoe, it's me – Mack. Remember? Come on boy, you know me!"

The malnourished Malinois was weak and startled. He expressed his displeasure with this visitor by displaying a mouthful of incisors and growling ferociously.

At this point, the sound of hundreds of animals howling in unison was nearly deafening. Mack knew their time was elapsing quickly and he had to get Roscoe out of the joint soon before the place was raining with security guards or cops or both.

The young police officer pounced upon the struggling canine and used his sizable right hand to cover Roscoe's snout and mouth. It took all of Mack's strength to hold the tenacious jaws shut. Mack reached under Roscoe's body with his left arm to cradle the seventy-five-pound police dog in his armpit and he began to run toward the exit.

"Come on, let's get the hell out of here!"

Out they ran, back through the roaring kennel and lobby and then out into the humid night. Duy led the charge, followed by a less agile Dave. Last in the procession was Mack, carrying a dazed and delirious police dog who was suffering from severe malnutrition, under his arm. Roscoe was no longer applying pressure and trying to open his mouth to bite, either because he now recognized his savior, or he was just too weak to continue.

The squad reassembled only fifty feet outside of the animal services building door when Mack nearly ran into the backs of the halted teammates ahead of him.

"Oh Fuck!"

Mack now saw what Duy and Dave had already seen. They stood frozen, staring at a slow but steady tidal wave of corrosion creeping all around Dave's truck parked on the street nearly half a block away. The lurking corpses had apparently been summoned from the woods by the looming sound of barking dogs from within the shelter and were now steadily approaching the men.

"I count at least twenty between us and the truck" Dave advised. "What should we do?"

"What if we went back inside and opened some of the kennels, releasing the dogs to go outside and serve as a distraction for us. Maybe the zombies will settle for canine tonight instead of humans?" reasoned Duy.

Mack wasn't nearly as fond of that proposition. "But the longer we take, the more of these fuckers will climb out of the woodworks. I say we go for it and try to make it to the truck!"

"I say we fight!" Duy shouted. He removed a black handled machete from his right pant leg pocket of his BDU's, and a set of three throwing knives from the large cargo pocket on his left leg.

"I don't even have a weapon guys, I left mine at the house. This was supposed to be easy," said Dave.

Duy held up his hands containing the various blades and said, "take your pick."

Dave grabbed for the machete, not being the skilled and accurate knife thrower that the Dew-man was.

"I've got my Glock and my sledge, but I don't know how much hammering' I can do without dropping Roscoe and he becomes tender vittles for these fuckers." Mack explained as he slung the weak and exhausted police dog over his neck like a furry, boney sack of potatoes. Roscoe's front and rear legs hung down in front of
Mack on either side of his head.

Mack used his left hand to reach back and hold Roscoe onto him tightly and he positioned his Glock in his right hand, preparing to rush headfirst into battle.

Duy commented, "All right, fellas, I hope everyone is good with the big man above, just in case we don't survive this. Godspeed!"

"I'm in like Flynn with the big guy!" Mack exclaimed. "I slapped him on the ass the other day and told him, 'Good game.' He gave me one right back."

Dave and Duy looked at each other, puzzled and unsure of what to think of Mack's last comment, but all three surged forward and began the onslaught of the *dead.*

Duy used his throwing knives like daggers, holding two in

his right hand and one in his left, jabbing the blades into the chest of the first of the jaw-chomping deadbeats he encountered. Duy stabbed repeatedly, shredding the heart and throat area of the creature, which continued to edge forward, still eager to eat.

"GUYS, THIS THING AIN'T STOPPING!!!!!"

Mack had already blasted three of the beasts to smithereens with single blasts to their heads from his Glock .40 as he took great care to prevent the macabre from biting or clawing at Roscoe. "Attack the heads, guys. Seems to be more effective…"

Duy sunk the two blades in his right hand into the forehead of his nemesis with a sudden upward thrust. The creature folded like a campground tent and collapsed to the ground at Duy's feet. A black gel-like glop seeped from its newly acquired cavity.

Dave swung his machete about as if it was a magic wand. He was slicing and carving at the creatures faces and removing noses and ears, but otherwise without much effectiveness.

The Chicago native found himself quickly backtracking as two zombies closed within three feet of him at the same time.

Unbeknownst to Dave, an already slain creature whom Mack had extinguished was now lying on the ground at Dave's feet. The tavern owner tripped over the carcass and fell backwards, landing on his hyper-extended right wrist, shattering the tiny bones within as if they were twigs beneath a Sasquatch's foot.

"AAAAAAAAAAAAAAHHHHHHHHHH!!!!!" Dave screamed in pain; his wrist was throbbing as one of the bones protrude through the skin. Blood squirted outwards from the compound fracture.

Duy had not planned on throwing his knives, for retrieving them wasn't nearly as convenient as just holding onto them in the first place. And there was no guarantee that once you had released them, that you would ever get them back.

But, recognizing the danger Dave was facing, the young Asian sensation took aim. He dispatched first one knife, then the second. They found their targets and like scalpels, made precise incisions. They pierced the skulls and brains of the zombies that were about to reach Dave. The bodies dropped to the ground, much to Dave's relief.

Now down to one weapon, Duy stood beside Mack. They

fought their way forward through the crowd of maggot herders who were collectively demonstrating their strong urge to BITE. Mack was carefully holding on tightly to Roscoe, while using his legs and feet to kick closing in creatures back long enough to buy the officer time to place a single shot through another one's head. He then would focus on another one and do the same.

Duy stabbed and stuck the monsters with a vengeance. This combination of Mack and Duy were able to clear a path much like the parting of the Red Sea.

Dave used his good hand to wrap his damaged right wrist under his shirt. He held it in place as he walked behind his comrades, and they all made it to the safety of Dave's truck.

"Duy, you gotta drive...I can't. Here are the keys..."

Mack jumped into the back seat of the crew-cab; his furry parcel unscathed.

Duy drove the Chevy Silverado like a demon possessed. He traveled at a high rate of speed and went over and through whatever got in the truck's path. He traversed over sidewalks to go around one pack of parasite incubators and then cut through a back alley, driving over abandoned furniture and trash cans alike.

"Woohoo!" Duy yelled as they lost sight of the crowd of creatures in the rearview mirror.

The trio headed back to north Dallas in search of medical attention for Dave, and Mack had Duy drop him off at his friend Michelle Valencia's two-story townhouse on the way.

Mack carried Roscoe in a bear hug, walking up to the front door and laying on the doorbell. A dreary and pajama-clad Michelle answered the door to see Mack holding what appeared to be a deceased Roscoe.

"Oh my God...is he... dead......????

"Not yet," Mack murmured. "You've got to help him."

Chapter 18 - Sex, Flies, and Videotapes

Michelle's residence, North Dallas

Jake and Mack, through their professional dealings with her over the years, had come to know and befriend Michelle Valencia. She was the lone female medical examiner for the Dallas County Coroner's Office.

Michelle was a titillating twenty-six-year-old Hispanic woman of short stature. She featured long, usually falling, chestnut brown hair with honey tinted streaks. She had gorgeous bulbous brown eyes with long thick lashes, and a medium build body with perky, bountiful breasts and curvaceous, feminine hips.

Originally from California, she had previously been married to a man named Miguel. Miguel had left her when their son Victor was just 6 months old. For the longest time she didn't have any idea where Miguel was, and she was grateful for that because she did not need his abusive behavior and negative personality influencing her young son.

When Miguel reappeared two years later; "changed, apologetic, and wanting to resume their relationship", Michelle moved herself and now five-year-old Victor to Dallas in the middle of the night. She did not tell anyone her plans and moved despite not knowing a soul in Texas.   Officer McElroy put the unresponsive Roscoe down on the living room couch and explained, "We found him like this in his kennel. I don't see or feel any wounds on him. I think he is starving. He's so skinny."

Michelle was not a veterinarian, but her medical training gave her enough knowledge to aid the animal and give him a fighting chance to survive. "Bring him in this back bedroom. Lay him down on the bed."

Michelle gathered makeshift supplies and medicines to prepare a makeshift IV for Roscoe. She hoped to replenish his vital nutrients and fluids in order to revive him.

"Okay, he's getting some fluids now, and he's going to need a lot of rest. But he should be fine in a few days."

Mack was instantly relieved to learn Roscoe was well on his way to recovery.

"Now that I have patched Roscoe up, how about you? I was so sorry to hear about the tragedy with Holly. Are you doing okay?"

"I guess you could say I'm starting to come to grips with the fact that she's gone. We never had a super serious relationship; we mostly were just good friends that liked to get together to have fun on a regular basis. It was cool to hang out with her because she wasn't a cop. I get so tired of talking about the job all the time and bringing work home with me. But I guess because her brother-in-law was a cop too, she wasn't always asking me to tell her my war stories.

"It's also nice to date someone who doesn't have a gun and shoots better than I do," he said with a half-smile on his face.

"Seriously, though, she was a great girl. I really miss her."

With a sympathetic tone, Michelle replied, "Well, when you're ready to have fun again, let me know."

Mack raised one eyebrow, obviously intrigued by Michelle's proposition. "What exactly did you have in mind?"

"Whatever you feel like, I guess the same sorta stuff you and Holly used to do."

"Whoa, hold up. I was always under the impression that you liked women. Not that there's anything wrong with that."

Michelle laughed heartily. "Haa, no. When I first started working here five years ago, I learned right away it was hard to be a woman in this field. Everyone that trained me and that I worked with were all men.

"It's hard to work on a stiff when your trainer is standing behind you and working with a stiff too, if you know what I mean. So, I came up with the idea to start wearing more masculine clothing and act disinterested in guys. Worked like a charm!"

"Okay, well, cool. All I know is I owe you one big time for fixin' Roscoe up."

"Yeah, you do! Why don't you stay the night so Roscoe can get rested up and recuperate and you can work on reimbursing me."

The next morning Mack was awakened by a cold sensation to his lower region but was soon overwhelmed by the luscious scent of fresh brewing coffee and fried eggs and bacon. He found his way to the kitchen and replenished his appetite with a beautiful breakfast that the ravishing lady had prepared.

"Good morning, handsome! How did you sleep?" Michelle gushed with gratification.

"I slept like a baby until you licked me on the ass a couple minutes ago," Mack said half smiling and still aroused.

"Oh, that wasn't me. It must have been my little Chihuahua,

Franky. He snuck into the bedroom when I opened the door. I think he likes you."

Mack quickly became unaroused.

After enjoying the fresh hot meal, Mack talked about his plan to set out on an expedition in search of his mentor. Mack decided that it might behoove him to acquire some information relative to the dangers and demons he might soon be facing. He recognized that Michelle was the one person he knew that could possibly assist him in his quest for this knowledge.

"You think maybe you could shed some light on this whole outbreak thing that's going on? Somehow, I think Jake is still possibly alive and wrapped up in this whole Infection Armageddon. Maybe if I had more intelligence on the matter, it might assist me in finding him."

"Well, I can tell you what I know so far" Michelle offered.

"I have been participating in this regular weekly info-sharing conference calls with other medical examiners, ER doctors and nurses, EMTs and fire personnel from across the country. They have all been seeing large increases in cases of people being attacked and/or transforming into these creatures."

"Yeah? So, what are these *things* anyways? Are they zombies?"

"Well, the dead and buried from before this plague was initiated are not awakening and rising out of their graves. However, we are seeing some more recently departed corpses who were somehow infected pre-mortem becoming reanimated."

Michelle recounted an incident she had personally encountered just days earlier.

"Just last Wednesday I was performing an autopsy on this older gentleman who had died of unknown causes. I was leaning over him from the side, working on removing the skull cap. I was about halfway through his skull with my mini circular saw when his eyes began to flutter. And then they opened. I freaked the fuck out and dropped the saw. Luckily, the blade didn't cut me on the way down.

"So, I screamed, and some of the guys came running in. One of the docs had his golf bag in his office. He grabbed a Ping wedge club to use as a weapon. Doc's got a pretty good swing; he whacked the THING's head off before IT could climb down from the table. I bet the funeral home had a hell of a time preparing that one for an open casket ceremony.

"So now we each have a nail gun by our sides when we are working, and we make sure these cadavers are always strapped down tightly to the worktable. At the first sign of them waking, we slam a five-inch steel nail through the side of their skull. It puts them down for good, and it's a lot easier to clean up then using the Ping."

Disturbed by Michelle's unnerving account, Mack posed a question for her.

"So, is there any word on what may have caused this to happen?"

"There are rumors out there that the initial outbreak was caused by the military somehow but there is no confirmation on that. But I have heard reports that authorities in Florida have found a dumping ground in the St Johns River, where up to fifty cadavers of previously missing and abducted persons ended up. All of them appeared to have been experimented on, they all seemed to be infected with an unknown virus. Officials estimated some of the corpses had been in the river for several months.

"There is no further information at this time about where these experiments took place or who may have conducted them. It is also unknown at this time if there are people out there who may have survived this testing and if so, whether they are carrying this virus as well.

"The St Johns River is a massive body of water. Thousands of vacationers and locals visit this river for recreation, swimming, fishing, waterskiing, etc. So, for the past several months these people have been flocking to this area for these reasons. However, unbeknownst to them, they were swimming in infected waters and contracting this virus. They might as well have been swimming in a pool of cyanide.

"These people returned home to their normal lives and over the days to follow, the infected ones start changing. For some the morphing was very gradual, but for others it was much more expedient.

"Scientists tracked down several people who entered the contaminated waters and conducted interviews and tests on them up until they eventually changed as well. In the interviews, they described gaining incredible strength and stamina early in the infection stages.

"But that didn't last long, because soon the plague began to take over, corroding their brains – turning them into angry, flesh starved beasts. They were devolving, dying, as they meandered through the five known stages of decomposition."

Mack was intrigued. "So, they are basically alive but dying at the same time?"

"Yes, pretty much. At first, internal bacteria start to digest the organ tissues and rigor mortis begins to set in. Insects such as blow flies arrive to deposit eggs in or near the natural orifices of the head and anus, as well as within any open wounds.

"All along their body is rotting out from under them, their brains do not receive or at least comprehend that message. It's as if they are unaware that they are dead, or at least refuse to accept it. Somehow there is enough brain activity to still make some parts of the body function, albeit at very low levels.

"Depending on the rate of decomposition and the development time of particular blowfly species, eggs may hatch, and young larvae begin to feed on tissues and liquids. Blood bubbles at the nose and anaerobic bacteria in the abdomen create gases, which accumulate and results in abdominal bloating. A color change is observed in the skin along with the appearance of marbling and the odor of putrefaction becomes noticeable.

"Ants, beetles and other insects have arrived by now and are feeding on the eggs and young larvae of the flies. Deflation of the body will then result as feeding larvae remove flesh from around the head and the anus, piercing the skin and causing internal gases to release.

"Eventually the bugs and larvae feeding frenzy ends and there is a mass insect exodus as the strong odors fade and the corpse is left dry, with very little remaining other than bones, cartilage and small bits of dried skin. I find it hard to believe a body at this level of decomposition could find itself upright without simultaneously collapsing into a pile of dust and debris.

"Oh, and all of those creepy crawlies who left the carcass are now infected. They subsequently move on to land on living people who are outdoors and not protected with pesticides. The bugs and flies land directly on people, or in their mouths. The bugs bite them, crap on them, get squished on them - everything. And the toxic disease is once again spread.

"The flies also lay their eggs in the water, creating more contaminated tributaries. It's like a never-ending cycle, there's no telling how long this will last and how many victims it will claim."

Mack paused to collect his thoughts and then recapped what he had just heard from Michelle.

"So, you're telling me there's partially living but dead people with maggots biting through their skin and feasting on their innards, with bacteria dissolving away the body organs and fluids leaking out and gases escaping. And these fuckers are still walking around?"

"Yes, and don't forget the most important part to remember; they are eating people!" Michelle emphasized.

"So how long does it take after someone gets infected before they are walking around with maggot pets in their face?" Mack half sarcastically questioned Michelle.

Michelle chuckled, not at the situation but at the way Mack worded his question.

"The amount of time depends on how the victim becomes infected. They can contract it either through contact with the compromised water or by one of these insects, or through a zombie bite. In the case of a bite from one of the infected creatures, then it all depends how badly infected the attacker was, over what length of time they had been inflicted, and the strength and age of the victim.

"And then the decomposition rates depend upon several factors as well. Factors like temperatures, external conditions, how much and what type of clothing the victim is wearing, any drug use, body fat, so on and so forth."

"So, do these *things* only come out at night?" Mack asked.

"They're not vampires." Michelle said. "They are out and about all the hours of the day, regardless of the light conditions. Obviously, they don't need sleep because they don't have to get up and go to work in the morning."

Mack grinned. "Haaa… very true. This is all so damn crazy.

"Thanks for enlightening me on this stuff. It should help immensely. Can you please keep me updated as you get more information? I would greatly appreciate it. And if anyone asks, you haven't spoken to me or know anything about Roscoe or me or what I am doing. I don't trust anyone other than you, Dave, Duy and Amanda."

"Anytime, Mack, I would be very happy to *enlighten* you again" Michelle responded with a glowing smile splashed all over her beautiful face. She was clearly just as appreciative of their symbiotic relationship as Mack was.

Mack left Roscoe resting at Michelle's house and he set out in his burnt orange Chevy Avalanche 4X4. The truck was nicely equipped with oversized mud tires, an eight-inch lift kit, and a front police vehicle type push bumper with a mounted winch.

He traveled across town to tend to some business before setting out on his excursion into this quickly devolving nation.

Mack idled his truck, made the turn onto Matilda Drive, and parked in front of the Talucci residence. Resting somewhat uncomfortably and high on his pain meds, Dave was now back home after having his fractured wrist surgically repaired.

Dave was groggy but recognized the bulky outline of Mack, who had let himself in through the unlocked front door.

"You really need to lock that thing," Mack commented as he proceeded to find a seat in the cluttered bedroom. "No telling who might let themselves in. How are you doing, man?"

The incapacitated Dave had his entire right arm in a cast. To the left of his bed was a black aluminum folding tray table upon which he had placed several empty Shiner Beer bottles.

"Hey, Mack! Umm, I'm doing all right. How's Roscoe?"

"He's gonna make it, just will take some time for him to be back at 100 percent. But he will be eventually. Thanks again for your help in getting him back."

"Don't thank me, I'm the dumbass who got hurt out there. I caused more trouble than good."

"What matters is you came. You didn't wuss out like plenty of others would have. You got guts, man. I respect the hell out of you for that."

Dave was happy to receive such high praise. "You and Duy call me if you need anything while you are out there looking for Jake. If you need money, supplies, information, anything. Just let me know."

Dave fell into a deep analgesic sleep and Mack left just as he had entered. He decided to stroll across the street to check in on Amanda before leaving town for who knows how long.

From the exterior, Amanda and Jake's modest house

appeared unkempt and possibly vacant. The lawn was uncut with crabgrass growing uncontrollably high. Within the picture windows, dark curtains were all pulled together and closed tightly. Unopened mail, advertising fliers and newspapers were strewn across the front step and a porch light continued to burn despite the light of day surrounding it.

Mack knocked on the front door twice and heard nothing from within. A third, louder pounding brought the unmistakable scuffing of house shoes upon a linoleum floor and Amanda appeared at the door, looking like all hell warmed over. "Mack. Hi."

"You okay?"

Amanda avoided the question and responded, "come in, that sunlight is blinding me."

Her skin pale from the lack of sunlight, her clothing was wrinkled as if slept in for days. Amanda asked Mack how his investigation into Jake's incident was going. Mack revealed some of the details he had uncovered but was hesitant to disclose his doubts surrounding the report of Jake's death. Mack felt it would be inappropriate at this early juncture to get Amanda's hopes up, especially if in the end he would be proven completely wrong.

"We got Roscoe back. Me, Dave, and Duy. Dave broke his wrist in the process, but he's back home now and healing. Roscoe was very malnourished and on his deathbed when we found him, but our friend Michelle from the coroner's office has got him back on track."

"Oh, that's so cool! Jake would have been so happy and grateful to you for saving Roscoe! He loved that dog so much."

"So how are you doing, Amanda?"

"Well Mack, I feel like shit, to be quite honest. I've been told I should seek some grief counseling to talk about my feelings - to get them all out so they don't remain bottled up inside me and cause stress and illness.

"So, I have been speaking at great lengths with Jack Daniels and Sam Adams, just to name a couple of my grief counselors. I also often find myself talking to Jake as if he was still here with me.

"I cry for him every single day. And as much as it pains me to cry so much, at the same time it somehow, oddly enough, soothes me as well. I know that wherever he is, he knows that I am mourning his loss and he knows that I will always have him in my mind."

Amanda's eyes welled up, and tears began to flow down her somber pale face.

"Mack, sometimes I really think I'm losing my mind. This is gonna sound really messed up and psychotic. There's a TV show where people have bizarre habits and addictions. There was one episode where a woman in her 30s lost her husband in a car crash or something like that.

"They kept showing her licking her finger after dipping it into the urn full of her husband's cremated remains. She was eating so much of these ashes that the whole urn was almost empty. She was making herself sick due to all of the chemicals mixed with the remains.

"Essentially she was poisoning herself but could not stop. I watched that show before Jake was gone and thought it was a hoax, so scripted and fake. But now that Jake is gone, I truly believe that story could have easily been true.

"I constantly long to touch him again - to smell him, taste him. I wish I could somehow contact him just one more time. I would gladly poison myself to be privileged enough to savor his remains, taste his ashes. Just to be a part of him again and him a part of me. Oh, God, I miss him so much!"

Mack was now himself shedding tears and speechless. He offered a comforting hug to the grieving woman.

"I'm sorry for being such a downer…" Amanda apologized.

"No, you're not being a downer. That is how you should be feeling," assured Mack. "So how is baby Carson doing?"

"Not great. He has been acting very rambunctious, hyper. I wonder if he might be bipolar. And now I need to find him a new babysitter too.

"His regular babysitter was this teenage girl named Tracey, who was about Austin's age. She watched Carson occasionally in the evenings when I would go out after work with friends. She was nice, prompt, and caring - up until one evening.

"I came home one night to find Tracey waiting in the driveway. She was upset that Carson had scratched her arm and gave her a small bite on her neck, which broke the skin and caused slight bleeding.

"I was so mad that she had left Carson unattended in the

house while she waited for me in the driveway. I stopped calling Tracey to sit for several months until finally there was an evening when I had no choice but to call her because no other sitters or options were available. Tracey did not seem her regular cheerful, attentive self that night. She seemed to have a dark cloud hanging over her. She was very rude, short, and unsociable.

"I became concerned and did not want to leave Carson with her that night, but I had no choice. I set out some hidden video recorders in Carson's bedroom and in the living room/ kitchen area and set them to record.

"I returned home at the end of the evening to find Carson in his crib crying and cranky and Tracey sitting in the dark on the back porch. I went to ask how the night went and noticed she had feces on the front of her shirt.

"I said, 'Oh, honey - it looks like you got something on you when you changed Carson. Do you want some stain remover?'

"Tracey just remarked 'no,' said she was fine and seemed to be in a hurry to leave.

"After she was gone, I curiously replayed the digital video recording of the night's activity. I was shocked at what I saw. Tracey changed baby Carson's diaper in the baby's room, then left him alone in his crib.

"She then carried the open soiled diaper into the living room where she promptly sat down, put the diaper up to her face and began to sniff at the contents like a dog inhaling a steak that was frying well within his reach.

"Tracey then began to lick at the stools and soon afterwards she was eating the feces as if it were a chocolate pudding treat!"

Amanda never told Tracey's parents about this; out of fear they would think she was crazy. Amanda never called Tracey again, but several weeks later she heard through neighborhood gossip that Tracey went missing from her home. It was believed that she did not run away, that there was foul play involved because she did not take any of her belongings with her like money, clothes, cellphone...nothing.

Mack demonstrated a sense of shock, unable to explain the sitter's outlandish behavior.

Amanda continued, "Also, Austin's getting into trouble. He is consumed with hatred for Jake, thinks Jake intentionally murdered his parents. I was thinking about putting him in military school. Sometimes he just up and runs away for days at a time, offering no explanation as to where he goes and why."

"I had no idea you were having so much trouble with him. If you want, when I get back, I can try talking to him if you think that will help."

"Sure, that would be nice, Mack. It can't hurt."

"Okay. Well, take care of yourself and holler if you need anything." Mack said goodbye and prepared to leave Ms. McKnight when she wished him a safe trip and kissed him on the cheek.

Mack drove to his police headquarters and gave written notice of his request for an undetermined length of leave of absence from work. He then returned to Michelle's house to check on Roscoe's condition.

Once there, he was pleased to find the Malinois in much better condition. He was still thin but appeared to be much more alert. So much so that he greeted Mack with a wet lick across the face and heavy tail wagging.

"Roscoe, boy, you ready to get back to work? Let's go for a ride!"

Mack and Roscoe jogged to the front door and prepared to exit Michelle's place when Mack uttered to Michelle, "I owe you one. Thanks again."

Michelle gave Mack an even wetter lick across the face, and Mack and Roscoe exited the residence. The duo of officers jumped into the waiting orange Avalanche.

Mack picked up the cellphone and pushed the call button for Duy Tran.

"Dew-man pack your bags. It's time for our road trip."

North Dallas (Present Day)

Ms. Valencia had heard Jake speak of his beautiful girlfriend often and with great endearment, but Michelle had not met Amanda in person. After talking to Mack and learning that Jake was possibly still alive, Michelle was compelled to reach out to Amanda for the first time.

Michelle messaged Amanda on Facebook and said she was sorry to hear about the tragedy with Jake and his reported death.

Michelle expressed her sympathy and added that everyone she works with at the medical examiner's office knew Jake and admired him. They all also felt he had been wrongly accused of the murders of his brother and sister in law, and it was obvious there was some sort of corruption and cover up underway.

Still grieving and in need of an outlet, Amanda took the opportunity to invite Michelle to meet her somewhere for drinks. The two agreed to join up at a nearby watering hole.

"I ache for him, Michelle. I thought it was bad when Jake was locked up, away from me, for months – on death row. But that was nothing compared to the way I feel now that he is dead. Before there was still a chance that he could get his conviction overturned and I could still at least visit him until then.

"But now he is gone forever. And I know this sounds selfish on my part, because he is the one who suffered, but I feel like I got screwed over too. He's all I can think of, from the time I wake up each day and realize it wasn't just a bad dream - to the time I cried myself to sleep at night. And when I wake up it starts all over again.

"Some days I spend hours in our closet just going through his stuff, trying to recall a special moment we may have had or something we may have done together when he was wearing each item. I hug his shirts, breathe in his clothes, trying to reach his aura. I just cannot get past the fact that he won't ever be back. EVER. Thanks a lot, God."

Michelle made a valiant effort to console Amanda, saying, "You know Jake would want you to move on, to …."

Amanda held up her right hand as if not wanting to hear another word. "Yeah, yeah, he would want you to be happy, I know…. blah blah blah. You know how many times I have heard that? Screw that.

"I have no desire to meet someone else. Maybe I don't want to be happy. Perhaps I just happen to be content in the state I'm in now – alone, missing Jake, wallowing in my misery.

"You know, sometimes I even feel like hurting myself. Not badly, but just a little. Even just the short time it takes me to fight through the pain, wash off the blood and triage my wound is just enough of a distraction to take my mind off Jake for a few minutes or so."

Michelle sensed that she had misspoken when she suggested

Amanda should someday move on without Jake. So, Michelle was quick to take the first opportunity she had to change the topic.

"So where are you working now?"

Amanda talked about having just recently resumed her career after a long leave of absence. She went on to describe the wealth management brokerage where she was currently employed.

"It helps take my mind off Jake for a few days a week. I guess that's a good thing."

Amanda then spoke about one of the agency's customers, an oil baron named Chad Tillinghast. He was hitting on her regularly, proposing to her in the office although he didn't even know her. He promised her wealth and was offering her expensive gifts to go out with him.

"Wow! Sounds like a hell of an offer. What's this guy look like?" Michelle examined.

"He's beautiful," Amanda insisted.

"Six feet tall, dark features. You can tell he runs and works out.

"But he's a cocky asshole, and I can't stand the sight of him. All the money in the world couldn't sway me into spending a single minute with him - whether I was looking for someone or not. I would take my new boyfriend Bob over him anytime."

Michelle was confused but intrigued. "Wait a minute. Who's Bob?"

"You know, B.O.B …. my battery-operated boyfriend…."

Michelle laughed out loud. "Hey, I've been seeing Bob too. That son of a bitch is cheating on us both!"

Chapter 19 - Loathing Love shack

Route 77, West Virginia

He had been driving off and on for a couple days now, still sticking with smaller byways and routes that were less likely to be traveled by the police. Although this was greatly prolonging Jake's trip, he preferred a slower, methodical trek to one that was rushed and unscrupulous. Jake could not risk being impatient and potentially ending his mission with him being captured.

Hathaway found himself to be somewhere in the West Virginia area not too far off the beaten path from Route 77. The stolen Oldsmobile was sputtering and fussing and blowing out blue and grey smoke along with its normal exhaust. The car was going to draw too much attention in this condition, and who knows how much longer it would even drive before it just couldn't go on any longer.

These factors considered; Jake decided it best to abandon the Olds. He drove the clunker into the middle of a corn field full of brown six-foot-high corn stalks that should have been harvested months ago.

Jake set out on foot and soon ascertained this Appalachian Mountain Area was not the easiest terrain to travel on foot. He was beginning to second guess his decision to hoof it. He trekked through the hilly, rocky region for a couple hours and was growing tired, thirsty, and hungry.

So, when the escapee happened across an old shed built beside a 20-foot-high cliff, he thought it might be the ideal spot to rest for a bit. Gathering from the homemade looking pots and pipes spread along the ground outside the shack, Jake assumed this was an old abandoned moonshine distillery.

The shed appeared to have been assembled utilizing recycled boards and materials. Jake quietly glided over to the small structure's door and listened for but heard no sounds coming from the inside.

He opened the squeaky, unsecured door, and immediately used his senses to discover that the lighting inside was dim. There was also an incredible stench of some type emanating from within. Jake entered and closed the door behind him but soon realized he had no flashlight, lighter, matches, or anything else he could use to illuminate the place.

He began to feel around in front of him with his hands. He was not searching for anything but was more interested in swiping away cobwebs. He also was attempting to prevent himself from walking into a tool or something hanging from the ceiling that might smack him in the face.

"GRRRRRRRRRRR!!!"

Jake heard this growl directly in front of him and he yelled in his mind, "OH SHITTTTTTT!!!" without making an audible sound. Stealth was an important attribute of the combat soldier and for police officers as well. Jake remained silent while backtracking swiftly to the entrance.

He reached behind him to open the door while still facing forward. He had not turned his back on whatever the possible threat in front of him in the blackness of the shack was. Jake gently pushed the creaky door open, slowly allowing the Appalachian sunlight to flow within.

The usually composed combat vet froze in fear and shock over what he saw next.

Now visible in the back of the shack was a nude woman chained to a work bench - bent over forwards. The female was tied with hay bale string around her wrists, ankles, and neck. "What the hell is going on here?" Jake inquired aloud, hoping to get answers from the restrained lady, who responded only with more "GRRRRRR" sounds.

Jake's eyes were still adjusting to the new light coming into the shed. He now noticed this tied figure was not a normal woman. She looked much like Holly had on that terrible day. Greasy, thin hair covered part of her head, while other spots were bare, as if clumps had just fallen out.

The lidless and brow less eyes were cold and inhuman with tiny black pupils. The skin appeared rotting, moist, varying in color, and in places was falling off. IT could not communicate and did not appear to be trying.

IT acted as if it were sniffing Jake and making biting and chewing motions with the mouth. The THING was acting almost as if it was enjoying the scent of Jake so much that it wanted to have a taste.

Not getting any answers from the subject, Jake pondered the situation. Had this been a family member or dear friend that someone could not find the means or finances to support any longer? Could they not seek medical attention for her in this horrible condition she was in? Or was this some female who had been kidnapped and left in the shed for weeks before some disease or thing got hold of her and turned her into this creature?

Jake had been so preoccupied with his living find that he had not even noticed that surrounding him, hanging on the walls, were an assortment of tools and devices. Some of these objects would serve quite adequately as improvisational weapons.

Jake removed a sickle, garden hoe, and large pair of pruning shears from the walls. Then he found a large metal file with which he began to manually sharpen the tools' edges and blades. The tied creature continued to pull at her ropes, trying to maneuver her biting mouth close enough to the hay bale twine. IT was attempting to chew her way to freedom and then most likely feast on Jake as well.

Between the metallic filing sounds filling the small shack, a faint sputtering sound of a vehicle engine and its squealing fan belt caught Jake's attention. Jake bolted over to the door and shut it quickly so he would not be easily seen inside. He peeked out through a knothole in one of the wall boards and saw an old, faded red, beat-up Chevy truck with side steps and no tailgate.

A white male about 55 years old, 5-foot-7 and 185 pounds with a beard and moustache exited the vehicle. Outfitted with a straw hat and overalls with no shirt underneath, this guy apparently hadn't set foot in a Banana Republic store for quite some time.

The barefoot hillbilly was smiling, holding a double-barrel 12-gauge shotgun under his left arm and using his right hand to unzip his overall fly. As he approached the shed and opened the door, he exclaimed: "Oh, Lucy, I'm home!"

Jake was hiding behind a large old wooden barrel. The lady THING began to growl and moan even louder than before. Luckily the bearded stranger had not even thought to make sure there were no uninvited guests in the shed.

Realizing this may be the best time for him to act, Jake jumped out from behind the barrel and punched the dude square in the face. The hillbilly dropped his shotgun to the dirt floor and Jake instinctively grabbed it before the overalls man could react.

The hillbilly slowly picked himself up off the floor and saw Jake's massive form. Holding his swollen face with his left hand, he said "damn, boy, you hit good! You didn't have to punch me though. Shit! My name's Ricky, by the way."

Ricky looked closer at Jake and paused before commenting,

"you that boy that's runnin' from the law, aren't you? They came by the house this morning showin' your picture around and such. Good for you. Fuck the law! Can't even run a little shine business around here without them motherfuckers sneakin' around with binoculars and shit. I forget what they claimed you done?"

Jake began to speak but then stopped himself, knowing that his Northeast accent might not be the best choice in this scenario. He opted to respond with a slight twang.

"Runnin' shine. Just like you, I'm just a businessman trying to get by. I saw yer shack here, thought maybe it had been abandoned and maybe there was some food or water inside. And so, I came in, and that's when I saw your friend here."

Ricky's smile returned to his face.

"Yeah, that's my girlfriend. She's a purty one, ain't she? Or at least I bet she used to be. I caught her a couple weeks ago chasing my chickens around in their pen. The bitch looked better then. She had more skin and hair and such, was wearing some Daisy Dukes and a white tank top that was covered with blood and somethin' that looked like meat.

"Guess she killed one of my poor hens and ate it raw. Knew I had to do the right thing and bring her here for her own safety. And my chickens' safety, too."

Jake was still thinking this was too crazy to be real but managed to respond. "Good thing you did! Is her name Lucy?"

"Haa. I don't know what her real name was. I just say, 'Lucy I'm home' every time I check on her, like Ricky Ricardo used to say to Lucy when he came home on the 'Lucy' show. Get it? My name's Ricky too. It's funny, right?"

"Oh. Yeah, I get it! Good one...."

Jake decided he needed to get going as soon as possible. The longer he stuck around, the greater the chance of the cops who were in the area earlier coming back around. Either that or some of Ricky's inbred family or friends could show up to "check on Lucy" as well.

Jake was still holding the shotgun in his right hand. He gathered up the sickle, garden hoe, and pruners that he had been sharpening and announced, "I best be leavin' now. Johnny Law's probably getting closer to sniffin me out."

Ricky agreed. "That's cool. Good luck to ya, man. Hey,

before you go – why don't you get you some... (motioning his head toward the she-creature in the Daisy Dukes). Besides, you may be back behind bars before long. You may not get any for quite a while."

Jake wasn't sure exactly what Ricky had meant by "git some" until the hillbilly stuck his hand up into the crotch area of the hungry zombie-lady. Jake nearly threw up in his mouth and thought to himself; *surely this inbred dumbass knows that it can't be healthy to have sexual relations with a creature that's more dead than alive?*

He had once again seen something that left him nearly speechless. Yet Jake regained his senses and said "that's mighty kind of you, Ricky. But I think she likes you better. Matter of fact, I'm gonna leave now so you two can have some alone time."

Jake pushed Ricky closer to his "Lucy," then swiftly swung the newly sharpened sickle about like a samurai sword, shredding the thin strands of baling twine that had bound the creature. Her arms, legs, and neck now freed, she looked as if she was smiling. Perhaps it was just that her nearly toothless mouth opened wider in anticipation of taking a chomp out of Ricky's thigh.

Ricky yelled, "NOOOO!!!! YOU MOTHA FUCKIN' YANKEE BOY!! I'LL KILL YOU!!!"

Jake tucked the tools and shotgun into his armpits to make room in his right hand for one more item before leaving. Inside the shack, beside the door on a small eye-level shelf was a mason jar about three-quarters full of a golden liquid. Jake grabbed the jar and ran out of the shed. Outside, he noticed a large log that was used as a chopping block. Dead chicken heads were lying beside it on the ground.

Jake set all his treasures to the ground and propped the log up against the shed door. Ricky's screams echoed through the valley, mixed with the sound of his girlfriend's growling, chewing, and slurping - all in harmony.

Jake retrieved his goodies and jumped into the driver's seat of the '74 Chevy pickup. He drove away northbound on the backwoods dirt road.

Although Jake was discouraged by the fact that his fake Southern accent hadn't fooled good old Ricky, this emotion quickly abandoned him in favor of his sudden urge to stop somewhere to get a bucket of fried chicken.

Chapter 20 - Dead Kennedys and Draggin' Slayers

Route 15, North Central Pennsylvania

Jake steered the throttling faded red 'shine wagon northbound along the tree lined Route 15 in North Central Pennsylvania. The gloom of this winter eventide was fast approaching, and Jake was content with his newly acquired booty and mode of transportation. It had been a good day in that sense.

But of even more significance had been Jake's chance meeting with Lucy. Lucy, or whatever its name used to be before she was changed, was the first creature he had encountered since the Birthday Incident. This Lucy creature exhibited the same mannerisms, shape, and demeanor as the Rich creature and Holly creature.

This discovery could prove to be monumental for Jake. There had been news reports of horrific nature involving similar personages over the past few months. But now Jake had visual proof that something very discomposing was taking place, whether it be due to a plague, radioactivity, or whatever it was.

If only good old boy Ricky back in West Virginia could have been a little more insightful in determining what brought Lucy to that metamorphosis. Still, now Jake had something he could work with. He had insight that would provide him with some hope and promise. He needed to stop somewhere safe to rest and camp out for the night, to brainstorm and project his next steps. Jake was on a mission to save his life and to get back to his family.

Surrounding traffic became non-existent, and Jake slowed down to about 20 miles per hour, attempting to find the perfect location to pull into the woods and hide his stolen ride. In the approaching distance he noticed two objects off to the left side of the two-lane route. The forms appeared to be two people dancing or struggling. He was unable to make out exactly what was happening until he was right up on it.

Suddenly the sight he had been straining to capture was as plain as day but as bizarre as a five-legged lamb. One of those creatures like Lucy, that was once human and had now morphed into something hideous, was grappling with a full grown, brown and white spotted doe.

The creature was biting the left side of the deer's large fur-covered venous neck. The deer was shrieking and bellowing while also kicking the shit out of the creature with its hind legs. It was using every fiber of strength it had to free itself from the carnivore's grasp, but to no avail.

Jake stopped the vehicle to stare dumbfounded. The doe's plight to survive the brutality ended in vain as the hungry meat-eater stood erect, holding its dinner in both arms and feasting away at the once glorious animal that was now nothing more than raw venison.

Jake stomped on the accelerator of the moonshine mobile and drove as fast as he could for another thirty minutes until he figured he was at a safe proximity. He then slowly pulled off the main road onto an overgrown, brush-covered dirt road. Shortly, Jake veered the truck into a large thicket of pines and saplings.

Jake drove deep enough into the woods to prevent the vehicle from being spotted from the roadway. He removed his sickle, shotgun, and Mason jar from the passenger floorboard, as well as a handful of maps from the glove box. Then he covered the old Chevy with broken tree branches to conceal it further, and he set out on foot.

He was tired, thirsty, hungry and still bewildered over what transpired just south down the freeway. Jake hiked through the dense thicket and came across a "No Hunting" sign nailed to a tree. In approximately every thousand feet, there was another identical sign.

Eventually Jake stumbled upon a large oak tree with wooden blocks nailed up the side of its trunk. These were man made steps used to climb up onto a waiting plywood platform. The platform was enclosed on all four sides but was lacking a roof. Jake didn't see or hear anything inside the structure, so he figured this was as good a place as any to gather his bearings and make a game plan. The weary traveler set his goods down on the floor in a corner, and he opened his maps.

The ability to map efficiently was an essential skill of a soldier and for police officers. So, Jake was quite capable of tracking his current location on the maps. He estimated his current location to be somewhere within the Loyalsock State Forest. This was a scenic forest that featured the "Endless Mountains" on its northern tier, as well as cascading waterfalls and flaming fall foliage over its 114,000 acres.

From out of nowhere Jake began to ponder. *Why would there be a tree stand in a state forest? Hunting is not permitted in such a publicly accessible area.*

His pondering quickly took a back seat in his list of priorities as Jake looked down at his large rubberized G Shock watch. The time was no huge revelation. It was about 2100 hours, or 9 p.m. But when he noticed that it was February 7th, he realized the significance of the date that would be arriving in just three hours.

It would be February eighth. The one-year anniversary of THE INCIDENT. The day that changed Jake's life and so many of his loved ones' lives forever. It was so much of a dramatic game altering event that Jake's mental calendar would never be the same. His new timeline began with THE BIRTHDAY INCIDENT as Day 1, and everything that happened before that was ancient history.

Jake reached for the Mason jar he had snatched while leaving Ricky's love shack back in West Virginia.

Please let this not be piss, he thought as he twisted off the lid and chugged down a mouthful of golden liquid. This was not urine, thank god.

It was a strong peach moonshine. It burned as it went down his throat and singed his esophagus. Not having eaten for a couple days, the lining of his stomach was wide open to accept alcohol, and it quickly took effect.

Jake continued to consume the backwoods swill, soon finding himself to be in a drunken stupor.

Flashbacks from that horrific date a year before ran through his mind. Random images from his entire life were jumping in and out of his head with no synchronicity or pattern. Thoughts of suicide struck his conscience as well. Jake could still not completely rid himself of his feelings of guilt regarding the incident.

There must have been something I could have done

differently. I didn't have to kill Rich and Holly like I did.

Jake plunged into a deep sea of unconsciousness and the empty mason jar toppled from his hand. It bounced off the plywood floor and flew out the entrance opening in the wall. The jar struck a couple of the wooden steps on the way down and smashed to the ground.

Dallas Police Sergeant Jake Hathaway suddenly found himself back in downtown Dallas. He was walking the beat again in his navy blue, short-sleeve uniform shirt and shorts.

A midnight blue 1961 model Lincoln stretch limousine slowly rolled past Jake and came to a complete stop about 20 yards ahead of him. This was not your typical limousine, for it had no roof and featured rear bumper steps.

Jake's unobstructed view into the open-air limo revealed that the vehicle was occupied by five people. At the very front was the driver. He was an ordinary looking guy wearing a grey suit and chauffeur hat.

Seated behind him was a white woman who had a man seated to her right. In the rear seat was yet another couple. Both women were seated on the driver side of the vehicle, and their accompanying men were on the passenger side.

None of the people looked back at Jake. They were all still seated and facing straight ahead. Jake noticed and recognized the woman in the back row. She was wearing a strawberry pink double-breasted Chanel wool boucle suit with a navy trim collar. She also had a matching pink pillbox hat.

The man seated to her left had neatly combed, noticeably red hair. He wore a black suit coat with a white shirt adorned with black and red pinstripes. His matching black tie was smothered with small navy crest patterns.

A man's voice from within the car called out: "Officer, how do I get to Dealey Plaza?"

Jake noticed not a single head had turned. All of the passengers still stared straight ahead. Happy to assist the tourists, Jake walked toward the car while pointing to the west, and replied, "you're on Elm Street now. Just keep going straight, and it's right below the hill."

Jake still got no looks from anyone in the vehicle. All he saw of them was the backs of their heads. It was odd that although he could not see their faces, Sgt. Hathaway felt as if he recognized these people. Yet he could not establish in his mind just who they were and why they were familiar to him.

A second voice emerged from the vehicle. This one came from the redheaded sharply dressed gentleman in the back seat. "Can you show me exactly where Kennedy got shot?"

Jake was now just a foot behind the vehicle. He took another two steps toward the passenger side of the vehicle until he was parallel with the red headed man.

Jake smiled, as he had been solicited this very question about a million times before. He was prepared to give his routine canned response. He took his right index finger and began to point it at the back of his head.

But from Sgt. Hathaway's new vantage point, he now realized exactly who he was in the presence of. This was THE Presidential Limo; code named the X-100. And he was face to face with President John F. Kennedy.

Texas Governor John Connally and his wife, Nellie, sat on the bench seat behind the driver. In the seat at the rear of the vehicle was none other than Jackie O sitting beside her husband, the president, JFK.

President Kennedy now had his head turned and was looking Jake right in the eyes.

Sgt. Hathaway unfolded all the fingers on his right hand to relinquish his pointing gesture. It probably was not proper to point out to the President of the United States the spot where a large rifle round had (or would) tear through the rear of his head, only to exit out the front, leaving a large gap in its wake.

"Oh, Mr. President. I'm sorry. Please excuse me. Dealey Plaza is about a block up, straight ahead."

President Kennedy replied, "Would you escort us there, son? I have a bad feeling about this."

Jake jumped on the rear bumper steps as the limo proceeded to slowly motor for another block. Suddenly, the limousines' engine blew. Hot steam and dark smoke belled out from beneath the hood. The expired motor had given out and the long car came to a sudden halt, resting directly over a large white spray-painted "X" on the center lane of Elm Street.

Jake realized the extreme danger they all faced stopped in that spot, particularly the President and Governor Connally.

"We can't stop here - we have to keep moving!" Jake yelled.

The chauffeur calmly uttered, "Calm down, young man, the car just stalled out. I can get it running again." The driver exited his seat, walked around to the front of the vehicle, and lifted the hood.

Four Dallas PD motorcycle cops arrived on the scene, riding large, loud Kawasaki police bikes. Two of them appeared on each side of the limo as Jake jumped down off the rear running board.

He appealed to the other officers, "we need to put the car in neutral and push it down past that overpass ahead. WE CANNOT STAY HERE!!!!!!!"

Jake looked to his right, seeing the green grassy knoll. A six-foot wooden picket fence separated the hill from the Texas School Book Depository parking lot.

The sound of dragging and clawing emerged from behind the fence. Soon what appeared to be mindless *dead* creatures began to stack themselves on top of the others fallen below them.

Zombies started to appear at the top of the wooden pickets and falling over the top, knocking pickets down with the weight of their falling masses.

Soon similar beings were pushing through the busted boards. A deluge of the *dead* began to flow down the green grassy slope. A couple of the creatures lost their footing on the steep grade of the hill and rolled down, smashing upon the sidewalk. Then slowly they gravitated back onto their feet and staggered into the road, toward the stretch convertible.

The horrified motorcycle cops began to fire their duty revolvers at the zombies. The cops were able to stop several creatures in their tracks. However, the revolvers soon emptied. When the officers began to reach for their speed loaders with extra rounds of ammo, the wave of *dead* washed upon them.

Several zombies now had the motor jocks in their grasp. The misfits began to gnarl on the cops, biting chunks of flesh from their necks and faces and heads.

Two zombies, one carrying an umbrella, then wobbled past the preoccupied motor cops. IT began to climb into the car, attacking Governor Connally and his wife.

Jake climbed back onto the rear step bumper of the car and

tried to enter the passenger compartment. But he could not do so. It was as if Jake was frozen. Not out of fear, he was simply unable to move. All he could do was watch as the creatures tore the Connally pair apart.

Another pair of flesh munchers finished their motor jockey meals and began to climb into the rear portion of the limo. The redheaded rear male passenger now turned his head around completely 360 degrees and again looked toward Jake. However, to Jake's surprise, this was not President Kennedy after all. It was sixteen-year-old Jimmy Griggs, from Exeter, Rhode Island.

Jimmy had a large section of flesh missing from the right side of his neck. He begged of Sgt Hathaway, "Jakey, please don't let me drown again!"

Jake tried with all his might to move his arms and legs, yet they still did not work.

He could not even flinch to save his best friend from being devoured by the cannibalistic mutants.

Loud chewing and slurping sounds enveloped around Jimmy's screams of "NOOOO!!! Jake, help me!!"

Soon those screams faded away and were replaced by the sound of footsteps, rustling leaves, and moans.

It was zero dead thirty, and the intoxicated convict Hathaway woke up with wood and pitch black all around him. He was thankful to realize he had only been imagining the whole Dealey Plaza scene, and he wondered what had awakened him from his deep moonshine slumber.

But soon the normal woodland sounds of crickets, mosquitoes, croaking toads and hoot owls were drowned out by guttural moans and growls, as well as rustling and scraping from below. Jake's heart was pounding, and his pulse was racing. Whatever was making these sounds was just below him on the tree trunk, about ten feet below the platform he was lying on.

Still lying on his stomach on the plywood platform and still quite drunk, Jake was not entirely sure that he wasn't imagining these sounds. Not willing to chance the fact that there might be a real threat approaching, he moved stealthily. Jake positioning himself in a manner so that he could peep through a crack between two plywood sheets that made up the floor he was on.

Peering through the crack, it appeared as if there were multiple dark figures below surrounding the base of the tree. One lone THING was also trying to maneuver its way up the wooden block steps, toward the tree stand.

Jake was familiar with this part of the country, being a Northeast native and all. He had heard the stories of black bears being in these parts and assumed that was what was visiting him in the early morning hours. Jake was thankful he had arrived prepared, bringing his weapons with him and not just leaving them behind in the vehicle. Jake had his Remington 12-gauge shotgun with five shells and his appropriately sharpened sickle.

Jake sat with his long shotgun barrels aimed toward the opening in the structure's wall. His finger remained on the trigger and he was ready for the first sign of an early morning unwanted wakeup call. He planned on staying put and as still as possible. But upon the first sign of that bear sticking his face into the deer stand opening, Jake was going to blow it to Kingdom Come with a shotgun blast straight in the face.

Surely after destroying the one bear, and with the loudness of a shotgun blast, the rest of the pack would flee quickly and head for the hills. Then Jake would be able to sleep off the rest of this peach haze and start out fresh around sunrise to continue his trek north.

The moans and groans became louder and louder as the top bear neared its destination. Jake lowered the weapon's barrel and steadied his aim as a dark head came into sight and the dark form curiously investigated the tree stand.

Jake's anticipation of a curious bruin climber turned to horror as the smell of death and decay poured from the open mouth of the creature that was now in his front door.

IT WAS ONE OF THOSE DEAD PEOPLE!!

ITs head was just four feet from Jake's face. IT was undoubtedly smelling his human delicacy, with nostrils flaring and closing, flaring and closing. IT seemed hungry, mouth wide open, yellow rotted teeth exposed and chomping at the early morning air.

Although horrified by this sight, Jake found himself not taking immediate action. Rather, he began staring in wonder at the nightmare before him. IT was by no means a beautiful creature. But this was like looking into the eyes of something that could not be explained. This was a manifestation of death itself, much more terrifying than merely spotting a Bigfoot, Chupacabra, or the Loch Ness Monster.

Here before him was the evidence he needed to prove to the world that somehow people were turning into monsters. Jake was not the type to normally take "selfies" with his phone camera, but if he had a camera on him now, he would probably entertain the thought. The next best thing would be to somehow preserve the body after slaying it, just long enough for the whole world to see.

The open mouth of the creature was now just one foot away from Jake. Jake thrust the shotgun barrel into the throat and pulled the trigger.

BLAMMMMM!!! The shotgun pellets exploded from the weapon, blasting the entire head off the creature with a spray of blood and vessels and decaying flesh pouring down onto the ground below.

The beast's body descended backwards, out of the tree stand and down below into a crowd of similar forms. That was when Jake finally realized the true extent and seriousness of the situation. He could sense the actual density of the shit he was now wading in.

There were several more of these *things* on the ground, probably between ten and fifteen of them. The lighting was still very dim, making it difficult to tell for sure. But THEY had not been scared away by the blast or in seeing their comrade miscreation blown to bits. If anything, it appeared as if the monstrosities were now even more driven.

They pushed and shoved at each other, trying to get into the pole position. Or to be more precise, the HOLE position. Each creature wanted to be the one to get up the tree first, to climb through the hole, and feast on the cornered human treat.

Jake was feeling like the only lobster in a seafood restaurant's tank. He was just waiting to be pointed at by a hungry customer, then plucked from the tank with some cold steel tongs. Jake knew his chances of surviving this were slim to none. But not being one to ever quit or count himself out when the odds were in someone else's favor, Jake sobered quickly and began to strategize.

Out of nowhere, a different noise echoed through the forest. A set of approaching headlights and fog lights appeared from one vehicle, with a spotlight shining onto the inhuman crowd. Jake flattened in the airborne shelter so as not to be seen by whoever was present.

No weapons could be heard. But Jake noticed that one at a time, as if orchestrated and rehearsed, the creatures' heads jarred just before their bodies collapsed onto the ground. In a matter of about three minutes they were all down for the count.

The escapee lay still as he heard two vehicle doors open and shut. Voices confirmed two different humans were converging on Jake's treehouse. A flashlight's stream of white light was pointed into the shelter's opening as footsteps of one began to climb the wooden foot pegs.

Jake again prepared his Remington to blow another mid-morning caller to smithereens when the squawk of a police radio filled the dead air.

"Central to 725.... status check. Do you copy, 725?"

"Dude turn your radio down! You're gonna give us away," one officer muttered to the other. They switched into silent mode as each pointed a weapon at the opening of the stand.

Jake knew that he was now in jeopardy of being identified and returned to death row in Texas. Even with that being a possibility, he could not bring himself to murder a cop who was just doing his job. Jake had been in that position many times himself and now wondered how close he could have come to meeting his maker at any given time in his career. Jake placed his shotgun behind him and opted for Plan B.

"I'm up here, officers! Thank god you found me!"

Jake vocalized in a somewhat convincing fashion. Jake showed the lawmen his hands to assure them he was not bearing any arms. He then climbed out of his shelter and stood at the base of the tree in what was now a cesspool of creature body parts, guts, ooze, and muck.

The two officers were dressed in all black from head to toe. Everything starting with their ball caps and plastic water-resistant jackets, down to their also-plastic pants and boots, was black. Their army green Hummer with brush guards over the lights was parked, still idling behind them. The truck's headlights were still aimed at and lighting up the area where Jake now stood.

"Are you guys the Forest Rangers?" Jake asked the uniformed men.

"We're with the Pennsylvania Wildlife Control. What the fuck are you doing out here? This ain't a safe place to be camping out. We need to see your identification."

Jake began to feel about his person, acting as if he was trying to find his wallet in his pants and jacket pockets. He was very thankful that his wallet and identifying credit cards were now locked up in the Dallas County property room and not on his person.

Jake replied, "I must have lost my wallet somewhere."

The older officer shined his small rechargeable flashlight at Jake's face, paused for a moment, then remarked, "I know who you are."

Jake knew his time was just about up. He had one last chance - to try and catch the officers off guard and then run like hell.

Jake turned away from the wildlife cops. He put his hands behind his back and said, "all right, you got me."

As soon as the closest officer moved toward him, Jake planned to beat feet as quick as he could. From there the only hope he had was to get behind a tree line before being shot in the back.

"You're that cop from Texas. Jake somethin, right?" asked the elder cop.

"Umm. Yeah." Jake said. He knew the jig was up.

"You got a bad rap man," said the elder officer.

Jake didn't know if the lawman was playing mind games with him or if he was sincere.

"Yeah, I'm Jake Hathaway," he affirmed with trepidation. He slowly turned to face his captors.

The younger of the two cops introduced himself as Owen and his partner as Harry. "Your family members that you killed – they had turned into zombies beforehand, didn't they?"

"They turned into something, all right. Is that what these *things* are?"

"Most people are calling them that. We call them 'draggers' cause they are so slow and drag their feet all around. That's how we track them, by the scrape marks their feet leave behind in the pine needles."

Owen explained that these forests and wooded areas were crawling with them. That every night the two "Wildlife Control Officers" went out in the Hummer to locate more 'draggers.' Then they would shoot them in the head with their AR rifles with built-in noise suppressors.

Or sometimes if they were bored, they would make the job a little more sporting. They would take to their tree stands with crossbows in hand to do some old-school "dragger hunting."

"But the most important thing to know about taking these *things* down," added Harry, "is that you have to cause them major trauma to their brains. You hit them anywhere else and you just slow them down. Not because they are in pain, but because when you shoot their legs off then they must crawl. But they still keep coming."

"How many have you guys killed so far?" Jake questioned, intrigued.

"Well, let's see. We have been doing this for about eight months now, probably averaging about thirty per day. Before us, the FBI, Secret Service, ICE – all of them were doing this when the draggers first started showing up. But then there were way too many of the draggers and not nearly enough Feds. So, they told us to start weeding them out ourselves, to burn them and to keep the mission top secret."

Owen was excited to finally be talking about the mission they kept silent about for so long. "We wear this rubber gear so we can hose off the dragger blood and guts at the end of the night."

Owen took off his black ballcap and showed Jake the patch sewn onto the center of the hat. "Check it out. Me and Harry made these hats up for us and all the other fellas here. See the zombie guy blacked out? We call ourselves the 'BODS - Black Ops Dragger Squad."

"Chief told us we couldn't make the hats, but we went and did it anyway. If the Mass State Troopers Cold Case Unit can have the Grim Reaper on their patch, we sure as hell can do this. Like the chief's going to come out here and catch us wearing them? I don't think so...."

Jake sought information of the duo as to why there was so much secrecy about the creatures.

Owen matter-of-factly said, "the government guys don't want mass hysteria out there. People would be freaking out and acting like it's the end of the world."

"How do we know it isn't?" Jake was quick to point out.

"But wouldn't they be better off informing the public about

how to protect themselves and on how to prevent them from turning into these *things*? You think maybe there's more going on here than we know about?"

"There always is," stated the elder and wiser officer, Harry.

"We are just the blue-collar guys. Like the trash guy. THE MAN doesn't tell us shit."

"Before you go, why don't you give us a hand with our dragger-fire?" Owen said.

Owen handed Jake a pitchfork and a pair of rubber gloves. The three men began to stack the creatures into a pile that was four wide and four deep.

Owen poured lighter fluid over the stack. He then pulled a Swisher Sweets cigar from a uniform shirt pocket underneath his exterior rubber raincoat. Owen sparked a Bic lighter to light the medium sized cigar.

Owen puffed at the fresh stogie for a minute, then used his finger to flick some still hot ashes onto the mound. The monster stack was set ablaze. "Grab the marshmallows," exclaimed Owen, who paused and then recanted. "Only kidding. They would taste nasty!"

Jake wished he had some way to capture this moment. A method of preserving some evidence of these beasts to take back to Texas and plead for a retrial. But he began to realize that, as many of these *things* as there were, there would be ample opportunities for him to capture some evidence. He expressed his gratitude to the BODS, then took his sickle, shotgun, and maps down from the tree fort.

Jake requested one last favor before heading out.

"I need to get going. Can you guys get a message to my partner back in Dallas? His name is Mack McElroy, and he works at the Central Division. Tell him #4856 is eating beans."

Harry replied, "No problem. Is he going to know what that means?"

"He will figure it out. And, just out of curiosity," Jake asked the officers. "What would you guys have done if I had run for it earlier on like I had planned?"

"Haa!" Harry laughed. "You'd be on top of that pile right about now with Owen browning marshmallows over your ass." The two Wildlife Cops continued to laugh out loud.

"And hey, if you were smart you would ditch that West Virginia stolen ride. And get you a disguise. There are pictures of you and that truck all over the APB's that the Feds sent out."

Jake moseyed down the trail back to the old Chevy truck as the malodor from the dragger-fire filled the dusk Pennsylvania daybreak. He removed the branches from the top of the pickup and fired the vehicle up. He then drove in a northeasterly direction.

Jake was overwhelmed with relief. He felt very thankful that he had not stuck with his plan to make a run for it when he had the chance.

Chapter 21 - The Organ Grinders

I20, Texarkana - the Texas/ Arkansas border

The majestic magenta hue of Texarkana's celestial sphere simmered just above the glowing Avalanche dashboard. Mack guided the SUV eastbound along Interstate 20.

Roscoe took advantage of the unoccupied back seat as he lay sprawled out, sleeping and snoring soundly. He was benefiting from this much needed rest because he was still recuperating from his lack of nourishment during his confinement.

Duy rode shotgun. He busily and with aggression was working on sharpening the blade of his newly acquired survival hatchet. He was cutting into a gray rectangular knife sharpening stone, turning the axe edge into a razor-sharp tool. When he was finished, this weapon would be able to slice and dice with the precision of a surgical scalpel.

Mack glanced to his right. He noticed that Duy seemed to be highly agitated and fuming. "Dude, you okay?" Mack asked. "You look pissed off."

"I've just been thinking about the way the whole Roscoe rescue went down. It's all my fault that Dave got hurt."

"How can you blame yourself for that? You and I were the

ones who got his ass out of there," Mack said.

"I know, but we never should have gotten Dave involved. He's not in great physical shape. We made him think the mission would be simple, with no risk of harm or danger."

"You can't worry about stuff like that, Duy. None of us saw that coming. But the important thing we got from that experience was that none of us gave up. We had each other's backs, and we will never go into another situation thinking that it will be easy. We all became stronger as a result."

Duy had taken a brief reprieve from the blade-sharpening as he thought about the words he had just uttered. The conversation now over, the Vietnam native resumed the procedure.

"Nice hatchet, dude. That's new?" Mack asked.

"Yeah, I got a few new toys." Duy began to remove his recently acquired arsenal from every nook and cranny of his clothing. "I got some more throwing knives that I keep in my inner coat pockets and I keep my hatchet in a carry holster on my back. This machete is carried in this sheath on my leg and I've got another pocket full of these ninja throwing stars. Oh- and finally is my old reliable Bowie knife with a 10-inch clip-point blade."

"Where are you gonna keep the Bowie?"

"Wherever it will fit. Right now, it's staying right where you see it, in my hand. I've been practicing a lot with these things, throwing them into still and moving targets. I spent a good deal of time unholstering and reholstering them while blindfolded or in the dark so I will be prepared for anything. Even in the pitch black I will be able to maneuver and fight as if it were second nature."

The cellphone strategically stationed in the center console of the Chevy Avalanche's cup holder began to vibrate vivaciously. Mack decreased the decibels of the old-school LL Cool J currently pulsating through the car stereo's amplifier and speakers. Then he took the call.

"Hey, Michelle. How's it going?"

"Hi, Mack. I was wondering how y'all were doing and where you were at?"

"Oh, we are doing all right. Moving right along and coming up on Nashville here pretty soon."

"Excellent! And exactly where are you going again?"

"Thinking we will probably start our search in Rhode Island.

We will start by checking Jake's hometown to see if anyone has heard from him at all lately. If that fails, then I know he has connections in Mass too."

"Well, Mack, I also wanted to give you some new information I just received in a conference call. It seems as if Uncle Sam has developed some new teams, called Containment Squads. They respond to areas highly contaminated to collect and quarantine those infected. But they are keeping this information from the general public. Outwardly, they still seem to be in denial about the whole infection thing.

"They are tracking and attempting to locate all of the offspring of the people who were in the military and took some so-called "Zeus Juice." They are also seeking any offspring of those who were experimented on in some secret labs. Apparently, there were at least two different experimentation laboratories, one in Florida and another somewhere on the west coast. Probably in California.

"These descendants are on a list to be hunted down. They will be dragged out of their houses to either be taken away and quarantined or, if there are no witnesses around, be executed on the spot. It's faster, easier, and cheaper than housing them in their Nazi death camp-like quarantine sheds."

Mack was astonished by the revelation. "Dang. I had no idea this was all going on. What do these 'Containment Squad' guys look like? Are they dressed like SWAT dudes and rolling around town in armored cars?"

"They wear face masks and haz-mat suits, with gun belts over the top and their government-issued Sig 45's within reach. They drive unmarked silver, full sized Ford Transit cargo vans with no side or rear windows. They are always moving around all stealth-like", Michelle said.

"These sound like some bad dudes, too. This one cop in Florida was in on the conference call. He told a story about a woman who had been abducted and held in the Florida lab. They injected her with the virus. This woman later escaped the facility along with all the other captives."

Michelle continued. "She later became pregnant and had a baby girl. But the same woman eventually was killed by the baby's father after the woman turned into a zombie. She was about to eat the baby when the father shot the lady down.

"Then just a few days ago, the team hunted down that father and the little baby girl in Winter Haven, Florida. At a trailer park. Tips led them to this one trailer, so they began pounding on the door. They demanded to be let in under the authority of the President of the United States.

"The dad told the little girl that it was time to play hide-and-seek. He said that she was 'IT.' He told her to climb down through the hidden trap door underneath the rug, and into a dark empty hole nestled into the ground, directly below the trailer. He told her to stay put and be as still and quiet as possible. He told her to stay that way until he came for her.

"The Containment Squad kicked open the door and found the father. He refused to reveal the whereabouts of his daughter. The team slaughtered the man where he stood, blasting him to smithereens with their automatic weapons. They eventually found the child, who was now crying uncontrollably under the trailer.

"They pulled that little girl out of that hole in the ground below the trailer. She has not been seen since," Michelle said as she shook her head.

Mack recalled the disturbing story Rich had passionately imparted on his video tape. He disclosed the fact that years earlier he had been held against his will in that same Florida lab. Baby Carson, Rich's only offspring, could undoubtedly be on that Containment Squad list, just like that little girl in the Winter Haven trailer park.

The lustful Latina continued her dialogue as Mack and Dewman listened intently. Her voice projected loudly over Mack's phone speaker.

"Mack, you guys really need to be careful out there. Every day there are more and more sightings and stories about these creatures. They even got one of the guys on one of my transport teams."

"No way! What the hell happened?" Duy asked.

"Well, there's a small three-bedroom house in a fairly quiet North Mesquite neighborhood. The house was occupied by a single mother of one latchkey twelve-year-old boy named Braylon.

"Apparently, a few days ago, Braylon's pet tabby cat named 'Tiger' disappeared after he went out the doggy door, as he normally did. However, uncharacteristically, he had not returned for several days.

"But on this day, the feline finally returned. It was in the early evening hours and the kid was home alone playing Xbox on the living room couch. Braylon was so fixated on the video game he was playing with his online friends, that he failed to notice Tiger stumbling through the pet door.

"The cat wasted no time before attacking the kid, lunging at and biting his jugular vein. Tiger began feasting on the kid's face and the juvenile began hemorrhaging profusely, unable to react.

Michelle continued. "The mom came home an hour or so later to find junior sitting on the couch, staring at a blank television screen. He was still holding the Xbox remote, but it was now covered with a black sludgy substance with the thickness and texture of coagulated blood.

"Before his mother could realize what was happening, Braylon attacked her. He killed her violently, chomping on her flesh as if she was made of Pizza Rolls. The neighbors heard her screaming and yelling and they called the cops. Police responded quickly and destroyed both the kid and his mom. But there was no report of any cat being present.

"So, then we got a call from Mesquite PD saying they had a couple of bodies for us to pick up. I dispatched Skip and Byron to that same house, and they responded. As they were putting Braylon on the body cart to take him to the car, the Tiger cat strolled back in through the puppy door.

"The once domestic tabby appeared as if he had been in a fight. He was covered with wounds and blood. His orange and white fur was falling out in clumps and his skin was rotting and stank of corrosion. Bugs were colonizing in the corroding flesh. Tiger used his front claws to grab Skip's ankle, and he latched on tightly. He mounted Skip's leg as if he was climbing a tree.

"Oh, fuck." Mack uttered.

Michelle nodded. "The Tiger zombie gnawed at Skip's inner thigh and groin, causing blood to spray out in thick splashes. Skip frantically tried to shake the hellcat off his leg, without success.

"Skip's partner, Devin, took off running. He offered no assistance to his partner and never looked back. He called us the next day to say he was quitting the job."

"Oh my god! So, what happened to Skip after that?" the

Dew-man asked.

"No idea. He's still out there somewhere as far as we know. So is the cat."

"I had to hire a new team of guys to take their place. I found a couple of young dudes who were already friends and applied for this job at the same time. Their names are Bobby and La Keith, but I call them Beavis and Butthead. They are both going through med school and are really into learning as much as possible about this recent epidemic."

"Michelle, thank you so much for the update," Mack said. "Sounds like things are getting pretty crazy everywhere!"

"No problem. You guys stay safe and keep me abreast of your location so I can be sure you're still okay!"

As soon as Michelle disconnected, Mack attempted to call Amanda to tell her about the "Containment Squad." Mack realized that Carson, being the offspring of a person who had been experimented on in the Florida lab (his father, Rich), was in grave danger. Amanda must be made aware so that she and Austin could keep the toddler hidden and safe.

Mack also figured it was time to let Amanda know that there was a possibility that Jake was still alive. He had waited out of fear of providing her with some false hope. But as time elapsed, he was becoming more and more able to confirm these suspicions.

Mack tried to call Amanda but was unable to get through. He was able to leave her the following voice message.

"Hey Amanda, it's Mack. I just got some information from Michelle. There are indications that Carson is in danger. And you could be as well. It is dire for you and Carson to stay hidden somewhere. And... there's something else I need to tell you. It's important. Call me back! And be careful!"

Mack had decided not to mention his hunch about Jake. That would have to wait until he could talk to her on the phone or in person. He needed to ensure she was sitting down when he revealed *that* news.

Chapter 22 - Dead on Their Feet

North East Pennsylvania

Jake's faith in mankind was somewhat renewed. He left Loyalsock Park in a northeasterly direction, headed for the great state of Massachusetts.

There, Jake had an old buddy from their high school days. A guy named Vinny DeAngelo. Vinny had family in Providence and Cranston who were rumored to be big-time players in the local mafia scene. Vinny moved up to Boston after high school, supposedly to continue in the family business and to become established in his own part of town.

But before Jake even started to locate his old friend, he would have to dump this stolen Appalachian-special pickup truck. He also needed a new set of clothes that would be more appropriate at his next stop. That hillbilly truck, grease-stained wife-beater, and "Get er' done" ballcap were not going to work up here in the Northeast.

Not only that, this wardrobe was doused in putrid body fluids and exuded a noxious odor. If these didn't draw unnecessary attention and make Jake stand out in a crowd, nothing else would.

Jake stopped in Brookline, a city just west of Beantown. There he found a thrift store on the main strip and parked the West Virginia Caddy behind a dumpster at the rear of the business.

He ran inside and quickly used cash to purchase a more commodious attire. He picked out a black toboggan hat, a used green and red striped Christmas-looking sweater, a torn pair of Levi's acid-washed jeans, and an old worn-out black pleather jacket.

He also acquired a decent pair of pre-owned sneakers. They still had a lot of wear left and were comfortable. Now in possession of his new costume and in the store's bathroom, Jake disposed of his old soiled garb in the trash can. He put on his new clothes and assumed his new identity, one that was better suited for this neck of the woods. He decided to adopt the name "Sal Armano."

He had no fake identification or documents to accompany his new name, so he would have to improvise as best as he could.

While paying for his new digs at the thrift store counter, a black and white patrol car drove slowly past the front of the store.

Jake was unsure if the cop was onto him or just performing random patrols. So, Jake decided to abandon his plan of driving the pickup truck into the Charles River, or burning it. Neither of those ideas was worth the risk of being captured in the process.

But then Jake remembered that he had left his weapons behind in the old Chevrolet. He would need some way to defend himself if he were to get in a jam while trying to infiltrate the mafia. Weapons would also be essential should any more of these "draggers" show up.

This thrift store had a small dishware/dining area toward the back of the store. Jake back-peddled to that area while keeping eyes on the plate glass window with a view of the street in front.

Two large matching kitchen knives with ten-inch blades and wooden handles would have to serve as his new weapons. He also grabbed a cheap blonde hair-dying kit and returned to the checkout area of the store. There he was able to scrounge up enough change to cover the cost.

Jake grabbed his purchases, waited a minute until the squad car was out of eyeshot, and then he exited the store. He set out on foot in the opposite direction from which the cop was headed. Jake now had no money to flag a cab to get into Boston. It was time to see how well his New Balance sneaker purchase would pay off.

Having walked many miles and now approaching the city, Jake got the feeling that the police were not looking for him yet. But it was just a matter of time until the stolen truck behind the thrift store dumpster was located. And then the cops would be crawling all over the place, hot on his trail.

He was doing well for now; the cool New England February temperatures were a nice change of pace. And as much as Jake was walking, he was starting to work up a slight sweat. He was also happy that he was not lugging around that large sickle and shotgun. His two new twin blades were much lighter and more appropriate for a foot traveler. Jake put one knife in each of his two inner pockets of his pleather jacket and continued his journey.

The Texas prison escapee knew he had to find shelter as soon as possible. He didn't know exactly where in Boston to start his search for Vinny, but he figured "Southie" was as good a place as any. "Southie" is a densely populated neighborhood in South Boston, known as a good old working-class, Irish American neighborhood.

However, it is also home to many of those who make their living in the crime syndicate business.

Jake made his way east through Dorchester Heights, one of the oldest and most historic neighborhoods in the United States. He had no idea he was following in decade-old footsteps once laid by George Washington. Washington had passed through while in the process of forcing British troops to evacuate during the American Revolutionary War.

A new Cumberland Farms convenience store was also along the route, and Jake ducked inside to take advantage of the restroom mirror. There he cut several locks of his hair from his head and subsequently applied the hair dye. Before long, he was now a bleached blonde.

Jake exited the store with his newfound "hair done in a blender" look as he approached Old Colony Avenue. The street was lined with lofty venerable brownstone buildings on each side. They loomed pleasantly, overlooking the cobblestone brick roadway.

Jake stumbled across a hole-in-the-wall pool hall called "The Eight Ball." It was a name that he recognized as a place Vinny would hang out at back in the day.

Jake walked into the front door and immediately had to pause for his pupils to adjust. There was but a minuscule amount of light emerging from the darkness within the game room.

The strong smell of burning marijuana immediately smacked Jake in the face. A cloud of smoke from the green leaf overwhelmed his eyes, nose, and mouth. Jake's eyes began to tear up and he started to cough. A pale white male sitting on a bar stool just inside the entrance of the establishment made eye contact with him.

This doorman was built like one of those inflatable punching bags for kids. He was rounder and wider at the bottom, making him nearly impossible to tip over. This dingy door guy was built like a Weeble. He was about five feet and four inches tall and wider than that around his waist. He was clad in Celtics T-shirt and black sweatpants with holes and was smoking what smelled like a very cheap cigar.

He stood up slowly from his perch to ascertain why this stranger had entered the private club.

"What the fuck you want?" he demanded. He stood in front

of Jake and looked upwards with his head only reaching just below Jake's chin.

Jake restrained himself from responding as he normally would in a situation such as this. But he realized that if he wanted to locate his buddy Vinny, he was going to have to play nice. Or at least *somewhat* nice.

"I'm lookin' for a dude named Vinny DeAngelo. You know where I might find him? I owe him some money."

The rotund door guy chirped, "Give me the fuckin' money. I'll make sure he gets it."

Jake declined the offer. "Nah, I think I'd rather pay Vinny face to face."

"How much you talkin' about? You must be a workin' girl. You been saving up your trick money, bitch?" he asked.

Jake quickly disengaged from his "play nice" game plan and responded appropriately.

"Who the fuck are you callin' a bitch, you mutha fuckin' troll! Now tell me where Vinny's at before I punt your ass out that fuckin' window!"

The astonished door-keep reached behind him with his right hand. He grasped for something from the top of a nearby cigarette pack vending machine. Duct tape covered a ten-inch long crack on the glass surface of the vendy. The door man revealed in his hand an empty Sam Adams Winter Lager beer bottle and prepared to smash it across Jake's left cheek.

Jake used his left hand to block the attack. He then followed that up by thrusting his right fist repeatedly into the lard covered rib cage on his assailant's left side.

Suddenly, emerging from the smoke floating around the rear of the brown nicotine encrusted pool hall, were three larger, less Weeble-like goons. These three were all dressed similarly to their now-rib-fractured door man comrade.

Carrying pool cues in their left hands and each holding a pool ball in their right hand, the three goons were as tall as Jake but not nearly as chiseled. The elder of the trio said, "you wanna see Vinny so bad? We'll take you to see Vinny, you lousy fuck."

Jake was escorted outside. Then he was shoved into the back

seat of a brown 1974 Ford Gran Torino sedan which was parked right in front of The Eight Ball.

One of the goons jumped in back with Jake, and the other two assumed seats in the front. "Pull that ski mask down over your eyes unless you want us to close your eyes for ya."

Jake did not feel comfortable covering his eyes in this situation. Realistically, if he did so, he may never see the light of day again. He could end up being knocked unconscious and taking a short swim at the bottom of a deep, freshly poured concrete foundation.

But to the contrary, this could be the opportunity he needed to establish himself in a new life under a new identity. Maybe not permanently, but at least until he could be proven innocent of his Texas murder charges.

Jake pulled down his toboggan to cover his eyes. The car trip to Vinny's hidden lair began. The car felt as if it went over a bridge and past a shipyard. These observations could be instrumental in saving Jake's life if he ended up being left for dead in some isolated part of the city and needed to find his way out.

The old sedan stopped suddenly and stalled out where it stood.

A voice called out, "you can look now, douchebag," as the thugs opened their car doors. The two from the front seats began to walk toward a fishing boat floating on the harbor. It was docked near a long wooden pier.

Jake lifted his hat and exited the back-passenger side door. It was apparent that dusk had set. Between the darkness and fog, the large older commercial fishing boat was barely visible. The back-seat goon exited on the left, then walked around the rear of the vehicle to approach behind Jake. "Follow them," he instructed, giving Jake a hard glance in the process.

The four men walked up the pier and stopped prior to boarding the sea-worn vessel. "You got anything on ya?" the elder wise guy put the question to Jake.

Before Jake could respond, the youngest wise guy, whom the others called "Junior," began to pat Jake down with both hands. Junior was going through Jake's pockets, looking under his hat. He was searching for anything that could prove dangerous to them or their boss.

Junior opened Sal's jacket and asked, "what you got in them pockets?"

Junior reached into both jacket inner pockets. He then removed the twin ten-inch-bladed wooden handled cutlery, saying, "what did you plan on doing with these?"

Junior put the knives in his own back pants pocket, and the three mobsters proceeded to pounce upon Jake. They were throwing punches at him and dragging him to the ground.

"You two hold him down. I'm gonna put a plug in this mother fucker" screeched Junior. He pulled an old black semi-automatic pistol from the front waistband of his pants.

The ruckus from the boat's exterior alarmed the lone occupant. That man exited the sea ship and yelled, "what the fuck's going on out here?"

It was Vinny DeAngelo. He didn't recognize Jake, due to the darkness and years that had passed. Jake hesitated to say out loud who he really was, for fear of his identity being known by the associates.

Vinny questioned his underlings, saying, "who the fuck's this?"

One of the goon squad spoke up.

"He came into The Eight Ball, claimed he wanted to pay you back some money. Then he broke Chuckie's ribs. We brought him here and searched him. He had two big-ass butcher knives in his coat. So now we are gonna cap this son of a bitch for you, boss."

Vinny squinted, trying to obtain a clearer picture of the dumbass lying idly by his feet. He noticed the guy on the ground was large and extraordinarily muscular. Vinny thought to himself, *this guy could probably take care of his own and dish it out to others pretty good too. He could prove to be an asset. But he also looks somewhat familiar.*

"Okay, let him up. I'm gonna take care of this piece of shit myself. You guys go wait in the car."

Vinny then bent over, positioning his face merely a foot away from Jake's, and said
"You're a dead man."

Chapter 23 - You're Dead to Me

"Southie", Boston Massachusetts

"Wait. Vinny, it's me." Jake replied.

The three goons retreated to the Torino as Vinny extended a hand down toward the downtrodden figure. Vinny grabbed Jake's hand, assisting the newcomer to his feet. Jake paused, unsure whether the mafia lord recognized him. Vinny got a hand full of Jake's collar, and pulled Jake's face within an inch of his own mug.

Vinny then quietly spoke. "Dude, I saw the news story about you. They said you died in some escape attempt from a prison bus?! So, I thought you were dead! I should'a known they couldn't have taken you out that easy."

Jake took a deep breath as he realized he wasn't about to be executed.

Vinny laughed. "What? Did you think I was gonna blast ya? Now that's funny! "

"Yeah. I didn't know if you recognized me. Anyways, there's a lot more to that story than what the media told," Jake explained. "Not to be rude, but if you don't mind, I'd like to have my knives back..."

Vinny led Jake onto the rickety old schooner filled with fishing nets, lobster traps, floatation devices, knives and tools. They sat down in a small back room that served as a makeshift office. This room was complete with a thirty-year-old schoolteacher's desk and an office chair with a cracked seat and missing one of its four casters.

Vinny reached into a small refrigerator and removed a couple of Saint Pauli Girl beers. The old high school buddies reminisced about the good old days for a spell. Then Jake told the tale of how his life had completely derailed since "the birthday incident."

Vinny explained that he was doing quite well with his own sports booking, loan financing, and "insurance" company. He said he was currently looking to hire someone trustworthy to be his personal driver and bodyguard because he had to "let the last guy go." Jake didn't ask for clarification whether that meant that he fired the last driver or threw him off a bridge.

Jake gladly accepted Vinny's offer of employment. He was also offered a dusty junk-filled room on the boat as a place to crash. A worn-out blue leather sofa in the corner would serve nicely for sleeping on, and a folding chair and a kerosene lantern were sufficient to complete Jake's new temporary living quarters.

Vinny manufactured two different forms of identification for 'Sal'. The first was a Maine driver's license and the second was a Social Security card. Jake was also given a black Beretta 92F 9mm handgun, a tool he would need in order to properly protect Vinny from the many disgruntled customers and business associates wishing to cause him irreversible harm.

Vinny threw a wad of cash at Jake. "Go get yourself some nice suits. You look like you live in a dumpster."

Dallas, Texas. Year 1 month 3 ATBI (after the birthday incident)

Mack had been gone from work for several days now, on an extended leave of absence. He, Duy and Roscoe were on their pilgrimage to find Jake.

Meanwhile, back in the Central Headquarters of the Dallas Police Department, a patrol administrative secretary was placing a note into Officer McElroy's mailbox. It was a small pink piece of paper marked "Important Message" at the top.

Below on the "Date" line, she had written "Tuesday," with no time inscribed. Further down on the paper was a line with the pre-printed word "Message" on it, followed by some handwritten words in black ink: "Pennsylvania Wildlife Control Officer Harry called, wanted to tell you 4856 is eating beans."

There was no phone number given or any email address. No contact information for this "Harry" guy whatsoever. 4856 was Jake's Dallas Police badge number. Not many people knew that off the top of their heads, without looking it up. Maybe the only ones who had that number memorized were rookies who trained under Jake and were constantly having to record both his and their own badge numbers in every offense, incident, and crash report they generated.

Even if Mack had seen this message, he might have believed it was a prank.

But if there really was a "Harry" with the Pennsylvania Wildlife Control, Mack would most likely wish to talk to this person and verify that he really had called. Also, Mack would try to decipher exactly what the hell this message meant. But for now, the message would lie dormant and the point remained moot.

Michelle and Amanda had become quite harmonious over time. They normally communicated every couple days or so. But as of late, Amanda was no longer responding to Michelle's texts, messages, or calls. Michelle had been trying for several days now to contact Amanda without success, causing Michelle to become quite worried about her friend's welfare.

One day Michelle was about to drive over to Amanda's place to check on her. Before leaving her house, she checked Amanda's Facebook posts and noticed a "life status update" that Amanda had recently posted online.

"Just married the most wonderful man in the world! I love you Chad Tillinghast!"

Michelle was dumbfounded by the blurb. She could not comprehend why Amanda would have married the same cocky, oil tycoon, asshole guy that she not long ago was disparaging critically.

It was readily apparent to Michelle that something was very wrong. She knew she had to seek Amanda out in person to get to the bottom of this.

Washington County, Rhode Island

Mack, Duy, and Roscoe arrived in the southwestern edge of the Ocean State after three long days of travel in Mack's Chevy Avalanche. The two humans had taken turns at the helm. They had been jaunting the interstates, dodging the once animal or human segments scattered across the roads between Dallas and New England. They did their best to avoid the countless dark lifeless figures walking in and out of the roadway. These THINGS would mindlessly step out into traffic to pick at the roadkill splattered on the concrete, in search of even the most minute morsels of meat and sustenance.

Although the Chevy truck's paint was a burnt orange, that color now only shone through in spots. The entire front half of the vehicle was covered with creature splatter; blood, guts, and other body parts coated the four-wheel drive pickup. It appeared as if it had been deep-fried in zombie batter at the Texas State Fair.

"So, Mack, are we gonna check his parents' house first? We can ask them if they have seen Jake." Duy queried.

"Man, I think we need to approach this more like a stakeout. I think we should conduct surveillance on a few select prime locations rather than actually contacting anyone" Mack said. "All it will take is for one person to be suspicious of us or our intentions, they call the local cops, and next thing you know them scoundrels with the Feds will be on us."

Mack continued; "if Jake is still alive, you know the government goons want to get ahold of him before he can talk to anyone else. They don't want him telling folks about the Feds framing him for the murders, and the reason why. We can't let the Feds get involved or it's game over for us and for Jake."

"But you're right about Jake's parents place," Mack said. "We need to sit up on that house. if that doesn't pay off, I have another place in mind as well. I recall Jake telling me a story about camping out as a kid with his little buddy over in this area around a 'Beach Pond'. There was a bad accident that killed his friend Jimmy. That might be a place Jake would return to. Possibly to pay his respects to his friend, but he could also camp out there and hide for a while. Plenty of fish, too."

Duy jumped on the Google Maps app on his smartphone and located Beach Pond. It was in the Arcadia Management Area in the town of Exeter. "Okay, I found it. Let's go there first. We're pretty close right now."

Mack steered toward the small Rhode Island town of Exeter. This was a town which coincidentally had its share of the un*dead* stemming from a tuberculosis outbreak in the 19th century.

In 1892, several members of George and Mary Brown's family passed away from the fatal tuberculosis disease (then referred to as "consumption"). The Exeter town folk began spreading rumors that the Brown family were 'un*dead* beings', causing mischief in the neighborhoods and places they had frequented while they were alive.

George was persuaded to allow the exhumation of the corpses of three of his family members. Two of these, upon examination, were very decomposed - as should be expected.

But the exhumation of George's recently deceased daughter, Mercy, created quite a stir among the town people. For unlike the other two, Mercy had been buried just two months earlier in an above ground vault. During the winter season, this vault acted much like a freezer. Thus, her body had little to no signs of decomposition, and her heart and liver still contained blood. These combined signs lead the investigators to believe Mercy Brown to be un*dead*. Her heart was removed from the corpse and burned. Subsequently, those ashes were fed to her still living brother, Edwin, to cure him of "consumption." He passed two months later.

Mack, Duy and Roscoe spent two days in reconnaissance of that Beach Pond area. They searched for any signs of Jake in the daytime, and then slept in shifts in the truck cab at night. These had been cold, rainy days, and neither of the men had prepared adequately for the potential of rainfall. They had anticipated the brisk Northeast air and had worn layers to combat such, but their failure to anticipate the necessity for rain gear was biting them in the ass. So, they soon found themselves cold and uncomfortable in damp layers of clothes, without anything else available.

By the end of the second night at this location, and now in the beginning of the third day of the mission, Duy found himself to be feeling quite under the weather. He was sneezing and coughing uncontrollably and slightly feverish.

"Mack, we don't seem to be having much luck here. Do you think we are wasting our time at this location? Maybe we should move around more, check out his parent's place for a change..."

"Yeah, we probably should go to another spot. This really is like looking for a needle in a haystack." Mack glanced over at Duy. "Dude, you look as sick as a dog passing peach pits. Maybe you should just sleep in the back while I keep watch."

Mack drove the Avalanche toward the next town over, West Greenwich. There he found the address for Jake's parents' house, and he parked on the edge of the wooded ten-acre plot. Mack began to veer through his binoculars to look for any movement at the house.

It was now 9:30 a.m. Eastern Time. They had only been in that spot for forty-five minutes when Duy began to tap vigorously on his comrade's shoulder. "Dude! Dude- look..."

Mack looked at Duy, who was pointing straight out through the front of the truck's windshield. They both saw the outline of a human form exiting the Hathaway property through a wooded southern property line. The person was obviously avoiding the driveway and opting to use a much more difficult-to-travel terrain.

Mack told Duy, "You stay here in the truck since you look like shit. Me and Roscoe will handle this. Come on, boy..."

Mack slowly and silently exited the Avalanche and began to tread stealthily toward the fleeing human form. "Stay here, Roscoe. Lie down."

Mack advanced closer and soon sought concealment behind a wide old pine tree with rotting branches and moss-covered bark.

The retreating hooded-sweatshirt-and-blue-jean-wearing person was about to pass by. Mack threw his beefy right arm out, wrapping it around the neck of the stranger and placing them in a chokehold position.

"Who are you?" Mack questioned the startled captive.

"Hey, let me go! I should be asking you the same thing!" a female voice emerged from within the sweatshirt hoodie.

Mack loosened his grip as the young woman began to remove her hood and show her face. "I'm Kristin Ramey. I went to school with Jake. I was just here visiting Mr. and Mrs. Hathaway. Now - who are you?"

"Kris Ramey! Oh wow. I remember you. What I mean is, I'm friends with Jake, and I remember him talking about you. High school sweethearts, right? He mentioned you fondly. He once made a comment that he would love to see you again someday just to catch up and see how your life is going."

Yep, he was a year older than me. We went to each other's prom together. So, why are you here?"

Mack found himself wanting to be honest with Jake's long-lost adolescent love and divulged that he might still be alive. But Mack knew this was a bad idea. Trusting anyone at this juncture could potentially cost Jake his life, as well as that of Mack and their friends.

Mack improvised on the spot. "Before Jake passed, I promised him I would tell his parents that he loved them and came to give them some of his things too."

"Oh, that's nice of you. I was talking to Charlie and Clara to see if they had heard the news reports about him. I was wondering if they were true or not. His parents said they hadn't heard any official news. But I guess you have confirmed the worst for me."

"It really sucks," Kristin said. "He cut ties from me back when he first got together with Amanda. I guess she was super-jealous, so Jake sacrificed our friendship so she would be happy. But I always wondered how he was doing and what his life was like. Way back in the day when we were together, he always made me feel special. And protected. He also seemed like the type of person that would do something really big or important someday."

Mack's cellular device began to rattle and hum in the front pocket of his BDU's. He removed the device with his hand and held it in a position to read the phone number of the incoming call. It was fellow Dallas PD Officer Campos, who had a mailbox next to Mack's in the Central Patrol Room.

Mack answered, "What's up, Campos?"

"Hey, Mack, I saw this pink 'missed message' sticky note sitting at the top of your inbox. I know you are gonna be away for an extended period, and I thought this might be important. You know, like from a hot woman or something.

"But then I figured if it wasn't important, I shouldn't bother you with it. So, I kind of read it. Sorry. But after reading it, it really does sound important. Weird, but important."

"So, what does it say?"

"It says you missed a call from some park ranger or something like that in Pennsylvania. He said to tell you that '4856 is eating beans.' What the fuck does that mean?"

"I'm not really sure, but thanks, man. Hey, can you do me a favor and burn that message. Oh, and by the way, you know nothing about it, right?"

"Yeah, sure, Mack. I mean… burn *what*? I don't even know what you're talking about."

Mack clicked off his phone, tucked it back into his pocket, and looked up at Kristin.

"Kristin, it was nice meeting you, but we gotta roll. Thanks for checking up on the Hathaways. Jake would have really appreciated that."

Mack and Roscoe climbed back into the Texas-registered pickup, and Mack piloted the vehicle in a northern direction. They had an hour-long trek ahead of them.

"All right, Dew-man, let's blow this taco stand. We're headed to Beantown. I mean Boston."

Chapter 24 - The Green Monster

Boston, Massachusetts

It was a seasonably brisk New England May morning. The Avalanche with bug-splattered Texas plates rolled onto the Massachusetts Turnpike and then exited onto Commonwealth Avenue. The truck was indiscernible behind the dense fog accompanying it.

"Dew-man, look! There's one of those Duck Boats they give the tours on. Every time the Patriots won the Super Bowl, they would use these things for the victory parades."

Mr. Tran, sprawled out on the Chevy's back seat, failed to respond.

"Are you okay, dude?"

Roscoe leapt from the front passenger seat to the center armrest/console, and then hopped onto the back seat. He began to lick Duy's hot, red face. Even this did not precipitate a response.

Mack pulled the vehicle over into a parking lot to assess the situation. Unable to wake his companion, Mack reached for his water bottle to splash some liquid onto Duy's face to wake him. In his haste, the nervous Mack grabbed his tobacco spit cup instead and poured a combination of tobacco juice and saliva onto Duy's face.

"Oh fuck! I know I didn't just do that," Mack scolded himself as Duy's open mouth now had tobacco juice trickling down into his throat. Duy began to cough, and finally opened his eyes. "I feel like shit, man" he said. "I'm burning up. I must have gotten pneumonia or Lyme disease from those stakeouts in the woods. Something bad. I think I'm dying here."

"All right, Dew man. Hang in there. We passed a hospital a few blocks back. I'll take you there now. You're gonna be okay."

The burnt orange Avalanche screeched out a U-turn in the middle of the street, with pedestrians and other vehicles yielding to avoid a collision.

The machismo mobile slid into the circular driveway beside the emergency room doors. The fit cop flew out of the driver's seat and opened the back-driver's side door to aid his passenger out of the vehicle.

Mack yelled, "Roscoe, STAY!" as he wrapped his arms around Duy's back and arms. He was practically carrying the young attorney, who was weak and hardly able to stand, let alone walk.

Upon reaching the Emergency Room entrance, Mack found the sliding glass doors to be locked. Visible on the inside were two people. One was an employee wearing blue medical scrubs and the second was a large security guard-looking dude with an AR-15 in his hands. The muzzle of the rifle was pointed at Mack and Duy from behind the glass.

The Scrubs Guy yelled through the glass, "what do you want?"

Mack explained, "my friend here has very high fever and he's very weak. He's been losing consciousness, blacking out. We need to come in."

"Where was he bit? "shouted the security guard.

Caught off guard by the question, Mack responded. "Bit? He's not bit by anything. He's probably got pneumonia or Lyme disease. Let us in!"

"We can't do that. We can't let anyone like that inside. All it takes is one infected person to get in and spread the virus to everyone else and we are all dead."

"You gotta be fucking kidding me, right? You're a GODDAMN HOSPITAL!!!"Mack shouted.

"We are only treating patients with traumatic injuries at this time. Gunshots, stab wounds etcetera - but no bites."

Mack said, "I bet if we were white, you'd let us in!"

Mack and Duy began the slow drag back to the car. Mack said half-jokingly, "damn that Jake. Of all times for our token white friend not to be around when we need him!"

"That's fine. We'll just get back in the truck and go to another hospit---- oh shit..."

Duy's head was down as he struggled to move one foot after the other without collapsing. "What's wrong?" he asked.

It suddenly became apparent why the E.R. staff was not letting everyone and anyone in without the proper screening.

Four once-living human beings now in various stages of less-liveliness circled the Texas truck. They were only about fifty feet away.

Based upon their soiled, tattered attire and other telltale signs, one of the DEAD appeared to have been a construction worker with his yellow safety vest and hard hat. Another appeared to have been a businesswoman in her once-smart-looking Macy's business skirt and blouse. The third and fourth may have once been some type of meter maids or parking lot attendants.

Nonetheless, they all were stammering around the Avalanche, black muck oozing from their orifices. Their flesh was corroding and featured the stench that comes along with that. And the other common denominator that they shared: they were all hungry.

They could all see and hear something yummy inside the Mack mobile. It was a beefy Belgian Malinois chicken nugget named Roscoe, pacing back and forth inside. He was nervous as hell and barking like crazy.

Mack asserted, "okay Duy, don't panic. But there are DEAD surrounding my truck. Just keep quiet, and I'm gonna carry you out of here."

Duy moaned, "no, leave me. I'm dying. You need to go on and find Jake."

"Quit being a wuss, no one's gonna die on my watch. Shut up and be still."

The muscled-up Mack threw the limp Dew-man over his right shoulder like a sack of red potatoes. He began walking down the street, with one eye on the mis-creations around his truck and another eye searching for a means of escape.

The street sign above read "Yawkey Way." Mack abruptly realized where he was: just outside the friendly confines of Fenway Park.

Mack was in dire need of a sound structural shelter and a place for Duy to rest and recover from his flu. Mack and his ailing cohort agreed mutually upon attempting to enter the ballpark as a temporary safe house. They also thought it would be badass to take a tour of America's best loved ballpark at least once before they died (or the world ended, whichever came first).

The desperate drifters began to walk the perimeter of the park. They were checking for unlocked doors, looking for holes in fences or walls short enough to scale and climb over. When they finally located a metal overhead garage door that was unsecured, Mack lifted it open just enough for the two to crawl inside. From here they were able to gain access to the loading dock area where food, beer, and game day souvenir vendors receive their deliveries.

"Okay, buddy, you wait here. I'll be right back."

Duy was so out of it that he didn't say a word. Mack crawled back out of the overhead door and ambled back towards the ER driveway. He was just in time to see a tow truck burning off from the location. The driver had probably been summoned there by the hospital staff then fled with his life when he saw the maggot farmers beside Mack's vehicle.

Roscoe was still inside the truck, his nose pressed to the glass as he looked out. Roscoe spotted his new partner, Mack, about seventy-five feet away. Roscoe's tail wagged and he began to whine as Mack made eye contact with the canine. Mack yelled, "Roscoe - COME!"

The creatures heard Mack's voice and began to turn in his direction. Roscoe leapt up through the pickup's moon roof and landed on the vehicle roof. The clatter of his nails on the metal lid regained the attention of the *dead* pack, and they retrained their gaze on the dog.

Roscoe took two running strides on the car top. He launched his body well over the heads and outstretched arms and hands of the beasts. His puppy pads landed safely on the asphalt street ten feet beyond the threats. Mack yelled, "Good boy!" followed by "RUNNN!!"

They made their way back through the Fenway Park overhead door to reunite with their sickly friend. Together they all made their way down through the various sections and rows upon rows of seats. It was hard not to take in the splendors and sights of this grand old relic. The left field wall, better known as the Green Monster, the one lucky red seat in a sea of green stadium chairs, and the Pesky Pole. Each of these icons had its own unique chronicle.

The muscular African American cop and the gimpy sick Duy made their way onto the natural grass playing field. Then they strolled over toward centerfield and the original non-electric, non-digital, *only* manually operated scoreboard that still existed in the major leagues.

They opened the door beside the scoreboard and entered the narrow structure behind it's face. Autographs from players and umpires, stars and starlets who were fortunate enough to visit there over the decades. Their names jumped off the interior walls, book marking their place in history.

"Mack, look! Bruce Lee was here!" Duy said.

Mack was about to admire the black permanent marker signature when the door that lead behind the scoreboard flew open without the assistance of an air current.

"That says Bill Lee, you idiots" came the voice of a stranger who was now pointing an improvised weapon at them.

It was a Caucasian male of about twenty-three years old. He was unshaven, with brown shoulder length curly hair and was attired in a Who rock band T-shirt and brown corduroy pants.

He also had a homemade white PVC pipe bow in his left hand. With his right hand, he was gently restricting the flight of a tin-tipped arrow.

"Who the hell are you dudes and how did you get here? You're trespassing in our house!" the stranger bellowed.

"Oh, so you *own* Fenway Park?" Mack asked. Roscoe was by Mack's side, and he began to eyeball the stranger and growl fiercely. "Easy boy, not yet," Mack said.

The voice of a twenty-year-old female emerged from behind the male and was also directed at the newcomers. "Well, we were here first and settled down here, so that's all that matters to you. We worked too hard to make this place our home and, we thought, safe from intruders. So, we are not going to just let some strangers come in and steal our place!"

"Look, we're just looking for a temporary place to seek shelter," Mack said. "My buddy Duy here is very sick, and, believe it or not, we just got turned away and threatened at gunpoint back there by the ER staff. If we don't find a dry, warm place to crash tonight, he might not make it."

The male party posed the question: "Has he been bit? "

"No."

"How do we know you're telling us the truth?"

"He's got pneumonia or Lyme disease or something like that - but he's not bit. You can check him."

Mack and Duy offered forward their wallets to show the young couple their Texas driver's licenses, and Mack presented his Dallas PD badge and credentials as well. Mack told the abbreviated version of the story about Jake and how they were hoping to find him, if he was still alive. If that were the case, they were prepared to tell him that they now had the evidence to get his murder conviction overturned, that he could be a free man again.

The female was curious. "Why don't you just call him and tell him it's safe to come back? And doesn't he ever call you to find out what's up?"

Mack said "he doesn't have his cell phone anymore, it's in the property room at the county jail. Besides, even if he had it, it would be so easy for someone to track it or trace it to him. And I'm guessing he doesn't call me from some payphone or something because he probably assumes that my line is being traced too. And it probably is. Those feds are pretty sneaky like that."

Now somewhat satisfied with the stories these two trespassers had told, the youthful male and female lowered their weapons. The male said "well, that guy (pointing to Duy) does look sick for real. He's about as green as that wall out in left field. You guys can stay one night, and you are out of here by 9 a.m."

And just as quickly as the hosts had raised their weapons a few minutes ago, they now lowered their guard as they began to exit the scoreboard. The young male chimed, "join us by the fire for some s'mores later if you like" as the couple walked back toward the infield. "Cool dog, by the way. What's his name?"

"Oh, that's Roscoe," Mack responded as he and Duy looked at each other. They were somewhat caught off guard by the invite to partake in the eating of s'mores at a time when one of them might be dying and they had just been chased by zombies. Yet, they fell in behind and followed silently.

The group all sat down around an open fire pit positioned at what was once the pitcher's mound. Burning baseball bats and large rectangular cloth banners which had been gathered from throughout the park burned ferociously inside a sawed-off metal barrel. Duy rubbed his hands together over the brilliant flames and soaked up the warmth his body so badly craved.

"So, I guess since we know who you guys are, we should introduce ourselves as well. My name is Graham. I don't know why I feel obligated to tell a couple of strangers my latest revelations. I usually save such stories for the fans of our YouTube video clips, but for some reason it seems important that you guys know our story too."

The internet hero pointed at his female companion. "That's my friend Nunu. She's from upstate New York. I am originally from Maryland. We are – were – students at Yale."

Graham's friend Nunu overheard the conversation and said "hi," although somewhat tenacious about joining Graham and the newcomers in their introductions and conversation. She was outfitted in a grey tank top, blue jean shorts, a plaid flannel shirt tied around her waist and Chelsea boots.

Duy inquired, "Not to be rude, but what kind of name is Nunu?"

"It's a nickname my dad gave me back when I was a little bitty thing. I have no idea what it means, but it seems to suit me just fine. Especially when some asshole asks my name and I don't want to put my real identity out there."

Mack was curious to hear the rest of the youngsters' story.

"So, what do you mean you *were* students at Yale?"

Nunu felt uncomfortable talking to these newbies about her life, yet she too was also oddly compelled to do so. Maybe it was because these dudes seemed to be showing interest in them as If they really cared, and not because it was currently "trending."

"Well, I was a journalism major, and he was studying political science. Graham was just a couple of semesters away from graduating. Everything was going great, until one mid-afternoon day about three weeks ago."

Nunu teared up as she recanted the horror that had unfolded nearly a month earlier. As she spoke, she removed a large backpack from her shoulders and unzipped the top compartment. Two brown furry rodents scampered their way out of the pack and scurried onto Nunu's lap, as if on command.

"Whoaaa...what the hell are those?" Mack examined as he leaned backwards, away from the rodents.

"Degus, "Nunu explained.

"Beansies and Diego, to be more precise. These are my babies."

She lovingly stroked the little furballs as she removed chinchilla food from another pocket to feed them.

Nunu continued. "So, we were sitting in New Haven Green, a park of over sixteen acres that lies at the edge of the campus and bordering the downtown district. Just a little history on 'The Green': It was once used as the main burial grounds for New Haven residents during its first 150 years. But by 1821, the practice was abolished and many of the headstones were moved to the Grove Street Cemetery. However, the remains of the dead were not moved and remain below the soil of the green today.

"Anyways, I was enjoying lunch - feeding curly fries to a friendly park squirrel with a jacked-up tail. It would eat right out of your hand. Hundreds of students were in the park either reading, sunbathing, or eating. I noticed one group of students playing Frisbee, and one kid chased the saucer into the tree line and didn't reemerge for several minutes. The second kid then went into the woods looking for his buddy, started screaming, and ran out of there. But he was followed by a creature!

"The second kid tripped and fell on the Green. A swift moving zombie landed on top of the student and began biting him on his shoulders and neck area. At first, the students were all awestruck by the scene unfolding. But many soon began to believe they were watching a joke or act by the performing arts students.

"Two more zombies exited the woods and attacked a sunbathing female. She had fallen asleep on the grass. And they bit another kid with headphones on, sitting in a cloth folding chair. But everyone still thought this was an act. That is, until old Professor

Willoughby, who was eating his apple in his suit and handlebar moustache, got tackled by a zombie. The professor's toupee went flying off his head and at that point this became very real.

Everyone who knows Willoughby realizes he would not let himself become part of a prank or a monster movie scene. Especially not if it meant revealing that he was as bald as a newborn baby's butt.

"Then the masses begin fleeing, running for their lives. They were dropping their lunches and leaving behind their schoolbooks and laptops. More zombies poured out of the woods and onto the green.

"The campus quickly became overrun with those *things*. The administrators had to shut the school down until the creatures could all be destroyed, and the campus was cleared out. But now they need to enclose and secure the entire campus before classes can resume. It could be quite a long wait."

Nunu set an exercise wheel and ball down for her pets to play with. Beansies and Diego both tried to enter the wheel together at the same time. It wasn't long before one became territorial, growling at the other. A fight was about to ensue.

"Stop it!" Nunu yelled, wiping tears away from her face. She paused to catch her breath.

Graham sensed that Nunu was upset. It wasn't so much with the rodent situation but more with overall life in general. He took over the conversation.

"We got evacuated along with everyone else. We decided to film the mass exodus, and I got attacked. Nunu started rolling the video and I barely thwarted off a couple of those *things*. We put it out on YouTube, and before long it went viral."

Mack looked confused by the viral comment. "That many people are watching that stuff on the internet?"

"Are you serious?" Nunu said. "Where else can they go to see honest reporting? Have you seen the local or national news lately? It's terrible, it's all lies - propaganda."

"All they show is what the government wants us to see. They completely run the media and the networks now. People don't trust the major networks' and media anymore, and for good reason. The news reporting outlets as we used to know them are going by the wayside, as did the newspaper not long ago.

"People who know us, they trust us. Because we are real. And every day more people are liking us and watching us and saying they can't wait for our next weekly videos."

The quadrumvirate began to settle down for the night in the dugout, when Graham said, "you guys are pretty cool. Even you, Mack. I've never known any cops before personally, but you seem like a good honest dude. Kind of like a normal guy."

"Thanks, man. You know, I just try to be a good person, just like y'all do. We all do things to help people when we can and to stop those who are trying to hurt or take advantage of others. I'd say that most of the cops I work with are the same way. But occasionally you do come across a cop who is all rogue, thinking they are above the law and can do whatever they want to without penalty.

"I had this one trainer in phase one of the Field Training Program. He was that way. His name was Senior Corporal Travis Ward. He was an older white guy with about 25 years on. Dude made me nervous. He would do things unlike any of my other trainers. If we arrested someone who was talking shit, he would occasionally get an extra shot in on the guy. After we got him cuffed up, of course."

"Sometimes I think he did stuff just to test me, to see if I would question him or even challenge him. I did once or twice, but it didn't go over very well."

Mack continued. "One time I bought a new compact Glock pistol to carry as my backup and off-duty weapon. I told Ward about it, and he told me to bring it to work one evening so he could check it out. So, one night as I was getting ready for work, I threw it in my duty bag and took it to work with me.

"When the shift started, I told Ward I had brought the Glock for him to look at. About halfway through the shift, when the call load had slowed down, Travis said, 'drive down to the river bottoms, let's see how your new piece shoots!'

"So, I did what I was told. I drove to the dried-up river bottom, and we parked below the Commerce Street overpass. My FTO told me to gather up some cans or some other shit we could blast to smithereens- so we could see how well the little Glock shoots.

"'Yeah, right', I said. I still really thought he was joking. It was illegal to shoot guns in the city limits. Never mind the fact that there were homeless people camping out underneath these bridges. A stray bullet could end up hitting someone or something. It was unsafe, unprofessional. Nonetheless, Ward said, 'come on, we're cops. We shoot guns. That's what we do. Who's gonna tell us we can't?'"

"So, did you shoot the gun down there?" Nunu quizzed.

"Yes. I was afraid if I didn't, they would make me fail Field Training or I would get the reputation of being a snitch."

All parties grew tired and decided it would be best to crash for the night. Mack asked, "where would be the best place for us to get some rest for the night?"

"We like to sleep here in the dugouts where we have a roof above our heads, but still a couple different escape routes. You know, in case the Dead or other enemies make their way onto the field." Graham followed up with a question he had been perplexed about regarding their earlier encounter. "So why did you tell the dog not to attack us when you had the chance earlier?"

"Let's just say I had a gut feeling that it wasn't necessary" was the lawman's response.

"Okay. Cool."

Midnight's full moon light filled the grand old ballpark, shining into the home team dugout and upon those sleeping within the shelter.

Duy was awakened by the bright light and assumed that someone had turned the infield lights on. He sensed motion to his right and figured that it was just Roscoe walking around in circles and trying to get comfortable. Suddenly a tug on his sleeve followed by a moaning sound got Duy's attention. He swiveled around to see a child-sized flesh muncher chomping onto his shirt. IT was attempting to snack on an adult-sized wing.

"AAAAAAAHHHHHHHHH!!!!! The Asian sensation began to scream and scramble for the dugout stairs. He tripped on the top step and rolled his ankle in the process. "Owwwwwww!!!!"

Mack was awakened by Duy's agonizing yell and he grabbed the wooden Louisville Slugger major league bat he had set beside him before falling asleep. There was no hesitation as he swung the wooden sphere in axe-like overhead fashion. He smashed the zombie kid's melon like a candy-stuffed birthday pinata.

"What the hell!? I thought it was supposed to be safe here!" Mack bellowed.

"For the most part it is. We have Constantine wire all along the top of the walls, but occasionally one will climb up and make it through. They are usually pretty shredded, but it's not like they care about being torn up. They still keep coming."

Graham led the group, searching the park for the place that the creature had gained access. They came across a flattened section of wire above the ten-foot-high brick wall behind the home plate gate. "Dammit, we need to fix that before any more get through."

Duy now was extremely sick *and* badly wounded.

Nunu and Graham told Mack that they had a friend nearby who could help Duy.

"Her name is Janice. She's known for helping those who require medical attention and need shelter. We can take you there now."

The foursome plus dog squeezed into Graham's micro red Toyota Yaris and exited the park through an underground overhead door. This driveway fed out into a little-traveled back alley. They scooted around the corner and up five blocks to a slightly charred red brick building.

"Janice is a wonderful doctor. At one time she had a thriving family practice at this clinic. It nearly burned to the ground months ago when the creatures attacked a nearby apartment complex. Amid the mayhem that ensued, electric poles toppled over and lines were downed. That caused a fire which devoured several city blocks," Nunu explained.

"But she is still here. Now she's running a safe house for those who have no other place to turn. She provides medical assistance and shelter. She even has a fenced-in outdoor area filled with raised bed box gardens."

The Yaris pulled onto the courtyard which was once part of the Haymarket. The Haymarket was Boston's centuries-old open-air market in the historic heart of the city. It was mere steps away from Faneuil Hall Marketplace and the elegant Millennium Bostonian Hotel.

"We are here. You guys go in and tell her that we brought

you over. She will take good care of you. We need to go back and secure our fence. So, if we never see you all again, we wish you the best of luck."

Hours later, Duy awoke. He found himself lying on his back on a cot and surrounded by pots and old soda bottle racks full of small vegetable plants. Among them were tomatoes, bell peppers, cucumbers, and green bean plants.

Duy had no idea where he was at the present time and had no recollection of how he had gotten there.

A familiar sight emerged as Mack approached from the courtyard area. "I thought I heard you waking up. How are you feeling, man? Hey look, I got you something on the way out of the park."

"Umm, what park?"

"Haaa, funny, dude." Mack handed Duy a green ball cap with the Red Sox traditional yet classic capital 'B' on the front. "It was just lying in one of the rows of seats."

"Oh, the Red Sox - Fenway Park. Okay I'm starting to remember now." Duy said. But I thought the Red Sox wore red and blue. Why is the hat green?"

Mack philosophized, "Well, I know they would wear green during St Patrick's Day games, but it may also be symbolic of the 'Green Monster.' You know, the nickname given to the left field wall decades earlier."

Duy stammered: "That's marketing genius right there, selling memorabilia relative to a wall in a ballpark. Who else would think of that?"

"No one else would. Because no one else has Fenway Park." Mack responded.

"So true" replied the Dew-man.

Over the next few days, thanks to some much-needed rest and the natural medicinal herbs, vitamins, and ointments that Janice provided, Tran began to feel stronger and healthier.

Although this down time was not anticipated at the beginning of their adventure, Duy and Mack did make the most of their stay. They made new acquaintances by spending time with some of the interesting people that called Janice's Lansdowne House their home.

One of the full-time residents of this place was a ten-year-old Puerto Rican/ African American kid named Carlos.

A couple of years ago, Carlos and his family were living in a makeshift house made of pallets and plywood below a nearby Interstate 90 overpass. They were attacked by a pack of the Dead. Carlos 'mother, father, and sister were killed. Carlos managed to escape. But he sustained a deep bite to his left arm.

In what could only be perceived as a medical miracle, Carlos merely needed stitches for the wound. In a rarity, he proved to be immune to the virus that infected so many others.

"I call him Bandit," Janice said. She spoke fondly of the boy, recalling for Mack and Duy the way in which the two met.

"One day he found a way to sneak into my garden courtyard from the outside. He was stealing a tomato from one of my plants in a garden box. I caught him in the act, confronted him. He didn't try to run for it. He just apologized and said that his family was hungry. So, I told him he could keep the tomato and return every day for one or two more. So, he did. And eventually he felt comfortable enough to tell me that he really had no family and was out on his own. I invited him to stay with us, and he has been here ever since.

"He's such a good little kid. He loves to read and loves to be told stories. There's one little tale I made up for him one night at bedtime, he asks me to repeat for him again and again.

Janice went on. "The story goes something like this:

"Once upon a time there was a little boy named Carlos. He liked to play stickball in the streets with other kids and eat hot dogs with catsup and mustard on them. Carlos was a happy boy who always wore a smile, even though the world he lived in was full of darkness. A world much like a black and grey watercolor painting.

"There was no light, no color. And this cold, dark world was full of scary monsters. Monsters that smelled horrible and did terrible things to the good people who lived in this place. All the good people lived in fear. They stayed locked up in their houses and never came out to talk to their friends and neighbors.

"This little boy ate a lot of vegetables and played a lot. But he also did his share of work too. He realized that there was time for play but only after all the chores were done. He also found time to pray to God to thank him for the roof over his head and the tomatoes in his belly. He was also thankful for the good friends that he had now, and for the wonderful people that were in his life before. Also, those that have moved on up to heaven to be with God. And Carlos asked God to say hi to his mother, father, and sister who were by God's side now.

"Carlos grew up to be stout and strong and courageous. He knew that he was faster and smarter than the monsters, and they could not hurt him. He did not live in fear of the creatures like everyone else did. One day he was walking down the street and found an old gnarly looking paint brush lying beside the curb. The flagged end of the brushes' bristles was all bent out of shape and the handle had dark green paint dried onto it.

"Carlos picked up this old brush and suddenly realized this wasn't a normal paint brush. It warmed his hand, and the longer he held it, the bristles began to appear cleaner and back to their original form. The dried paint on the handle disappeared as well.

"Carlos knew he did not have any paint. But that did not stop him from running that brush up and down the strip, stroking its bristles across everything he saw and dreaming up brilliant colors for each object. Carlos noticed that everything he had brushed changed to whatever color he imagined it should be. He was ecstatic! Carlos began to paint everything in sight, adding brilliant bright colors to the whole city.

"People saw the bright lights and colors illuminating outside. They opened their curtains and blinds on their windows for the first time in years. They came outside to see what was happening. They introduced themselves to their neighbors and struck up conversations about this radiant new neighborhood.

"The monsters were blinded by all of these bright colors and lights. They could not find sunglasses that would stay on their ugly faces, so they all left to find a new home. They went to places where they could roam around in the dark and chase people and strike fear in their hearts.

"Carlos was an instant hero, and the town people carried him through the streets on their shoulders. They paraded him around for all to see and thank him. The end."

Carlos had stealthily walked up upon Janice when he heard his favorite fable being told. "I love that one," he said, glowing as he spoke.

"You know what the best part of it is?" Janice quizzed the boy.

"No, what?" "It can all be true someday. It's totally up to you."

Chapter 25 - Massholes

Boston, Massachusetts

Another inhabitant of the Lansdowne House was a twenty-two-year-old, heavily tattooed white male dwarf. He had shoulder-length jet black hair and gauges in his earlobes. Anthony grew up in nearby Amesbury and managed a tattoo shop, where he also worked as a tattoo artist and body piercer. In his spare time, he often practiced on himself, and thus he was covered with ink.

Anthony's Body Arts shop closed shortly after that entire area was overrun by the Dead. When everyone fled town, so did Anthony's clientele and livelihood. Anthony did not flee. Rather he continued to live in the vacant tattoo shop and building, climbing through the boarded-up windows to pass in and out when he needed to go on supply runs.

One day he had to leave the building to find some food. He found himself surrounded by a herd of the disgruntled decaying who mistook Anthony for a "fun size" human treat.

Janice and Bandit happened to be in the area. They too were scavenging around for supplies. They heard the short-statured one yelling and cursing at the creatures. He was stabbing them in their heads with the flat head screwdrivers he held, one in each hand. He had already finished off a couple of them but was tiring quickly.

Janice and Bandit were quick to act. They provided a distraction to the demented, buying Anthony the time to backtrack away from the stampede.

The Lansdowne leader asked the misplaced man if he needed a place to stay. He accepted the invitation, and they led him back to Janice's place for food and shelter.

Anthony is like family there now, volunteering his time to be their security/door man. He has since upgraded his weaponry. He ditched those old screwdrivers for a battery-charged power drill and nail gun. He found these power tools abandoned in one of the nearby shops. The owner used these in boarding up the place when the town was overrun.

Anthony is also now an avid lifter of the free weights. He has been working out with dumbbells and kettlebells since his close call with the monsters. Anthony was eager to have his lack of height overcompensated by his muscular physique.

Thanks to Janice, Duy was beginning to feel more himself. And, being the social butterfly that he was, figured he would strike up a conversation with the vertically challenged one. "Hey, Tony, I dig your tattoos, man."

Janice was several feet away but heard Duy's statement. She began to look at Duy and shook her head "no" as if he had done something unacceptable.

"What did you just call me?" Anthony asked. Unbeknownst to the Dew-man, Anthony absolutely despised being called 'Tony' because it sounded way too much like "Tiny."

"I called you Tony. Do you not like that?" Duy and Mack looked at each other, each quite befuddled as to why the little guy seemed irritated suddenly.

"Oh, are we supposed to be all buddies now because Janice let you stay here for a couple of days?" Anthony barked. "Listen *friend,* you don't mean jack shit to me. Not you, not that big cop, not that stinky dog. You guys are nothing to me."

"Hey man, I'm really sorry. I meant no disrespect."

"Haaa. Man lighten up. I'm just fuckin with you guys."

The ice now broken, Anthony and the guests began to trade stories. The Lansdowne doorman felt comfortable enough to discuss some of the hardships he has faced throughout life as a dwarf in a land of bigger people.

"I was always being made fun of as a kid. So as soon as I was old enough, I got some tattoos to serve as a distraction from my size. So now people ask about my ink rather than asking me stupid shit like, 'What's it like being that size?'"

"I mean, so what if I am only four foot ten. So what. I'm still a man. I'm not that different from everyone else. I even had a girlfriend once who was five-nine. I was crazy about her, but we had to end it."

"What happened?" Mack asked.

"Man, did you ever see a Chihuahua trying to hump a Great Dane? It just doesn't work too well.

"So, when we split up, I was bored and lonely. I decided to make a career out of the circus. When I started, they had me walking behind the elephants with a broom and dustpan to clean up the large piles of crap they left everywhere.

"Eventually they started to let me perform in an act where I was all done up like a clown. I would stand on a pony's backside as it ran around in circles in one of the three rings under the big top" Anthony said.

"Then one day they asked me to become a trapeze artist, swinging back and forth on a thick rope swing about fifty feet above the crowd. I had a Russian female partner who was of normal size and sexy as fuck. We both wore sequin-covered jumpsuits which sparkled under the bright lights of the big top. I had a wicked crush on her, but I never told her because of that whole Chihuahua and Great Dane situation.

"But one day I was swinging high above the crowd during a show and heard screams from down below. I looked down to see what appeared to be hysteria, screaming audience members running for the exits in masses. Zombies had found their way into the circus tent and were feasting on crowd members. One of the creatures had a pink puffy poodle in his mouth and was snacking on his appetizer as he was making his way over to a crowd fighting for the exits.

"I swung down and landed on the back of the pony that I used to stand upon in the old act. I rode that young horse out of the tent, staying just ahead of them and luring away the hideous monsters. The audience and other circus members then were able to flee to safety."

Duy was impressed. "Damn, man, that's crazy. You're a real hero. "

"Yeah …. umm, no. I made all that shit up about the circus. You see that? Most people think the only job or life a little person can be successful at is in the circus or some sort of freak show.

"Do you not know that little people can lead normal lives in society? We work bullshit 8-to-5 jobs too, you know. We pay bills and taxes, beaten down by THE MAN daily, just like you. But you guys probably wouldn't know about all that, would you?"

Anthony apologized and continued. "Anyways, ever since I started to get tats at eighteen, I had this dream to one day own my own tattoo place. Wanted to make a name for myself as a tattoo artist. My dream was finally realized, and then these sons of bitches' zombies destroyed them all. Along with just about everyone else's, I suppose."

Undoubtedly, there wasn't a single human being alive in the contaminated areas of the United States whose life wasn't going to be affected by this ruinous outbreak, if they hadn't already.

But like many other noxious plights that occur throughout different parts of the world, regularly there are some people somewhere who find themselves in situations that will ultimately make or break them. Those who can adapt and overcome will survive and the others fall along the wayside.

The people of Lansdowne House learned from the start that they were in this deep doo-doo together. They all had grown to depend upon each other and help each other survive this wicked plight. As a result of this teamwork, some great friendships were born, and alliances created. One such bond, for instance, was the one formed between Anthony and Bandit.

Although they were ten years apart in age, these two were nearly inseparable. Perhaps they felt some type of brother-like affinity, or possibly it was merely because they were about the same height. Nonetheless, they enjoyed going on supply runs together, avoiding the Dead and crawling through smashed fences and doors and unlocked windows to get into abandoned residences and/or businesses in search of food and other essential goods.

However, each of them displayed their own unique individual style in their choice of apparel and weaponry. Bandit was fond of his black cowboy hat and dual leather cowboy holsters which strapped a pair of .22-caliber Smith & Wesson revolvers (Anthony found these at a pawn shop a few months back and taught Bandit how to shoot and exercise gun safety).

Anthony looked more like an angry heavy metal construction worker type of guy in his Dickie shorts and his light blue work shirt with customized 'Anthony' patch sewn on the right breast. The sleeves had been cut off in Belichikian fashion to reveal his full-sleeve tattooed arms. His weapons of choice were the battery-charged drill with a zombie skull-piercing drill bit attached and his favorite Makita nail gun.

"Southie", Boston Mass

Meanwhile, on the other side of town where the "Dirty Water" could be found, Jake (now using the alias "Sal Armano") was wearing his regular work attire of black or grey Ermenegildo Zegna and other high-dollar suits. He has been working as a bodyguard/driver for his old friend Vinny DeAngelo. For the last couple of weeks, this new lifestyle had gone smoothly and seemingly without anyone having recognized him. That had not even been suspicious of him. At least not to his knowledge.

Everything seemed to be going swimmingly in this partnership between Jake and Vinny. Jake's identity was being protected and at the same time, he was protecting Vinny's ass from his living enemies as well as from the DEAD. Jake would clear those THINGS out of his path, allowing Vinny to be able to continue his family practice without the threat of being gnawed on by the flesh mongers.

But one day, just as Jake was beginning to feel comfortable in his new role, a new wise guy rolled into town. His name was Frederick Szharko. He was a short and petite runt of a cocky fuck with a blonde buzz cut on top of his head. Szharko had what some people call the little man syndrome, always trying to talk and act big to make up for his other shortcomings. Perhaps this was the reason Frederick demanded that everyone call him "the Shark." A big tough name for a little sawed-off jerk.

This guy had been doing business for the DeAngelo family in Hartford for several years. But now he had been promoted to the Boston job to partner up with Vinny. And this meant that he would be also dealing with 'Sal' on a regular basis.

Shark never messed bothered 'Sal' when Vinny was around to keep the Shark preoccupied. But the day finally came when Shark showed up and Vinny was nowhere to be found.

Bright and early one Friday Massachusetts morning,

Frederick Szharko made his way onto Vinny's fishing schooner and found Jake reading the Globe. "Hey douchebag," Szharko instigated, "let's go for a drive. I need your help with a job."

"Sorry, man, I don't work for you. I work for Vinny. I need to stick around here. If he shows up needing his driver, he'll be really pissed off if I'm not around."

"He'll be even more hacked off if I tell him that I think you're a filthy pig ass cop," Shark threatened.

"Shut the fuck up, Shark. He knows for damn sure that I ain't no cop" Jake said.

"Yeah? We'll see. Now let's go for a ride. You're driving…." Shark dictated.

Jake and the Shark headed out in the Shark's black Escalade with Connecticut plates.

"Jump on the 95 until I tell you to exit. We gotta go pay our competition a visit and explain the rules of interstate commerce."

About thirty minutes later, the black Cadillac SUV pulled onto the long Foxborough, Massachusetts, driveway of a rival family member, Mr. Giovanni Portelli. Portelli was an overweight, balding 55-year-old Italian man known for his love of Hawaiian shirts and all things golf related.

Jake parked in front of the massive two-story raised ranch. Jake and Shark exited the car to instantly hear a golf club meeting ball. The sound was coming from the driving range behind the house.

Jake and the Shark walked around the house and toward the driving range. They caught Giovanni off guard, to say the least. As soon as "Gio" saw the two rivals approaching, he turned toward his golf cart and attempted to reach for something below the seat.

"No, you don't, Portelli," Shark said as he lunged at Gio and pushed him away from the golf cart. "Sal, go look and see what our friend here was reaching for on that cart."

Sal (Jake) located a Sig Sauer .45 on the floorboard of the golf cart, holding it up to show Shark. "I bet he was looking for this beauty."

"Now Gio, that's not very nice of you." Shark said. "So, where's your boy Benny at? I never seen you out when he wasn't by your side to protect your plump ass."

"He's gonna be here any second. After that, you guys will be wishing you never came here."

"Actually," Shark responded, "I remember now. I ran into Benny down at the Dunk earlier this morning. He was getting his cup of black coffee and blueberry muffin breakfast, like he does every single morning. He said to tell you he's not gonna make it to work today. Actually, he's never coming back to work."

Giovanni began to struggle with the puny Shark. Shark was losing the struggle and pulled his 'piece' out of his waistband. He pointed the muzzle at Gio's head. "If you know what's good for ya, you'll quit fighting and take it like a man. You know you've had this coming for a while now. Vinny warned you weeks ago not to be operating on his turf."

"Now walk over here and sit down. Take a load off. Make yourself comfortable and put your back up against that tree."

Szharko said, "Sally-boy, watch him closely. I gotta get something outta the car."

Shark walked over to the Escalade and returned moments later with a large roll of silver duct tape. He placed Giovanni's arms behind Gio's body and had one on each side of the elm tree's trunk. Then he duct-taped Gio's wrists together so that Gio couldn't pull away from the tree.

Shark had another item with him as well. He held up a fifteen-pound bag of off-brand ant granules and said, "look what I found in the backyard. Looks like you got a problem with little pests just like we do. Maybe we can help each other get rid of some pests today."

Shark pulled a switchblade knife out of his left sock and extended the blade. He began to slice open the top of the ant granule bag. He then lifted the bag and began to pour ant granules all over Portelli's beet red, sweat covered face.

"Why don't you open your mouth, you fucking piece of shit. I'm trying to feed you, you fat fuck. You know what, that's fine. Keep your fuckin' pie hole shut."

The scrawny, buzz-cut Szharko took the now-half empty bag of ant poison and placed it over Giovanni's head. Then Shark told 'Sal' to hold the bag in place as Shark duct taped the bag opening tightly around Gio's neck.

Shark took a step back to admire his work as Gio, with his head now inside the insect poison bag, began to gasp. Needing air, he involuntarily opened his mouth. And the more he struggled and squirmed to try and free himself from the duct tape, more ant granules poured down into his mouth.

"You watching this, 'Sal'?" Shark was amused by his own actions. "Sometimes it's more fun to snuff a guy out using random shit you got available to you rather than just blowing a guy's brains out with a pistol in the mouth. You gotta mix it up, be fuckin' creative."

Gio continued sucking the small trace of O2 remaining inside the bag. But in the process his lungs were being filled with the poison granules. 'Sal' and Shark watched on as Portelli continued to struggle, his back against the tree and his wrists still bound. He was just minutes away from imminent suffocation.

Jake's mind was racing. He was filled with thoughts and reflections on discussions many years earlier in the police academy about ethical dilemmas and challenges police officers would encounter. But this situation was far above and beyond the level of those talks about whether it was right to accept free cups of coffee at the 7-11.

This Gio guy was a very bad man. He was responsible for countless crimes against small business owners, financial institutions, the poor and the oppressed. Anyone this guy and his family could take advantage of to benefit themselves in any way, became a victim. And many who further tried to stand up to him or stop him found themselves taking a long walk on a short pier.

There were undoubtedly several law enforcement agencies and agents tracking and investigating this man. They had every intention of developing or uncovering any piece of evidence that could contribute to a meaningful prosecution and incarceration of this individual. And here he was, at Jake's disposal. With no one other than Shark around to witness or judge what Jake did with him.

Jake had changed over the years. He was not the naïve rookie cop he once was. Nor was he that eighteen-year-old kid with no real-life experience to speak of as he entered the Marine Corps, wet behind the ears.

As a child, Jake had been reared by his parents with the understanding that there was a "right" and "wrong." He also understood that sometimes there is a fine line between the two. At times the line is blurry, making it that much more difficult to distinguish exactly where in the sand that line should be drawn.

And although he was feeling less like a law enforcement officer as each day passed, he still had that guardian mindset instilled within him. The "Protect and Serve" mentality of a cop. But even more importantly, he was still a god-fearing Christian and believer in the Fifth Commandment "Thou shalt not kill."

Jake was also not an animal. He was a human being. For the most part.

His decision made now and with unknown consequences pending, Jake jogged toward the elm-strapped Giovanni Portelli.

"This is bullshit, Shark. It's too fuckin easy to do him this way," 'Sal' yelled. This asshole doesn't deserve to go out this easy, without any body damage or bloodshed. And he needs more time to think about us coming back for him later. Coming back to mess him up so bad that his family won't be able to show him off in an open casket."

Jake removed his cutlery from beneath his coat. He severed the duct tape binds that had attached the rival gangster to the large tree beside the driving range. Gio used his now-freed hands to rip the tape off his wrists and then pull the poison bag off his head.

Jake kicked Giovanni square in the back, saying, "here, let me help you spit that shit out, bitch." Gio began coughing up ant pesticide granules through his mouth and nostrils.

Turning away from the freed mobster, 'Sal' resumed his strut toward the waiting Escalade while Shark targeted him with a long-frustrated stare. "Why'd you do that, you pussy?"

"Because that's not how a real man takes care of business. So, fuck you, Frederick."

Szharko drove the Escalade back to the city, while Jake rode shotgun for the thirty-minute return trip to the harborside. The trip seemed never-ending to Jake, who had more than enough Shark for one day.

It was early evening when they arrived back at Vinny's schooner. They soon discovered that the patriarch still had not returned from whatever business had kept him away all day.

"Looks like your daddy's not home, Sally. You're lucky, because I was about to give him an earful about what happened today. Letting Portelli get away like you did. Tells me you're either a cop or a pussy - I'm not sure which. Either way, you're not to be trusted. Vinny's not gonna like this one bit. And neither are the other fellas."

Shark shooed 'Sal' out of his car. "All right. Run along, bitch. Enjoy your last night here. I 'm gonna go get my dick sucked."

"Oh, nice. Dinner with mom?" Jake quipped, unable to resist swinging at the slow-pitch softball that had just been lobbed at him.

Jake climbed back aboard the makeshift fishing vessel, and he began to relish the fact that he was alone again. It was times like these that "Sal" could be Jake again.

Although, as time went by, he was feeling less like Jake and more like someone he really didn't know or recognize.

It had been nearly six years since United States Marine Captain Jake Hathaway began the first of many doses of the experimental Zeus Juice. Originally, he took the serum under the premise that he and his soldiers could be the best they could be, making them the ultimate military combat personnel. They were bearing super-human strength, able to endure pain like none other, tireless and full of energy 24-7.

It wasn't long afterwards that the Corps captain was doubling down on the doses, as different priorities began to emerge in his thought processes. For the longer that chemical was raging inside his body, the more he found himself feeling the need to seek POWER.
This longing for power has been inbred in biological organisms dating back to their origins of life on Earth. And this was exactly what the drug had been designed to create; the intensification of that desire - a hunger and need to be the most powerful being in the universe.

That coupled with a body that had morphed into one able to sustain and endure trauma, while dishing out much of the same to lesser beings.

The unfortunate side effect of the Zeus Juice was the way blood cells and tissues were dying. This caused certain brain and bodily functions to be diminished at varying rates.

As with any drug, every person's body reacts differently to them. Some fail to react at all. But the way Jake had been feeling lately, he was quite certain that his body was reacting more rapidly than when he first began to take the serum.

Jake found his physical body to be stronger than ever, without having been exercising or weight training. He also found himself struggling more with cerebral activities such as decision making and poor long-term memory. He had already completely forgotten about his high school sweetheart, the name of some of the guys who he hung out with in the Corps, and some of the officers at DPD with whom he shared camaraderie.

Jake Hathaway's soul was changing as well. He often found himself feeling alone, delusional, and expendable. He had been betrayed and blacklisted and left for dead by his beloved Corps and government who no longer had any use for him or his services. At times he felt like the one remaining human on this desolate, unfamiliar planet.

Several hours after the Shark dropped Jake off at Vinny 's ship, the Shark returned. He was alone, intoxicated and agitated. He stopped his Caddy alongside the docked fishing vessel and rolled down the windows. "Yo, Sally. You up there? Get the fuck out here! Now!!! Do you hear me?"

Jake walked up to the deck and looked over the side of the boat to see what the commotion was outside.

The obnoxious one below yelled up towards 'Sal', "Yeah, you heard me. Get your ass down here!"

Jake exited the vessel and met the sawed-off Shark by his car. "What's the fucking problem, Frederick?"

"You think you're so bold and clever calling me by my first name when you know I demand and deserve your respect. You can call me Shark like everyone else does, you pathetic go-fer. That's all you are good for - go get this for me, go get that for me. You're just Vinny's big bitch, his go-fer. Nothing more."

"And you're nothing but a little prick always running off your big mouth. How about I call you 'the Guppy' instead. That's more your speed."

Szharko became furious at this point, his voice now as unsteady and shaky as his balance. "We need to talk. Get in."

Jake hopped in the passenger seat of the Escalade, and the Shark began to drive. He headed toward the Prudential Center in the Back-Bay neighborhood just blocks from Fenway Park.

He parked the black Escalade in a large parking lot below a sign that read "Boston Duck Tours - 20 years of smiles." Sal asked, "What the hell are we doin' here?"

"I got some connections. I got us our own private boat so we can talk business without interruption."

The two adversaries walked up a plank to board one of the large WW2 amphibious style landing vehicles used for the tours. This one, painted jet black, was named "Longfellow Bridge" after the nearby Longfellow Bridge, which got its name from the poet Henry Wadsworth Longfellow.

Shark handed the driver a wad of large bills and whispered, "crank up the radio and don't turn your head around if you know what's good for ya." Shark and 'Sal' then walked to the very rear of the large boat-like bus and sat in the last row of seats. They were approximately twenty-five feet behind the driver.

The Duck Boat driver started to proceed along the tour's normal historic route. They passed the once-well-known landmarks that used to be known as the golden-domed State House, Bunker Hill, the TD Bank Garden, Boston Common, Copley Square, Newbury Street, and Quincy Market.

The large iron vehicle passed through an open chain link gate. The bus rolled slowly down a boat ramp into the dark and murky Charles River.

The vehicle was no longer operating like a bus. It was functioning as a watercraft. The river was calm and tranquil, and other than the driver, not another soul was in sight.

Shark was still obviously agitated and became more vocal with 'Sal'.

"Okay," Shark said. "I got you all the way out here in the middle of the river. If you don't come clean with me now, I'm gonna leave your ass in the river and I'm going back alone. Sal, tell me who the fuck you really are, or else you can start swimming."

Jake looked up toward the milky full moon. It was shining brilliantly down upon himself, Shark, and the great Sir Charles.

"You wanna know who I am?" Jake said. "Let me start by saying who *you* are. You are a piss ant little shit who lies in his bed, afraid to look in the closet or underneath the bed because you know there's a big bad monster watching you. He's just waiting for you to slip up and peek out from under the covers so he can chew your fucking pin head off. Well guess what? I'm that fucking monster. And you better get your needle dick back under that blanket before your fucking nightmare comes true."

The highly inebriated one, now blinded by fury, reached into his right black nylon sock to reveal a switchblade knife. Swinging the knife in his hand and allowing earth's gravitational pull to open the blade, the Shark used a quick underhand stabbing motion to stick the blade about two inches deep into Jake's rock solid lower left abdomen.

Shark let go of the edged weapon then took a step backwards, either because he was trying to admire his work or because he was in shock that the knife hadn't penetrated deeper and created more damage.

'Sal' grimaced, feeling very slight pain. Pain similar to having been punched in the point of impact. He looked down at the knife, then looked up at the Shark. And then 'Sal' smiled.

And Jake (Sal) said, "You know what, Frederick? I think maybe you should have stayed under the covers."

Jake pulled on the switchblade handle, extracting the steel from his gut. Then he waved the knife's razor-sharp edge across Shark's neck from left to right, as if swinging a magic wand to cast away the evil.

Shark's head fell back away from the base of his neck, which was now wide open.

The bloody Shark head was nearly decapitated. Jake grabbed the body and used his powerful tattoo covered arms to, with one clean jerk, hoist the blood oozing, lifeless jerk over his head.

Jake tossed the seeping carcass into the grand Charles River. It floated on top of the choppy waves for a while. Seaweed, plastic bottles and various forms of filth began to cover it. Some of this debris floated into the cavernous gap between the esophagus and chin.

Slowly the dead Shark descended into the watery grave and was out of sight.

"Driver. Turn this thing around, let's head back," Jake said.

The Duck Boat driver steered the now slightly lighter craft toward shore. The dark of night was now brightly illuminated and with the downtown Boston skyline behind him, Jake did not feel happy, anger, remorse, guilt nor regret. He felt NOTHING…

Chapter 26 - Dead Beat

Jake returned to the mother ship and slept like a baby that night, into the following morning.

Upon his waking, he welcomed the start of a fresh day. It would be the first of many days which held the spectacular promise of a Shark-less serenity.

As Jake was on deck basking in this new light, Vinny returned from his business trip. He was immediately suspicious that something out of the ordinary had occurred.

"Hey Ja - I mean Sal. Have you heard from or seen Shark lately? That son of a bitch won't answer my calls. Some of my Hartford people are telling me that he may be taking more than his cut on some of our services rendered."

"Yeah, Vinny. Last night he came around here all drunk and messed up. He said he needed to talk to me about some stuff. So, he drives us out towards the river, and we get on a Ducky boat, then he starts accusing me of this and that."

"And... How did that go? "Vinny questioned.

"Let's just say that when I was ready to leave, he felt more inclined to take a late-night swim. Who am I to tell him he can't?"

"Oh fuck, Jake...."

As the next few days went by, Jake resumed his role as Vinny's driver. Jake escorted the head of the DeAngelo family throughout Boston and further parts of New England in his shiny black Caddy with the limo tint glass.

Vinny's associates seemed to be nicer than usual to Jake. For that reason, Jake was extremely cautious about walking into any rooms with plastic tarps strewn across the floor.

"Vinny, why do I have the feeling one of these associates of yours is gonna step in behind me with piano string in their hands and try to tune me up?" Jake asked.

"Actually," Vinny replied. "Word got out on the street about you and Shark. This is their way of showing you respect. They all hated that squirrelly little cocky fuck Shark. It was just a matter of time until one of them did whack him. So, they are glad he 'went for a swim.'"

Now somewhat relieved and less concerned about getting ice-picked, Jake went on doing business as usual. However, the following week, the media began to pick up on the report of a possible homicide investigation. This investigation followed the discovery of a body wedged up in the propellers of a large ferry boat in the Charles River.

DeAngelo's sources also began to warn him that the local police and feds were in contact and working together. They were closing in on the wanted escapee fugitive from Texas, Jake Hathaway.

The authorities all believed that Hathaway was currently in the area, and they also recently learned that Hathaway had been friends with Vinny DeAngelo back in high school.

"I guess the jig is up," Jake said after Vinny gave him the news. "I guess it's time for me to fly."

Jake wasted no time grabbing his handful of personal effects and throwing them into his black Swiss Army backpack. "Come on, man, I'll give you a ride," Vinny said as the two jumped into the Escalade.

It was now early evening. As they drove down Landsdowne Street, the two compadres observed a white female standing on top of a small red Toyota Yaris stopped in the middle of the street. The female appeared to be in extreme fear and was screaming something at the top of her lungs.

Meanwhile, a white male, also apparently in his early 20s or so, was standing in the roadway in front of the car. It appeared as if the vehicle had broken down there and he was attempting to repair something under the popped hood.

Jake and Vinny remained in the stopped Escalade. They peered down the dark adjacent alley to see three shapes dragging slowly toward the curly headed brunette male.

The young male remained still, as if frozen in fear. And upon further review, when they emerged from the darkness of the alleyway and onto the lit roadway, the three staggering forms were not intoxicated winos - they were DEAD!!!

Jake opened the Escalade passenger door and prepared to exit. Vinny cautioned, "dude, what are you doing? It ain't worth it, man. We need to get you out of town before the cops show up and identify you."

Jake said, "they're just kids, Vinny. I can't stand by and watch them die. What if they were your kids?"

Vinny jumped out of the vehicle prepared to help with his Ruger .45 pistol in his right hand. He was ready to blow the DEAD away. Jake realized Vinny was right about not wanting to make a scene. He left his Beretta in his waistband when he realized that firing shots would be loud and draw much undesired attention.

Jake used both hands to reach into the inner pockets of his black leather full-length coat. Within a split-second, the hands reemerged. Each hand was now bearing a large-wooden handled steak knife with a ten-inch blade.

"I got this." Jake stated as he placed himself between the stragglers and their millennial prey. Jake efficiently began to carve up the DEAD, making mincemeat of the feet draggers. At one point he paused to catch his breath when the twenty-something guy angrily shouted, "what the fuck, man?!"

Jake looked at the kid, who was obviously pissed off about something. Then Jake glanced over at the twenty-something-year-old girl, who jumped down from the vehicle with a video camera in her hand. She was aiming it at Jake and Vinny and yelling sarcastically, "thanks for ruining our shot, jerkoffs. We gotta eat too, you know."

Jake was astonished that he was now catching heat from two kids he had just saved from creatures.

"We didn't need your help, old man. I was about to test my latest homemade weapon, this PVC pipe bow-and-arrow set, on those creatures for our YouTube series and our vlog."

"Are you serious? You both risked your lives for a lousy video?" Jake quizzed, stupefied.

The male responded, "You don't get it, dude. Do you know who I am?"

"You mean besides a dumbass?"

"Who are you calling a dumbass, you musclebound moron? You have no idea what's going on in this world today. I am Graham Pruitt, better known to our countless viewers as the 'Urban Survivor.' Every week we show a new video where I demonstrate new survival techniques or utilize another improvised weapon to live another day in this zombie-infected Armageddon. We are out here struggling to survive - and you just cost us some advertising money and a meal."

"Advertising? You mean people actually watch that stuff?" Jake queried.

"Ohhh, wait a minute. You're not planning on releasing that video, are you? Probably not since we ruined it for you, right?" Jake reasoned.

The female, otherwise known as Nunu, replied, "We can still work with it. Maybe edit it up and do some feature story on how *even old people* can defend themselves."

Jake chuckled maliciously, then held out his open hand and roared, "give me the fuckin' camera."

Nunu and Graham looked at each other and laughed. They darted into the Yaris as Nunu sped the compact car down the alley, squealing around garbage cans and narrowly avoiding dumpsters to escape before Sal and Vinny could even get reseated in the Escalade.

"Did that really happen?" Jake queried. Now fearful of the possibility of being identified by the police, Jake and Vinny climbed back into their ride. "Okay, so much for good deeds. Let's head south to Little Rhody."

Graham and Nunu whizzed down Lansdowne and parked at the rear of Janice's shelter. They ran up to the back door, where Anthony greeted them and welcomed them inside.

"Are Mack and Duy still here? We think we might have just had a run in with their buddy that they are looking for!"

Mack had been standing beside the once bed-ridden Dewman. Duy was now on his feet again and feeling nearly like his previous, energetic self. They both heard the youngsters enter and heard what they had been carrying on about.

"Y'all saw Jake?" Mack asked in a hopeful tone.

"Let's just say we saw a big muscled-up white dude probably in his 30s, with blonde hair and wearing a suit, and he was with another shorter and chunky guy about the same age, also wearing a three-piece. They were in a black Escalade, and the big guy ruined our weekly vlog by killing some DEAD that we were gonna shred ourselves.

"Gotta admit though, it was impressive. He went through them creatures like they were made of butter. Looked like he was enjoying it too. Oh yeah, and the shorter fella kept mentioning something about leaving before the cops showed up. Look - we got a video of them."

Mack and Duy began to watch the video that Nunu had captured. Duy perked up. "Oh shit! That's Jake! What the hell happened to his hair?"

"Well, it sounded like he was planning on leaving the area after the encounter with our zombies. He may be long gone by now," said Graham.

Mack said "Dew-man, you think yer gonna be strong enough to head out in the morning so we can get back on his trail?"

Duy assured, "I think so."

"Hey, Anthony," Graham announced. "We finished working on that weapon you had asked about. I think you're gonna love it."

Earlier in the month, Anthony had graciously hooked Graham and Nunu up with some free tattoo sessions. He gave Nunu a six-inch squared black ink scene of Saint Francis of Assisi, the patron saint of animals, on her left backbone.

Nunu had always wanted this symbol on her as a remembrance of her mother, Suzann. Suzann had passed just a few months earlier at the age of forty-seven, as a result of a heart attack.

Suzann had been a devout Catholic who had loved animals and rescued them whenever she could. When she saw an animal that had been run over by a car or otherwise dead in a street or elsewhere, Suzann would make the sign of the cross and be deeply saddened within.

Graham had opted for a black circle tattoo with black flames within, on his right bicep.

When Anthony asked what this symbolized, Graham said it was a "ring of fire."

"Oh, are you a big Johnny Cash fan?"

Graham said, "somewhat. But this is more a symbol of the world we live in today. It's like a black hole straight to hell. Even the flames are black, there's no light or warmth at all anymore. This place is cold and barren, and it's spreading like wildfire. If this isn't the end of the world, I'll be friggin' shocked."

"Okay, Anthony, here it is!" Graham produced the masterpiece he had created in the metal shop in the basement of Fenway. The shop had formerly been used to repair the metal seats, poles, railings, and stairs of the ballpark as needed.

Anthony picked up the weapon. It was once a police baton with a handle that expands with centrifugal force. "So, we cut off the metal striking end of the baton, and in the hollow center I welded and secured a double-sided dagger blade. So, when you swing the baton horizontally, it will expand from three feet long to about four and a half feet long and the spring-loaded dagger blade pops straight out and locks into place. This will make it much easier for you to be able to reach up with it and poke a zombie right between his eyes.

"And when you're done, one push of this button will cause the blade to gently submerge back within the depths of the baton. The expandable portion will then retract back to its compact position."

Anthony inspected his new plaything. He realized that if the rechargeable batteries in his nail gun and power drill should ever die on him, this weapon could be removed from the ring on his belt and save his life. He began to smile and chuckle. "Oh, this is so badass! "

Graham and Nunu had a surprise for Mack as well.

"Mack, we made Roscoe something as well. Check out this little gadget," Graham announced.

He reached behind him to grab hold of the object and pulled it toward him for show and tell.

Obviously proud of his creation, Graham began to describe the item. "I took an old police flak jacket and tailored it to fit Roscoe's neck and body. Attached to the neck cover is an extension that serves a couple different purposes.

"First of all, it is a muzzle intended to prevent him from biting those nasty *things* and inhaling or ingesting all their blood and nasty decaying flesh. I'm not sure if that would affect animals the same way it does with humans, but you never know. That shit can't be good for him. But in preventing him from being able to chomp on his enemies, we took Roscoe's only weapon away from him, and his ability to defend himself and you guys.

Graham continued, "so, we had to find a new weapon for him. Look at the four mini daggers spot-welded onto the snout area of the muzzle. They are located precisely where his main four incisors, used to tear and rip, are located. So, when Roscoe acts as if he is biting these creatures with his own teeth and shaking his head side to side and all up in these monsters faces, he's still gonna be shredding them to bits with these blades. Just be careful because these daggers are not retractable. For those, you will have to wait for version 2.0.

"The only negative aspect of this Kevlar vest is that it adds five pounds to him. That will slow Roscoe down slightly. But I think the rewards will positively outweigh this one negative."

Mack expressed his heartfelt gratitude. "Man, that means a lot to me, to Roscoe. And Jake would be extremely happy to know we are doing everything we can to keep his partner safe. Thanks, Graham."

West Greenwich, Rhode Island. Year 1 month 6 ATBI

Jake told Vinny to drop him off at the side of Nooseneck Hill Road in West Greenwich, Rhode Island. Jake's hair was still dyed blonde, and he had shed his three-piece suit in favor of something that would be a little more appropriate for his hometown. He felt much more comfortable in what he wore now - that same thrift store get-up that he purchased when he first arrived in the Boston area.

Jake walked a mile or so down the long, narrow, winding roadway, before approaching the long gravel driveway that led to his parent's house. This was his childhood home. He walked up onto the ten-acre farm, which was dwarfed by many of the vast farm spreads Jake had seen in his travels. But this was just the right size for his parents.

As far back as Jake could remember, his father, Charles, had been growing all the fruit and vegetables the couple would require for survival. He had raised cows, pigs, and chickens for their meat as well. Charles did all of that while working for more than thirty years as a caretaker and landscaper for a nearby state-owned facility and campus.

Jake's walk up the driveway revealed familiar sights. He saw rows of corn off to the right, and fruit bearing trees to the left. There were rows of assorted vegetables fenced in behind electric wire to keep them from being eaten by the migrating deer that pass through almost nightly. Jake strolled further. He could see the enclosed porch on the north side of the old white Victorian style house.

The porch had a concrete floor, a screen door, and screen windows. Jake could see through the window screens to see a figure sitting within. The person did not seem to have noticed the visitor and was rocking slowly back and forth on a gliding red rusted metal swing. This bench swing was covered with cushions adorned in a yellow and white flowered print.

Jake walked slowly closer and was able to recognize the figure on the gliding bench to be his father, Charles. Charles wore his traditional plain colored T-shirt with a breast pocket on the left, a brown pair of Dickies pants, and his brown Timberland work boots.

Charles was 68 years old, and still in good health other than having minor typical old age issues with his eyesight.

"Dad, it's me," Jake said as he reached within ten feet of the screen porch door.

Charles did not recognize the person who stood before him, but he thought he recognized the voice.

"Is that you, son? You don't look like my Jake."

Charles knew there was one certain way to determine if this was truly Jake. Charles would ask him a question that only Jake could possibly know the answer to.

"What was the name of that tremendous bullfrog you caught down at the pond back in grade school. You won that frog jumping contest with him. Remember?"

"Ribbit" Jake said without hesitation.

Charles knew that no one else would have known the answer to that question. He leapt up from his seat and hugged his son, his arms unable to reach completely around Jake's wide statuesque physique. Jake was taken aback by this. It was uncharacteristic of his father to show emotions of any kind.

Before Jake could comprehend his father's display, that flash of emotion ended just as rapidly as it started. Charles asked, "what the heck did you do to your hair?"

Before Jake could explain, Charles again quickly diverted topics. "I need you to sit down. There's something you need to know."

Jake and Charles sat side by side on the porch's gliding red rusted metal bench. It was reminiscent of many previous evenings from at least fifteen years prior. In the past, there was a lot less conversation then time spent just taking in the scenery. The two would relax, watching the breeze waft through the pines and the hummingbirds jettisoning back and forth.

But this night would be much different. Conversation would be flowing here like- never.

Charles said, "Your mother is dead, Jake."

"Oh, no. I feared as much when I saw you alone on the porch," Jake sympathized.

"She was very sick going back a few months. The doctors never could seem to pinpoint exactly what it was. Towards the end, Clara became incoherent. She wasn't eating. Sometimes it was as if she had no memory or recollection of who I was or who she was, or where we were. One day I was out in the garden digging up potatoes with a hoe when she came speed walking out the front door of the house. She came right towards me. I yelled, 'Clara, what's wrong?' She didn't answer. She just kept coming. And then she attacked me.

"She was biting, scratching, trying to ravage me. Her eyes were glazed over and cold. Not human. She showed no emotion. It wasn't as if she was angry or enraged, she was acting more like a starving, deprived, vicious animal attacking its prey.

"I knocked her in the head with the metal end of the hoe. Once was not enough; it really didn't even faze her. She kept coming, still fixated on trying to gnaw on me. I had to strike her again, and again. I lost count of how many swings I took."

"Dad, it's OK. I know you didn't have any choice. You did what you had to do. The same thing happened to Rich and Holly. And I was placed in the same situation as you were."

Charles was now sobbing, something Jake had never seen his father do. EVER. "I knew the stories about you were untrue, Jake. There was no way you would harm your brother and his wife. Your mother knew it too. In the last couple months, she was talking about you a lot. She sensed that you were alive and nearby and coming home soon. As a matter of fact, she wrote you a letter. It's in the living room on top of the fireplace mantle."

Struggling to hold back his emotions and anguish, Jake walked into the living room and found the letter. It was tucked into a white sealed envelope with the word "son" neatly handwritten in cursive on the front.

He opened the envelope and removed the thrice-folded stationery. Jake read it silently after looking over his shoulder to see that his father had not followed him into the room.

"Jake - if you are reading this, then I was right all along about you still being alive and coming home to us. I knew you were too strong and stubborn to let anyone get the best of you. You're a fighter, just like your Grandpa Bill. It's important for you to know that your father and I know you did not hurt Rich and Holly. They were sick, much like I am now. I don't know what it is, but it's horrible. At times I hate everyone and everything and want nothing more than to go on a rampage and... never mind that. While my mind is clear now, know that I love you. WE love you. Your dad never says it just because he was raised that way. But he really loves you and he loved your brother. Nothing can ever change that. We are constantly told by other people that we did a good job raising you. You have grown up to be such a caring, respectful, successful man. You make us proud to be your parents. Love, Mom."

Jake's heart filled with remorse and heartache. He paused momentarily in order to regain his composure before returning to the kitchen to face his father. This was never a family that showed emotions of any sort. Jake's eyes flooded, but he wiped them dry before a semblance of a tear could make its way onto his weather-worn cheek.

"Jake, can you stay a little while and have dinner?" Charles asked.

Jake nodded in the affirmative. The two men walked out to the garden to pick some fresh, ripe ears of corn and tomatoes to eat alongside their main course of pork chops that Charles had earlier retrieved from the freezer.

Father and son returned to the kitchen of the old ranch house, and Charles sliced the tomatoes. He laid the slices down onto a plate of breadcrumbs, then flipped them over to cover the alternate sides as well. He then sent the crumb-covered slices into a sizzling oiled frying pan on a stove top burner to let them brown slightly. Meanwhile the corn ears were cooking in a saucepan one burner over, and the pork chops were baking in the oven below.

After consuming their dinner, the men decided to play billiards and devour some Narragansett beer. Jake had never known his father to be much of a consumer of alcoholic beverages, drinking only on occasion when offered a beer but never purchasing any on his own.

Charles removed a vinyl protective cover from his old mahogany eight-foot-long pool table with cracked leather pockets and legs carved with eagle claw feet. The cover had a thin layer of dust on it.

They each selected a cue stick from a rack mounted against the wall. Jake proceeded to swivel a blue square chalk cube back and forth against the tip to prevent slippage upon contact with the cue ball. A cassette featuring classic George Strait country music was prompted to provide a fitting soundtrack for the tournament.

Neither of them had played pool in quite some time, so it took a while for the players to reclaim any semblance of their once fluid strokes or precise aim.

Between their pool shots, the duo reminisced about years past. They reflected on visits that Charles and Clara had made to Texas. Twice a year the Rhode Islanders would leave the small-town solitude of West Greenwich to make an expedition to Dallas to visit their two sons and their families.

As one large group, the family would visit tourist attractions like the Stockyards in Fort Worth, the Dallas Arboretum and the zoos in both of those cities.

Also memorable was an outing they all made to the Sixth Floor Museum in downtown Dallas. This was the building that was formerly known as the Texas School Book Depository. It was here that Oswald supposedly pointed a rifle out of a sixth-story window to gun down President Kennedy as his limousine drove westbound along Elm Street, just south of the building.

After several games and with the score being even at four wins apiece, the competitors retreated to the living room and found themselves watching an ancient rerun of a "Rockford Files" episode. After that ended, Charles switched the channel over to the second half of a live baseball game in Tampa, Florida, where the Boston Red Sox were matched up against the Tampa Bay Rays.

"I hate to watch games that are played in that ballpark, with that damn dome and ladder up on the ceiling. Why the hell would they build a domed ballpark in Florida, anyways?" Jake commented.

"Yeah, it was a poorly designed stadium for sure," Charles agreed.

The topic of conversation soon took a solemn turn as Charles asked, "so what's causing all of these people to turn into monsters or zombies or whatever?"

Jake told his father the little information that he knew about these incidents. His knowledge was particularly limited due to his efforts to maintain a low profile while on the run and hiding from the law.

"I'm not sure what is causing them or where they are all coming from. I just know in order to destroy them you must cause serious trauma to their brains or else they keep on coming. Nothing else seems to work."

"A couple months back your mother and I were walking at the pathway that circles the cemetery on Weaver Hill Road. We would go there every couple of days to get some exercise and to get to know our future neighbors," Charles chuckled. He was proud of himself for coming up with that humorous aside.

"You can't walk on the side of the road out here anymore because there's so much traffic. Those cars are all flying up the road. It's a good way for a person to get their ass run over! Anyways, we were walking around the new section of the graveyard when we noticed one of the fresh new graves seemed to be caving in. The topsoil and sod grass were slowly sinking into the grave. That one had only been occupied for about a week. The name on the head stone was Rosemary B Standifer.

"Each day we returned and looked at it. And each time it appeared to have sunk deeper into the ground. We didn't know who to call to notify them about the situation. We just kept going hoping to see a caretaker or grave digger working there so we could let them know about it.

"Then finally one day we returned and saw a gaping hole where the grass had been. We could see all the way down into the depths of the grave and noticed the lid of a simple pine box casket. You know Clara's hearing was much better than mine was. As we were standing there, bent over and looking down through the crevice, she told me that she heard something. It sounded like a clawing or scraping sound from inside the coffin. Clara shrieked, 'I think Rosemary is trying to scratch her way out!' and she took off running out of the cemetery plot like she had just seen a ghost.

"I decided not to stick around either. I just took off after Clara. I was so flustered I tripped over a tree root and twisted my ankle. I fell to the ground, and before long, my ankle swelled up like a balloon. So much for my plan to try out for the Pats this year."

Again, Charles smirked at his humorous side note.

Charles continued his tale. He said that when he caught up to

Clara, he told her she was crazy and that she had imagined hearing sounds from within the grave. But the next day they returned to see the entire top of the casket unearthed, the coffin lying empty, and no sign of Rosemary B. Standifer.

Clara was convinced Rosemary had been buried alive and dug her way to freedom. Charles was more inclined to believe that a grave robber had been digging away at her grave a little at a time for several nights. Then last night the robber came back and finished the job, stealing the body for whatever morbid reason.

But Charles knew this did not appear to be the work of the body snatchers. The casket lid apparently had been broken from within, not from the outside.

The elders returned to the cemetery the next day to find the entire property surrounded by a six-foot-high woven wire fence and a gate that was fortified with a padlock.

Charles and Clara wondered if the fencing was meant to keep the human walkers out or to keep the DEAD walkers in?

Now time was slipping by, and it was getting late. Jake knew that the Boston cops were probably closing in on. By now they probably know where his father lives and would be arriving any time now to look for him. Jake could not chance staying there any longer, as much as he would have loved to stay forever.

Jake told his father he had to leave.

Charles was now looking slightly different even from when Jake had first arrived. He was looking older, more weathered and worn down.

"I understand," Charles said. "It's probably for the best anyways. Do you need a ride?"

"No, Pops. But thanks anyways. I don't want you to get involved in this any further. You already took a risk by letting me stay as long as you did."

Jake began to turn toward the door to make his exit. Charles extended his right arm and placed his right hand on Jake's shoulder. "I'm proud of you, son. You turned out to be quite a fine young man."

"Thanks, Dad. I owe it all to you and Mom," Jake said as he removed his flat wallet Dallas Police badge from his billfold and handed it to his father. I don't need this anymore. I want you to have it if you like."

Charles opened his hand to receive the gold shield. "I would love to have it."

Jake handed the metal over and walked out the front door. He whispered, "I love you, Dad." It was a sentiment that his father had never felt necessary to express verbally to Jake. But Jake knew that the feeling was mutual.

Jake began walking back down the long, winding gravel driveway toward Route 102. Now that Jake was out of earshot, Charles sighed and murmured, "I love you too, son." He then went back inside the modest white single-story house as he studied the new shiny hardware in his right hand.

Charles depleted the final two cans of Narragansett while watching the finale of the Sox game. It was a victory for Boston thanks to another late inning comeback, led by some clutch hitting by Mookie Betts.

Charles stood up from his La-Z-Boy recliner and walked over to his dormant fireplace. He methodically removed his shotgun from a rack above the fireplace mantle. He walked out to the back yard and into his hand-crafted chicken coup painted in brick red to match his barn and tractor garage.

Charles proceeded to provide food and fresh water for his rooster and six hens as he did routinely every evening. However, Charles acted out of the ordinary when he left the newly laid eggs behind in the nesting boxes and neglected to shut the coop door behind him as he walked away.

Charles proceeded east on his property to his once dark brown stained barn. Over the years, the tone had faded into more of a grey. He set the loaded shotgun down on a grain barrel and climbed up the ladder leading into the hay loft. He threw down a bale of hay and then climbed back down the ladder.

Charles used his trusty pocketknife to cut the string on the bale, then spread the hay all over the floor of the stall. This stall belonged to Charles' only remaining cow; a Jersey named Martha. Charles left Martha's stall door wide open as he reclaimed the long gun and walked out further east on his spread. He went out through his pasture and toward a thicket of pines.

A sixty-foot-tall majestic pine tree was one of many lining the eastern border of the properly. Tied around the base of that tree was one end of a cow lead. The other end of the rope was tied around the neck of one Clara Hathaway. But Clara was not Clara. She was now a creature. A once-human entity that now was more monster than homo sapiens.

IT was growling, moaning, pulling the rope taught and trying to reach Charles with its extended arms and clutching hands. IT began to gnaw at the knot in the cow lead near its mouth.

Beside the looming tree was a hand-dug, three foot by five-foot rectangular hole in the ground, three feet deep. A blood-covered shovel was lying within. Charles climbed down into the pit. Dusk was approaching, so Charles removed a small six-inch flashlight from his front left pants pocket.

He turned the light on and placed it in his mouth, biting down gently to hold the device in his dental vice grip. He picked up the soiled shovel and illuminated the bottom of the hole, then dug another three feet lower.

Charles threw the shovel back up to ground level. He jumped up and grabbed a handful of level ground, then pulled himself out of the earth's depths. He took the shotgun in hand and placed the double barrel between the eyes of the frustrated, hungry monster.

Charles looked skyward, then used his right hand to make the symbol of the cross to his head, chest and arms.

"I love you, Clara. God forgive me."

His right index finger squeezed. An explosion ripped through the weapon, propelling a handful of lead pellets through the barrel and outwards. The force of which struck the creature's forehead, completely blowing off the skull cap. The creature's body fell backwards into the pit. Then, without taking a glimpse within, Charles began to shovel soil back into the pit.

Charles walked back inside, feeling cheated and angry and hostile. He peered into the mirror of his bathroom medicine cabinet and lifted his John Deere T-shirt to reveal a blood-soaked bandage wrapped around a large deep gash across the center of his torso.

Charles put his shirt back down then ambled into the kitchen. He removed a clear glass bottle of Cuervo tequila from the top cabinet. He held the bottle to his lips and chugged down a mouthful of the alcohol. Charles retreated to the living room and resumed his oneness with his recliner. He watched an "All in the Family" episode on the boob tube before falling into a deep slumber.

The patriarch of the Hathaway family woke up at about 3 a.m. He was devoid of any human emotion and feeling hungry for flesh. He walked north through his vegetable garden in a state of DEAD. He fumbled over the stone wall that separated the Hathaway property from the Stanley property to the north and got within fifty feet of Fred Stanley's grey colonial homestead.

Charles walked with the speed and resemblance of someone sleepwalking and in a trance. He got caught in three strands of barbed wire fence and his clothes and flesh began tearing. He continued to struggle as his arteries and veins were being severed.

Tin cans tied to the fence clanged loudly, and Mr. Stanley came outside along with Smith & Wesson. Stanley pointed his .357 at Charles' head and apologized, saying "I'm sorry, Charles. I'm gonna take you home."

Fred Stanley shot once, striking what was once his neighbor Charles in the middle of his forehead. Stanley's teenage son ran outside, and he helped his father carry the creature's body back onto the Hathaway property. Mr. Stanley guided his son.

"It's over by that tree, right where he told me it would be. Looks like Clara is waiting for him already." They placed the body of the Charles-creature inside a second waiting grave and then utilized the same blood-stained shovel, taking turns spreading the dirt over the top of the still corpse.

With the Hathaway couple now in their final resting place, Mr. Stanley located two hand-carved crosses. One cross read 'Charles' and the other 'Clara.' They sat on the ground and leaned against the base of the grand pine.

The Stanleys placed each cross at the head of its corresponding occupant. They began to walk back to their house as several chickens scattered across the Hathaway property. Some of the hens pecked at bugs in the garden soil while others chased flying beetles across the yard.

Fred and his son had not noticed in the early morning black; Martha the brown and white spotted Jersey milking cow was sleeping comfortably. She was lying down just a few feet away from the new resting places of Charles and Clara Hathaway.

Part 3 - Blinded by the Science

Some days it seems as if everyone you come across or hear about in your travels is bad, the filth of the earth, pure evil. One explanation for that could be as simple as this: That is exactly what people want to hear. So that's precisely what the media gives you. It is what sells newspapers (or used to before all the news went online) and what makes people tune in to that awful TMZ crap on television.

But not all beings are wicked (being used in the malevolent context). For there are those members of mankind that occasionally find themselves leaning upon their right cerebral hemisphere, sometimes displaying acts in which they utilize their physical and mental strength, and/or exhibit feats of bravery and courage, in order to help another in need while at the same time placing themselves in potential danger.

Often, although aware of their inescapability of death, they still confront such threat head on without the slightest hesitation, out of the knowledge and reassertion that what they are doing is right and just. Often, they find themselves standing up to face a challenge, finding the stamina necessary to assist a brother or stranger, even when they had no idea previously that the vigor even existed inside them, or from whence it came.

Chapter 27 - NOT So Convenient

I 95, Connecticut

Jake had left his hometown hours ago and was now walking in a southwesterly direction away from Rhode Island. He soon found himself in the neighboring state of Connecticut.

Tired and hungry, Jake decided to stop at a Cumberland Farms convenience store in Stamford at about 2:00 a.m.

The weary traveler walked into the well-lit shop to find the place empty. There was no sign of life. He walked over to the coffee island and poured himself a large cup of black coffee in a tall disposable paper cup.

Although there were no employees in sight, the jumbo-sized hot dogs were turning behind the clerks' counter. It was as if someone had been there recently. Jake cautiously perused around, hoping to locate a store clerk. He noticed a "Caution Wet Floor" sign lying on its side out near the refrigerated foods area at the rear of the store.

A large yellow janitor's plastic mop bucket on wheels was tipped over with dirty floor water spread all over the floor. A mop with a cracked wooden handle was sprawled out flat in aisle five.

The cash register appeared to be secure. The drawer was closed. If this had been a robbery, most likely the till would have been opened or the robbers would have just taken the whole register with them.

Jake stopped short. He had stumbled upon a trail of blood that led past the building's single restroom and lead into the back warehouse. The blood did not appear to have dripped or splattered but was thick and vast and spread across the floor. It was as if something had been dragged through it.

Jake began to follow the bloody path. Suddenly a sound, barely audible but resembling a female crying, came from the lavatory. The door handle began to shake violently as if someone inside was attempting to open the door.

Jake returned to the sales floor and picked up the abandoned mop. He snapped the wooden handle in half over his knee, then clutched the half without the mop head. He was wielding the stick in his right hand like a club. With trepidation, he used his left hand to turn the bathroom doorknob and slowly opened the door.

There was no light on in the bathroom. It was consumed with darkness. Jake opened the door wider to allow the fluorescent light from the main portion of the sales floor illuminate the small bathroom.

Jake could now see inside and saw straight ahead was a wall-mounted hand dryer beside a small white sink. An oval mirror with various rock bands and gang names scratched into the surface hung above the sink.

"Hello? Are you okay?" Jake asked. He turned his head around the door opening to investigate the right corner of the lavatory.

A large, beefy, black arm smacked Jake across the face. It knocked him backwards a few feet and out of the bathroom doorway. This caused Jake to drop his improvised club in the process.

The large arm smelled of rotting flesh, was oozing a dark fluid, and had gaping holes through which brown bones were visible in between missing wedges of skin and muscle.

"ARRRGGGHHH!!!"

The sound echoed from within. For the large beefy arm that had just swatted Jake was attached to a creature who now came looming out of the Cumberland Farms potty.

IT was once a large African American male who stood about 6-foot-2 and weighed 280 pounds. IT had a dark complexion, long braided dreadlocks that hung out from beneath ITs Washington Nationals baseball cap and was wearing a New York Yankees' Alex Rodriguez jersey.

The zombie lunged at Jake. ITs catcher's-mitt-sized hands reached for Jake's torso. ITs mouth full of rotten yellow teeth were biting near the former police sergeant's head. Jake instinctively assumed a fighter's stance, with his body bladed and using his left hand to block. He used his right fist to throw several upper cuts into the beast's abdominal region.

Realizing these had no effect on the zombie, Jake had to rethink his approach. This was not a human competitor that was sparring with him. This was a monstrosity hell bent on killing Jake and devouring his innards.

While blocking and ducking the lurching zombie's advances, Jake backed his way into aisle five. He grabbed the second half of the mop handle, which had the mop head attached.

Jake had both hands on the stick. He swiveled to the left and made an upward thrust to spear the grandiose oddity below its chin and then upwards. The splintered wooden mop handle careened through ITs mouth, nasal passages and brain.

The defeated beast tumbled to the floor. A young white female who had been huddled in the corner of the supply room walked out into the retail area of the store. She was sobbing loudly and obviously relieved that the threat had dissipated.

She had jet black hair, black nail polish, and was dressed in a white T-shirt featuring the caricature of a skull head with a pink bow on top. Her wardrobe also included a pair of pink pajama pants with an elastic waistband, and black and white canvas sneakers.

"Do you work here?" Jake demanded of the shaken-up youth.

"No, she's in there."

Denise pointed in the direction of the metal walk-in freezer just inside the storage room.

Jake ran into the supply room. He noticed the blood trail he had observed earlier led into the walk-in freezer. He used a paper towel to cover the blood-smeared freezer door handle and he opened the door to find the store clerk inside. She was lying face down on the floor.

She was a fifty-something-year-old Middle Eastern woman with the name plate of "Alice" on her blue Cumberland Farms smock. She was barely alive, her body horribly bitten and clawed by the now-defunct creature.

Alice struggled to speak. Jake attempted to comfort her by holding her hand. To hear her flaccid voice, he put his ear closer to her mouth to hear her urging.

"Please, please... not want ...die ...like this. End it!"

Alice begged the stranger to get her gun from underneath the front counter near the cash register. She wanted him to end her misery. Jake hated to see an innocent person suffer, but he also knew what would happen to Alice if she were to "change over."

Jake made his way to the area behind the checkout counter. He looked around for, and finally located it, underneath the "Big Dog" hot dog wrappers. Lying there on the shelf was a worn-out snub-nose .380-caliber revolver.

The scratched and dented weapon had seen better days. Black electrical tape held the plastic handle grips in place and the trigger was loose and wobbly.

Jake retrieved the gun and returned to Alice to oblige her in her final request. He covered her eyes with his left hand, then placed the snub nose to her left temple and squeezed the trigger.

The .380 projectile went through Alice's skull and into her brain, putting her out of her misery. Her limp, mangled body toppled onto the dingy back room floor. Jake noticed a set of keys fall out of the employee's work apron and onto the tile. Jake snatched up a Kia car key and thought to himself, "I guess she won't need this anymore."

Jake returned to the coffee island and finished getting his java. Then he ambled over to the hot dog rotisserie and grabbed three of the "Big Dog" hot dogs. He bedded them inside of fresh white buns and loaded them down with two very different toppings.

This was a recipe he had developed years earlier. It was something he called the "Mason Dixon dog." It featured one ingredient from the north, dill relish, and another ingredient from the south, salsa.

The girl, now standing a few feet away, reacted. "That's gross! Have you ever heard of mustard?"

Jake ignored the juvenile and began to eat one of the dogs as he prepared to make his leave.

"What about me?" the teen requested.

"Take what you want. This asshole is paying," Jake commented as he took a wallet out of the male zombie's pants pocket and placed it beside the cash register.

Seemingly offended by the comment, the young female yelled, "Shut the fuck up. That's Curtis. He's my brother."

Jake was rendered speechless and stood silent as the girl related her story. She told Jake how her parents had split up when she was ten. And then her mom remarried Curtis' dad.

They had all made a new life for themselves and settled down in a quaint town in Delaware. She and Curtis did not get along well from the start. However, they had matured since. Curtis was fifteen and Denise was now thirteen. Their sibling relationship had improved considerably over the last three years.

One of the highlights of their family outings was the time their dad took them to a Yankees game at Yankee Stadium.

"Curtis begged dad for a jersey. The only XXXL sized jersey they had in stock was that Rodriguez jersey he's wearing now. Curtis was really a Washington Nationals fan but wore the A-Rod jersey to remind him of that special day we had with Dad."

Jake felt sorry for having called the girl's brother an asshole. Especially now that Curtis is dead. Concernedly he asked, "Where are your parents now?"

"We were all on a road trip together, traveling from Delaware to Massachusetts. Then we had car trouble. Dad exited off the freeway and parked in this Cumberland Farms parking lot to check under the hood. That's when zombies started to pour out of that wooded area back there.

"The monsters attacked Dad and killed him, while Mom, me and Curtis all watched from inside the car. Mom and I tried to call the police, but our cellphones were not working. Curtis started to go out to help Dad, but Mom yelled 'No!' and locked the car doors and windows from the front seat.

"They ate Dad! We were honking the car horn, yelling and screaming for help! But no one would stop. Either because they thought we were crazy, or they just didn't care. And the monsters kept on eating dad!

"Then they got a chunk of concrete and smashed out the front seat passenger window. One of them grabbed Mom, started biting her through the open window as she sat there. Mom yelled for us to run for it and call 911. So, I got out of the car and ran like hell inside the store. Then I looked back and saw Curtis trying to pull the creatures off mom.

"One of the zombies bit Curtis, then another and another. Curtis dropped to the ground and looked dead. I told the clerk to call for help and then I waited inside the store.

"The Cumberland Farms lady locked the doors. Me and her hid behind the magazine rack.

About twenty minutes later Curtis was outside pounding on the doors and trying to

get in. But he was not the normal Curtis. He looked dead."

Denise paused and looked at Jake. "I thought zombies weren't supposed to be real!!??"

Jake found himself sympathizing with Denise. He was enthralled in her story.

"Hold on, back up." Jake said. "Did you say you called 911?"

"Yeah, the cops are on their way."

"Oh man, I gotta go!!" the former lawman announced. He looked out the front store windows to the left and right, ensuring that there were no zombies or cops in sight. The coast was clear. He ran out towards the vehicles parked outside.

Jake pushed the unlock button on the key fob he had taken from Alice. The lights flashed on a granny-smith-apple-green Kia Soul parked on the north side of the building.

Denise ran after him begging, "Don't leave me here alone!"

Jake hurried along and insisted, "The police are coming. They will help you. That's what they do."

She said "I don't like cops. They're assholes. Please let me go with you."

Jake reluctantly agreed. "Geezzzz. Okay, come on."

The two jumped into the square vehicle. Jake drove away hastily and headed southbound. Seated in the front passenger seat and holding on for her dear life, the girl introduced herself.

"I'm Denise. What's your name?"

"Sal," Jake said.

"Where are we going?"

Jake replied, "Just out of here for now, until we can find a safe place to stop and figure out what to do with you."

"I have nowhere to go. Where do *you* live?" she said.

"I'm not going home. I actually don't have a place to call home anymore. So, I don't know where I'm going. All I know is I'm dropping you off somewhere as soon as I can."

"Whatever," Denise mumbled under her breath as she pulled a large smartphone out of her back jeans pocket.

"What is that? One of those tablet things?"

"No, it's my cellphone."

"You gotta have huge pockets to hold that thing," Jake said.

"Are you saying I'm fat?"

"No. I'm saying, why do you need a phone that is mammoth?"

"Why, what do you have?"

"I don't have one now, but I used to..."

Denise chirped, "Let me guess – a flip phone, right?"

"It worked well enough to make calls with."

"What are you, 70?" Denise chuckled.

Jake did not respond. It was obvious these two were from two different planets and had nothing in common to discuss. The youngster began to access the internet on her device.

She quizzed, "I guess you don't do Facebook, do you?"

"I guess you're smarter than you look. No, I rarely do' Facebook."

"What's your last name?"

"Armano."

She typed the name "Sal Armano" into her smartphone and studied the screen momentarily. Then under her breath she murmured "oh, shit!"

Denise began to fidget with the passenger door handle as if trying to open the door. She was about to jump out of the still-moving vehicle.

"Whoa- hold on." Jake pulled the Soul over to the side of the road. "What the hell's wrong with you?" he asked.

Denise flew the passenger door open and was halfway out of the car.

"That's why you took off before the cops showed up! You're some mafia dude wanted for murdering some other mafia dude on a boat in Boston!" she yelled.

Jake explained that was just his alias name. He told her his real name was Jake Hathaway. Denise remarked, "that's a stupid alias. You need to use the name of someone who ain't killed people!"

She quickly typed in the new name and recounted, "sooo... now you're a cop? And they got a murder warrant out for you for killing your brother and sister-in-law! I felt safer with you before when I thought you were just some mafia hitman!"

"Sorry to disappoint you," he grunted sarcastically.

Although Jake did not owe her any explanation, he began to spill out his life story to Denise. She respectfully and silently listened to the unbelievable tale. He explained that he had been accused of murdering his own brother and sister-in-law.

"They were not in their normal state. They were like your brother. And that happened a while ago, before most people knew anything about the creatures. Now they seem to be all over the place. The government was trying to cover up the whole thing for some reason which I still don't understand, and they used me as a scapegoat."

Jake also described his abbreviated stint as a mobster. Denise was confused. "So that Shark guy you slashed and threw into the river, was he a zombie too?"

"No, he was just a douchebag."

When Jake was done, both sat silently as the Soul rolled down I 95. Jake broke the silence by changing the topic. "Can you see if my lady is on there? Amanda McKnight."

"Umm. I found some lady named Amanda McKnight-Tillinghast. Here's her picture. Is that her? She's pretty!"

Jake looked at the Samsung Galaxy screen to see the face of an angel. It was Amanda, his soul mate, his personal celestial being who now apparently belonged to another.

Denise narrated, "this says she married some dude named Chad Tillinghast. Looks like he is some crazy rich oil man or something. Wait a minute. She posted that her previous boyfriend died. How come she thinks you're dead?"

Jake offered an explanation.

"It seems like someone with the state or the feds wanted everyone to think I'm dead. So, they fed the media some bull crap, and the media blasted it out there for everyone to see. I guess Amanda believed it was true."

Jake clenched his jaws and squeezed the Soul's steering wheel hard enough to make his knuckles glow white. He continued to drive onward, maintaining his strong, tough exterior while within him his heart was melting into a puddle of gelatinized mush.

Chapter 28 - In the Flesh

Boston, Massachusetts

Mack and Duy had been at the Lansdowne House for over a week now. Janice and her fellow compassionate constituents had done the best they could for Duy, who appeared to be on death's doorstep when he first arrived there. The group provided the Dew-man with necessary nourishment through intravenous fluids and cleaned up some minor scrapes, cuts, and scratches he had obtained throughout their venture. He still wasn't feeling wonderful, but the young attorney at least now had enough strength to stand up and walk about.

"I wouldn't get too overzealous if I was you, Duy," Janice cautioned. I'm still not exactly sure what it is you had or have. It's not completely out of your system. At first, I thought it looked like the flu. But then you were also showing symptoms that were like Lyme disease, which is quite prevalent in this region. I really think it would be best for you to stay here and get more rest."

"That's kind of you, and I truly appreciate everything you have done for me. But we really must get going. Jake is probably on the move again. The news stations are all talking about him, showing his picture on TV. They say he is wanted for the murder of some well-known mobster known as 'Shark."

Mack and Duy began conducting a quick inventory of the supplies within their backpacks. They were preparing to head back out on the road in search of Jake. Anthony ran into the room and said "dudes, take me with you!"

Janice was shocked and saddened at the thought that her good little friend Anthony wanted to leave. Young Carlos overheard the commotion coming from the front parlor, and he went to investigate further. "What's going on, Anthony?"

"Hey, little buddy." Anthony began his explanation. "As long as this city is overrun with these creatures, there will never be the potential for me to achieve my life's dream. I will never get the chance again to own another tattoo shop here. So why should I stay? I want to get out of here, see the country. Or what's left of it. Hopefully it's not like this everywhere, but I won't ever know if I don't go see for myself."

Carlos' eyes began to well up and fill with tears. "I don't want you to leave, but I can't stop you either," he said. "Take this - it will keep you safe from the monsters." The little boy handed the little person a super soaker water cannon that was nearly as big as Anthony.

"Oh, little dude. That's awesome! Thanks, buddy." Anthony felt bad about leaving his little amigo. He began to search for the perfect token of his appreciation for someone who Anthony had considered much like a younger brother. "I've got something for you too!"

"Aaahhhhh, here it is," Anthony said as he reached into his backpack. He pulled out the square clear plastic compact disc case, which contained his favorite band's best compilation of rock music. "Van Halen 1! Little dude, it's all yours now. Someday you will thank me!"

He handed the masterpiece over to Carlos, who took possession of the prized CD. Carlos realized that whatever this thing was, it must be special. Anthony had tears running down his face as he handed it over. And Anthony never cries. Never.

"All right, Anthony. If you want to come with us, you're more than welcome. We're gonna find Jake and tell him what we have learned about his wrongful conviction. We will probably have to kill a few zombies along the way. So, if you're down with all that, let's go."

Mack, Duy, Anthony and Roscoe all bid farewell to Janice and Carlos and they shoved off, out to the mean streets that awaited them.

"So where to now, Mack?" Duy asked as the group climbed up into the filth- covered Avalanche.

"I've got to think that Jake, being on the run again, would probably try to stay in areas he is somewhat familiar with. Sometimes that means it is easier for others to predict where he will land, but Jake can handle himself. I think he may be willing to risk it. Especially when he is comfortable and knowledgeable about his surroundings and can use them to his advantage. I know we already checked his parent's place once, but it's less than an hour south of here. Shall we give it one more shot?"

"Shit yeah, why not? "Anthony chimed in. He was already feeling accepted and welcomed with open arms by his new band of brothers.

West Greenwich, Rhode Island

The Avalanche pulled up to the closed gate across the front driveway to the Hathaway residence. Upon a closer look, the guys were able to see that the gate was padlocked shut.

"I don't recall that gate being closed last time we were here" Duy recalled.

"Yeah, it wasn't." Mack affirmed.

"Hell, let's just go blast the lock off," Anthony said, new to the team and full of piss and vinegar. He reminded Mack of himself when he was a rookie and Jake was training him fresh out of the police academy.

"Nah, that will make too much noise. Let's just leave the

truck here and hop the gate and walk up to the house. Gear up, fellas. Who knows what we will find when we get there?"

Anthony strapped the untested muzzle blades onto Roscoe's snout, then they made their weapons ready and exited the Chevy. They all jumped over the gate and strolled up to the front door of the old white Victorian with dark green wooden shutters. They found the door unlocked and slowly opened it as Mack announced their arrival. "Hello? Mr. and Mrs. Hathaway?"

The men cleared the house, finding no trace of Jake or his parents. They were about to leave the premises when Duy walked into the living room. He approached the large oak mantle shelf above the fireplace. "He was here."

Duy reached up to the mantle, retrieved an item from the shelf, and handed it over to Mack. "What is it?" Anthony asked.

The blue and silver paint on the Dallas Police Sergeant badge wasn't bright and shiny anymore. Not like it was when it was presented to the newly promoted Sergeant Jake Hathaway not that long ago. Now it was somewhat dull and worn and scratched. But it had plenty of stories to tell, if it could only speak.

"How do you know that hasn't been here for quite a while?" Anthony asked.

"I don't believe Jake had been home since promoting to sergeant." Mack recalled. "I bet we're not that far behind him. I just don't have any idea where he would have gone from here, unless he's just headed back home to Dallas."

Mack placed the badge back upon the wooden mantle, and they all began to exit the house. Suddenly they heard the bellowing sound from a Jersey cow coming from the back pasture.

The team walked out to the back pasture to see Martha pacing back and forth. "Hey, old girl, what's wrong?" Mack spoke to the light brown mature milking cow who stood beside a four-foot-high stonewall that marked the east border line of the Hathaway property.

That was when the guys noticed the two gravesites just a few feet away from the cow.

"Oh shit. What the hell happened here?" Mack asked. "That's not good. These are fairly fresh, too."

Several hundred feet away was a brick red garage with three separate bays. One of the sections housed a farm tractor and the other two hosted a variety of other equipment, such as a hay baler, hay tedder, rake, and snowplow.

    The guys decided this would be a good opportunity for them to stock up on supplies while they are here. They should gather up some fuel, tools, weapons and so forth now that the Hathaways would not need these items any longer. They were mindful that a lot of the service stations in the area had closed as a result of the Dead Armageddon, which made gasoline and other supplies that much more difficult to come by.

    Mack entered the tractor shed and began to unscrew the gas cap to the old dirt encrusted orange Allis Chalmers farm tractor in the first bay. "Cool, it's got about half a tank left. You guys see if you can find a hose somewhere."

    Duy spotted a garden hose just outside the garage and brought it over to Mack. Then he obtained three large portable plastic gasoline containers in the corner and moved them closer to the tractor.

    Mack and Duy began to work on siphoning the fuel from the tractor tank and into the portable cans. Meanwhile, Anthony and Roscoe began to scout out the rest of the utility building.

    The pint-sized one came across a selection of smaller gasoline powered tools such as chainsaws and weed whackers. He began to pour the remaining fuel from them into the water chamber of his super soaker cannon.

    At that moment, Anthony noticed that Roscoe was no longer by his side or inside the tractor garage. The police dog was now standing just outside the middle bay door but facing the opposite direction. He was growling fiercely, his gaze focused upon the tree line and what he heard directly behind the wooded property line.

    A seemingly hungry pack of horribly demented dogs and contaminated cats had been scouring the area. The sounds and scents of the human group on the Hathaway property had caught their attention. Some of these dogs and tabbies were formerly house pets that became infected along the same lines of their human counterparts. Others had always been out on their own and never had a place to call home. Nonetheless, they were all together now and with one thing in common: the need for feed. Preferably human or other animal flesh.

    The herd of approximately a dozen mutated monstrosities

began to make a beeline toward their living feast. They were much slower than normal animals, moving with a cynical stagger and an unbridled enthusiasm to devour.

A black death vomit drained from their nostrils and mouth, all were missing at least chunks or all their fur. More than one was missing an eyeball. One of the canine creatures at the rear of the pack was once a collie. Now, only ITs upper torso remained. IT was using its two front legs to pull the stumpy carcass forward. The group smelled of a combination of garbage and death.

Anthony called out to his friends, "umm, guys... we got trouble. "

The other two men looked up to see the approaching maniacal mutts and looked around to each find an improvised weapon within a close proximity. Mack reached for a wooden-handled, ten-pound sledgehammer. Duy grabbed a short-handled, curved-blade sickle. The pair exited the garage and began to march toward the pack, sledging and slashing the heads of the chaos breed.

Anthony recognized that as effective his comrades seemed to be in stopping some of these beasts, they were still severely outnumbered by this pack of crazed animals. He accessed his freshly fueled super soaker and began to shower the demon beasts with gasoline. He then pulled a large metal Zippo lighter from his pants pocket and flicked the metal spark wheel with his left thumb. Holding the flame up in front of the water cannon's muffle, he effectively turned what was once a child's squirt gun into one badass flamethrower.

Anthony torched the beasts as his comrades stood back, watching as the creatures matted fur, muscle, and tendons melted to the ground. The creatures were not fazed by being barbecued or acting as if they were experiencing pain.

Now they were completely scorched, like beasts in a petting zoo from hell. A couple of the zombie dogs and attempted to continue forward but their legs just crumbled below them, and their advance was thwarted.

"I hope you all like your meat well done," Anthony said. "Let's finish them off and get out of here."

Roscoe ran up to muzzle slash the first line of roast beast, while Mack and Duy utilized their garage tools to finish off the rest.

The team then gathered their filled gas cans and garage gold. They retreated to Mack's truck, still parked in the driveway on the other side of the Hathaway's closed gate.

It was now nightfall, and Mack parked the Avalanche in a nearby church parking lot. The group opted to get some rest in the secure vehicle rather than risk their safety by camping out in the unknown.

New York Interstate

Come sunrise, the crew was back on the road again. Dewman was now driving the begrimed king cab pickup.

They began to recount their experience on the Hathaway property with the anthropophagous animals. Anthony asked, "So what the hell do you think caused those animals to change into what we saw?"

"I don't know for sure. But being stray animals and with no steady food source, I imagine they were probably feasting upon infected carcasses that had been discarded in the streets, the forests, everywhere," Duy replied. "Thank god Graham made that muzzle for Roscoe so he's not ingesting any of that nasty shit!"

They were about to enter the lower tip of New York state from Connecticut when McElroy picked up his cellphone. He noticed that the ringer was still turned off and muted from when he had shut it off to sleep the previous night. He also discovered that he had missed an incoming call about an hour earlier, and there was a message on his voice mail in-box.

Mack began to play the recording and held the phone to his ear to listen. He suddenly began to feel his jaw drop. The eerie voice on the recording was one from the past. It was a voice he was not sure if he would ever hear again.

Duy saw the stupefied expression on Mack's face and pulled the vehicle over to the side of the road. "What, man? What is it?"

Mack pushed play again on the voice message and then set it to 'speaker' for all to hear. "Hey, brother. It's me, Jake. Maybe you're not answering because you're still upset about Holly. I really had no choice, man. You must believe me. She wasn't herself. Neither was my brother. I guess by now everyone has seen these *things* and noticed what's happening to people. I just heard that

Amanda thinks I'm dead and she went and married someone else already. What the hell is that all about? Anyways, sorry I missed you but maybe I'll get another chance later. Stay safe buddy."

Duy looked at Mack and astonishingly said, "Oh my god, he really is alive!"

Chapter 29 - Us and THEM

New York Interstate Hwy

Mack attempted to find the phone number Jake had called from, but there was nothing showing on Mack's cell phone caller ID. "He must have used *67" Duy said. Why would he not want you to be able to call him back? "

"Maybe he is afraid that the people who are hunting him as a prison escapee have access to my phone records?" Mack wondered.

"But just because I can't get a name or address from the phone he used, maybe I can find out which cell tower he was closest to when he made the call. I've got a dispatcher friend who might be able to help me out with this."

The DPD officer searched through his contacts on his cellphone, located the correct one, and called. "Hey, Tracy, it's me, Mack. I received a call on my line just a little over an hour ago. Any chance you can find out which cell service provider that call was from and then try to ping it for me? It's important. I need to know the location that call was made from."

Tracy advised it would take a few minutes and said she would have to call Mack back. Twenty minutes later, the dispatcher rang back and said, "okay Mack, the phone that called you is serviced by T-Mobile, and they were able to ping it for me. The call you are referring to was made within a three-mile radius of the southwest borderline of Newport News, Virginia."

"Hmmm. Newport News...Newport News.... I have heard someone mention that place before." Mack thought aloud. It didn't take long for him to recall who had spoken of that Virginia town.

"Jake was telling me about his old DPD buddy who resigned and left to move to Virginia. Now he's an air marshal."

Tracy offered, "That was Stanley Glazier."

"Yes, that sounds right. Can you look up his new address for me, please?" Mack got the address from Tracy and said, "All right, fellas, looks like we need to head towards Newport News."

"Hey, Mack, one more thing," Tracey added. "This may prove to be interesting to you. Remember that Gladys woman that testified against Jake at his murder trial? She was found murdered the other day."

"Really? That *is* interesting! Do we have any suspects yet?"

"I don't know. I'm just a dispatcher, Mack. No one tells us the GOOD shit. Except I heard that she was hacked up pretty good."

"Wow. Hey, thanks for all your help, Tracey. Bye."

Anthony was beyond curious. "Who is Gladys!?"

"Gladys Torrence; she was the nosey neighbor who testified against Jake," Mack said in response to Anthony's question, but then continued to think to himself out loud. "So, she *was* correct in some of her statements during her testimony. Rich probably *had* changed over time, in appearance and behavior, considering the way his carcass looked. She assumed he might have been doing drugs or excessively drinking alcohol, but there was something far different going on with him. His posture became hunched and slumped over; his appearance and hygiene deteriorated noticeably. Who knows what was really happening to him? My guess is that he was changing as a result of being infected. He was probably turning into one of THEM.

"Gladys also said that she observed on several occasions that there was a different vehicle going in and out of Holly's garage. She said the car was white and large and looked like a police car. She was right about that part - but it was MY unmarked Tahoe take home police car, NOT Jake's. The prosecutor put his own little spin on this bit of information. He was attempting to convince the jury that Jake was the one driving that car into Holly's garage and having a secret affair with her. But it was really me," Mack said.

Anthony interrupted. "Whoa. Hold on. You were banging *who?*"

Mack continued. "And then Ferron speculated that Holly

ended this fling with Jake, causing him to go there on that February 8th to seek revenge. Ferron's theory was that Jake plotted to kill Holly for dumping him. And when Jake tried to get away after that murder, Rich tried to stop him from leaving with Carson. And then Jake had to kill Rich so Jake could get away with the crime. All lies! Every word!" Mack said.

Anthony asked, "so why were they framing Jake for murder when it was clearly something very different?"

"That's a great question," Mack said.

Duy continued to navigate the orange Avalanche toward Virginia as Mack continued to work through his investigation. "I need to call Michelle. Maybe she has some answers for me."

Mack picked up his cell to call her.

"Hey, Michelle. How's it going? "

"Hi Mack, good to hear from you! Any luck finding Jake? "

"Nahhh, not yet. But we are still out and about searching for him. I was wondering if you had any new information for me that might help us make sense of what is going on with this whole plague thing going on. Maybe a little scientific and medical expertise as to what turned these people into creatures may also assist us in our goal as well."

Mack put his smartphone speaker on as Michelle began to recite some of her findings. "Well, I've been working on a timeline and conducting studies based upon some of the specimens we are examining here in Dallas County. I have also reviewed several reports from the cases of my colleague medical examiners throughout the country.

"It seems as if the first of the infected started out as either military personnel or small groups of people who reportedly were abducted in Florida and California. They were basically guinea pigs in some superhuman type drug experimentation.

"And then it appears as if some of the infected wandered northbound up the coasts. Others went more inland toward the center of the country," Michelle said.

"How long after they become infected do they switch over to those other *things*?" Anthony asked.

"That's difficult to say exactly. But it seems that, much like with other diseases, it takes varying periods for a person to contract the disease or, in this case, to transform. It all depends upon several different factors; the size of the dose, the health of the person, the temperature, and so on," Michelle said.

"So, we are seeing once-humans, who should be dead, still up and walking around. Meanwhile, their bodies are in one of the five stages of decomposition. Blowflies and other insects are laying eggs in them and eating the infected flesh.

"The flies then land on living people, usually in their sleep. Most of them are outdoors; campers, firemen battling a wildfire, road construction crew, the mailman, etcetera. That's how the flies spread the toxic disease to new living hosts. As a result, it has led to mass amounts of these creatures. And then, as these 'zombies' travel and kill, their victims turn as well. And they multiply again.

"I have read reports of the *dead* being dumped by the masses into lakes, streams, and rivers. This is polluting and contaminating those bodies of water. Mosquitoes and other bacteria-carrying insects spend some of their life cycles in that water. So then they get contaminated too. Then they go all over the place, landing on healthy humans and spreading the disease even more."

"Oh my god." Mack suddenly began to feel itchy. "So how many of these THINGS are they estimating to be out there? And are they everywhere?"

"The numbers are roughly between three to five thousand right now, with many of them along the coasts. But there are pockets scattered throughout other regions of the U.S. as well.

"Some different teams and neighborhood watch groups have formed up and gathered with the intentions of going out to eradicate them from their towns. It's like Salem all over again with these modern-day witch hunts. Some groups have had some success, while others never made it back home."

"It's all so crazy. Hard to believe this is real and not some bizarre movie from the science fiction channel," Mack said in amazement.

"Oh, by the way Mack. You remember this Camacho asshole with the FBI that testified against Jake? So, he's been showing up everywhere asking about Jake, saying he's going to track Hathaway down for his escape charge. Said he's gonna also charge him for the murder of the prison guards on the bus as a result of Jake's get-away plot."

Mack became incensed. "First of all, Jake didn't murder any

HUMAN. Second of all, why would he plot an escape when it was just a matter of time until his conviction would be overturned on appeal?"

"I know, I don't get it either. And that jerk Camacho has been harassing me ever since the day he met me at Rich's house on the day of the birthday party."

Mack said, "Wait a minute. Dallas PD never called your agency out to that scene. And I thought you all didn't get involved in the federal cases."

Michelle hem hawed for a moment, acting suspiciously uneasy and searching for an answer. "Oh, that's right. Our office received an anonymous call that there were bodies to be picked up at an address on Matilda. I was close by and went there to verify whether a transport team was needed. By then, Mack, you had already left the scene. The FBI, Camacho, told me they were working the case and did not need our help. I told him it was protocol that all bodies in the county be examined in our office. Agent Camacho then told me there was a new protocol called the 'Camacho Rule'. He told me I needed to leave or be arrested. So, I left. I have no idea what happened to those bodies or where they were taken."

Eager to change the topic, Michelle mentioned, "Oh, I finally got in contact with Amanda. I asked her how she was doing, told her I was concerned because I hadn't heard from her lately."

Mark was intrigued. "What did she say? Is it true that she really married that other guy she had been telling you about?"

"Yes. And I asked her what changed because last time we spoke she said she hated the guy. She didn't respond and stopped talking. I had to ask if she was still on the line and she said, 'I'll be okay.' It was a weird conversation, to say the least."

The Hail Mary, Dallas Texas

Talluci returned to manage the sports bar/restaurant that he owned. His right arm was still in a sling as a result of his role in the K9 jailbreak, but he was healing rapidly. He was still relying on some strong pain meds and a lot of booze to get through the sleepless nights. This allowed him to function relatively well during the daytime so he could get back in the saddle and operate his business again.

Dave was making his rounds, chatting it up with his regular patrons. They were happy to see the chipper bar owner back tending to his establishment. A news story flashed upon the flat-screen TV above the bar: exorcisms were reportedly on the rise.

These increased occurrences were a result of the numerous infected persons who appeared to be acting irrationally, as if they had been possessed by demonic beings.

They were not responding when spoken to and exhibited far-off glances. They were making sounds sometimes misinterpreted by others who believed them to be "speaking in tongues." Families and/or caretakers of these victims, not knowing any better and without the knowledge of the current state of infection in their area, believe their loved ones may be possessed by evil forces or demons. Many were calling upon the church for help.

On a related note, the number of priests who had since become infected through bites from the befouled had risen by the same percentage.

Meanwhile, a familiar blonde female customer sat alone at a booth in the far back left corner. Mack's friend Megan Anderson, the sensational-looking lady law enforcer, appeared to be down and distraught.

Dave moseyed up to her and remarked, "Hi. Megan, right? How are you?"

"So, you are friends with Mack, and you were with Jake too, right?"

"Umm, yeah."

"Have you heard anything from Mack since he left on his trip?"

"No. Nothing."

Megan sighed and returned to her tall glass containing a fruity mixed drink.

Dave gingerly set his repaired right wrist onto the table as he lowered himself to sit down on the bench seat across from Megan.

"Can I ask you something off topic?" Dave asked.

"I guess so."

"It's just – you're beautiful. How did you decide to be a cop?"

A roll of the eyes and a pause by the young woman was

followed by, "Aren't you kind of old to be hitting on me?"

"I'm not - I'm just saying..."

"Do you know how many times I have heard that? What is wrong with you men? Are you all so inadequate that you cannot handle seeing an attractive woman in any sort of position of authority? I guess you all are too busy imagining us in OTHER positions. If I wasn't pretty but more masculine, you wouldn't have a problem with me telling you what to do, right?"

Dave sat speechless, fearful and smart enough to know better than to try and interject at this point of the conversation.

"And the guys at work are just as bad. It's such a male-dominated career. If you are even a decent-looking woman and you are a police officer, you are screwed. All the guys you work with either want to bang you or they don't like you because you won't *do* them, or they have this male chauvinistic attitude that women don't belong in the profession. Even other women cops who aren't as attractive are jealous of you because the guys aren't interested in them... so basically you have no friends and no support system. Wonderful career choice, huh?"

A thick sap of sarcasm was oozing from her lips.

"It's no wonder cops' lives are so dysfunctional." Megan went on. "We have some of the highest divorce and suicide rates, and short life expectancies after retirement. And not only that, we are living in a society now that is full of cop haters, cop killers, etc."

"So now, you tell me...how do YOU think I feel about being a cop?"

"Ohhh. I'm sorry I asked." Dave said. "I didn't know..."

Having just unloaded on the well–meaning bar owner, Megan finished off her cocktail and began to feel badly about the pounding she had just unleashed on Dave.

"Hey, I'm sorry. If you're friends with Mack and Jake, then I'm sure you are a good guy. I just have a lot of shit going on right now."

"It's no problem. I get it."

"Hey, if you do hear from Mack, will you let me know?" Megan asked.

"Of course. I sure hope that he was right about Jake possibly being still alive."

"Say what???" Megan was caught completely off guard.

"Oh, you didn't know?" Dave asked.

"No - what's going on?"

"Let me get you another drink. You're gonna need it. I better get one for myself as well..."

Chapter 30 - The Dead Precedence

Newport News, Virginia

Alice's green Kia Soul was riding on fumes, with the gasoline level showing less than a quarter tank of gas.

"I'm starving," Denise declared.

"Here, have a hot dog," Jake offered as he pulled a napkin-wrapped Big Dog from his pants pocket.

"What the...? That's shoplifting. And you're supposed to be a cop?"

Jake philosophized, "It was shoplifting back when we lived in a society with laws and rules. This is not that anymore. I'm not sure exactly what THIS is, but it's not THAT. Now it's all about survival and not much else."

Denise began to utilize the camera on her smartphone in order to take a picture of her Cumberland Farms dinner. Jake chuckled. "Really? Don't tell me you're going to post that? You really think people care about seeing what you're eating for dinner at this point? Do they know we just survived a friggin' zombie attack? "When those abominations were lumbering after us in the parking lot, why didn't you stop and say, 'Timeout, creatures! I need to update my status to *'currently running for my fucking life?'*"

"You just don't understand - you 'Boomers are too old to get it..."

"Oh yeah, I'm sooo old. At least I, unlike you millennials, can communicate with people in conversations, face to face, and not just through my smartphone or on Instasnap or FaceChat. If it wasn't for social media I don't know if you kids would be able to communicate at all."

"That's not what they're called..." Denise smirked.

The elder continued. "It's no wonder so many job forces are struggling to find good, qualified college grads with adequate people skills anymore. We were struggling even with the rookie cops we were hiring in Dallas. They were having trouble asking even the basic questions they needed answered in order to take simple reports. They were struggling to take control of scenes and situations, had a lack of initiative, no command presence."

The elder of the two halted as he noticed the troubled teen began to tear up and had suddenly become silent.

"Jake... "

"Yeah? "

"I miss my mom and dad. Even my brother. Me and him weren't super close because we each had a lot going on in our own little worlds, I guess. But I do miss him too. I can't believe they're all gone."

"I know, kid. I'm sorry you have to go through that."

"Have you ever lost anybody you were close to like that?" Denise asked.

Jake replied, "My mom recently passed away. And my brother and sister-in-law got taken from me much the way your brother was. And losing family is the most difficult, of course.

"But I also lost a couple close friends in the Marine Corps when we were deployed in the Middle East. It really sucked. Even though when you are enlisted in the military, it's in the back of your mind that you could be killed or hurt badly. But you don't think about the fact that you could make good friends and lose them there just as easily.

"And as bad as it hurt when those buddies of mine got killed, it still was not nearly as life-changing as the time my fellow Dallas Officer Derek Parrish perished."

"What happened to him?" Denise asked.

"Me and Derek were in the same academy class. When we graduated, I was assigned to the Central Division, and he was sent to Southeast. We saw each other occasionally at the jail when we were booking our arrestees in, but that was about the only time. We didn't hang out off duty or even keep in touch really. One night he was working his patrol beat when he heard another officer was in pursuit of a kidnapping suspect's vehicle. The car chase was headed in his direction, so he pulled his squad car over and grabbed the spike strips out of the trunk. He went to deploy them in front of the bad guy's car. He was hoping to flatten the tires and get the vehicle stopped so they could rescue the kidnapping victim. But when the kidnapper approached and saw the strips lying across the freeway, he swerved hard to the right to avoid them. The bad guy's car struck Parrish as he stood beside his car. Killed him instantly."

"But if you guys weren't that close, why did you say it was worse than when your soldier friends died?"

"I guess because when we signed on to be cops, we really didn't think of it as that dangerous of a job - not like going off to war. Cops weren't getting killed every day in this country like they are now. Or at least you didn't hear about it if they were, before social media took off like it has. So, to lose someone that I know closely and trained with, and in the way that he did… he was a great guy with a wife and a couple kids. It's sad. It really caught me off guard and made me stop to re-evaluate my career decision and life.

"But then again, even before this whole zombie thing began, the job had changed. The WORLD has changed. Society has no respect for law enforcement, or for any authority - for that matter. Cops began to get killed much more often than they used to - being assaulted, ambushed while they are eating at a restaurant or stopped at a red light in an intersection. It's as if we are at war here in our own backyards."

All his stories having bored her to sleep, Jake sympathized with the teen traveler. Not only had she lost her family recently to the infected ones, but he truly felt himself commiserating for her and this younger generation. He pitied those who might never again be able to experience life in a world free of the disease and devastation that they currently were on the fringe of experiencing.

Hathaway eased the Soul eastbound down the Newport News street called Haystack Landing Road. This was a similar trek; one he had taken a couple years earlier when he spent a week of vacation at his buddy and former co-worker Stan Glazier's house. At that time, the Glazier homestead was your average American three-bed, two-bath with a white picket fence along the front sidewalk.

Jake did not recall the exact address of the Glazier residence but figured he would recognize the dwelling upon driving past it. However, much to his amazement, the surrealistic scene which was strewn out before him made that assumption quite asinine.

Haystack Landing Road was now much less a nestled comfy community than an obvious reminder of previous conflict, ruin, and disorder. The three-bed, two-baths were still there, but many appeared to have been deserted some time ago. Backyard fences had been trampled down, windows smashed out, and doors forced in. Cars were wrecked and strewn along the street, a couple of the habitations showed signs of having been on fire, and the carcasses of once-family pets and even a couple human-shaped forms littered the sidewalks and yards.

Much like many other neighborhoods that were in its path, this one also appeared as if a herd or migration of cannibalistic corpses had swept through the area. They had left nothing but bad memories and destruction in their wake.

But as the procurer of the Soul-mobile continued onward, he came across an utmost anomaly. At the end of the dead-end street stood an erect steel monstrosity of a structure that resembled a three-tiered fortress much more than that of a residence. The two-and-a-half-acre property was lined with a titanium-like, twelve-foot-high wall and an electronic sliding gate of the same height which bore the name GLAZIER on its exterior, facing the roadway.

Upon further investigation, Jake noticed the three-foot-high rolls of Constantine barb wire on top of the walls. There were long, deep trenches around the outsides of the walls. These had been dug by backhoe and now contained still-kicking INFECTED - skewered on vertically positioned and pointed bamboo poles rising from the trench's depths.

Another dire diseased one appeared to be pacing slowly back and forth in front of the main entrance. It was almost as if IT knew that there were living beings inside that IT might potentially be able to feast upon soon.

With the creature only about fifty yards away, the street-savvy sergeant pointed the Kia at the diseased one. Jake stomped onto the accelerator with both size 11s, and the Soul car's rear tires chirped lightly on the pavement.

The vehicle's front grill KIA emblem struck the rotting, walking corpse around the knee area, cutting the mutant in half. The lower portion of IT, the ankles and shoeless feet, stayed put right there in the street. Meanwhile the upper torso, arms and head, went airborne and flew ahead about thirty feet. It slammed down onto the road surface just before the speeding Soul drove forward over IT again.

The automobile ground the demented one into the asphalt for another twenty feet or so before Jake threw the car into reverse and stopped suddenly in front of the Glazier property.

"Hey, kid. Denise. Wake up - we're here."

The teen passenger awoke to see Castle Glazier outside the car window. "What the ... this is where we are going?"

"Yeah, come on," Jake said.

"OMG!" Denise said. "Look at all of the freakin' zombies in the ditch! Creepy!"

An intercom button on the front gate was not accessible now due to an overturned U.S. Postal Service mail delivery vehicle blocking the way.

The odd couple exited their vehicle and made their way around the mail Jeep and up to the intercom. Denise pushed the gate button and then stepped back away from, not quite sure what to expect at a place such as this. Jake's head was on a swivel as he stood postured to attack any potential threat. Each hand was holding one of his thrift store kitchen knives that were straight outta Jersey.

Inside the steel domain, Stan Glazier's sixteen-year-old daughter Hannah had heard the intercom buzzer. She pulled up the front gate camera video on her monitor from the front door entryway/living room area.

"Hey, Dad, there's a dark-haired goth-looking girl at the gate. She's with a big white guy with a bad blonde dye job on his hair. And it looks like they drove up in a toaster. "

"Don't just buzz them in - let me see them first," the former Dallas Police Officer cautioned Hannah.

"But, Dad, I can handle them if they're bad people," the young girl said. She clutched her black and blue crossbow tightly.

Stan wheeled his chair over to the monitor and was unable to recognize the girl or big guy on the screen. He pushed the intercom voice controller and asked, "Who is it?"

The somewhat recognizable voice replied, "Stan, it's me - Jake Hathaway. I know I look different, but it's me. My badge number is 4856."

Stan was stupefied, to say the least, and under his breath he replied, "No fucking way. They said he was dead."

Stan buzzed the visitors into his estate. As the gate slid shut behind them, Hannah opened the large double front doors and said, "Come on in. My dad's in the living room."

Jake noticed the once-fit ginger hardly appeared to be the same person. Stan, once a physically fit and strong man at 5-foot-9 and 160 pounds, was now something quite different. Now wheelchair bound, his thin frail body was battered and scraped beyond repair and he was paralyzed from the waist down. His head once full of thick, red hair, this white male was now hard to recognize with his thinning splotchy white hair and the skin on his arms, legs, and face all horribly scarred and damaged.

Jake was as surprised about Stan's appearance as Stan was of Jake's. They both gave each other the once-over look and simultaneously they said, "What happened to you?"

"Jake, what can I say? I'm still in shock seeing that you're alive, after all I've read and all that's been reported. How are there so many conflicting stories about you?"

"Let's just say that it's been an interesting time in my life, for sure. First I get set up on a bad murder charge for what was really a self-defense shooting, then someone breaks me out of the prison bus and sets me free, only so that I can be on the run from the law and trying to avoid an escape charge on top of the murder. As if this world hasn't gotten crazy enough already. Some days I have to pinch myself and hope that I will wake up from this nightmare."

Jake's former co-worker sympathized with him. "I know, man. This shit doesn't seem like it can be real. I'm sorry you have to deal with all that side bullshit too. So, what happened to your hair? And what happened to your Soul?"

"Oh, yeah. I need to dye my hair back to brown. I changed it up as a disguise when I first got to Jersey and the cops were hot on my trail. As for ME, I have changed. Everything that has happened has me thinking differently, feeling less or other than usual emotions. I feel numb on the inside sometimes. It's amazing how you were able to pick up on that so fast."

"What do you mean I picked up on it?"

"Stan, you asked me what happened to my soul."

"Haaa, Dude..." Stan chuckled.... "I asked about your car - your Soul.... there's half of a corpse moving around below the engine block. I can't tell if he's stuck under there or giving you an oil change."

Glazier was happy to provide a guided tour of the homestead for his guests. He placed special emphasis on his secure fortified basement with distant escape hatch, the pressure chamber with fresh oxygen pumped into it, and a supply of food and rations vast enough to last five people for up to three years.

Afterwards, the guys began to catch up with the past as the girls quickly became bored and departed to hang out in Hannah's study. Jake and Stan continued to swap stories into the late night as they also indulge themselves with some of the finer spirits of Chardonnay from Glazier's liquor cabinet.

Stan soon found himself recalling one of the many true tales that he experienced on the job as a federal air marshal.

"One week I was in Raleigh-Durham, North Carolina, waiting to board my assigned plane for the day. In the same gate area was a woman sitting in a wheelchair, covered in a pink bathrobe with hood.

"Airline employees saw her itinerary and boarding pass sticking out of her purse and they were able to scan her papers without waking her. There was a boarding announcement overhead, and then the airline employee pushed her and her chair into the ramp and onto the waiting plane. There, other flight attendants then assisted the elderly Middle Eastern woman into her first-class seat. She appeared to be sick, sleeping and mumbling in another language unknown to me.

"The Airbus A320 took off for its three-hour flight to Atlantic City, New Jersey. There were rows of three seats on either side of the center aisle. I remember seeing a couple all dressed in wedding clothes apparently set to marry as soon as they reached their chapel destination in Atlantic City. Some members of their wedding party were seated near them also. And there was a large group of senior citizens on board too, apparently on their way to the casinos to gamble and enjoy the shows.

"So, the lady in the wheelchair appeared to be sleeping at first, then she woke up and tried to communicate with the stewardess. She was pointing at the restroom at the front of the plane. So, the stewardess helped push her wheelchair into the plane's restroom. The lady was in there at least thirty minutes. I'm seated at the rear of the plane, kind of observing and taking in everything and everyone all at once.

"Eventually I start to hear other passengers talking amongst themselves, and I see them standing up and pointing toward that restroom. I got up from my seat and began to walk up the aisle toward the front of the jet. All along I was thinking to myself that maybe the lady had fallen, and she couldn't get up, or something like that. We all began to hear banging sounds, moans and groans from within the lavatory. At that point a flight attendant knocked on the door to see if someone was inside and needing assistance. There was no verbal response, but the moans and groans from inside were turning into growls and snarls. It sounded like there was something very peculiar going on within the plane potty or else someone was joining the mile-high club. But since I saw who had entered the restroom, I was betting on the first option.

"The concerned head air steward waved me over. I went up and pounded on the door, announced myself as a police officer. More growling, more heavy breathing and snarling continued. I pounded my fist on the door and it popped right open. I had been leaning on that door so now my weight shifted, and I stumbled forward into the lavatory. My hands latched onto the sink and I was able to suspend my forward motion.

"What had been a frail old disabled foreign woman was now a hideous, wiry, blood-thirsty *dead* thing covered with death vomit and smelling of the same. It lunged at me from the corner of the latrine and savagely tried to bite my chest and face. I tried to spin out of ITs path and my face smacked into the small metal mirror above the tiny sink.

"I pulled my gun out of the concealed holster below my suit jacket, and I fired two 9mm rounds into IT's chest. The creature wasn't even fazed by this and showed no signs of pain.

"I figured I better shoot it in the head, like they have been telling us in our training. I went to shoot this thing in ITs head, but the demented creature struck me on my arm, knocking the gun out of my hand and causing a misfire. A man from the economy seating area of the jetliner ran up the aisle toward the struggle and tried to help me fend off the beast. I told the guy to find something that we could use to tie IT up with.

"So, he tore that curtain down from its rod, the one that had been separating the seating areas. Two air stewards assisted us. It took all four of us to get it done but we finally wrapped the curtain around the creature, restraining ITs arms by strapping them down tightly by ITs side.

"We planned on taking IT alive. But the plane was damaged when my bullets went through the monster's body and projected into an electrical panel. As we started to prepare for an emergency landing, IT began to fight again and nearly broke free from its curtain restraint. I resorted to smashing in the creature's head with repeated whacks from a fire extinguisher.

"Unfortunately, the good Samaritan guy was bitten in the process. If he had just stayed in his seat like a pussy and hadn't helped me, I would have probably been chomped instead of him. It really sucks that he got bit."

"Wow, that's intense, man. So that's how you got all beat up?"

Stan explained, "No. I was in a motorcycle crash."

"Huh?" Jake said.

"Yeah, one night I was up on I-95 riding my black Kawasaki Ninja when a large SUV came into my lane. It bumped me while doing over 80 miles per hour. I slid about sixty feet on the freeway until a guardrail stopped me really quick. It snapped my spine in half, and now I'm a paraplegic."

"Oh, fuck, man."

"No, Jake. The good news is my bike slid about thirty more feet than I did, and it got mashed by an eighteen-wheeler. So, I was the lucky one that night because I *didn't* stay on the bike.

"Also, it turns out, the driver of the SUV was a coach for the Redskins, driving home drunk from a club. So, I ended up with a fat settlement check from the team and turned my house into this fortress."

Meanwhile, Denise and Hannah had no choice but to become acquainted. Upon first glances, and based upon each of the other's appearance, neither of them seemed interested in learning more about the other. And even less interested in befriending the other.

They were quite apparently exact opposites. Hannah was the type of girl who dressed preppy and neat in pinks, whites and yellows. Denise on the other hand, preferred the attire of a punk rocker. She wore dark, torn outfits, concert tees, and plenty of black makeup and fingernail paint.

Nonetheless, the two struck up a conversation to at least kill time and the awkwardness of their silence. Denise began to talk about her love of music and the artists that she primarily listened to, such as Nirvana, Rob Zombie, and Marilyn Manson.

"Eww," Hannah murmured.

"What kind of music do you like?" Denise teased. "Oh, I know, I bet you like Taylor Swift and probably Bieber and all those mainstream pop tarts out there, right?"

"Yeah, they're okay. So what? But my favorite artist is Kina Grannis. She's really popular on YouTube, she's got a great voice and writes beautiful songs. I saw her in concert once and met her backstage. I love her. She is so sweet!"

The thoughtful teen paused and then added, "Oh man, I hope she hasn't been eaten by a zombie."

The ice now having been broken, Hannah began to talk about losing her mom to breast cancer three years earlier, as well as the more recent hardship of her father being paralyzed from the waist down in his motorcycle crash. She revealed that he was able to do a lot for himself now, but it had been a long, hard road they both had to endure in order to get to the place they were at now.

"After he first had his accident and got out of the hospital, he had already pretty much given up on his life. I remembered feeling the same way after mom passed. I didn't feel like I wanted to or could go on. But that was when dad told me to 'suck it up' and 'quit feeling sorry for myself.' He just got real frank and said that Mom wasn't going to be around to help me with everything anymore or to protect me from the world. He said I was going to have to start doing things for myself and grow up.

"And that's exactly what I told him after his crash."

Denise somewhat sympathized with Hannah. "But now you're filthy rich and live in this mansion and can buy whatever you want, so it's all good, right? At least you still have a dad - or any family at all. Because I don't. The closest thing I have right now is

Jake, and I've only known him for three days. Plus, he doesn't even like me."

Hannah was incensed by Denise's "rich" remark and expressed herself with "I'd give all this money and stuff away in a heartbeat to have my mom back and my dad healthy again." But she also felt sorry for the dark-haired teen as well. "What happened to your family?"

The jaded juvenile related her traumatic tale, attempting to stifle any emotion. She soon broke down, sobbing. Denise told her story and Hannah was surprised to see such heartrending sentiment from the one with the hardened façade. The preppy one then felt inclined to hug Denise tightly in a comforting gesture.

The unpleasant conversations now out of the way, the girls compared notes on their likes and dislikes, favorite hobbies and fashion preferences, and so on.

Denise was particularly fond of welding, creating the likes of industrial-themed art pieces and weaponry out of metal. Hannah shared her love for the crossbow and archery, which quickly led to the girls comparing zombie survival stories. A friendly debate followed, over which of them could better survive if they were ever stranded alone somewhere in zombie apocalyptic territory.

"I'll tell you what," Hannah challenged her new friend. "Let's see how good you really are. Let's have a scavenger hunt challenge. We will go out to a neighborhood in search of food and supplies. Whoever comes back with the most valuable and best finds wins."

"How is that going to be fair? I have no weapons, and you have that fancy crossbow. Also, you probably know which houses might still have good stuff in them and which ones have already been raided."

"Let's go down into Stan's bargain basement," Hannah quipped "I bet there we can find you a good deal on some gently used tools of destruction."

"You call your dad Stan? "

"Sure, that's his name. What should I call him? Pablo? "

"How about, maybe…Dad? "

"Yeah, I guess that would work. I like 'Stan' better. "

They walked down a long wheelchair accessible ramp into the nether regions of an underground storage room. They began to sift through piles of old computer parts, police equipment, sporting goods and motorcycle gear.

"Oh, badass!" Denise exclaimed. "I found an arc welder over here! Can I use this?"

"Yes, of course. Everything here is fair game."

Denise was stoked. "So cool! I found some things over here I can use. Why don't you run along and go play with dolls or something while I build my weapon?"

"Bitch, I'm about to kick your a___"

"Save the hostility for the monstrosities out there, honey. You're gonna need all the help you can get."

Hannah left the room as Denise began to implement her new creation, a zombie slayer constructed with the likes of an aluminum softball bat and the blades from two ice skates. Denise forged the blades onto the barrel of the Louisville Slugger, with the business end of the blades facing outward. These had now been sharpened on a grinding wheel and were capable of slicing through zombies like a hot knife through butter.

Denise had impressed herself with her freshly fabricated armament.

"Okay, I'm ready! Let's do this!"

Without alerting the adult type people in the place, the duo proceeded out a side exit of the building. They walked through the foot-tall Bermuda grass in the backyard toward the rear gate of the compound. Each contestant had her weapon of choice in hand, Denise her Louisville Slicer and Hannah her favorite micro crossbow.

"Okay, here are the rules," Hannah pronounced.

"We will go out onto the street over there - Mountaineer Drive. It's one that I have never explored, and I don't believe anyone has lived in any of those homes for several months. Most of the people either were eaten or fled when the last herd came through. I really don't think many of the survivors packed stuff up. They probably just got the hell out.

"So anyways, we each will choose a house to pillage. We are looking for food, weapons, medicine - anything that can be considered of use to us. Whoever returns back to this gate with the best booty wins."

"The best booty? Looks like I already won!" Denise smirked.

"Let me rephrase that; the more valuable collection of items." Hannah clarified.

The girls headed out, each with an empty pillowcase to fill and their weapon of choice in hand, ready to deploy.

The street was crowded with single-family detached homes. Hannah had her eye on a large gray two story modern-conventional structure that appeared to be in decent shape. The front picket fence apparently had been trampled over by a herd of *dead* heads and the large front picture window had been shattered. Large pointed glass shards hung like icicles from the top of the window frame.

Denise made her way toward a large, much less modern appearing, white Cape Cod-style house with brown shutters. She found the front door to be barely hanging by its hinges, as if it had been kicked or forced open previously. The adventurous one cautiously walked into the front entryway and heard classic country music echoing from the downstairs corner kitchen area.

Denise located a large walk-in pantry and scored her some cans of Chunky soup and pork and beans. She then made her way to an adjacent bathroom where she began to load up her bag full of prescription meds and aspirin, band aids, razors and toiletries.

The country music still blaring, Denise heard the county classic "All My Exes Live in Texas'. But the song was suddenly interrupted by the sounds of Hannah yelling "GET OUT! THEY'RE COMING!! DENISE!!!!"

The goth girl grabbed her goodies and ran back through the house and onto Mountaineer Drive. She was just in time to see her competitor running past, in the opposite direction of Stan's safe house. Hannah was followed by about fifteen much slower, drooling, oozing foot draggers of mixed gender and race, size and shape.

Denise began to sprint alongside Hannah when they noticed directly ahead of them, at the intersection of Mountaineer and Morning Glory Drive, was another larger mass of munchers. So many, in fact, that they were breathing down each other's corroded necks.

"Okay, plan B," Hannah shouted as she made a 45-degree turn to the right. She jumped onto and climbed over a six-foot picket fence, then cut in between two houses. This led to a large wooded backyard which eventually led to the adjacent street to the east. It took all Denise had for her to keep up with Hannah, but Denise never fell too far behind.

"Haaa! No problem at all! See how easy it is to outsmart those fuckers?!"

Having said that, Han realized she had spoken too soon. For she had just run through a thicket of shrubbery and now, was right smack in the middle of a pack of about eight more zombies. They were effectively blocking the girls' path back to the rear gate of the Glazier compound.

At this point the teens were exhausted from all the running and climbing fences and hurdling corpses in the street.

Hannah reached back to remove the crossbow from her back harness and began flawlessly shooting the mini projectiles right between the creatures' eyes. Denise deployed her improvised Louisville Slasher weapon and began to swing the bat furiously. The freshly sharpened ice skate blades were easily taking off the heads of the decaying deformities they encountered.

But for every cadaveric creature they stopped, another would join the ranks. Hannah was soon down to her last two arrows and began to hold them like knives, using the tips to puncture the heads of the *dead*.

Denise was steadily slaying the *dead* but was also running out of gas. She noticed Hannah was struggling to push creatures back and said, "Oh no, rich girl. Did your daddy not buy you enough darts?"

Denise went Wade Boggs on a couple of the mis-creations that were closing in on Hannah but was now too exhausted to swing the bat any longer. "Oh no, white trash girl. Is someone getting tired of swinging their ghetto bat around?" Hannah jabbed back.

"Shut the hell up! Why did I let you talk me into this stupid shit anyways?!"

More of the demented breed began to close in, as there were now fifteen of them between the girls and the back gate.

"Oh, are you scared? Okay, watch this," Hannah quipped as she pulled out her smartphone and pushed an app, which opened up a screen with control levers and gauges to operate something or other. Hannah began to feverishly push buttons on her touch screen.

"In three, two, one... here we go."

A three foot by three-foot drone with video camera rose up

off the ground in the Glazier compound and lifted over the rear fence, then hovered approximately twenty feet above the abysmals.

"Whoaaaaa." Denise was stupefied. "What the …?"

Hannah yelled, "Get behind this car!"

The couple retreated and took cover behind a disabled, abandoned silver Nissan Sentra. One more push of Hannah's finger onto the screen caused the unmanned aerial vessel to drop a stun grenade smack in the middle of the DEAD crowd.

A BOOOOMMMMMM!!!! rang out as several zombies were blown back from the concussion of the device, clearing a path for the teens.

The girls began running through the newly created opening to the compound. Denise said sarcastically, "Why didn't you just deploy a drone that has a flamethrower on it and barbecue them with that?"

"Oh, I would have. But that one is on backorder," Hannah said.

Chapter 31 - Dead Meet

Newport News, Virginia

Mack's mandarin machine turned onto Haystack Landing Road. The truck pulled up along the huge privacy fence that lined the front of the three-story monstrosity of a steel-fabricated structure. On the structure's exterior was the number 501, which matched the address Mack was given for the Glazier residence.

"This should be it," Mack asserted.

"Damn, looks like a steel castle," Anthony chimed in. "Only thing missing is the moat.

"And what's up with all these junk cars lining the street and blocking the gate and driveway? It's as if they were driven here and then destroyed somehow and then just left behind."

"I don't know, dude. But nothing better happen to my baby."

Mack parked his Avalanche on the pothole-covered concrete roadway in front of the solid abode. The three men and a Malinois prepared to exit the vehicle to make their way over to the gate's intercom system.

Before the doors could open completely, the vehicle began to get showered with flaming plastic sacks. They were pounding hard against the windows, hood, and roof of the truck. Once they impacted the vehicle, they exploded and immediately discharged a thick brown substance consisting of feces and urine.

Although these bag bombs bounced off the windshield and doors without causing any harm to the vehicle, Mack's SUV was now covered with this malodorous, putrid element.

"Oh shit! IT'S SHIT!!!" Duy negated while gagging. "Thank god we had the windows rolled up!" he exclaimed, just as another flaming feces bag was catapulted in through the open moonroof and exploded on the back of his head.

SPLUSHHHHHHHHHH!!!!!!!!!!!!!

"FUCKKKKKKK!!!!!!! EWWWWWWWW!!!!!" Duy screamed while Anthony instructed, "Close the roof!!! Shut the moonroof!!"

The interior of the Avalanche was now not only sewage-soaked but was on fire as well. The travelers had no option other at this point other than abandoning the ass-smelling Avalanche.

"ABANDON SHIT!!! I Mean SHIP!!!!!

They began to walk past the other trashed-out vehicles, and Mack looked back to see his carbonized Chevrolet now becoming fully engulfed in flames. The pickup was rapidly becoming EXTRA Burnt Orange.

Mack was in shock and devastated at the same time. "SON OF A BITCH!!!!"

The foursome approached the front gate, looking up at the twelve-foot steel wall with coiled barbed wire surrounding the top. There was an intercom button by the front gate, which Mack pushed, and then he paused. There was no response.

He pushed it again and put his face close to the microphone/speaker.

"Hello? My name is Mack McElroy. I am looking for Stan Glazier...and by the way, whoever trashed my ride owes me a new fuckin' car too."

Apparently, all of the previous loud noises; the flaming sacks smacking the SUV, the screams from sewage-soaked citizens, and the sizzling and crackling reverberations of a Barbecue, were all enough to wake the DEAD.

For the human group had suddenly become surrounded by clumsy carnivores, and each of the missionaries was quick to defend themselves with their weapon(s) of choice.

Mack pulled out his Ruger .45-caliber and blew out a couple of zombie brains before running out of ammunition. At that point he had to adapt and overcome. He grabbed the weapon by its long barrel and began to smash the butt end of his pistol grip into the faces of filth. He pistol-whipped several of the dying humanity until the Ruger and his hand were covered with stinking, rotted brown flesh.

Roscoe was as persistent in shredding mutants with his muzzle blades as he had always been in performing tasks for his favorite reward - tennis balls. He continued to thrash the domes of the demented while Duy, machete in one hand and a stainless-steel battle axe in the other, was busy cutting and pasting his own share of wretched worm food.

Anthony, though small in stature, was holding his own. He was kicking the legs of the decayed out from under them, bringing their disgusting heads down to his level where he would put the final nail in their coffin. They were five-inch stainless steel nails which he fired into their brains with his cordless Makita nail gun. After going through several nails and wearing down some battery, Anthony switched over to deploy his new expandable police baton with the retractable switchblade. He found this weapon to be quite capable as well.

Just as they were finishing off the final sludge monster, all looked up to see the sliding front gate open about a foot, just wide enough for a small crossbow to fit through. A crossbow which was now pointed at Mack's head. And standing behind this weapon was a brown-haired teenage girl who abruptly bellowed, "You're trespassing! What are you doing on our property?"

A second teenage female, this one with jet-black follicles, walked up behind the first. She was carrying a metal softball bat with improvised blades attached to the barrel and looked as menacing as the first female.

Mack reasoned, "Maybe I've got the wrong house?" The black-haired, bat-toting girl enlightened him with, "Yes, I would say so. Now you need to leave while you still can."

Caught off guard by the tenacity and toughness of these two young girls, Mack explained, ladies, calm down. I'm just looking for Stan Glazier. He used to work for Dallas PD where I work now. I was hoping he might know where I might find our mutual friend, a guy named Jake Hathaway."

Hannah radioed inside the house on her two-way radio. "Hey, Dad, this guy claims he knows you and Jake."

Stan looked at the monitor in his living room and questioned his friend who was seated nearby. "Hey Jake, do you know that guy on the screen? He told the girls his name is Mack and he is looking for you. And there's an Asian guy with him, too. And either a kid or a little person."

Jake peered at the monitor screen, saw his good friend, and shouted in jubilation. "I'll be damned! Yes, that's McElroy! He's the guy I was telling you about. And my other friend, Duy! I don't know the little guy."

The gate began to slide open just wide enough to be accessible for the visitors to pass through.

"Okay, follow us," Hannah chirped somewhat untrustingly as she and Denise began the five-hundred-yard trek back across the front yard to the front door of the homestead. The small group followed behind and made their way into the Glazier dwelling. Jake and Mack spotted each other from across the vast living room and approached each other. They stopped about three feet apart.

"Dude," Mack exclaimed. "You're a sight for sore eyes! We've been searching for you all over the eastern half of the U.S.! We were unsure if you really were alive or if we were just chasing a ghost. But it's really you! You look bigger, like you've been working out twice as much. Your hair looks kind of fucked up with those blonde highlights, but you look good, man."

"Thanks, Mack! Hey Dew-man." The three men shared bro-hugs and continued catching up.

"You guys look great too," Mack said. "It's nice to be around people I trust again, I'm tired of being on the run and not knowing what the hell is going on in the world. Sometimes I wonder if I would be better off still locked up in the pen rather than out here in these apocalyptic conditions. I still wonder why I'm not sitting on death row right now, but..."

Mack interrupted, "Oh shit. I forgot, Jake - I have a surprise for ya!"

Mack yelled out, "Angeriest kommen!" - the command of "come here" in German. Everyone soon heard the prancing of heavy paws coming from the front entryway. Jake's eyes were wide open in anticipation, hoping that he was right in his assumption of whom was running his way.

Suddenly, through the double doors of the living room ran a full-grown little person man.

Jake was quite caught off guard and somewhat disappointed as he had been expecting someone quite a bit furrier to make that entrance. "Umm, am I supposed to know him?"

"Dammit, Anthony, not you!" Mack said.

One second later, a happy, healthy Roscoe ran around the same corner and saw Jake. Reunited with his best friend and partner again for over a year, the jubilant K9 leapt into Jake's large sculpted open arms and proceeded to wash Jake's face with his tongue.

Jake was overwhelmed with elation. "Oh my god, buddy. I thought I would never see you again! Good boy!"

Stan and Hannah hosted the diverse assemblage, providing them with a scrumptious, hot, home-cooked meal. All had all sat down to enjoy the dinner when Mack's cell phone began to buzz.

Mack stood up from his chair at the large dining table and motioned for Jake to follow him into the adjacent room. There he would be able to talk without the other party hearing any background noise.

"It's Michelle. Don't make a sound, "Mack whispered to Jake.

Jake was puzzled but complied.

"Hi Michelle. How's it going? "

"Hey, sexy. I got some information I thought you might be interested in."

"Oh really? Cool- what you got?"

"It seems as if multiple sources of intelligence are indicating that there is some sort of secret laboratory operating out of a house down near Hidalgo, Texas. But it's on the Mexico side. Apparently, there's been many zombie sightings coming from that area over the last few months."

"Hmmm. Why the hell would there be a lab in Mexico? That's crazy, Michelle..."

"Yeah, I really don't know the answer to that one. So where are you guys at? Have you found Jake?"

"Nope, still no signs of him. I hate to say this, but I'm starting to wonder if some of the Jake stories and sightings were not accurate. Maybe he never even made it out of that prison bus crash alive."

Jake remained silent, but his facial expressions were screaming, "WHAT???"

"I think he's out there somewhere, Mack," said Michelle. You gotta believe that. Trust your instincts and you will find him."

"You're right. Thanks, Michelle. I'll let you know if we get any closer."

Mack disconnected and responded to Jake's bewilderment. "I know you're wondering why I'm lying to her. Something she told me a few days ago - it just didn't make sense. She told me she was out at your brother's place the day of the birthday party, after you and I left. She said that her office received an anonymous call about a body being at that location and needing transport. I don't think in real life they would respond to a pickup call from someone other than a law enforcement agency. Responding to an anonymous call? Sounds like bullshit to me. So, my question is: why was she there?

"And furthermore, when I called her on it she really started stepping on her own feet. I'm not sure what 's up with her, but I'm having a tough time trusting her now."

"So, do you think this whole Mexican lab thing is not true?" Jake asked.

"It's odd. She has been giving me information that has panned out and been accurate, but I just don't feel safe in giving her any help back."

"Something does smell fishy. You're probably right."

"So, Jake, now that we have found you, what's next? Do we need to find a way to get your name cleared? Because I think I have the evidence that we need to do that. I came across a video taken at your brother's house that captured the whole Birthday Incident. It's obvious from the footage that Rich and Holly were no longer Rich and Holly.

"But I also came across a video your brother made not long before the incident. He talked about being abducted in Florida some time ago, having crazy experiments done to him in some bizarre secret lab that he was eventually able to escape from. Michelle had told me before that there were apparently reports of experimentation and testing being done on *both* coasts."

Jake was flabbergasted by the news. "Well, that may explain why his whole life went to complete shit after he came back from spring break. His personality and behavior changed completely - he was unrecognizable.

"So, Mack, do we know if there's any link between the Florida lab and the west coast lab and this one in Mexico that Michelle is talking about?"

"I really don't know about that part, Jake. Maybe if we can go to locate this place south of the Texas border, we can get some answers."

"I think you're right, dude. At this point it really doesn't seem to matter anymore whether my name is clear or not. That's the least of my worries. Of OUR worries. And as crazy as this sounds, I wonder if we may be the only hope for the future of our nation. Because I don't know if anyone else out there will be able to get to the root of the problem. And it needs to be done soon. Someone needs to slow this decimation down. And it's just a matter of time before this epidemic begins to spread worldwide."

Mack nodded in the affirmative. "Okay, I'm in then. Let's do it. We can head out in the morning."

They rejoined the party in the dining room and partook of the first quality meal either of them had received in a very long time. It was one that they would savor, understanding fully well that this could be their last supper. There was no talk of the abominations that had become all too often seen shuffling and smudging their way into rural neighborhoods and city streets, claiming lives and completely redefining a "normal life" as they once knew it to be. Tonight, the assemblage would celebrate being alive and being together. Tomorrow would be a completely different story.

The following morning, Jake and Mack thanked Stan for his hospitality. They announced that they and Roscoe had to hit the road even though Stan and Hannah had been gracious enough to extend an invitation to all present to stay if they wanted.

Duy and Anthony found themselves wanting to contribute to the cause and agreed to tag along and take the trip south.

Denise stepped forward from the back of the room and said, "I would like to stay if that's cool with everyone. "

"Yayyyy!! Yes, you can live here! Right, Dad?" Hannah was overly excited, as she had made a great new friend in Denise and was happy to see her stay.

Denise walked over to her short-term travel companion and gave Jake a big hug.

"You know, Jake, for a big goofy old cop you're pretty cool. Thanks for saving my life and putting up with my attitude like you did. And for not kicking me out of the car. And for the hotdog."

"Of course, Denise. You're a good kid. Take care of yourself, okay? "

Now that Mack's mango machine had melted into the ground, and Jake's Kia Soul was somewhat out of order, the guys had to arrange for an alternative means of transportation. About three blocks up the street was a locked, unoccupied navy-blue Chevy Silverado crew cab with Virginia tags. This vehicle would suit the fellas just fine.

Anthony had come prepared for such a situation and pulled out a slim jim. He slid it down between the driver's window glass and frame to manipulate the lock buttons and to set them into the "unlock" position. Next, he opened the driver's door and used his power drill to force open the steering column and then flip the ignition switch. Within a matter of a couple minutes, the crew was all loaded up and rolling southbound on Interstate Highway 64.

Mack was driving the rig while Jake rode shotgun and Duy, Anthony and Roscoe occupied the back seat. Roscoe sat in between Duy and Anthony.

"Umm, Jake... Is it safe for us to be riding back here with this killer police dog?" Anthony nervously inquired. "And I think maybe he's hungry too? He's looking at me and drooling like I'm a chicken nugget or something..."

"Nah, man, that just means he likes you. Roscoe, er ist ein freund."

"Okay, Anthony, you can pet him now if you like. He loves

to be scratched behind his ears too."

"What did you just say to him?"

"I said you would taste better with some sweet and sour sauce."

Duy chuckled. "Haaa, very nice."

"No, seriously," Jake explained. "I just told him you were a friend. Just don't make any sudden moves toward me and he should let you live."

"Gee, thanks, I'll be sure to move nice and slow around him." Anthony said. "So… he doesn't look like a German shepherd, I thought all police dogs were shepherds."

"No, many police agencies are using the Belgium Malinois now as well. That's what Roscoe is."

"So why did you guys decide to get the Malinois?"

"We actually have some of each. When a handler is looking for a new dog, the department sends them out to a breeder who has both Shepherds and Malinois. The K9 officer will then get to spend time with the dogs, see how they react to him or her and what their relationship is like. It's really more about choosing the individual dog more than selecting which breed you prefer, because both breeds have their advantages and disadvantages. The Malinois are smaller but faster and slightly more aggressive, whereas the Shepherds are larger and maybe a little smarter..."

"So, what was it about Roscoe that made you select him? "

"He was just a badass little dog. We got along great from the start. But that's not what sold me on him. This dog had something the others didn't seem to possess."

Duy asked, "What was that?"

Mack said, "I bet it was his flatulence!"

"Sounds like you've gotten to know Roscoe quite well, haven't you, Mack! You're exactly right! This dog loves nothing more than to catch a bad guy, bite him on the ass and then rip a juicy one in their face as they're being cuffed and stuffed."

"Oh, that's what I'm smelling back here," Anthony remarked while trying not to breathe in the malodor. "I thought it was Duy."

"Heyyy…" Duy chimed in.

With a long trip ahead of them, the bunch began to take advantage of their down time by getting each other caught up with the details and events leading up to this very moment.

Duy was curious, as were the others. "So, Jake. How the hell did the whole prison bus crash and escape thing go down? The news reports were so sketchy and so different that no one could tell what really happened out there."

"I'll tell you what, guys - that was some crazy shit that I still have questions about myself. This group of masked dudes in some hopped up four by four get the bus to flip over on the freeway, and then they come on board and demand the guard to set me free from the cage. No one else, just me. They kill the guard and cover my head with a pillowcase or something and then they started driving me somewhere. Next thing I know, the van stops, they knock me in the head with something, and I wake up alone in a swamp a few hours later.

"So of course, I was wondering who the hell would have broken me free like that. Initially, Mack, I thought it might have been you who freed me, but then I knew you wouldn't have knocked me out and left me out in the middle of nowhere. So now I'm wondering if they meant to release someone else and got the wrong person, and then when they realized they screwed up they just discarded me? I don't know what to think.

"One thing I do know. The main man in that heist was a big friggin' dude. Strong as an ox too, picked me up and threw me around like yesterday's trash. Of course, I couldn't get a look at his face with his mask on.

"Anyways, "Jake continued. "Is what I'm hearing about Amanda really true? "

Mack said "well, I spoke to her about two weeks ago. She mentioned some guy that's been annoying and bothering her. But now Michelle is telling me Amanda posted something on social media about her previous relationship ending when her man died, and that she has just married some rich oil man."

"Wow. Didn't take her long to get back in the saddle again, did it?" Jake said.

Officer McElroy took this opportunity to change the topic. He told his former partner about everything he had learned from his personal investigation as well as that which Michelle had told him.

He also talked about some of the mind-boggling things that had been happening on duty, and how these incidents have now become more of the norm. For instance, he had seen increasing numbers of people taking their own lives. People who have become infected were attempting suicides by cop, jumping off freeway overpasses, intentionally being run over by cars.

"Every day we were getting multiple rescue calls too. People being chased by these creatures, getting trapped up in trees trying to escape. The *dead* are growing in numbers. It's bad."

"We actually have come up with an officer safety roll call training that we call the 'Twenty Foot Drool Rule'. Basically, it's been determined that twenty feet, give or take, is the average distance one of THEM can travel in the time it takes us to recognize whether it's still alive or one of the DEAD, pull out a weapon, and stop the threat before IT's mouth full of mini-sharp edged weapons can reach us and chomp into us."

"You gotta be kidding me. The twenty-foot drool rule?"

"Man, I didn't come up with it. Kinda catchy though."

The team was now navigating westbound along rural Route 58 in the central North Carolina town of Danville. They passed a flat black unmarked Dodge Charger that appeared to be idle on a dirt patch on the north side of the roadway.

The tint on the vehicle's window glass was too dark for anyone to determine whether the car was occupied, and in their brief glimpse of the vehicle the guys were unable to notice if it was equipped with emergency lights or any sort of police package.

"Guys - was that a cop car we just passed?" Anthony offered.

"Not sure if it was or not. Were you speeding, Mack?" Jake asked.

"Of course, I was."

"Okay, then I guess we may be about to find out."

Mack continued rolling at the same pace, with one eye on the road and the other fixed upon the rearview mirror. Jake, in the front passenger seat, was focused upon the right-side mirror, and all the heads and eyes in the backseat were completely turned toward their six.

The Silverado traveled about another mile further before everyone noticed the red and blue wig wags activated on the front of the unmarked Charger, which was closing in quickly behind them.

"Oh fuck. It's about to go down. "Mack muttered.

"What's the big deal? "Anthony inquired. "So, what if we get pulled over by a cop for speeding. You guys are cops too. All you gotta do is identify yourselves as police officers and they will cut you loose - that whole 'professional courtesy' thing."

"Dude, have you not been listening to our conversation up here? About how there's two groups of law enforcement out there after Jake: the real police who have been told he's a wanted convicted murder escapee and then there's the federal cops who for some reason are involved with that crazy Camacho guy and seem to have a vendetta against Jake for something that happened between them in the Corps."

"All I can hear is this dog snoring and farting back here."

"Mack's right," Jake intervened. "Either way, being stopped by any cop is a bad thing for us. I'm not going back to prison on a bogus murder or escape charge. And as for the feds - if they were putting out information to the public that I was dead, they most likely intend to see to it that I end up that way."

Anthony absorbed the recent revelation and paused briefly. "Oh FUCK! It IS about to go down! "

Now the cop car was directly behind them, weaving back and forth, still flashing the reds and blues and pointing a spotlight in their faces.

Mack suggested, "I think we should pull over and just explain the circumstances to them. After all, you told us how you were able to successfully communicate with those Pennsylvania Wildlife cops who believed you were innocent, and they sent you on your way."

The seasoned Sgt. Hathaway disagreed. "How do we know these guys are that cool? Maybe these dudes are complete opposites. For all we know these could be some of those crooked feds ready to kill me and all of us on this very spot."

"I don't know, Jake. Let's just stop and see what happens, then improvise if we need to. Let 's just be prepared for the worst and hope for the best."

Mack slowed the crew cab truck down and pulled onto the narrow shoulder of the highway in preparation to stop. Suddenly, the Chevy got rocked by a hail of AR-15 rounds fired directly at the truck.   RATTTTTATTTTAAATTT!!!! RATTTATTTATTTTATTTT!!!!!!

"SHEEEIIITTT!!!!! SEE!!!! TOLD YA !!!!" Jake bellowed

as Mack punched the accelerator and the rear tires chirped, charring the concrete black. The tires finally grabbed traction and the steel sled sped up and pulled from the Charger. For the moment.

Mack had driven in many police pursuits previously, but this was a first for him. He had never been on *this* end of a chase, being the pursued rather than the pursuer. Mack was now imitating all those criminals who had tried to outrun and outlast him, some successfully. Others, not so much.

Knowing that the police interceptor would be able to catch up to them soon, Mack determined that technique might beat out tachometer in just such a situation.

Predictably so, the deputy in the Dodge was soon on their heels again. Mack meanwhile was driving the acquired Chevrolet at top speed, moving like greased lightning along the left lane of the two-lane highway. He approached an exit and, at the last second, swerved all the way over to the right lane and exited, hoping the cop car would be following too closely to respond quick enough and miss the exit entirely.

The maneuver was unsuccessful in losing said pursuer, as the Charger was able to exit and maintained its close distance behind the pickup.

"Come on, man!" Duy yelled. "Drive it like you stole it! You gotta do better than that!"

"All right, all right. I got one more move. This one should work."

McElroy killed the truck lights and shuffle steered to the right. He made a sharp quick turn onto a narrow, rocky dirt back road which cut through a thick wooded property. The smooth squad car was still on his ass.

"All right, guys. Muzzle Roscoe up and tell me when you're ready to bail!"

Anthony fastened Roscoe's muzzle mount onto his snout as Duy grabbed his edged weapons. The entire group inched open the four pickup doors and prepared to run for it. "OK, we're ready when you are!"

"As soon as I yell 'now ', jump out and run like hell in different directions. If he's lucky he might get one of us."

"Umm, which one of us? "Anthony asked.

"The slowest, "Mack said.

Mack dropped the speed down to roughly 25 mph and then slammed the automatic shifter into reverse. "NOW!!"

The four men and a dog all hurled themselves from the vehicle passenger compartment and took off running through the dense forest as the Silverado's rear bumper trailer hitch careened into the grill and motor of the tailgating, pursuing Charger.

Everyone fled in separate directions through the North Carolina woods, with Jake having run eastbound. The lone officer, his Charger now disabled with a Silverado in its grill, entered the thicket where he had last seen the biggest and slowest suspect running.

The North Carolina state trooper soon saw a huge looming form attempting to hide behind the trunk of a grand oak tree.

The highwayman drew down on the figure behind the tree and commanded, "all right, asshole! Stop right there and drop whatever weapon you got!" Jake stepped out from behind the massive oak with his hands held high.

"Damn, you're a big-ass corn-fed motherfucker, ain't you?" the trooper retorted.

"I would say I'm probably gonna be justified to shoot if you do so much as blink. Hell, even if you *think* about blinkin' I might have to shoot your ass…"

What had appeared in the darkness to be a small stump or log under the ground cover of leaves and pine needles sprang toward the ankles of the officer.

This was Anthony, who grabbed the officer around the shins and pulled his legs out from under his body. The young law man dropped to the ground, firing off a round from his Sig Sauer service weapon as he went sprawling backwards.

The projectile missed its target. The officer was quick to his feet and stood upright while Anthony held onto his legs with white knuckles, restricting the trooper's motion. Mack and Jake each darted over to share a football style sack on the startled young North Carolina cop.

Jake disarmed the trooper, then called Roscoe over to intimidate their pursuer.

Jake announced, "You see this demon dog? He's just chomping at the bits for me to give the attack command so he can shred you to bits with those titanium blades on that muzzle of his.

"If you don't want that to happen, get on your portable radio and tell the other officers out there that the bad guys got away. Say we car-jacked someone in a green Camaro and fled in an unknown direction. Don't say anything cute like numbers or codes or else you won't live to tell this story to your kids."

The nervous patrolman held his portable radio shoulder mic to his mouth and said exactly what he was told to say.

"That was great," asserted Mack. "Now this time try it with the radio keyed up, you douchebag."

The officer transmitted the information requested and was abruptly snatched up off the ground. He was then handcuffed to a supple birch tree by the former DPD Sergeant Hathaway.

"Is that really necessary, Jake?"

"What? "

"Cuffing him to a tree."

"Mack, you heard all that shit he was talking about shooting us if we blink, calling me a corn-fed motherfucker. I don't even like corn."

"Funny, Jake. But you know you were in his position hundreds of times, chasing bad guys and talking shit when you caught up to them. You know you can't be a cop and sound weak or scared or unconfident."

McElroy continued, "remember what you told me back in field training? 'You must come off strong, brave, determined. Ready to kick some ass and take some names. It's also a mind game you're playing on the suspect, the more confident you are and sound, the less likely they are to try and fight you or flee, and the more apt they are to give up and surrender. So, if by talking a little bit of trash to the suspect, the cop is able to take the suspect into custody without having to use force, all the better it is for everyone involved.' YOU said that, Jake. That kid's just doing his job."

"Fine, Mack. If you want to let him go so bad, you make him strip down to his skivvies and he can walk. If you let him go as is, with his uniform on, I guarantee he's got a back-up weapon on him or something like that and your kindness will bite us in the ass!"

Mack removed the trooper's gun belt and then addressed the young man. "You heard my partner. Take off your uniform and hand it to me if you want to leave here on foot. If you don't mind being chained to a tree, then that's your prerogative."

The trooper said, "I'll walk." He stripped down to his boxer shorts, handed his uniform over to Mack and said, "until we meet again..." as he began to walk off.

Mack interrupted, "Umm no, dude. You need to go THAT way - away from the vehicles." The trooper did a slow 180-degree spin and began to hike off in the opposite direction, further from the group and into the woods, until they all lost sight of him.

The four men and their canine friend walked back toward the dirt road and abandoned vehicles, cautiously looking and listening for more responding squad cars. The coast appeared to be clear, so they exited the woods and traversed the dirt road. Soon the two crashed vehicles appeared within their sight and Anthony excitedly blurted out, "Let's take the cop car!"

"Oh hell, no!" Mack cautioned. "Not only does it have a blown radiator now from where we backed into it, but those things got all kinds of electronic devices inside that can be tracked. Heck, it's probably got video cameras recording in there right now."

"We really need to shut those things off." Jake suggested.

Anthony was curious to find out exactly how that could be done.

Duy suggested, "Anthony, why don't you do that car like you did to those crazy doggies and kitties a while back?"

"Really? Sweet!" replied Anthony, who promptly used his super flamethrower to torch the flat back Dodge police interceptor.

The team re-entered the Silverado. The truck now had a caved-in rear bumper, a crumpled tailgate and smashed-out taillight lenses from where Mack backed into the closely pursuing squad car.

A group decision was made to quickly leave the area and locate a clean vehicle. The team fled rapidly as the charred Charger ignited and exploded, illuminating the hordes of black blow flies swarming through the North Carolina sky.

As they were driving away in the Silverado with the newly bashed-in rear bumper, Mack began to reflect upon the fact that his re-found friend and mentor, Jake, seemed different. As If he had changed physically and emotionally, as well as mentally, since his arrest and subsequent adventures.

The former Marine and DPD Sergeant now appeared to be harder, colder, and less human. He also appeared larger and more muscular than ever. This was hard to explain since Jake had been on the run the entire time and had not been working out or eating properly.

"Hey, man, can I ask you something?" McElroy asked.

"What's up?" Jake responded.

"What *really* happened to you out there? What happened to your soul?"

"My Soul? You too?" Asked Jake. "Why is everyone so concerned about my fucking Soul? Yeah, I ran over one of those creatures back there. I think it got stuck in the fan belt. So now the car is still parked there in front of Glazier's place and I imagine that THING is still struggling to separate itself from the motor."

"No, man. I mean your *soul*, your personality, your being."

"Oh. I thought you meant my Kia."

"No, Jake. Not your Kia. And how the hell do you explain your physique? For a guy who has been on the run, hunted, and *not* working out, how is it that you are still built like The Rock?"

"Maybe he exercises by lifting his Soul?" Anthony chimed in from the back seat.

Jake suddenly felt compelled to confide in his comrades about the skeleton in his closet.

"You're correct, Mack. I'm not the same Jake Hathaway you knew. I think the Zeus Juice is really starting to catch up with me. I can't remember. Did I ever tell you about the experiments from back in the corps?"

"No, you didn't. But Michelle mentioned something about them to me awhile back. I had no idea you were involved with them, though."

"I authorized some of my men to take experimental serums in the hopes of turning them into the ultimate warriors - with uncanny strength, and ferocity surging through their veins. They would be unaffected by pain, fatigue or illness and consumed only with the desire of fighting for the freedoms of our great nation.

"I figured if my guys were going to submit themselves to the testing, I should do the same. But it also just sounded too good to be true - who the hell wouldn't want to be Captain America, right? So, I took the Juice as well, but without telling the others. I took a lot more than I should have - more than what the Marine scientists were prescribing for the volunteers.

"As a result, I have experienced a growth in muscle mass and strength, and I do not tire or endure pain much at all. However, pain is not the only thing I fail to experience anymore. I struggle to feel emotions other than rage and an unquenchable thirst for enemy blood. I don't even recognize myself now. Sometimes when I look in the mirror, I see some stranger looking back at me. On more than one occasion this has resulted in my brain being overwhelmed with rage.

"My ability to rationalize or comprehend things like I have been able to in the past has been eroded. All told, it's as if I'm dying on the inside while my body is thriving on the outside."

The other men within the van all looked at each other, now somewhat anxious about the prospect of traveling any further with this cold, inhuman being that they once knew as Jake Hathaway.

"Do you feel like you want to kill or eat us?" Anthony half-jokingly questioned.

"Come on, don't be ridiculous. I don't feel like I want to eat any of you. At least not until our quest is over."

Everyone got a good laugh over Jake's cannibalistic crack, and then Duy became quite perplexed. "So, do we know if there's any correlation between the Marine Corps Zeus Project that you were associated with and the reported labs on both coasts?"

"God, I hope not. Because at least we in the Corps volunteered and somewhat knew what to expect the results of the serum to be. But if civilians were being abducted and shot up with this stuff like guinea pigs, that's inhumane. Hopefully we will be able to make that determination soon enough" Jake speculated.

As the Silverado continued to trek westbound and crossed the Tennessee state line, it was a mutual group decision which led the wayward travelers to find an appropriate vehicle to appropriate.

The pickup pulled into a half-full Walmart parking lot and began to cruise the rows as the guys were in search of their next mode of transportation. They soon located a beige Honda Odyssey van with tinted windows and Tennessee handicap plates.

Anthony piped up, "That one will work, right? Drop me off here. I can get it going for us."

He of small stature, with power tool in hand, drilled out the driver door lock and pulled the door open. Then he began to work on the van's steering column and ignition switch.

Mack parked the battered Silverado behind a large RV at the rear of the lot where it was not clearly visible from the main roadway. By the time he, Jake, Duy and Roscoe joined Anthony, the van was running and ready to roll.

"Can I drive for a while?" Anthony asked.

"Sure, man, that would be great." Mack agreed. "Just keep us headed in a southerly and western direction."

As the squad headed toward the south Texas border in their newly retained vehicle, Hathaway began to speculate aloud. "Mack, maybe it would be best if we let you off in Dallas so you can attempt to track down Amanda to make sure she is okay. And to also check on Austin and baby Carson."

Mack agreed. "Yeah, I need to tell Austin about Rich's video that he made in reference to his abduction and experiences at that lab in Florida. I also need to make sure Austin can keep Carson safe and hidden from the 'Containment Squad.'"

"But are you sure that you guys don't need an extra hand looking for that Mexican laboratory? You sure you don't want me to come along to watch y'alls' backs?"

"Nah, we will be fine," Jake asserted. "Shouldn't have any problems getting into Mexico. Then we just gotta find the lab and this doctor guy and get whatever information we need from him. Hopefully they have an anti-serum there as well so we can figure out how to mass-produce it. And then we will shut the place down once and for all."

"Besides, I've got my Roscoe back. This will be a piece of cake."

The Odyssey pulled into Mack's Dallas neighborhood and stopped a few doors door from his house.

"All right, good luck you guys! Keep me updated. Go kick some lab coat-wearing motherfucker's ass!"

Part 4 - What Happens There Slays There

In the end, no matter which cerebral hemisphere of your brain you favored throughout your existence, whether you leaned more toward the good or evil side, humanity eventually all falls dead. Every being eventually becomes one with the earth in the very place it was birthed. Mankind evolves into worm food and daisy fertilizer on a regular basis.

But one can possibly take solace in this theory. That those who, in life, preached their continuous and repugnant legacy of hate against others will, in death, meet "ANOTHER."

"ANOTHER" who, like them, preyed upon the weak and the downtrodden. And furthermore, perhaps that "ANOTHER" was now looking upon his predecessor with a gleam in his eye and necrophilia on his mind.

Chapter 32 - Just Another Chapter

Hidalgo, Texas / Mexico border. Year 1 month 7 ATBI

Recently, the American president had announced he was tearing down the towering walls along the north and south borders of the country. The previous POTUS had raised these walls during his last term in office. This new Amcrican leader claimed to be removing these barriers as a sign of peace and reconciliation between the nations.

However, as reported by Graham and Nunu on their underground podcast, many believed there was another underlying reason. Apparently, the U.S. government really wanted the borders opened again so they had a way and place to run all the DEAD out.

For the first time ever, more people were leaving America for Mexico rather than the other way around. And they primarily were fleeing America in order to escape *the infection.*

Resultantly, Mexico was now protesting the walls being removed. The Mexican President threatened to construct their own obstacles, although they realistically were not in the position financially to do so.

Mexico had begun to change drastically over the last few years. The pigmentation of the country had become a little bit lighter as the gringos from America were starting to infiltrate the nation.

The drug cartels had been negatively affected by the decline in demand for marijuana and other drugs when several states in the U.S. legalized them. It was then that the American entrepreneurs began to produce the drug legally and took over the U.S. market.

Additionally, law enforcement agencies in the U.S. had recently become so involved in the zombie-slaying business that they were too busy to enforce drug possession and other non-violent laws. American drug dealers became free to peddle their goods openly and thus, Mexican drug suppliers no longer had a market in the states. So, they ended up moving their businesses to other more profitable locales.

And with the cartels bouncing out, so did most of the violent crime. It made these territories more open to commerce again, providing many work opportunities and slowly driving the poverty level downward.

Anthony steered onward as the guys began their slow south - Texas odyssey from within their tan, Tennessee-placarded Odyssey.

And when the Honda van arrived near the McAllen-Hidalgo International Bridge at the Reynosa Texas/Mexico border, Jake and Duy were completely taken by surprise. They were shocked to see the American side of the border gateways were completely unmanned. No one was asking for passports, checking ID's, or searching vehicles. No access was being denied or even delayed. It was a mass exodus. Long lines of cars were proceeding through the border gates, as were many pedestrians. But they all came to an abrupt halt just a short way south of the border when they came upon the Mexico side.

For, equally as baffling was the sight of heavily armed police and federal military personnel on the Mexican side of the border crossings, threatening to shoot anyone trying to enter without clearance.

And so, it became abundantly clear to the men that it would not be nearly as easy getting into Mexico as they had originally anticipated. Rather than continue toward the border crossing gates, Anthony turned the soccer-mom-mobile around and headed back into Hidalgo.

"There's got to be another way! Let's just cruise around near the border and see what we can find," said the Dew-man. Jake and Anthony agreed. "Maybe we can find someone who can help smuggle us across. "

The van navigated east through the town, and it wasn't long before the team came across a shopping plaza. It was the home of an AutoZone auto parts store, a nail salon, and a Whataburger restaurant.

Anthony was somewhat baffled. "Dang, looks like we are back in Dallas again. It went from war zone to AutoZone in one block. I'm gonna drive around the back of these stores to see if there's some access to the border back there."

As he rounded the corner with the family wagon, Anthony noticed a shady-looking dude eye fucking their vehicle hard. "Fellas check this freak out. He looks like he thinks we are cops or something."

The lanky, nervous Mexican was wearing a white T-shirt, khaki pants, and a Houston Astros baseball cap. It appeared as if he was trying to keep a low profile, acting like he was just dumpster diving in the back. But he continued looking over his shoulder at the van while maintaining constant conversation on a disposable burner cell phone.

"Dew-man, let's go talk to this joker and see if he can get us across."

"Duy, Jake, and Roscoe hopped out of the sliding rear door of the Honda minivan and made eye contact with the nervous Mexican. The character took one look at the two men and their police dog and he abruptly took off in a sprint.

Jake was lagging, carrying much muscle mass which caused him to be somewhat slow. Meanwhile Duy and Roscoe remained hot on the stranger's trail, chasing him down one street, into an alley, then into an adjoining residential community. They continued between several rows of houses. Roscoe passed Duy and was barking fiercely as he nipped at the fleeing man's heels.

But just as quickly as this foot pursuit had started, Duy now realized he had lost the shady character. He could still hear Roscoe barking in the near distance, but he had completely lost sight of them both.

Anthony pulled up in the van directly behind Duy. Duy saw the gassed former Marine, Jake, gasping for air in the front passenger seat.

Duy was quick to ask Jake: "why are you riding in the van?"

"I was saving my energy for the fight that would have occurred after you caught him, but it looks like someone didn't do their part."

Roscoe was now bellowing from somewhere close, and Anthony parked their ride so all three men could search on foot.

Jake called out, "Roscoe!! Where are you, boy?"

The Belgian Malinois began to howl even louder in order to summon his human companions hither.

"He's over here," Jake advised the others as he began to sprint in that direction.

The three men came upon a wide-open galvanized chain link gate which led to the backyard of a white double wide trailer home. The rear door of the trailer appeared to be open as well. The adventurers entered the yard and then the trailer home. They exercised extreme caution, all with their weapons in hand and ready to be deployed. They fully anticipated finding their furry friend inside but were not expecting what they now saw before them.

There, in the center of what would normally be the living room of this residence, was nothing but dirt. No concrete, no tile, nothing whatsoever, except for soil. Dry, hard, reddish claylike ground that surrounded a large manhole cover-sized opening in the center of what should be the floor.

Roscoe stood at the top of the crevice, his eyes darting into the dark tunnel as he continued to howl.

"What is it boy? Did he go down the hole?"

"I think we got us a rabbit to catch, fellas. Let's go get him! "Jake rallied the team as he began to step into the aperture.

Anthony hesitated and was quick to voice his concern about such a venture. "Uhhh, I don't know if I mentioned this to you guys yet, but I'm seriously afraid of going into small spaces, like underground and stuff. What if we go in there and someone behind us up here starts to fill the hole with dirt? And they bury us alive? And also, what if there's huge rats down there and we can't see them, and they start gnawing on us?"

Just as Anthony was contemplating backing out of the hole idea, several DEAD began to stumble into the open trailer house door. They had been alerted to the location by the shrieking Roscoe.

"Oh shit!" Anthony echoed. "Let's go chase that rabbit!"

Man and dog alike began to climb down into the hole. The gargantuan, musclebound Jake entered last, barely able to squeeze into the opening. There was a sawed off 3-foot x 3-foot square of quarter-inch plywood above the ground lying beside the hole. The former police sergeant pulled the fabricated board over the opening behind him, hoping this would keep THEM from following him into the abyss.

Dropping a couple of feet to a lower level within, the men found a lengthy wooden ladder leading downward still. Leaning against the cavern wall beside the ladder was a filthy, rusted pickaxe which Sgt. Hathaway acquired just because it may come in handy down below.

Roscoe began to descend the ladder, his snout still tracking the scent of the fleet footed suspicious guy.

The further the team climbed downward, the darker and more humid the atmosphere became. About fifteen feet lower, all stepped down off the ladder. As they did, they felt the glitching beneath their shoes upon landing into piles of a very foul-smelling substance.

"Oh, perfect," Anthony spouted. "So, it's not enough that I have a fear of being buried alive and we are about twenty feet below the ground, but it's hot as hell and dark and we are walking around in shit!"

"I bet this is an abandoned drug smuggling tunnel" Jake said. It probably runs all the way from the U.S. side and under the border into Mexico. You could see where the Border Patrol or someone had cemented in that entrance to the tunnel, but someone had come through and jackhammered it back open again."

"Oh, by the way guys - that's not shit." Jake informed.

"What do you mean it's not shit? How can you tell?"

"I can see quite clearly down here, seems like I'm acclimating to the dark quite nicely. I believe we are trudging through fermenting innards. I think I just kicked a spleen."

"Ohhh!!!! Eeeewwww!!! GROSS!!" Anthony jumped upwards to remove his Nikes from the magenta flesh flush. However, he was unable to defy gravity and his Airs quickly splashed down again. This splashed slaughter sauce all over Duy's face.

"Hey!! Quit jumping around, dumbass! You got that stuff on me! My mouth was open!"

They continued shuffling slowly forward as a team. Roscoe continued his track followed by Jake with his newfound night vision capabilities. Behind him, Duy and Anthony remained closely together. They clung onto each other's shirt out of the fear that they could become separated and or lost in the blackness.

Onward they trudged, in a long, dark dirt tunnel that seemed to be spiraling deeper and deeper into the chasm. The thick, noxious air was becoming more and more overwhelmingly toxic with each step.

They marched further into the seemingly endless void, for what seemed to be at least a mile. Jake could see that several feet ahead of them was another tunnel that crossed the one they currently were traveling.

"Oh great!" Anthony squealed in a somewhat stifled voice. "Now which way are we supposed to go? It's like a friggin maze down here. We're not getting out alive, I just know it! "

"It's gonna be okay, man. Look, Roscoe is still tracking straight ahead. You watch, I bet soon we will see light at the end of the tunnel." Duy comforted his wee amigo.

No sooner had Duy spoken, a clan of musty, underground dwelling endoparasite packers rounded the corner from that crossover tunnel. They now blocked the path that the humans were traveling. It was plain to see that there would be no getting around them, the only possibility was to go *through* them.

"Oh shit," Jake said. He was not too keen on Roscoe's odds of making through
the line of DEAD ahead. Not even with his muzzle daggers.

Jake grabbed Roscoe by his tail and restrained the valiant K9 from venturing further toward the HUNGRY.

"Roscoe, BLEIBE! "

Roscoe promptly sat and stayed put as commanded. The brawny law officer, armed with his newfound pickaxe, marched forward.

"ARRRRRRGGGGGGG, BLEAAAAAAAHHHHH" was the horrible eerie intonation echoing through the clay chamber.

"FUCKKKK YOUUU MOTHAH FUCKAHSSSS!!!!!" Jake screamed as he went Super Mario on the FLESHWROUGHT, slinging his miner's pick in short quick strokes. His size and the tight enclosure would not allow him to swing the tool over his head as it's customarily utilized.

"GLUNKKKK, GLOOOOOOOOPPPPP." The once rust-encrusted axe blades were now shiny and sharp again as the bones from the beasts had revived their vibe. They sliced and diced zombie heads, necks and faces. The axe detruncated their limbs, separating the flesh from the bones as the laceration mantra played on much like an orchestrated composure. It was a meat hook masterpiece.

This nauseous genocide of the grotesque and flagitious concluded as abruptly as it began. Jake the morbid angel was now coated with the substance and stench of splattered slaughter sludge and decay.

"Holy fuck, Jake! How many were there?" Duy asked, awestruck.

"Man, I don't know. I was too busy to count them. Ok Roscoe, JAGEN!"

The canine leapt over the pile of rotted entrails and eventual maggot meals, as the pyramidal of humans followed suit.

They marched onward for approximately fifty more yards until they came across another wooden ladder. This one went upwards to a steel manhole cover. Jake pushed upwards on the silver steel disk and sent it airborne for a few feet before it smacked down in the middle of a dirt road.

The team climbed out of what might have become their underground tomb. Anthony took a huge breath of fresh air and gasped, "I can't believe we made it! "

"Where do you think we are?" questioned Duy.

"If I had to guess I would say we are in Mexico," guessed Jake as he observed a street sign and advertising for a couple of small shops which were all written in Spanish.

They all began to walk several feet before they realized how tired they were from their adventure within the labyrinth. It was also getting quite late in the day.

"I think we lost the suspicious guy. Or he lost us, one or the other. For all we know, maybe that was his spleen we trounced on down in the tunnel at the bottom of the ladder," Jake recalled.

Duy agreed. "Yeah, maybe we need to rest up for the night and start out fresh tomorrow. Let's find a safe place to set up camp, there's no telling how long we might be here."

Montpelier, Vermont. Year 1 month 9 ATBI (October)

In the small town of Montpelier, Vermont, a group of a dozen young students from a Sunday school group ranging from the ages five to fifteen were on a church-sponsored fall pumpkin patch hayride. The kids were seated on hay bales on the back of a fifteen-foot-long wooden flatbed trailer, towed by a medium sized green John Deere tractor.

It was evening time. Dusk was settling in and there was a slight roll of fog lingering about. Soon the tractor came to a stop in the pumpkin patch and the kids sprang off the trailer to pick out a free pumpkin of their choice to take home and turn into a wonderful jack-o-lantern.

Most of the children became focused upon searching for their prize orange gems. But one of the more observant children pointed over toward the adjoining corn field and loudly exclaimed, "Whoa! Look – monsters!!"

The kids looked over and saw slow moving figures dragging their way through the fog-covered corn field. They were now only approximately a hundred feet away. One of the older kids excitedly jabbered, "Haa, that's cool! They got some people out here dressed up like zombies!"

Steve was an eighteen-year-old farmhand who enjoyed driving the local church kids around through the patch each year.

Steve looked at the figures wobbling through the golden stalks and he knew there was trouble brewing. For he knew that no one on the farm had planned for any sort of monsters or creatures to be looming through the fields. Steve didn't want to panic the little ones, so he abruptly announced, "Kids, everyone get back on the trailer…"

"But we haven't picked out our pumpkins yet…"

"We have plenty of them to choose from back in the barn. They are, even better and bigger than these. Come on, let's go!"

The children jumped on the trailer and Steve punched the accelerator, sending one lightweight seven-year-old kid flying off of the back.

Steve slammed on the John Deere's breaks and the tractor skid to a stop.

Steve ran to the rear of the trailer and grabbed the tot by his scruff. He picked up the little dude, hoisting him back onto the trailer.

"Okay, everyone hold on to the person next to you, especially you smaller kids, hold onto a bigger kid nearby."

Steve again stomped onto the accelerator pedal. He was still looking back at his cargo to make sure no one had been thrown off the back again.

But because he was not paying attention to what was in front of him, the John Deere veered directly toward a large boulder. The tractor abruptly collided with the large rock. The front wheel warped around the stone, bending the front axle and rendering the farm vehicle inoperable.

Dusk was near and a heavy fog blanketed the pumpkin patch. This fog cover concealed the close gravitation of the lucid figures that had been looming in the corn patch.

Their speed increased gradually as they sensed human flesh. Their sustenance of choice was dead ahead.

Steve yelled, "Everyone run for the barn! Older kids grab the little ones! RUNNNN!!"

Everyone abandoned the tractor and trailer combo. They were all sprinting, stumbling through the pumpkin patch and tripping over vines and rocks, pumpkins, gourds, and squash.

Some of the children who tripped, dropped to the ground. Of those, some regained their footing and ran fleet of foot back into the barn safely. Others on the other hand were not as fortunate. Three of the children tripped a second time and were swallowed up by a sea of DEAD. Nearly a dozen zombies swarmed over the exhausted kids and in a frenzy. They relished the carnage by feasting on the innards of the kiddy cadavers.

Chapter 33 - The Anthropophagus Among

Us

Fort Leavenworth, Kansas

The United States Disciplinary Barracks, more often referred to as Leavenworth, is the U.S military's only maximum-security facility that houses male service members. They have all been convicted of or court-martialed for violations of the Uniform Code of Military Justice.

Although this was an Army facility, the two outcast Marines, Barrett Blackhoof and Levi Fiedler, found themselves committed to being longtime residents. They had been sentenced to twenty years apiece for their roles in the Al Anbar incident.

So far, the two inmates have been incarcerated for over six and a half years. Although they entered on the same day and were scheduled to leave at the same time, their incarceration experiences had differed vastly.

Barrett Blackhoof since childhood had been cursed with a very poor attitude and a quick temper. So, while others in the prison were trying to make the most of their stay by reading, getting an education, or at least pumping iron for muscles, Blackhoof opted out. Rather, he chose to pick fights with fellow inmates, steal their rations, and direct cat calls to their wives or girlfriends who sat across from their loved ones on visitation days.

Because of his erratic behavior, and because he was one of the most dangerous inmates there, Blackhoof was considered a Level 5 inmate. He was moved to the Supermax base, where he was kept in solitary confinement for twenty-three hours every day.

On the other hand, was Levi Fiedler. Ever since he had joined the Corps and was deployed to the Middle East, had become interested in Islam. He spent most of his time studying the Koran in the prison library.

He already held a strong hatred for the U.S. government as a result of the Zeus Project and his sentencing from the Al Anbar Incident. And it became fueled even more when he began to study and idealize the writings of Osama Bin Laden.

Over time, Levi, much like the others who had taken multiple doses of the Zeus Juice in the Corps - Blackhoof, Camacho, and Jake - had become much larger. He was the beneficiary of incredible strength and stamina. They all had become able to endure extreme pain while also possessing amazing healing powers.

In addition to all of these, Fiedler had over time also been able to develop one other capability that the others had not. Fiedler was still in the process of mastering the skill but was becoming somewhat proficient in the practice of psychokinesis. This was the psychic ability allowing a person to influence a physical system without physical interaction.

With his unique and powerful attributes to propel him, Fiedler now had plans to recruit others around the world to assist him in his cause. He had become obsessed with the goal of making not only America, but the entire Western World, pay.

Year 1 month 10 ATBI (November)

One brisk November Tuesday morning in Leavenworth Kansas, two Army prison guards escorted the leg-shackled Barrett Blackhoof to the outdoor exercise yard.

On each side of the yard stood a fourteen-foot-high fence. A second fence, just a few feet away, was equally as high. But this one was charged with a lethal current of electricity.

Blackhoof, who was as tall as the biggest guard but twice as wide, wasted no time in using his left hand to grab the guard to his left. He used his right hand to clasp the prison guard to his right. He then utilized his sheer strength to bash their heads together as if he was playing the symbols in a marching band. Both guards lost consciousness and collapsed to the ground.

The behemoth Blackhoof then released the guard to his left. Blackhoof grabbed the right guard, tucked him up under Blackhoof's right armpit, and began to climb the towering fence much like Kong.

A guard in a nearby watchtower began to fire his rifle at the escaping inmate. In little time, Blackhoof was already jumping down off the first fence and running toward the second. He was using the unconscious guard's body to shield him from the hail of bullets being sprayed at him.

Barrett threw the guard's body about halfway up the second

fence, and it remained stationary as the electrical currents fried the body like Spam in a greasy, hot frying pan. The fence shorted out rapidly, and the Native American was up and over that barrier in no time.

The disenchanted Blackhoof, now on the exterior of the secured facility, came across an occupied Army mail carrier Jeep. He extracted said letter deliverer before driving off with her vehicle.

With one more piece of business to attend to, Blackhoof drove the Mopar mail truck back onto the Leavenworth base and through the wall of one of the minimum-security habitation barracks. The eager escapee had done his homework and determined that this wall separated his compadre, Levi Fiedler, from certain freedom.

With the Jeep now halfway into the building with brick and rubble having been thrown all about, Blackhoof yelled from the driver's seat, "Come on, Levi! Let's get the fuck out of here!"

Fiedler replied, "no, you go on without me. My work here isn't finished yet."

Reynosa, Tamaulipas Mexico

Just on the outskirts of town, the band of brothers had found a wide-open field to park their Odyssey in. Then they set up some basic trip wires with aluminum pop cans attached, all along the perimeter. This would allow them to sleep in the van and remain relatively safe while giving them notice and time to react if some of THEM entered the camp site.

Jake, Duy, Anthony and Roscoe spent several days scouting out the area. They had noticed that there was a large concentration of the creatures not far from where they exited the tunnel, through a manhole in the street.

For this reason, the guys knew that the secret research facility they had heard about had to be close by.

Abruptly, a Hispanic teenage kid came running up to the guys, breathing heavily and fearing for his life. His name was Rafael Torres. He was a seventeen-year-old who was about six feet tall and very lean from having played a lot of soccer. He surprisingly had a better than average understanding of the English language. "Please help me!"

"Kid, what's wrong? Is someone chasing you?" Jake

inquired.

"You gotta help me. I left home a few days ago without telling anyone where I was going. And then I was hanging out in the street, kicking the soccer ball with my friend. A black Range Rover pulled up.

"A sleazy-lookin' Mexican-American guy wearing a baggy black pair of swat cop pants and a black T-shirt, ballcap, and aviator sunglasses jumped out of the front right seat. He walked up to us. He said he was some agent for the Federal District Police, or something like that. He flashed a badge.

"He sounded American, speaking good English. Weirdest thing was that he had very long, wavy black hair. Like Troy Polamalu. He didn't look like a real cop to me with that hair," said Rafael.

"My buddy took off because he was afraid. I don't know why I didn't, too. He said I could make money if I helped him do some labor at some rich person's house. I agreed.

"The cop guy and some other white dude drove me over to a boarded-up grocery store, the 'Super Mercado.' Once we got there, we went inside the back way - through a solid white metal door with a peep hole.

"So, when we get inside, there's like three or four people wearing white doctor coats. They told me instead of doing labor that they needed someone to sample these new vitamins that they were wanting to put on the market in America.

"After I said yes and took them, they said I have to stay for a few days to see the results before they pay me. But later I began to hear some other people in another room. They sounded like they were sick or crazy. Moaning and screaming and stuff. It freaked me out. I wanted to leave now, so I pushed one guy wearing a white jacket away, and then I ran out the front door."

"Okay. Rafael, right? Do you think you could lead us to that grocery store?" Duy asked.

"Yeah, I think so. "

"So why did you run away from home in the first place? "Anthony asked.

"I have this dream to be an international soccer star. But my dad has different plans for me.

He wants me to learn the family business and take over when

he retires. He had tutors come teach me and my brother English so later on we can do business with Americans."

"But I don't want that."

"What exactly does he do?" Anthony asked.

"My dad is Juan Carlos Aguilar."

"Oh shit." Duy exclaimed. "He's the head of the Aguilar drug cartel."

Rafael nodded. "Yep."

"All right, guys. Rafael says he can take us back there. Let's arm up and get ready to roll. Anthony, can you put Roscoe's muzzle mask on?"

"Yeah, no problem."

So, the four live crew and Roscoe climbed into their conversion van and began to scour the area looking for the monster shop.

"This looks right - I think it's down there." Raphael instructed as Anthony drove onward. "There it is. "

Anthony parked the Odyssey war wagon on the side of the once-supermarket building, then proceeded to the back door. The entire building was completely blacked out, and there was no sign of activity around.

Jake muscled the back door down with a lowered shoulder. The team was instantly greeted by a gaggle of gore. Several DEAD pushed their way toward the scent of fresh meat as they moved in to devour the living ones who had entered.

"Let's waste them inside before they can get out and surround us!" The Herculean Hathaway commenced to slaying the mis-creations with his miner's pickaxe. He began swinging, poking, jabbing the blade and flogging THEM in their noggins.

Duy began slicing and dicing zombies left and right with his pair of nickel bladed Karambit combat knives. He was slashing and shredding the beasts, creating a sanguine spray.

Anthony, being of a shorter stature, was handling business down below. He was utilizing his nifty cordless reciprocating saw to remove the legs from the lethargic and bring them to the floor. There, Roscoe took over with his membrane-destroying muzzle blades.

During this battle, a handful of white lab coats escaped

through the front. They had released the DEAD from their cages in the warehouse when they heard the back door get destroyed.

THEY were now all immobilized, and the team began to walk throughout the facility. It had the appearance of a hospital emergency room in some areas, with beds and curtains and goo-soaked surgical tools lying around. Other sections of the place looked more like a zoo with large cages all about and blowflies lining the walls.

"Jake, look what I found hiding in the attic crawl space above the old manager's office" Duy said as he shoved a lab coat wearing medium-sized man of Middle Eastern descent into the space in front of Jake and his cohorts.

"So, who the fuck are you, and what's been going on here? "the former police sergeant interrogated.

"I am Dr. Abraham Gideon. I have been expecting a visit since I let the boy escape. I am so fortunate that you are here now so I can be free of all this.

"I am just one of the many doctors and scientists that the U.S. Government brought in several years ago. Our jobs were to implement ways to develop 'Invulnerable Warriors' for their military and 'super athletes' for their Olympics and sports programs. They had us working directly with the Marine division. They set up two labs for us in the States, one on each coast, and then this one after the Florida lab got shut down.

"I was initially just an assistant to Dr. Sonjay Muhammed, who has since left us when he got a little too absorbed in his work."

Jake offered, "That name sounds familiar. I think he was one of the consultants the Corps was using for our Zeus project."

"Yes, that is correct."

Jake needed some clarification. "Okay, Doctor. I don't get it. So, it all started out with you guys trying to develop these ultimate warriors with us in the Corps. But we all know that didn't work out. What went wrong?"

"At first the serum seemed to be working. It was intended that we would give the soldiers their 'Power Rations', daily subjecting them to minuscule portions of the formula.

"But then there was talk that Camacho, Fiedler and Blackhoof had stolen some of the vials and then consumed amounts *way* over what we had prescribed. Very dangerous. So of course, the effects on those guys were incredible. Damaging, but incredible at the same time. A few months later, there were accounts of them pulling three-foot diameter trees out of the ground and lifting automobiles.

"But for those that were taking the rations as suggested, they were benefiting quite nicely. That is until it eventually destroyed their brains, and some could not think for themselves any longer. They began attacking and eating their own comrades.

"But even when the generals over the project learned that the new drug had turned their own people into monsters, they did not stop the program. They said that as long as the soldiers did not turn into monsters right away, if their transformations could be controlled and delayed for a few years, then the soldiers would be extra powerful while they were still active officers. And if they *turned* after their military commitment was over, no big deal.

"Eventually though some of the soldiers were turning much earlier than others. This is because all people are unique and are affected differently by various strains of viruses and drugs.

"You know, it is very likely that someday we would have been successful. But like always, the government people were impatient. They would not allow us the proper amount of time that we really needed to perfect the product before they started using the drugs on their men."

Gideon continued. "Isn't that just like the impatient Americans to throw billions of dollars at something that doesn't even work? Hell, where do you think they started spending all of the money that used to go towards the space program?"

"We used to joke about that. We would call these experiments 'one giant leap backwards for mankind" Gideon snickered.

"I tried to get out of this long ago. What they were making me do was evil, immoral. I tried to stop the whole project, but they would not hear me out.

"Then the whole Al Anbar thing went down, and this project became exposed to the world. They sent us all packing. I was so relieved, I felt free again. I planned to start out on my own and aimed to develop a performance-enhancing product for the top athletes in the world. I could have made millions.

"But then he found me."

"Who did?" Hathaway asked.

"The one who calls himself Camacho.

"After he was forced out of the military because of his role in the Al Anbar incident, he testified in the court trial against soldiers Barrett Blackhoof and Levi Fiedler to avoid his own prosecution.

"After that, he tracked me down. He informed me that he would bring me to the authorities and have me prosecuted on a variety of charges if I did not set up this new lab here in Mexico. I had to do it in exchange for my freedom.

"Anyways, it's still Camacho and who knows who else is running the show. They are still hoping to develop some type of indestructible warrior or super athletes. When we needed to find volunteers to participate in the testing, it was his idea to go out with his cronies to collect the homeless, illegals, druggies, runaways; the dregs of society, to be brought to us to experiment with.

"But you watch - Camacho only cares about himself. If he gets some foreign nations interested in this work, I could see him jumping ship and selling out in a heartbeat. Anything he can do to make himself a fortune in the end."

"So why would you take a risk and let the kid escape and cooperate with us *now*?" Jake was curious.

"I don't have much life left to live. I was accidentally exposed to the virus. I am doomed. I don't want to die without doing something valiant before I pass. For the sake of all humanity, someone needs to put an end to all of this.

"Oh - and on a side note, I hear that within the last few months all of the branches of the military started to use the serum again. But now, as a weapon. It's part of their Zeus to Zombie plan, or Z squared."

"Huh?" Jake was stupefied. "They are still using it?"

"Yes, now they give the serum to soldiers even more slowly, with tinier doses over long periods of time. It increases their strength and will, but the side effects don't set in as quickly.

"Then, if the soldier becomes badly injured or ill when in enemy territory, they have been instructed to administer to themselves one final mega-dose with their Z-pen. They shoot it up in the leg.

"This turns them into zombies, and they continue fighting the enemy long after they would have if they had died. And then they bite the enemies who in turn will eventually turn as well and eat their entire ranks. The victims multiply.

"They like to refer to this as 'slaying it forward'."

"So, break it down for us then in terms we can understand. What exactly were you guys giving to these people you are experimenting on? And what was in our Power Rations or 'Zeus Juice' in the Corps?" Jake demanded.

"Well, there was some HGH for building muscle mass. Also, some prostaglandins to promote inflammation by diluting the blood vessels and letting blood flow into body tissue to build more mass as well. It also provided quicker recovery from vigorous training and exercise.

"There was also some creatine to boost levels of adenosine triphosphate, or ATP, in the muscle tissue. We added erythropoietin to increase red blood cell production, increasing endurance and allowing the recipient to train or fight longer and harder.

"Then we sprinkled in some bromantane for good measure. This is a chemical the Russians used to give to their soldiers and cosmonauts to make them more alert and to fight fatigue."

Jake offered, "Doc, I ain't no scientist but none of those substances you described should be making people turn into walking cadavers that want to eat other folks..."

"You are correct" Gideon said. "Except that somewhere during the process of creating this compound substance, some protein-aceous infectious microscopic particles, or prions, found their way into the synthesis process. These prions are pesky pathogens responsible for a variety of neurodegenerative diseases such as Mad Cow Disease and scrapie.

"Mad cow disease affected cattle. And scrapie is a painful, fatal prion disease that attacks the nervous system of goats and sheep.

"These diseases also attack brain tissue, often leaving mini craters in the membrane. Now imagine a disease that can influence humans in a similar manner. That is what we are seeing here now."

Anthony scratched his head and contemplated the doc's last sentiments. "Okay, so you're saying these *things* are not dead. They're not zombies? They are just people who are *really* sick and fucked up?"

"No, I would not consider them to be zombies as portrayed in the traditional movies and TV shows. They don't climb out of cemetery graves after being embalmed and inactive for years. Everyone knows the *dead* cannot suddenly reawaken and emerge from their dirt beds to plow upwards through six feet of soil and pop their heads out of the ground like that Whack-A-Mole game at the video arcade."

The science guy chuckled to himself, then halted. He quickly ascertained that no one there was amused.

"It would probably be more accurate to describe these as something else. Beings that are not clinically dead or living - but somewhere in between. Thus, I like to call them the 'in-betweeners.' Their hearts can be defunct, blood no longer flowing. They should be deceased and down for the count, but they don't feel the pain and don't know they are dead, so they continue to sludge around.

"So, to answer your question, I don't know what they should be called. But they are something quite different from your Hollywood zombies. However, I would say they are still zombies, nonetheless. The only difference is that these ones we are seeing- are real.

"Some of us in the laboratory were referring to them as 'Anthrops,' short for the term 'Anthropophagi,' which means an eater of human flesh. They exist merely to eat and devour animal and human flesh.

"And they are very difficult to stop. One must destroy their brain."

Gideon continued. "Some others started calling them 'carnies' for carnivores or 'chemically altered ravenous nonhumans', whichever you prefer. I didn't like the term 'carnies' because apparently that is the nickname given to those people who wear old Motley Crue concert shirts cut into 'wife-beaters', chain smoke cigarettes and put your kids on the rides at the state fair. Quite scary characters themselves."

Duy quizzed the science guy.

"Then how does one account for the reports of people waking up after being pronounced dead in emergency rooms or sitting up straight during their autopsy? And some even climbing out of their graves? These are accurate accounts from morticians, emergency room doctors, paramedics, and grave diggers. These aren't just headlines from the National Enquirer. This is the real deal."

Gideon responded. "In order for any being to move at all - anything from opening an eyelid to sitting straight up on a coroner's table - there has to be at least a minute portion of the central nervous system; the brain and spinal cord, functioning.

"Now when a person has been infected with these prion-based neurodegenerative diseases, it seems as if many of the body's key organs and systems become lethargic. Much like when one falls into a coma.

"This could make it virtually impossible to detect a pulse, heartbeat, blood pressure, and brain activity. There would even be a good chance that the body temperature would be reduced and there could even be signs of rigor mortis.

"These characteristics combined would easily make someone infected with this malady to appear deceased. Thus, they are being pronounced dead, being sent off for autopsies or going straight to funeral homes for burial and awakening from their slumber with some very inconspicuous timing."

"Okay, it's starting to make sense to me now. Except for this: how are people who weren't even experimented on or been given the 'Power Rations' now becoming infected through bites?" Jake questioned.

"It's simple - any transfer of body fluids from an infected one to another is just like being injected with a loaded syringe full of the serum. The disease cannot be transmitted through skin absorption alone, but it can be contracted when these diseased fluids enter into a previously healthy recipient's mucous membranes such as the mouth, nose, and eyelids to name a few. Or even open wounds."

Jake, Duy and Anthony all looked at each other. They were obviously concerned about this newfound information they had previously been completely unaware of. Duy declared, "Jake, remind me to get some goggles, face masks and a raincoat as soon as we get outta here."

Jake nodded in the affirmative and redirected his questioning of the doctor. "So, once infected, how long does it take before you …?"

"Before you are stricken and mutate?" Gideon completed Jake's sentence for him.

"You know, everyone's body is unique. Much like each fingerprint or retinal blood vessel pattern. So, there are many factors to be considered, but a lot depends upon the means in which the virus was contracted.

"A person who receives a transfer of infected body fluids through an open wound is going to mutate slower. Slower than one who is bitten and receives that contagion directly into their bloodstream. And they are also losing their precious untainted hemoglobin simultaneously. This person could switch over in a matter of minutes..."

The science guy was on a roll. He was feeling somewhat satisfied in the fact that he may be helping these young men in their efforts to understand and fight this epidemic.

"So, what you are wondering now is - what can one of these creatures do? Can they think? Can they run? Can they fight or maneuver a weapon or turn doorknobs or climb trees?"

"Yeah...?" Jake said.

"Well, again – every person and body is unique. But some obvious factors can determine these answers. Physical abilities and/or limitations are the primary factor.

"A person who in life was old and slow from arthritis or missing a leg is not going to change and become any quicker after the morphosis. Then you also factor in some rigor mortis, which is the stiffening of the limbs following death as muscles decay. This seriously slows them down, depending how far along into the process they are.

"Throw in the fact that there is also autolysis, or postmortem cell disintegration, and putrefaction, the decomposition of proteins by anaerobic microorganisms. You can see that most of these mutants are going to be slow because their bodies are shutting down and struggling to function at even the lowest levels.

"Another element to consider is the condition of the brain in that who has switched over. As we discussed already, the infected have cerebral disease. Corrosion is eating away at their membrane.

"I don't know how much you guys know about the human brain. But in a nutshell, there are two hemispheres which are linked to the corpus callosum, which is just a large bundle of nerve fibers through which the two halves communicate back and forth.

"This communication is what coordinates such various functions of the body as motor, sensory, and mental functions. So, if the portion of the cerebrum that controls motor skills is diseased and/or damaged from any type of injury, the Anthrop is likely to be dragging some limbs around and functioning much slower.

"A 'throp that has holes blown out of its mental function fuse box may have the ability to use its hand to turn a doorknob but will have no clue as to how or why to make such an attempt."

Anthony was chomping at the bits to ask his question: "Okay, doc. Now tell us how the nation and mankind can survive this plague."

"Well, the solution is no secret. People must stop injecting themselves or others with the serum at the front end. Additionally, all of the infected must be eradicated, and then all of the water and soil that has been corrupted with the toxin from the dead remains must be decontaminated, as well as all of the various mosquitoes and insects that may carry the germs. They must also be eliminated.

"And as for those who have already been exposed, there is no cure available. The only one who could create such a thing, an antivirus or vaccine, was Dr. Muhammed. And he has since flown the coop. Other than tracking him down or someone else concocting such an antidote, those who are infected like me are nothing more than ticking timebombs."

"So, in short, fear the Anthropophagus. Because they sure as hell do not fear you!"

KAAABOOOOMMMMMM!!!!!

An earth-shaking explosion erupted in the near distance, followed by a thick grey smoke which propelled all around the men where they stood. In a caricature of chaos, Duy became separated from the rest of his crew.

He was suddenly smashed in the back of his head with a solid hard wood rifle stock, sending him straight into dreamland.

Chapter 34 - Wake Up Call

Reynosa, Tamaulipas Mexico

Duy Tran woke up at the crack of dawn, with a seventy-five-pound Belgian Malinois police dog licking his face. His head was pounding like a heavy metal drummer's bass drum. He was sprawled out on the ground outside the now empty and abandoned structure that just days before was operating as a secret laboratory.

Duy had been rocked by someone or something that abruptly ended his consciousness of the evening before. Now in his blurry of indescribable head trauma and pain, he sat upright on the sunbaked, red Mexican soil. And all he could wonder was: where the hell is Jake?

A few feet away from Duy was the body of Anthony, face down in the dirt and disturbingly still. Duy instinctively presumed he was dead at first sight, but quickly proceeded to wake him up. "Little man - you okay?"

"Yeah I guess," Anthony weakly retorted. "And don't call me that."

Duy stood on wobbly legs and began to look around for Jake, telling Roscoe "Find Jake, boy. Find Jake."

Roscoe, although trained and educated in the German language, could not comprehend Duy's commands, but he knew what Duy was getting at. Roscoe put his nose to the ground, searching for the familiar scent of his best friend.

Within a few moments, a mud-encased tan Toyota Sequoia pulled alongside Duy and Anthony.

Inside the crew cab of the Sequoia sat four heavily armed Mexican men. Each was gripping their own automatic rifle to their sides with the stock ends on the floorboards and the barrel ends facing up toward the inside roof.

"Hey, we know where your big muscle-bound friend is at" remarked the rear left passenger. Roscoe was going crazy barking at the men and eager to jump in through the lowered back window.

"My name is Humberto. These are my employees. Word on the street is that my boy Rafael and your friend got taken at gunpoint by several undercover agent-looking guys. One of my people was able to follow them and is still tracking them currently. Seems they are headed north into the U.S. and continuing northbound up through the states.

"We are gonna get my boy back. If you care to help us with that, we will see to it your amigo is saved, too."

Duy and Mack looked at each other as if to say, "should we?" But after a mere few seconds of hesitation, Duy coaxed Anthony with, "we got nothing else to go on. I guess we need to do this."

Tran tried to settle the anxious K9 down so that he could climb into the Sequoia with the duo. "It's okay, boy. Calm down."

They hopped up into the open rear hatchback of the spacious luggage area of the SUV. Then it proceeded to burn off with them inside.

"So, what were you guys doin' here in Mexico in the first place?" Humberto asked. "And what's up with that dog? Is he vicious or what? He's making me nervous."

"We were here looking for these crazy people who have been doing experiments on innocent people and turning them into monsters. We actually found what we were looking for but got ambushed before we could leave."
Duy replied.

"Oh, and this is Roscoe, he's a pol…. umm… trained security dog."

The driver, Felipe, continued northbound at a pace best described as "balls to the wall." He was driving about as fast as the vehicle could go without the wheels falling off, and only slowing down or stopping when necessary.

The two newest passengers held onto whatever they could to avoid being slung around in the back of the sport utility vehicle, as Anthony moaned, "I'm gonna be sick."

Upon their arrival to the closest border gate to the U.S., the Toyota got to the rear of the line, about twenty cars deep. The Mexican militia working the gate recognized the vehicle and flagged the driver to pull into the next lane over, which according to the signage was closed.

Felipe handed the gatekeeper a stuffed plain white envelope, and the gate popped open.

"Okay, we are right around the corner from the airstrip. My people have been in communication with me. They have tracked the people who have your friend and my son - all the way to Nevada. So, we will fly into Las Vegas and take it from there."

The large Toyota squealed onto a Hidalgo private airstrip

where attending gatekeepers automatically opened the double entry gates upon sight of the vehicle.

"Hey, Humberto, can we make a quick pit stop in Dallas to pick up a buddy? He will prove very helpful if we get in a shit storm."

"You know this is not a 'for fun' trip, right? We're not going to see a show with those gay gringos and tigers."

"Yeah, no - I know. This guy is big, good with weapons. He likes to fight."

"Very well then," Humberto conceded.

Duy phoned Mack with the news.

"Dude, we need your help. Jake's been abducted, and they took him to Vegas. We are flying now, and we will pick you up at this little airstrip in Waxahachie. I'll send you the GPS coordinates."

"Whoa, hold on. Who has Jake? It must have taken about twenty guys to get him detained and abducted - aaand who are you guys with?" Mack asked.

"We can explain later. But have you had any luck? "Duy questioned.

"Kind of. I found Austin, and he's taking care of Carson. I showed Austin the video, tried to explain to him as best I could about what really happened to his dad, Rich. But he acts like he doesn't believe the whole Florida lab story. He said his dad was probably just drunk or high when he made the recording, possibly mentally disturbed."

Mack continued "So, it seems as if Austin is still mad at Jake and he doesn't believe that Carson is in any danger either."

"As for Amanda, she really is gone and has not spoken to Austin at all. He has no idea where she is."

Mack's iPhone buzzed and blared as a message flashed across the screen. "Hey Mack, it's Megan. So, like - Campos is spreading rumors around here that some cop in Pennsylvania saw Jake eating some beans?? What's going on? Can you call me please?"

"All right, Dew-man. I gotta call Megan. I'll see you in Waxahachie in a bit."

Mack returned the call to Megan and gave her the latest updates concerning Jake. "I need to go with you," she said. "I can help. I'll meet you at the airstrip. "

An hour later, Megan met Mack at the secluded air strip in Waxahachie. They had not been there long when a small Cessna 120 propeller-driven plane came into view. It made an abrupt, jerky landing and wobbled its way another two hundred feet down the line before coming to a standstill.

The passenger door opened, and the attached built-in stairway lowered to the outside. Mack and Megan jogged up the stairs to join Duy, Anthony and Roscoe on the plane.

Mack then looked around and saw their other travel companions. He immediately recognized Humberto Aguilar as the head of the Aguilar drug cartel.

He casually worked his way over to Duy and said, "You didn't tell me we would be traveling with drug kings."

"You didn't ask that," Duy responded. "But it's all good, they are looking for their kid just like we are looking for Jake. We are in this together. At least we know they're not afraid to get a little blood on them."

"True that. Okay." Mack settled into his seat next to his steamy academy classmate, Megan Anderson.

"Ok, Megan. So, tell me why you are so willing to risk everything to help us rescue Jake."

Megan began to bare it all. "I told you, there was a connection between us. On those days he trained me. It was life changing. We both felt it, and we both tried to fight it. I was married, we worked in the same division, our age difference... Everything about it was taboo. The repercussions we would have been dealt were extreme, we each could have found ourselves dumped, unemployed, chastised.

"So, we went our separate ways, I requested a transfer to Northwest just to make sure I would not be tempted to stray.

"It worked out fine until one morning we ran into each other in traffic court downtown. The case was the result of a traffic stop we had made together on one of the training days. Our setting was postponed until after lunch and court intervened until the afternoon session would start back up. We had two hours to kill.

"I told Jake it would be a good opportunity for me to get a workout in, and he said he would like to lift as well. He suggested we go back to the Central Division where we could workout close by and make it back to court on time.

"I grabbed my workout clothes and gear out of my car and we drove together to Central. We separated at the station and I went into the ladies' locker room to change into my exercise outfit, a white jogging bra with a half shirt over it, and pink spandex shorts with running shoes. I then went to see if Jake was ready and knocked on his office door. He opened the door and was already changed into a white wife-beater and black running shorts. When he turned to grab his shoes, I followed him into the large unoccupied single office and shut the door behind me. I don't know why I shut the door; I just did.

"That was it. The point of no return. We just sprang at each other like two hungry wild animals attacking their prey. Hugging at first, then groping. That led to light kissing and then a hard-core make out session. There was a large wooden door behind the desk which led to a large walk-in concrete storage closet beneath the stairs that led to the second floor of the building.

"Jake opened the closet door as we waltzed our way into the dark storage room. We could hear heels going up the stairs above us, but it merely acted as a white noise filter in the background. We barely noticed those sounds over our heavy breathing, moaning, and whispering sweet nothings into each other's ear.

"Although the room felt cool as we first went in, before long it felt steamy and hot like a sauna. We were both sweating, panting, lusting. Before long, each of us had frantic hands in the other person's shorts. And without going into detail, let's just say that at least one of us got *off* before we got out.

"And the rest is history. We began seeing each other regularly and religiously for a couple of months. We would meet in parking lots, hotel rooms. It was incredible. And then it was over as abruptly as it began."

Mack was intrigued. "What happened?"

"I ended it. I got scared. It was getting too serious too fast. I was young, immature, confused about what I really wanted. I also was extremely busy with many side ventures I was working on. In addition to my full-time career with DPD, I was into Crossfit training, and doing some modeling. I also created a website to promote fitness in law enforcement and was selling gym apparel and other fitness gear. That was a full-time job.

"My whole life became centered around social media. I had my website that I constantly had to update, as well as accounts on Facebook, Instagram, Snapchat, Twitter. I had to interact with everyone, while marketing myself and my products nonstop. I never actually used vacation time to relax or go anywhere or do anything other than work on my business ventures. I felt like a damn social media whore.

"I got stressed out over my many self-imposed deadlines and determined that something in my life had to go. So, I figured, now is the time to cut ties with the one thing (or person) who I feel guilty about even having in my life in the first place.

"I wasn't even nice about it when I ended it with Jake. I didn't think a cordial goodbye would work. Fearing a long drawn out discussion and debate, and questions, I thought it would be so much easier and more effective just to pretend I was mad at him. That I thought all he wanted me for was sex, that he really couldn't care less about me or my feelings. I know that was all bullshit, but I was a mean bitch.

"I said I never wanted to speak to him again, and I blocked him on everything. He sent me some text messages and tried to call me, but I never responded. Eventually he stopped trying to reach me. Now so much time has gone by, it's like he's just somebody that I used to know. I'm not sure if he even considers us to be friends. He probably hates me with a passion, and I can't say that I would blame him.

"But over time I have come to realize how badly I fucked up. I realize how much Jake truly cared about me, and I love Jake like no one else ever. I was about to leave my husband and had hoped to reunite with Jake to tell him how I felt. I was going to ask if he was wanting to be with me. That was when the whole birthday party thing happened.

"Now Jake is gone, and I feel like my life is over. I want to find Jake and let him know how I feel. That's why I am here. Let's go get him!"

Mack was awestruck, mouth wide open and completely speechless for what seemed like minutes.

"Umm, I had no idea Jake was cheating on Amanda... with you ... wow!! I never would have guessed that."

Las Vegas, Nevada. Year 1 month 11 ATBI

Sin City, a place where dreams are made. Some are pleasant dreams; others are not nearly as delectable. Some are just downright disturbing nightmares.

At this juncture in what some have deemed the "Infection Armageddon," most of the major metropolises along both coasts of this once great nation were infested with THEM.

THEY were everywhere. Sometimes scattered, occasionally in clusters. When they weren't aggressively pursuing the humans, who dared even enter those areas, they were rooting around in dumpsters and dark alleys searching for scraps of sustenance.

Prior to the outset of this "Apocalypse of the Unliving," the worst-case scenario one had to worry about in many of the larger cities was being harassed by a panhandler. Now that same person was risking their life by entering the same zone, with a good probability of being accosted by a pancreas pirate.

This was an accurate depiction of most of the metropolises in America. However, it was NOT by any means, an authentic characterization of Las Vegas.

Being in the center of the nation, this was one of the last areas to be reached by the migration of the mutated. Vegas still stood unfathomed for the most part. This city was now, more than ever before, the mecca of the United States.

People from all over flocked to the city to gamble, party, take in shows, be entertained. And all that without the risk of becoming a TV dinner for the DEAD.

The municipality did not remain unblemished on its own, however. Realizing that this city was nearly the last revenue-generating locale in the country, the United States government had decided to provide a vast number of resources to assist the State of Nevada and the city in keeping the province pure.

All the equipment and personnel that had previously been used to keep America's southern border secure had now been redeployed. They had all been shifted to surround and protect the interurban limits of Las Vegas. These protectors of the people resembled the wagon forts of the 19th century American settlers. When faced with a potential attack by their enemies, they would "circle the wagons" by rapidly joining their wagons together into a circular shape and strategically keeping women and children safe in the center.

The modern twist on the "wagon forts" was that now the wagons were Humvees, and they were equipped with M4A1's with Close Quarter Battle Receivers instead of push rod loading muskets. And these modern-day settlers' (members of what was once a group called Homeland Security) primary function was to keep the DEAD *out* and the tourists and their money safe *within*.

On the inside of the perimeter, usually posted up on or close to "The Strip," was a "Containment Squad" featuring several men and women fully geared up in white hazmat suits and helmets. Their gun belts, worn over the top of their hazmat suits, secured their Government issued Sig 45's.

This Vegas Containment Squad featured several team members on bicycles, along with a mobile incinerator. To prevent the incinerator from being so obviously visible, possibly causing the tourists to question the safety of the area, it was disguised as a normal looking, completely white, sanitation truck. This squad and vehicle allowed for the abrupt neutralization of any DEAD that may somehow get through the outer circle, with their quick disposal by cremation to follow.

At the far, less traveled end of the main strip, stood the Venetian. This was a twelve-story, two-hundred-room hotel/casino that originally opened in 1970 as the Royal Inn. It didn't have the lights of the Bellagio or the allure and glam that some of the other high-end places had, but it possessed a feature that could be found at no other place in the world.

For, far below the hotel's main structure, was a secret below ground five-thousand-seat arena. The atmosphere was dark, and there was a distinct animal-like scent hovering about. The seats within were not very lush or even comfortable. Alcohol and water were served here but nothing more.

This theater was not meant for musical performances or wild cat acts. It was equipped for and only offered one means of entertainment: underground cage fighting.

Saturday, February 3rd. It was Super Bowl weekend. The big game was here in town. For the last few years, *every* Super Bowl was played at Allegiant Stadium, home of the Raiders.

Since the "Spread of the DEAD" caused many cities to become overrun by the unliving and forced humans to vacate, several NFL and other professional sports franchises left the United States for healthier markets. Resultantly, attendance was way down in the cities that still had a franchise. The leagues were barely hanging on by a thread to survive.

So, Vegas, now being clearly the safest city in America (maybe the ONLY safe city) was the obvious choice for a Super Bowl location.

This championship match between the Quebec Titans and Saskatchewan Chargers was not exactly going to be a barnburner. The league would be lucky to fill half of the seats in this massive Raider stadium.

However, a few thousand wealthy gamblers from across the globe had still gathered in this city. They were not here to wager on everything championship football game related, from the coin toss to whether there would be a wardrobe malfunction at halftime.

These high rollers were in town for the *"Fright Fights."*

The leviathan former law enforcer awoke, unable to see anything other than the burlap sack tied over his head.

Jake could hear another's heavy breathing close by. In a snap, the bag was removed from his face.

Hathaway looked about to assess his situation and learned that he had been hog-tied. His hands and feet were now bound together behind him with rope and duct tape.

He was inside a sterile glass-enclosed cube, feeling much like a small creature inside a very large, covered terrarium.

And then, there was Camacho. He looked larger than life, bigger than even Jake. As if sculpted from a mountain, he was huge and muscular, but now with long, flowing, black wavy hair that fell halfway down his back.

"Good morning, sunshine. I mean Captain Jake. Good to see you again! You must have dropped my name at the ticket window to get backstage! We have so much catching up to do. We go way back, don't we, sir?"

"You always thought you were so much better than me, didn't you? Back in the corps, you got promoted instead of me. You somehow stole Amanda from me. I did beat you in that boxing tournament we had on the base, even though it was only through a

TKO. If the referees hadn't stopped it when they did, I would have knocked your ass out cold!

"Do you remember those 'immunization shots' and 'vitamins' you and your staff recommended we all receive regularly back in the corps? Your so called 'Power Rations'. I know you commander types called it the 'Z Serum'. All part of your idea, your secret project. The Zeus Project, isn't that what you called it?

"You all gave us grunts the serum without full disclosure as to what it *really* was meant to do. It was supposed to turn us into 'Invulnerable Warriors.' Maybe you weren't the one who created the formula, but the whole concept was your baby."

Jake was still trying to clear out the cobwebs in his head, come to his senses and figure out exactly what kind of predicament he was in. "Where the fuck am I?"

"You're in Vegas, about eighty feet below the Venetian Hotel. Not only that, you are the star of tonight's show! I will explain that here in a minute. But first, why don't you start by admitting that you're a worthless piece of shit for ruining our lives with that Zeus Juice, as you called it."

Hathaway was taken aback by Camacho's comments. "You all volunteered for the experimentation. No one else was supposed to be exposed. And I had no idea what that stuff really was or what the generals had told the scientists they wanted it to do. I truly thought our intent was to make Marines stronger and better able to endure pain and lack of sleep."

Camacho countered: "We only volunteered out of fear about the assignments we might get fucked with if we declined. And for your information, *everyone* got tiny doses over a long period of time, not *just* the volunteers.

"Except what you did not know was that me, Blackhoof, and Fiedler learned what the serum really was. So, we stole some extra bottles of the stuff and began to double and triple down on the doses. It was painful. The shit burns your throat as you swallow it, and it's like acid to your innards. It literally leaves you feeling like you swallowed fire. But in the long run, we became twice as strong as everyone else, twice as fierce and hungry. We never tired, and we felt no pain. We became something other than human. We were invincible! We became half human, half GOD. Basically,

DEMIGODS."

Confused, Jake pondered aloud. "So, let me get this straight. One minute you are crying about me ruining your life and the next you're telling me how wonderful it is to be this amazing DEMIGOD. So, which is it? Am I here for you to punish me or praise me?"

"Actually, you did both of those things to me. Nonetheless, you and your high-ranking official buddies wouldn't know anything about how it feels to have been experimented on with that stuff. You wouldn't touch the stuff. You were scared, and justifiably so. It's not like you all needed it anyways. You don't need to be strong and fearless to sit behind a desk and push a pencil around.

"And then you had the nerve to have us court martialed and prosecuted. You testified as a government witness against us. You threw us under the bus for that whole Haditha scenario, saying that Blackhoof, Fiedler and I shot up that village, slaying people in the streets for no reason at all. But you know damn well that everyone we killed out there was a fucking Al Qaida operative terrorist."

Jake interrupted, "Wait just a fuckin' minute, Camacho. You apparently have become delusional over time. First, we don't know that those people were Al Qaida or terrorists. And second, you guys made matters worse when you went and injected an innocent family, even the little kids - with the 'Z Serum'. No one told you to inject civilians with the Power Rations. That drug was still highly experimental and classified, not intended to be used on anyone outside of the Zeus Project.

"Hell, I still don't understand how your role in Al Anbar didn't get you treason, murder, and war crimes charges. You should have been hung out in public, right outside the Capitol Building or the Pentagon, for all to see.

Jake continued; "is that why you're not with the FBI anymore? Did they fold under the public pressure to let such an evil predator as yourself go before causing any further scrutiny? Is that why you are here, hiding underground like the worm that you are?"

Camacho interrupted, "Shut the fuck up, Hathaway, and let me finish. So, then you ended up testifying against us, your own fucking stool pigeons. And we end up getting sent away to lockup. Once again you came out on top, looking like some great American hero - so high and mighty.

"And you made us look like the bad guys, portraying us as

immoral traitors. We did what we were instructed to do, and you threw me, Blackhoof, and Fiedler under the bus.

"So now Blackhoof and Fiedler are doing twenty years in Leavenworth. I was supposed to be joining them there, but I made a deal with the devil otherwise known as the United States government. They were so worried about their secret getting out, your whole Zeus Project, that they traded me my freedom for my services. All I had to do was cover up their role in the military project and the civilians who got flipped as well."

"When this whole zombie thing was first starting up, they needed someone to clean up the mess, cover up the loose ends. So, your case, that whole birthday party massacre thing, was one of the first major DEAD incidents to get media attention. It became quite obvious that I should make you be our scapegoat."

Jake asked, "What are you talking about? How does the Zeus Project relate to my brother and his wife?"

"How ironic was it that just a few years after you ruined our lives, you would get yours in return. You end up being attacked by your own brother and sister-in-law after they got infected by the very Z Serum you masterminded! Then you end up destroying them and charged with and convicted of their murders! It's some crazy shit, ain't it?" Camacho chuckled evilly.

Jake was still not himself, weak and listless but struggled to speak, "What do you mean they were infected by the Z Serum?"

Camacho laughed aloud.

"Oh, you really don't know. Oh, that's right, I guess you have been a little out of touch with the news, running from the law and playing mafia badass will do that to a guy.

"Well, it seems that back when your labs were up and running in Cali and Florida, they were snatching up people to test. The homeless, vagrants, runaways, were all being experimented on because those involved figured no one would miss these people or be looking for them."

"No. I never was advised about or gave approval for any laboratories in the civilian world. And I had no knowledge about any kidnappings or abductions of people for experimentation. The scientists who we were working with said nothing about testing these drugs on anyone other than the Marine Corps volunteers in the Zeus Project.

"And those same scientists told me after the initial wave of tests had been analyzed, that the drugs were showing only positive signs. They were working as planned, making the soldiers stronger, increasing their pain threshold, giving them energy and making them tireless. They said we were creating 'invincible warriors', and without any negative side effects. And definitely without any civilians or the public being exposed."

"Wow, Hathaway, you really believed that shit? You probably think there's really a Santy Claus too, don't you?

"Anyways, let me continue this fascinating story. So, I guess your brother was in Florida for some reason and somehow got abducted. He ended up in the lab. He became a lab rat for a while until he escaped and disappeared. Sounds like he made it a few years after that but, as you know, the symptoms grow worse with time. He eventually ended up succumbing to the stuff and changing over to one of your zombies. Then he must have bitten, clawed, or scratched his wife and then she 'turned' as well. Well, I guess you already knew that part, didn't you?"

"Then there was that nosey neighbor lady, Mrs. Torrence. She saw exactly what happened the day you got attacked by Rich and Holly. She was in her house, watching through binoculars into the open windows of Holly's house.

"I contacted her the night of the incident and she told me she saw you go in the house without your dog, saw you looking around. Then you found Austin tipped over in his highchair, and you set him back upright before being attacked by Holly, who was now a zombie. You finished her off, then went outside with the baby and got attacked by the Rich-monster.

"Gladys drove a hard bargain when it came to us bribing her into testifying the way we wanted her to. But I guess the five grand we offered her could feed all of those dogs for quite a while and pay for a lot of Bingo games."

Jake remarked, "I heard someone killed Gladys."

"A funny thing happened to her on the way home from court. Seems like someone had punctured her car tire while it was in the court parking garage and she got a flat while driving home. She pulled over to look at the damage, and I just happened to be driving behind her. Being the nice guy that I am, I drove the smelly old broad home and escorted her inside."

Jake recalled the horrid details of the condition in which Mrs. Torrence's body was found. "So, you are the one who tied her up and carved out her eyes and tongue? You're a sick fuck, Camacho."

"Hey, she was just a crazy, nasty hoarder woman with a bunch of pathetic stinky mutts. I did her a favor by putting her out of her misery. Besides, that old lonely biddy was dying to be relevant. So, I granted her wish. Now she's famous! And she would be glad to know that after she died, her little dogs ate pretty damn good. They snacked on her big body for a couple weeks to follow!

"Now this whole 'Infection Armageddon' as they are calling it, is spiraling out of control. It's like a landslide. We can't possibly cover *everything* up anymore, so we started to put a new spin on it. Now we are reporting this to be some unknown bacteria or strain that's causing the outbreak. People are so gullible; they seem to be falling for it," said Camacho.

"Oh, by the way, your hot girlfriend Amanda; if it's any consolation for you, she still had some feelings for you even after you went to the pokey. She was the one who funded your escape from the prison bus, too. Well, it was her new rich husband that paid for it. You will find out why soon enough. Boy, she wasted no time in getting remarried, huh? Hooked up with some wealthy oil man from Texas. You know she got an upgrade there!

"So, my boys and I set your punk ass free. As much as I hated to do it though, because I so much loved seeing you imprisoned, your freedom taken away, caged up like an animal.

"Oh, by the way, hope I split your skull open when I gave you that little love tap, before shoving your bitch ass out of the van back in Louisiana. And don't feel like you have to say thank you because we freed you, but you're welcome anyways. It was my pleasure, because if we hadn't released you back then, you wouldn't be here today."

Clapping his hands in a slow, steady rhythm, Camacho continued... "Oh, by the way, let me congratulate you for following all of the clues me and my friends put out there for you. And for successfully overcoming a few obstacles we put in your way. Not that I had any doubt that you would. I knew you would find your way here to me.

"Oh yeah, sorry I got sidetracked. I just have so much to tell you, old friend. So, after we saved your sorry ass from death row, I told Amanda you got killed in a shootout with the troopers. She has no idea you're alive.

"I wonder why she didn't wait to verify the reports of your death before moving on and seeing someone new? Maybe she had been screwing around with him all along? Maybe she was hooking up with other people too. Like me."

"Fuck you, Camacho."

"What's wrong, Jake? Just telling you the truth about your lovely Amanda and how she couldn't keep her hands off me. She said she should have chosen me from the start, way back in our San Diego days. She just loves my long sexy hair.

In a fit of rage, Jake yelled, "I'll fuckin kill you!" and struggled, flexing his muscles and rocking back and forth on the cold galvanized steel floor. Jake was attempting to break free of the titanium restraints that were restricting his movement.

"You probably thought she had no idea you were fucking that cute little blonde cop chick either. Am I right? You're such a moron." Camacho said, grinning.

"Or maybe Amanda was ready to forget about you because of the story the prosecutor fed the jury during closing arguments at your trial. Before the trial started, Ferron told me that we would need to come up with a motive for which you slain your own brother and his wife.

"So, I came up with the idea that Ferron used in court. We made up those allegations that in the months leading up to the birthday party massacre, you had been screwing Holly. That you decided you were going to leave Amanda to be with Holly, and you went to the birthday party with the intentions of killing Rich to get him out of the picture. When you got to Holly's place that day, you told her of your plan, and she wanted nothing to do with it. She tried to stop you. Pretty convincing story, wouldn't you agree?"

Camacho continued. "But it gets even better. I'm not sure if you know this yet or not. But the person who was really bangin' Holly was your old partner and best buddy, Mack. Sometimes real-life events are even better than fiction!

"But over the years I decided that it wasn't fair for me and all the other low-ranking Marines to have this advantage over you. You deserve to have the power too, to be indestructible and godlike. I knew we would be running into each other again. It was our fate.

And that way you will have no excuses when I still kick your ass in our rematch!"

"What the hell are you talking about - rematch?" Jake asked.

"So, when we had your ass knocked out unconscious in the back of our van in Louisiana, I gave you a dose of your own medicine. I used a syringe to give you two vials full of your 'Zeus Juice' shit.

"Have you been feeling weird lately, Jakey boy? Making any irrational choices? Having any anger management issues? You sure look strong though. You been feeling power hungry? Or are you hungry for something else? Like, say…human flesh?

Camacho went on … "you know you're turning into one of those *things* that your scientists warned you about. They told you there was a high risk that these experiments could go awry. But you insisted they continue to inject us with this stuff. And now the public has been contaminated by your diabolical doping and the whole country is in the middle of an epidemic. It's all your fault.

"About the only vindication all of your victims can receive from this is the satisfaction of knowing that you yourself are turning into one of those *things*. So how does it feel to be a freak? I know how it feels because I have been there since the start, back when I was getting all those daily doses of the Juice back at camp. Every little drop tearing away at my humanity, changing me into what I am today. A freak. But also, a DEMIGOD!!!

"I have you to thank for that. I have become a divine, supernatural being. Even after we are long gone, *I* will be remembered as a mortal. Much like the offspring of a god and a human, "Camacho said.

"You haven't been taking the stuff as long as me, so you can't relate. And very soon you won't be in any state to remember any of this conversation, because all you will have on your mind is the desire to eat someone.

"Well, let me explain what we have going on here. Every Saturday night for the last couple of months we have been having these 'Fright Fights.' It's like a combination of two different events. It's one-part circus side show and another part cage fighting, all rolled into one huge party.

"I am like the animal tamer under the tent, and each week I battle an assortment of *dead* ones with my bare hands. With no weapons or assistance whatsoever I enter a locked cage with those mal-formations and destroy them while being showered with applause and cheers."

"You're so vain, Camacho. So.... you avoided the question earlier. What happened to your fulfilling FBI career?" Jake sarcastically queried.

"Fuck the F.B.I. with all their rules and policies and dress codes and shit. I left on my own so I could be free again."

"Yeah, right. That means they shit-canned your ass."

Camacho ignored the comment and continued his utterance.

"But this weekend will be extra magnificent! This stadium is going to be rockin '! The richest, most relevant, celebrities, politicians, kings, and business owners from around the world have gathered here in Vegas this weekend to celebrate the 'Fright Fights'! Fuck the Super Bowl. They are here to see us!

"Anyways, prior to our big fight, the audience members will be encouraged to walk through the backstage area here. They will be able to observe the vast selection of combatants we have on display in these glass cells, just like the one you are in now.

"They will then place their wagers on their selection. And when the show starts, they will watch the fights and cheer on their favorites.

"Now let me tell you what is going to make tonight's showdown even extra special! As tonight's highlight, YOU are going to be the main attraction! The once great American War Hero turned Super Cop turned murderer and escapee - America's Most Wanted - will be battling several of the backstage participants.

"You can see some of them from here. They have already received the first few injections in the series of the Z Serum that you were so proud of. But before the fight they will get their final, large doses. This will make them even fiercer, hungrier, stronger, and faster for the big grand finale death match. The last person, or creature, to remain in the ring wins.

"I sure hope you survive that fight, Jake. It's been a blast having you as my personal plaything. You were like my little pet bug that at any time I could grow tired of and squish. I would occasionally reach down and snatch you up from your own little terrarium and put you in a new one to see how you would react. Like when I set you free from the prison bus and put you in that swamp.

"Then I watched you do your little thing up north, acting like Mafioso and shit. And now I've brought you here. All good stuff.

"I've enjoyed playing God with you, like you did with us in the corps. You let me, Blackhoof and Fiedler dabble with dangerous drugs for the betterment of your beloved corps and the government, only to eventually be turned into freaks. Every one of us.

"But now I control your every move. Until I get tired of playing with you. Then you will be of no further use to me. I will be bored and just end your miserable existence. But I will make damn sure that in the end, any loved ones you left behind will get to see you suffer. And then, I will kill them too. After I am done playing with them of course."

Chapter 35 - Fight or Play Dead

Jake sat on the floor, still groggy from what they had done to him. He was chained to a pole and unable to roam more than a couple feet away. Jake began to size up the glass-encased, zoo-like cage in which had been imprisoned. He was looking for a weakness, some possible way to escape. He could see that Camacho and others were escorting several well-to-do-looking people throughout the holding cells area.

These fight fans began to look at all the evening's contenders. They were, pointing at certain specimens and having meaningful conversations with one another about who they should put their money down on.

One of these wealthy gamblers was a man named Chad Tillinghast. Jake was not privy to the fact that Tillinghast was a rich oil man from Texas. *Or* that he was Amanda's new husband.

Chad never made eye contact with Jake, or even acted as if he saw Hathaway. He
briefly remained in the contestant's area before returning to his front-row cage-side seat and sitting beside his companion for the evening.

Several minutes passed before four men in grey jumpsuits with helmets, masks, and gloves simultaneously entered Jake's cube. Three of the men pointed their automatic rifles at Hathaway, and one carried a large syringe. This needle had been prepared specifically for Jake - one large final dose of the "Z serum" to turn him DEAD, once and for all.

"Oh hell, look at his eyes." the syringe holder said. "Someone already gave this one the juice. He's already changed over."

Jake was now shackled around the ankles and wrists, barely able to move as the four jumpsuits put a leash on his dog-like collar. They began to remove him from the cage. They put the burlap sack over Jake's head and led him, still at gunpoint, by pulling the leash and prodding him with large spears. They forced Jake from the backstage kennels and toward the large caged-in stage at the center of the packed arena.

Jake could see through the pin-sized holes in the burlap that the bright stage lights were becoming even more brilliant. He could hear the roar of a crowd and it became louder the further he walked. Jake was pushed through the steel cage door. Unable to stay on his feet because of the ankle chains restricting his motion, he smacked down hard face first onto the solid wooden floor. He tried to get to his feet but felt other bodies colliding with him, as if they had been thrown onto him.

A too-familiar voice then reverberated through the building as Daniel Camacho held the microphone to his mouth. "Ladies and gentlemen, now for the main event, the fight of the night! It's the one we call the 'King of the Cage'!"

Jake was forced to his feet, as were the other bodies in various stages between human and DEAD. Camacho's jump-suited goons began to walk around, unmasking the contestants from their burlap bags. They were also removing the fighter's handcuffs but leaving the leg chains in place.

Camacho continued: "Okay, people; here are tonight's fighters. You have only five more minutes to place your bets, so get a good look at these contestants and pick a winner!"

All but one of the combatants were revealed. For one of the forms was not like the other. That person or thing remained seated and was at the back of the pack- wearing a full-bodied green and brown warrior ghillie suit.

Camacho was enjoying his game show host role. He strolled past some of the other contestants, who tried to grab at him or bite him as he passed. He ignored their attacks and went straight to Jake, in the center of the cage.

Camacho snuck up behind the still-befuddled Hathaway and extended his arm to reach over and grab Jake's shirt by the rear collar behind his neck. Camacho yanked downward, completely ripping the shirt off and revealing the former lawman's upper torso and tattoos for all to see.

Sitting beside Chad Tillinghast in the front row was none other than Jake's last lady love, Amanda.

She had shown little interest in the happenings on stage until this point. She had no idea that the massive white man on stage was anyone she had ever known, never mind one she had loved and spent so much time with.

Amanda noticed the Catholic archangel Saint Michael tattoo on the left peck of the being who was on stage. She suddenly grew quite engrossed with the show.

Her mind began to race: *That fighter up there kind of resembles Jake. My mind is obviously playing tricks on me... I'm hallucinating. I mean, Jake is dead. Then again, the guy on the stage looks half dead himself - unshaven and pale with splotches of tan and brown all over his body. The hair on his head looks greasy and thin, his eyes look noticeably inhuman with dilated tiny pupils. And that putrid scent that I can detect from here....*

Amanda turned away for a second, sure she was still imagining things. Then she looked back up on stage to do a double take, which was followed by an unanticipated outburst. "OH MY GOD!!! JAKE!!!"

Amanda jumped up from her chair, yelling his name repeatedly. "JAKE! JAKE! It's me, Amanda! Down here! Look at me! You're alive! What has happened to you?"

Hathaway heard a commotion from the front row and turned in that direction but was blinded by the spotlights luminating his face.

Amanda smacked her husband in the back of the head. "You knew he was here! That's why you insisted I come along to this stupid thing. You knew he was alive and never told me!?"

Mr. Tillinghast looked at Amanda and, appealing to her, said: "You needed to see what he really is, always has been. He's a monster. He was when he killed his family, and he still is today. You are so fortunate that he is out of your life now and I am here to protect you from him."

"That's a bunch of hogwash, and you know it, Chad. His family were the ones who had turned into monsters. He was the brave one who faced them and ended them before they could hurt baby Carson or anyone else.

"You are nothing but a deceitful snake, hiding the truth from me so you could take me for yourself. I only married you because you said you had dirt on Jake. You said you had information that he was involved in the Marines coverup of that Al Anbar incident with the family that was injected with the Z serum. You said if I didn't cooperate with you, that you would have released that information to have him court marshalled. And then, soon after that, you and everyone else led me to believe that he was dead. I *never* loved you. I *never* will. So, screw you, Chad - I'm out of here!"

Amanda began to walk away from her new husband, but Tillinghast wrapped his hands over her shoulders and reeled her back in closely to him. "You're not going anywhere. And don't think that making a scene will get you any help. I've got friends here who will throw you in that cage if you really want to see HIM so badly."

Jake was still unable to detect any one voice or see anyone in the audience due to the crowd noise and bright lights glaring in his eyes.

He had noticed, however, that Camacho had now freed the one still-disguised person in the ring. The one wearing the ghillie suit was no longer cuffed or ankle shackled.

Even in his haze and cloudy mind, Jake was suspicious that this could be someone he knew. It was possibly even someone close to him.

Why would Camacho release this one from his restraints but not the others? For some reason he wants me to fight that one first...

The ghillie-suited opponent was bumping into the hulking Hathaway, not in a hostile manner but more as if he was trying to get closer to the cage door to escape.

Jake lightly pushed him away to avoid a possible attack, but also to move the suited one a bit closer to the exit.

The lack of aggression on Jake's part began to anger Camacho. "Fight him, Jake," Camacho yelled. "What are you, a coward? Are you afraid of that one?"

Meanwhile, the other opponents all now had their hands and arms free. Only three-foot-long leg shackle chains remained to restrict their motion.

These antagonists were clearly DEAD, unlike the ghillie-suited one.

Jake began to wake up, snapping out of his treacherous trance and realizing that he could beat these THINGS in one-on-one fights. He was twice their size and doubly strong.

Hathaway began to approach the THINGS closest to him. He made mincemeat of the first creature and second, pummeling their heads in with precision punches to the heads. He then walked over to another and proceeded to utilize his steel-like fists to perform a frenzied skull-fucking on IT.

He began to destroy the next beast up, throwing punch after repeated punch to the face of this now ruptured, infected mass.

Jake moved on to start pounding another one. He pushed two others down to the floor when they tried to gang up on him.

He grabbed one of those two by waste and lifted it straight up over his head. The ankle chains severed the beast at the shins, and the feet remained on the floor. Jake began swinging the rest of IT around full circle above his head for a couple of rotations. He then slammed ITs head into the face of another DEAD, causing both brains to explode and splash upon impact.

The irritable Camacho had seen enough. With his microphone in hand, he walked over to the ghillie-suited contestant and ripped off the face mace. "Look who we have here! Jake, do you know this young lad?"

Jake stopped mid-pummel and peered over at the face of the now unmasked subject. The young male's cheekbones were swollen, his eyes were sunken, and his skin was colored in an unhealthy shade of decaying brown. But Jake knew who it was.

"Rafael! "Jake exhorted. "He's just an innocent kid! What the fuck is wrong with you Camacho? Let him go!"

Camacho said, "you know what Jake, I was just an innocent

kid too. Until you turned me into one of THEM.

"I'll tell you what I'm not gonna let the kid go. I'm gonna do something even better for him. "

Camacho promptly placed his hands on each side of Rafael's jaw. Then, with extreme power and torque, he twisted the head counterclockwise, completely separating it from the neck, spinal cord and torso. Rafael's decapitated body fell limp onto the floor.

"NOOOOOOOOO!!!!!" Jake yelled and lunged toward Camacho who effortlessly pushed the weaker Jake away. Camacho inserted his index and middle fingers into the now severed head's eye sockets then pulled backwards. He completely ripped the top of the scalp from the head, and then squeezed the skull to pop the top open.

"OHHHHH, look at the brain on this kid!" Camacho yelled distastefully. There was an initial roar from the crowd. An audience that may or may not have realized what they were witnessing was real, not some staged act.

Camacho spiked the freshly plucked cranium to the canvas. The audience slowly began to realize what they had just witnessed was an actual and bitter dissection. Done with revolting and savage annihilation, to an innocent youth.

The crowd began to voice their distaste of his actions by booing loudly. Individuals began throwing bottles and trash at the caged-in Camacho.

Camacho paused, enjoying the crowd's bilious reaction. He was now basking in the bloodbath of his victim, the black blood had sprayed all over his face, covering his teeth and lips. The life liquid was dripping down his chin and onto the floor.

"There. That was excruciatingly entertaining!" Camacho said laughingly.

"BOOOOOOOOOOO!!!! BOOOOOOOOOO!!" The crowd was in an uproar.

"And now he's free," Camacho continued. "That's what you should have done for the kid when you had the chance. Why do I always have to be the bad guy, Jake?"

"That was just your warmup, Captain Jake. You and I are going to have the rematch that I have deserved all along. This will be the title fight of a lifetime! The winner will get the title, riches, fame and glory that go along with being the champion."

"They will also win their freedom" Camacho said. "But the loser, on the other hand, will be given a final extreme dose of your precious serum. Enough to make that person turn once and for all. This will make them a mindless unliving creature forever, or at least until someone hurls a fucking spear through your grey matter. Pretty large stakes, I must say..."

The self-deemed DEMIGOD began to battle his counterpart.

Meanwhile, now assembling in the lower depths of the arena, were the team of Mack, Megan, Duy, Anthony and Roscoe. Alongside them were Humberto, Felipe and two other cartel members who had been tracking Jake and his captors.

The gang soon encountered a squad of security minded militia, who were quick to commence firing their AK's at Mack's crew and the cartel guys. Meanwhile, several mega sized wall-mounted monitors showed a live video feed of the events in the center ring.

Anthony had taken cover behind a bar and eyeballed the big screen to see Jake clashing with Camacho. Behind them, the remaining DEAD were still leg-restricted but attempting to break free and nibble on Jake's loins. "Guys!!! It's Jake! He's in trouble! We need to get to the arena!"

Jake's intellect began to waver as this present-day reality was beginning to blur with his past. In a muddled confusion he flashed back to his childhood, training with Grandpa Bill. Suddenly, Jake was the new and improved, heavy weight version of Vinny Paz.

Announcers:

On our left is the Evil Incarnate, Daniel Camacho, with long black hair and blood running down his face.

And across the ring in the blue trunks is his opponent, six foot three and weighing in at 235 pounds, it's Jake Hathawayyyyyy!!

He's the way maker with the haymaker

Okay, we are underway...

Camacho throws and lands the opening blow, there's another uppercut

Good left hand to the midsection by Jake, he's right in front of him now

He doesn't have to use his jabs to be creative, he can afford to throw power shots

He's trying to load up with that left now

Another right by Camacho scores, and a left as well

Good right hand by the evil one again, and a left follows it up, but Jake is still there

Lack of strength may be costing Hathaway a little bit there

He doesn't appear to be as strong as we have seen him in the past

Maybe he's starting to feel that, slow down a little bit

Now Camacho is taking his time, placing his shots, stepping to the side

He's looking for an opening that he might not see in front

He has the liberty to do that with no jabs coming back at him

Camacho's flying off the ropes, ripping off his left hand

He comes at you from odd angles you don't expect

Jake's doing a nice job of slipping punches - that kid has plenty of heart, but he's not fighting the smartest fight

He's fighting back but really doesn't have the power to do anything significant

Jake needs to be busy all the way thru because he is behind

Now Grandpa Bill was yelling at Jake from his corner. "Get your hands up! Move your head!"

The announcer continued to call the fight.

Camacho has been the aggressor so far- look at the punch numbers. He landed 30 punches to 17

About 85% of his punches are power shots

The kid from Little Rhody is a little bit close right there

He wants to be on the outside

He needs to use that six-three height of his and his long reach to his advantage

Jake has too much heart to go dead for a whole round

He's punching at the wrong time

"Come on, kid!!" Pops yelled.

Announcer.

Now there's the left hook and the left uppercut from Jake!

He's going to fight in spots

Camacho's covering up. Some pretty good offense from both men in this round. He's trying to use that jab.

OHHHH!! That looping right hand of Jake's was very

effective

Some guys can catch them, but Camacho could not

You can see how this bout has turned

Hathaway's pretty smart in there now

He still has hand speed, maybe not like he did in the past, but you would expect that

He's looking to pick his spots, to pace himself

Experienced fighters will do that, especially when they're in there with someone who has dynamite in their gloves

Now Jake delivers body punches

Very brisk pace

Uppercut right behind it!

Camacho may be wearing down a bit

He has to pick it up

Oh, here are the antics you expect from him

Camacho's doing some clowning, and he's not having any luck with those power shots

More Hathaway! One punch at a time. Now he's throwing combinations, being more effective.

Camacho should have jumped on him when he had the chance

Now he's trying to turn it on but it's too late

You can see it- normally he likes to stand up straight, statuesque

But now you notice, when he's showing signs of wearing down and fatigue, one of the things that goes first is the chin, then the legs

BAMMMMMMMMMMMMMMM!!!!!

One final right bare-fisted battering ram from Jake pulverized the evil one's left cheek. Camacho's blood-percolating brainpan lead his body in a downward tailspin, sending it on a collision course straight into the cold canvas.

Jake had knocked Camacho down and nearly OUT. The frenzied crowd was
pleased as punch.

With chants of "JAKE!! JAKE!!" blasting through the arena, Jake began to talk as he walked away from the defeated one. "It's over. You wanted your rematch, there it is. You lost fair and square. Don't let me ever see you around me or my family again, asshole."

Camacho, now seated on the floor, managed to get on his knees. He replied, "No, it's *not* over."

The long-maned one pulled a large Ka-Bar carbon steel-bladed Marine Corps knife from his pants leg. He walked over to the back of the cage and severed one rope, which had held eight more cannibalistic mutants secured in place.

Now freed, the zombies began to walk about the cage as Jake was attempting to open the steel pen's door. A couple of THEM approached Camacho and sniffed at him but quickly lost interest. They continue to drag onward, seemingly now more interested in Jake.

"You see that, Jake? They have no interest in me, because I'm no longer human. I'm more like them than I am like you. They fear me! I'm the Big Dog, the Big Bad Wolf. No, I'm more than that - I am immortal! A divine being! A GOD!

"You created me, Jake, the way you gave me and Blackhoof and Fiedler those small portions continuously over time, slowly allowing our bodies to absorb the poison. What amazing attributes we received, power like none could ever imagine. But you also are responsible for these wretched creatures as well. How fitting is it now that you should be devoured by the very poor souls that you destroyed? And all while the immortal ME that you also created, stands by watching every square inch of your flesh being chewed and torn from your skeletal system!"

Jake walked over to the nearest zombie and put his neck right in front of its mouth. The zombie inhaled a face full of Hathaway scent and then turned its head away in disgust and disinterest.

Jake approached two more DEAD and placed his arms in front of them, but they obviously lacked interest and turned away.

Camacho was stunned. "WHAT THE FUCK?! Wait - no way. You - you took it too! You drank the Zeus juice all along? You're just like me, Fiedler and Blackhoof!?"

"Not quite. Because the truth of the matter is, I started to take those supplements weeks before you guys were even selected to participate. But I did it for completely different reasons than you guys did. I went first to see what I was getting my troops into. That's what leaders do. They don't ask their men to do something that they wouldn't or haven't done themselves.

"The stuff made me stronger, made my endurance peak. I didn't tire. I didn't feel pain. It was incredible. I didn't realize until much later in the program exactly how devastating and dehumanizing this stuff was, or else I never would have asked you guys to participate."

Meanwhile, Jake's friends and their cartel partners were still in the lower depths of the building. They were attempting to make their way toward the arena. But they had their hands full; Camacho's heavily armed guards and security officers were intent on keeping any of the uninvited from ruining the big show.

Anthony knew that at this point he was the only one in position to get past the security guards to aid Jake. He waited until all the watchmen were fully engaged in their combat so they would not be able to prevent him from passing by.

Anthony snuck past the militia undetected. He opened the doors to the long runway leading up to the stage area and ran as quickly as his short legs would allow. He jumped up onto the stage and dashed up to the cage door. Anthony began to use his cordless Makita drill to bore into the steel lock just above the door handle.

Camacho, now realizing that Jake was more powerful than him, had made his way closer to the door in preparation of an escape. Seeing Anthony working on the door lock, Camacho kicked the door open from the inside. The solid chain-link gate smacked the wee warrior hard, sending him airborne. Anthony's body flew back about ten feet and he landed on his back, still on the stage.

Camacho ran over to Anthony, picked him up, and pulled the drill from his tiny hands.

The over-sized long-haired villain then put the small man under his arm. Anthony was punching and kicking as Camacho walked back into the cage and began to squeeze the life out of his victim.

"Anthony!!" Jake roared as he raced to his friend's aid. Hathaway drew his fist back, but not before Camacho began to use the hijacked power tool and penetrate Jake's forehead. The drill bit slightly punctured Jake's skin, causing blood to trickle down into his eyes.

Jake stood still, taking the drill bit to the head. It didn't hurt him, and he had serious doubts that he could be injured with much less than a missile blowing his head clean off his torso. "Give it your best shot, Camacho!" he challenged.

Camacho continued to bore onward, the high speed and torque of the drill bit continuing to penetrate flesh, with the odor of parched body pulp wafting through the air.

The penetration concluded abruptly as the drill bit struck the original Invulnerable Warrior's skull. Then the drill bit fractured.

Camacho continued to mash the trigger on the tool in a maniacal fashion, and the drill bit then snapped in two. The momentum of the break sent the borer backwards.

The portion of the high-speed drill bit that remained inside the drill now bumped into Camacho's long flowing mane, tangling up and swirling around in his fleece. The evil incarnate did not realize what was happening and never let up on applying the power to the tool.

The menacing Makita now appeared more like a fur-covered cotton candy stick; locks, tresses and curls were all packed onto and wrapped around the machine.

Camacho was unable to see what was happening, as he now had hair down over his eyes. VRRRRRRRRR, VRRRRRRRRRR!!!!! The drill bit continued spinning, twisting the hair taught, until the Makita apparatus itself flew from Camacho's grasp.

Jake grabbed hold of the blue power drill and, with an incredible feat of strength, jerked the drill so hard that the momentum began to pull Camacho's scalp clean off his head. Jake continued to tug, causing more flesh to peel off.

A congealed, brownish-red blood was now pouring down Camacho's bewildered face, onto his neck and down his chest.

What had been advertised as a cage fight between man and DEAD had precipitously turned into nothing less than a feeding frenzy. All the creatures instinctively focused upon the source of the sauce.

The DEAD could not resist their carnal temptations, and they followed their noses to the flowing fountain of blood and epidermis.

One final yank and Camacho's face skin was cleanly jerked away from his head. The zombies piled onto the expressionless evil warrior and began to devour. They feasted upon the fallen, bloody, incised face skin much like a teenager would eat the top layer of mozzarella cheese dripping off a freshly baked slice of pizza.

Once the face was gorged, the UNLIVING ones, all in their hungry daze, dove in. They proceeded to devour the screaming Camacho in what would be a horrific cannibal carnage.

"NOOOOOOO!!! GET OFF OF ME, YOU GODDAMN MIS-CREATIONS!!!!! YOU CAN'T EAT ME!!! I'M JUST LIKE YOU!!!!! I'M NOT HUMAN!!!!! YOU CAN'T EAT ONE OF YOUR OWN!!!!!!!! AAAHHHHHHHHH!!!!!!!!!!!!!!"

It truly is a dog eat dog world.

Jake had a rare flashback and was reminded of a time when he was a kid back in Rhode Island. It was an instance where he had been at the beach eating fried chicken when a swarm of hungry seagulls began to swoop down upon him to get his food.

He found it odd that these birds ate other fowl, and they loved it. Seemed quite cannibalistic at the time, yet not quite as stupefying as what had just transpired before him.

Jake and Anthony fled out of the cage.

Hathaway was barely able to stand as they walked down the runway back into the lower depths of the arena.

Meanwhile, some of the Vegas Containment Squad assigned to the strip had been called over to the Venetian. They arrived to provide support to their fellow security personnel as Mack, Duy and Roscoe, along with their cartel allies, were still battling with and taking gunfire from the hotel's hired goons.

All the gun fire and fighting in the cage area had caused the transparent glass holding cells of the creatures to smash and crack. The UNLIVING began to forge their way through the weakened structures, freeing themselves.

The zombies made their way through the premises and began flooding out into the arena, and among the audience members. Many of the crowd were still under the impression that this was all just part of the show.

These blood-thirsty, organ-hungry oddities began to feast upon the humans in the building. Before long, the entire structure was encompassed by these hungry maggot-colony creepers.

Jake and Anthony joined the rest of the gang in hysteria, struggling with security and now also flogging the DEAD that had escaped their restraints.

Jake began looking around in a frenzied state. He started calling out, "Amanda! Are you in here? Amanda!!!"

Mack found Jake in the crowd. "Dude! Jake! Are you okay?"

"Yeah. But where's Amanda?"

"Amanda is here? Jake, are you sure?" Mack asked.

"I could have sworn I heard her voice in the audience, but I couldn't see because of the bright lights. We need to look for her!"

After several minutes spent searching, Mack said, "man, I hate to say it, but I think your mind is playing tricks on you, Jake. And with all these flesh-famished creatures lingering around, we need to hurry up and get the hell out of here."

The crew all ran up the underground sports stadium ramp toward the above ground exit. Mack was now the one who was frantically looking about. "Who are you looking for?" Jake questioned.

"A friend came with us wanting to help, but I don't see h…"

Before he could finish his enunciation of the word "her," an extended white catering company van came flying in reverse out of a side overhead garage door. A cloud of dust and a pack of the *carnally obsessed* emerged behind it.

"THERE SHE IS!!!!"

The group all swiveled in unison and stared. The beautiful blonde former sprinter was driving a white Ram Pro Master 2500 van much like a Hollywood stunt woman would.

Jake was blown away by who he saw before him. "Holy fuck! Megan!?!"

She slammed on the brakes, spinning the vehicle around in a 180-degree half circle, bringing the vehicle to a screeching halt with it now facing forward. Megan leapt out of the driver's door and into the hulking Hathaway's tattered arms. She began to smooch him with a hard, passion felt kiss, like the one she had planted on him when they were in that storage closet at Central a year or so earlier.

However, this kiss was one-sided. Jake failed to reciprocate the sentiment this time.

"I thought you hated me," a surprised Hathaway remarked.

"We need to talk about that when we get outta here," Megan replied sheepishly.

Anthony hopped into the driver's seat. As the crew loaded into the van, Duy saw Humberto Aguilar emerge from the underground tunnel. He was carrying the body and head of his deceased son, Rafael.

Aguilar's men flanked their boss to the front, rear, and sides as they all walked away. They were using their AK's to mow down the creatures around them, parting the sea of DEAD and clearing a pathway for their boss.

"That's the cartel guy that helped bring us to you, Jake," the Dew-man said.

Jake got out of the van and met Aguilar in the roadway. "Mr. Aguilar, my friend tells me I owe you and your men my gratitude. But I'm very sorry for your loss also."

"You know, amigo, I wish my son had survived this ordeal, as did you. But I know that you did everything you could to try to save him. You're an honorable man. Maybe someday we will meet again. If you ever need anything, you call me."

Aguilar shook Jake's hand and carried his son's remains into a waiting limousine.

Jake re-boarded the van and Anthony drove them all away, traveling southbound out of the Vegas city limits.

The former Marine sat in the center of the cargo van, propped up with his back leaning against the interior wall. Jake was not sitting straight, his posture exuded frustration and sheer consternation.

Megan wormed her body up beside his as she revealed, "I left my husband, Jake. I want to be with you."

Jake rolled his eyes. "Really? Don't you understand what is happening here Megan? You expect me to just forget the way you wronged me? You think I should be highly flattered and excited at the prospect of being with you again?

"All you care about is YOU and your fucking website and social media bullshit. What's wrong? Is that failing? Are you no longer the flavor of the month?"

"Jake, let me explain. I was young and immature. I've grown now. You don't know the real me."

"I think I do. You used to be a sweet girl, great cop, and good friend. All that changed when you turned into a social media sweetheart and celebrity. Then the only thing you cared about was having fresh material to post on your fucking websites.

"But that's okay, Megan. I hope those websites loved you back as much as you loved them. And guess what? You have made a huge mistake in deciding you suddenly want to be back with me. Because I'm not who or what you think I am, either."

A sobbing Megan responded, "I know who you are. So, you messed around on Amanda. I messed around too. We just fell for each other; we couldn't help it. We
didn't do it on purpose, we did not plan for this to happen. It just did.

"And you should not feel guilty about what we did. No one should have to stay with someone forever if they don't make you happy... whether you are married to them or not."

Jake was compelled to explain further. "No, that's not what I mean when I say you don't know me."

Jake paused, and diverted his eyes from gazing directly into Megan's stare and aimed them at his feet instead.

"I have the virus inside of me. For quite some time now. I'm practically one of THEM..."

Megan veered into Jake's dead serious expression and she broke down. Tears fled her eyes like flood water through a storm drain.

She breathlessly murmured, "Oh. My. God... Noo!!!"

The shaken but also stirred, petite yet sensually sculpted blonde attempted to hug Jake or to be held in return. But the solemn ex-Marine felt no inclination to offer her any solace.

Rather, he scooted away from her and said, "Now you know how it feels."

He relocated himself to another seat in the van, several feet away from her. Megan felt isolated and foolish and covered her face to conceal her dismay.

Normally in a situation such as this, the real Jake Hathaway would have felt guilt since he was not able to rescue Amanda from the devastation back at the casino, and he would have felt sorrow for her loss.

He might have felt the desire to reconcile with Megan, to bask in the fact that there was still someone in his life who loved him and longed to be with him.

But the military veteran felt none of these emotions. He felt *nothing*.

Mack, Duy, and even Roscoe all stared out their respective windows, trying to remain isolated from the awkwardness of the situation surrounding them.

Anthony stared ahead out the front windshield as he drove. He then attempted to converse with the closest passenger to him, Duy, about the "Fright Fights" finale.

"Dude, that was crazy. At first, none of those THINGS would even get near Camacho - they had no interest in him at all. Then, when his scalp was gone and the blood started gushing out the top of his noggin like the Fountains of friggin' Bellagio, it was ON!!! It's like that old story about how the Eskimos kill wolves with a frozen knife covered with blood."

"Huh?" Duy asked, seemingly somewhat out of his normal sorts as he gazed out of the catering van window.

"First the Eskimo coats his knife blade with like some seal blood or something, then lets it freeze over before putting another layer of blood over the blade to conceal it.

"Then the hunter plants the knife in the ground with the blade up. The wolf will follow the blood trail and his scent to the knife, then begins to lick it to taste the fresh blood. He begins lapping it up more steadily and before long, his own tongue is slit open from the sharpened edge and it is now his own blood that he is tasting.

"But he doesn't notice or care. And out of his insatiable appetite and thirst for warm blood, the carnivorous wolf begins ferociously smacking his tongue against the weapon until he has completely bled out and is found lying dead in the snow.

"You get it, Duy? The wolf is just like these creatures. Even though Camacho was basically one of them, they still could not resist tasting his blood and flesh when it was gushing out of his head and all over the place. They couldn't help themselves. After all, they are just mindless creatures."

The Dew-man did not respond or even acknowledge Anthony's attempt at a conversation. For he was currently struggling with a real-life dilemma that was quickly approaching him, with the force and impact of a runaway freight train.

Chapter 36 - A Death in the Family

It was a solemn vibe that filled the air in the catering van as Anthony headed southbound in the early stretches of a roughly eighteen-hour trek back to Dallas.

Mack attempted to talk to Jake to discuss their next plan of action.

"So, Jake, what's next? We have a lot more information now about what these THINGS are and what it was that created them. Should we get this information to someone who can develop an antivirus or a serum to combat it or reverse it? Or do we need to go after Blackhoof?"

The former Marine was unresponsive, acting oblivious to any of the people or conversations around him. He seemed to be completely out of it, indifferent to where they were going and how they needed to proceed.

Mack turned toward Duy to get an opinion on the matter and noticed that Duy was bright red, burning up, and sweating profusely. "Duy! Are you okay, man?"

The aspiring young attorney was now lying down on the bench seat. He began to moan as if in extreme pain and promptly commenced in disgorging projectile style.

Anthony asked, "Dude, what's wrong?"

"Stop the van," Mack advised.

"But if he's REALLY sick we need to get him someplace where we can get him some medical attention."

The Dew-man raised his head up from the seat and bellowed, "STOP THE VAN!!!! NOW!!!!!!"

Anthony pulled the white Ram Pro Master 2500 over to the side of the road.

Duy tried to walk toward the front of the minibus but was unable to stand. "Jake, help me out of here."

Jake picked up Duy and carefully carried him off the bus.

"Jake," Duy began. "I can tell I don't have much time left. I can feel a change, my vision is nearly gone - but I feel the demons all swarming around, like vultures... circling around me. Do you see them too? They think I'm roadkill."

"Duy, you're burning up, delusional. What's wrong? What happened? Did THEY get you back there?"

"No, Jake. It happened way back when we went to rescue

Roscoe from that Dallas dog pound. As we made our way out of the place... tons of THEM between the building and our truck. I got scratched. Not bad - I really didn't think anything of it until... I started getting really sick up in New England."

"Oh fuck, man. Hang in there, we can get you some help."

"No, Jake. Here..."

Duy removed his trusty Bowie knife from his leg strap sheath and handed it to his mammoth amigo.

"I need you to end it for me."

"Come on, man, don't give up," Jake pleaded.

"It's almost time. I can tell I'm about to ... no longer be me. I've been saving this special knife my grandfather left for me. Been saving it for such an occasion... I haven't dirtied it by wasting any of THEM with it. It's still clean. For me...

"I want to apologize for not being able to clear you in your trial, Jake."

Jake said, "it's not your fault. That whole thing was a setup, crooked. Besides, it really doesn't matter now, the whole world is changed, different."

Duy said, "Jake, do you believe in God? In heaven?"

"Oh, man, I wish you hadn't asked me that."

Jake looked upwards searching for the answer to his waning friend's question.

"You're really asking the wrong person, Dew-man. You know, there's nothing I would like better than to be able to tell you what you want to hear. Something that will make you feel better about where you're going.

"I'd love to tell you that someday I know you and I will be in a beautiful, warm sunny place reflecting on our life on earth and surrounded by gorgeous women angels and drinking beers and watching from above as the Pats and Sox win more rings."

"I hate the Patriots," Dew-man struggled to verbalize.

"Oh, right. But I used to believe in all that stuff. I was raised that way. I believed in God, Satan, heaven and hell, and the places in between.

"But over the past year or so I've really begun to wonder how a 'God,' if one really does exist, could not protect my family from turning into monsters, or from placing me in a situation where I have to kill them or be killed myself. I have lost my freedom, my career, the woman I love. And the earth as we used to know it is being slowly taken over and inhabited by carnivorous flesh-feasting demons that were once our friends and neighbors and relatives. What kind of 'loving father' would allow the world we live in to turn completely upside down like it has?"

Jake continued, "but, having said all that, even after all that shit has happened and there seems to be no explanation why, I still believe there's an almighty one. And heaven. They say he works in some mysterious ways. Maybe someday it will all make sense to us. So, I know for sure that you are going to a place better than where we are right now. And I sure as heck hope that someday I will see you there and that we meet again."

"Will you do me a favor, Jake?"

"Anything, dude."

"Will you try to get in touch with my parents in Minnesota? Their address and phone number are in my cellphone. Tell them something good about me? Something to make them proud of me, of the way they raised me. Even if you have to make shit up."

"Of course. That won't be difficult at all. I'm sure they're already proud of you, and they should be very gratified with themselves as well, for raising you the way they did. You turned out to be a great man."

"I love you, brother," Duy said, closing his eyes for the final time.

"I love you, man," Jake whispered as he gave his close friend the merciful peace he had asked for.

Jake began to walk away from the body and in the opposite direction of the van. He was trekking with a steady pace toward the vast, punishing desert.

Mack jumped out of the driver seat and ran toward Jake, who never slowed down or missed a beat.

"Jake! Dude! Where are you going? The van's in the other direction!"

"I gotta go, Mack. I'm not like you and everyone else on that bus anymore. I've changed. I'm no longer Jake. No longer human. I don't feel, I don't need. I don't sleep... I'm better off alone.

"All of the things Duy just described to me, the way he was physically feeling and the things emotionally he wasn't feeling. The visions, the delusions. I've been experiencing all of that for months now.

"Duy Is the lucky one, he doesn't have to endure that pain any longer. I am not so lucky. I can't even die properly. Trust me, I've tried to end it. But that didn't work. So now I try to just remain numb to this life since I can't *feel* it anyways. It's best for everyone that I leave. I need to be alone; it feels better.

"Plus, I have some unfinished business with Fiedler and Blackhoof. After I take care of a promise I made to a friend. And then I am going to stop this virus from spreading before the whole world is infected."

Jake paused, then extended his right arm forward to shake Mack's hand. "We will meet again, dude. Who knows? Maybe it will be at the Steak Pit?"

"Umm, probably NOT at the Steak Pit. But somewhere, for sure." Mack smiled.

"Haaa," Jake grinned. "Strong, my friend. You sure have come a long way since field training. Stay safe brother."

Jake, the **wicked awake,** colossal Caucasian, clad in his black BDU style pants, combat boots, and black Killswitch Engage concert t-shirt, walked toward the uninviting, sizzling desert before him.

Daylight turned to dusk; the absence of light was something that Hathaway relished. The obscurity offered a concealment which made it that much easier for HIM to blend in with THEM, the evil ones that he has vowed to destroy.

Or rather, was it THEM, the **wicked-** who would be merging with *him*?

THE END

Made in the USA
Middletown, DE
30 April 2020